Fairy Godmothers Aren't Cheap

FAIRY GODMOTHERS AND OTHER FIASCOS
BOOK ONE

JEAN ORAM

Fairy Godmothers Aren't Cheap
A Sweet Romantic Comedy Romantasy

Fairy Godmothers and Other Fiascos, Book 1
By Jean Oram

This is a work of fiction and all characters, organizations, places, events, and incidents appearing in this novel are products of the author's overly active imagination or are used in a fictitious manner unless otherwise stated. Any resemblance to actual people, unicorns and other mythical creatures, alive, dead or extinct, as well as any resemblance to events or locales is coincidental, except for when it isn't. (See Author's Note and Glossary, or check a map of Canada.)

For nondigital editions, the print location of this book is stated on the last page. Published by Oram Productions in Alberta, Canada.

Front cover design: Elizabeth Mackey

COMPLETE LIBRARY OF CONGRESS CATALOGING-IN-PUBLICATION DATA AVAILABLE ONLINE

Oram, Jean.

Fairy Godmothers Aren't Cheap / Jean Oram.—1st. ed.

Ebook: 9781998476510

Paperback: 978-1-998476-77-0, 978-1-998476-78-7

Large Print: 978-1-998476-79-4, 978-1-998476-54-1

Audio: 978-1-998476-80-0

First Oram Productions Edition: September 2025

Because if not me, then who?

That was what kept going through my mind while writing this very Canadian book near where I grew up, and debating using Canadian spelling in a published work for the first time.

If not me, then who?

Why was this particular phrase going through my head?

For some time now, I have noticed the slow loss of Canadian spellings here in Canada. Even most Canadian books use American spellings and not Canadian spelling. Including mine.

Therefore, if I care about preserving Canadian spelling, and feel as though it is a part of our culture... if not me, then who?

But also...who cares?

Well, it seems I do! I believe that language is part of one's culture. Language is a way of expressing ourselves and our culture and, therefore, spelling is an extension of that.

Language distinguishes us. Separates us. Identifies us. And in that identification, it can also bring us back together. Language is comfortable. It is home. And quirky Canadian spelling is wholly me, and feels comfortable and homey.

This all probably sounds like a big fat, juicy nothing burger. (But I'm not a trained sociologist for nothing, I suppose. I ponder odd things.) Here's a little backstory, if you're so inclined....

Normally, in the past, I would write my books using Canadian spelling, and then run the book through a spellchecker to make hundreds of tiny changes to switch the book over to American spellings. That was an extra hour or two of my life for every one of my 39 books. That's a lot of hours spent fighting with stupid spellcheckers.

Then, I tried skipping that step and writing solely using American spellings. It was fine. I'm a decent bilingual speller. But as I'd be writing, in the back of my head I'd constantly be thinking, drop the 'u', don't use a double-L here... That isn't a word that Americans use.

Really, it boiled down to this: be more commercial.

In other words, fit in.

Hon, I'm almost fifty, and I've never fit in. This book won't fit in, either.

And what is 'fitting in,' anyway?

Does anyone truly fit in?

This book is a lot of things, but really, to make a long story short...it's very Canadian. So, I'm using weird Canadian words and spellings in this series, because this quirky series is me. It's Canadian. And we're both deeply rooted in the heart of a land where I grew up. This story has big chunks of myself stitched into the pages. Thus, if not me, then who?

I hope you enjoy this taste of where I grew up. And I hope you are charmed by the cultural touches that feel like home to me, and maybe to you as well. Or maybe they simply feel warm and welcoming, and like a place you might want to visit one day. Look me up if you do.

Hugs, love, and maple syrup,

Jean Oram

To cups of tea, doggy and kitty snuggles, and mini chocolates for getting me through over a year of completely rewriting this book several times over. Because I am very aware that I could have written about five other novels in the time it took to beat you into submission.

But truly, this dear sweet book is for everyone who's ever made a wish, and had it come true. Keep dreaming. Keep wishing.

(Like that time in the 1980s when Cabbage Patch Kids were *The Thing* and impossible to get, as well as expensive,—especially for some farmers just trying to hold on. Naturally, I wanted a Cabbage Patch Kid. Being me, I wished on the first star I saw one night, and the next morning a large box came for me in the mail. I announced to my mom that it was my Cabbage Patch Kid. She was certain I was going to be crushed.

Because what were the odds?

But do you know what was in the box?

The box without a return address?

Inside was my first Cabbage Patch Kid, Katrina.

Sometimes the magic is real. Trust.

FAIRY
GODMOTHERS
AREN'T
CHEAP

Quick Note

To add to the authentic Canadianness of this Canadian story, this (Canadian) author uses Canadian spellings. Enjoy!

(Be sure to check out the glossary at the back of this book.)

CHAPTER 1

~ *Char* ~

Mail. Who sent mail anymore? I snagged the envelope addressed to me—Char McDonnell—from our cubby on the main floor of the renovated, clapboard rooming house. It didn't look like junk mail and, standing in the middle of the entry, I hooked a thumb under the envelope's flap. I froze as a tiny metallic scritch from a nearby apartment door echoed across the entry. Randy. I flew across the ancient checkerboard tile as his door creaked open. I slipped behind the door that led up to my shared second-floor apartment and flicked its lock into place with an exhale of relief. Randy, our building manager, was having a midlife crisis and had a tendency to corner the five of us women from upstairs. He wasn't an awful person, but he wasn't the person I wanted to spend three quarters of an hour with every day.

James, the security guard at the nearby museum, however, was a different story. Hence my always-renewed annual membership. Not that I ever cornered the poor, sweet hottie. At least not for very long. He didn't seem to mind, though, and I did also go to the Museum of Culture for the ancient pottery

1

displays. Sometimes even when my favourite Viking-like security guard wasn't on shift.

I climbed the stairs that led to the top floor space I shared with four friends. We had the run of the whole level, unlike the main floor, which was divided into three apartments along with the shared entry. All five of us had our own bedrooms, a giant four-piece bathroom, a generously sized powder room, and plenty of living space to share. We even had our own secret roomie, a Richardson's ground squirrel (otherwise known as a gopher in these parts), Felipe, who'd adopted us before last winter.

"Were you good today?" I asked him as he met me at the top of the steps. "Were you quiet so Randy wouldn't hear you?"

Felipe chittered.

"Good boy."

He sat up on his hind legs and impatiently stretched his tiny, tawny paws upward.

"Hold your horses." I dug into my canvas courier bag and pulled out my lunch leftovers. "Apple core, who's your friend?" I sang, handing our chubby little buddy the core.

He grabbed it with both paws and began gnawing.

I hung a right into the living room, dropping my bag on the faded red sofa along with my mail. My friends had cleared out for the May long weekend, leaving me kicking about on my own just like at Christmas. Only this holiday, I hadn't planned a one-day visit to go see my dad who lived two hours away. And even though it was only Friday night, I was already lonely and wishing for something to keep me occupied.

Right. The envelope addressed to me. Probably junk. I flopped onto the cracked leather armchair Samantha had found in a thrift store, then muttered "sacrilege" under my breath while moving one of her half-full coffee cups off my new stack of Grecian pottery hardcover books. Too lazy to get up again to retrieve my slate letter opener from my display of ancient pottery fragments near the window overlooking the street, I tore the envelope, curious about the sender, some place called YFGM.

Unfolding the enclosed invoice dated two days prior—May 15—I frowned. How could a place I'd never heard of be charging me for something? It didn't even list what I'd purchased. I scanned the bottom line and choked at the amount due. Over one-hundred thousand dollars? Yeah, I would most definitely have recalled racking that up.

It had to be an error or a scam.

I toed off my pink slides and, tossing the invoice aside, rubbed my tired, blurry eyes. A day of data inputting at my temp job had done a number on them today. But I was one day closer to having enough money to take myself and my father to Athens on an ancient ruins and pottery tour.

I grabbed the invoice, double-checking the name and address. Nope. That was me. Oprah Charmaine McDonnell, Apartment 2A, Stone Street SE, Calgary, Alberta, Canada. They even had my first name, which basically nobody—and I mean, *nobody*—knew, because I went by my middle name, and always had. Tamara, one of my roommates, who I'd graduated from high school with, knew about the Oprah thing and that was it. Well, I guess, technically, my boss at the temp agency knew, too.

My first name was a shout-out to my mom's most-favoured daytime TV host. I was lucky she hadn't named me Oprah Howie Maury Joy McDonnell.

I flicked the invoice. My name had to be the key. Chewing on my bottom lip, I considered the possible implications of ignoring the invoice. Maybe it was like the dust in this place—if we ignored it long enough, Gabby took care of it. If I ignored the invoice, maybe it would go away, too.

But what if this was a credit-rating-impactful error or an identity-theft scam? There could be consequences if I didn't pay up. But what if it was a scam, and I paid it?

Ha. That was funny. I was lucky to have an extra two-hundred dollars in my account by the time the end of the month hit—especially with our financial savvy roommate Samantha making the group of us act like grownups. A year ago, she'd sat us all down and made us set up automatic deposits that went into our new tax-free saving accounts and RRSPs.

Despite her influence, I still only had enough money to buy a one-way ticket to Athens with my savings, as well as maybe retire for two whole weeks if I cashed in my RRSP. Which she'd told me numerous times to *not* do. Ever. Not until I was a withered old senior citizen. Yes, withered.

Which meant I probably needed to act like a grownup and deal with this invoice or suffer her wrath if she found out about it.

I considered the invoice. What did YFGM stand for? Your Financially Gouging Mega-Scam?

I laid back on the couch, thinking and rubbing my eyes, not caring if I was blending mascara and eyeliner into my cheeks.

Maybe this was just a prank. A financial test from Samantha. I could see her pulling something like this if she discovered my legal first name. Last year she'd managed to convince me that our boss had shut down the whole temp agency where we worked in honour of my birthday. Sure, I'd been flying high due to recently earning employee of the month, but still. I'd fallen for it. Hook, line and sinker. Gulp, gulp like a baby fish who didn't know any better.

She wasn't a regular prankster, just like I wasn't a sucker. But every once in a while....

It didn't help that she had a certain regal gravitas about her, like pranks were beneath her. Although, just because she'd been born with a silver spoon in her mouth, unlike me and our other roommates, it didn't mean she wasn't human. In fact, in some ways she was more down to earth than the rest of us and was probably the biggest prankster of us five.

So maybe it wasn't the gravitas. Maybe it was those practiced innocent eyes and fluttering fake lashes that made me want to trust her. Every time.

Hook. Line. Sinker.

Even when my brain was saying "Nah. That can't be true. She's got to be pulling your leg." I found myself believing that an agency of a hundred people got the day off because it was my birthday.

Yeah. She'd made me look ridiculous, and I absolutely adored her for it.

Thank goodness she hadn't noticed my crush on James, or who knows how she'd torture me over that.

I opened the group chat on my phone that the five of us had going. Tamara, who loved to name things, had called it GAL PAL, which was an acronym for something I couldn't remember.

I typed out a one-word message and attached a photo of the invoice.

ME

Samantha?

While I waited for someone to reply, I shuffled to the thermostat, upping the heat. I knew Josie, the most environmentally conscious of us five, would turn it back down to save on fossil fuels when she came home Monday night, but until then I could happily bake in our drafty little abode.

SAMANTHA

Is this what you owe Book Emporium? 😆

Ha, ha. Yeah, okay. So I had a little book problem, which was especially noticeable at the moment, since both Samantha and I were currently temping at a book depository. Everyone said I had a horseshoe up my you-know-what, because I always seemed to get the best temp jobs. Which was true—the job part, not the horseshoe.

Not to brag, but I was a fantastic manifester. For example, I'd wanted the apartment to myself for a few nights to binge watch some Discovery Channel history documentaries without judgement, and to drool over possible tours I could book as a surprise for my dad, and suddenly my roomies all had plans this weekend. (That *never* happened.)

As for my book hoarding? I firmly believe it's not hoarding if it's books—unless the stacks become so numerous and precarious that they threaten to topple and kill you on a regular basis. And even then, I could just buy more shelves or get creative. For example, a solid stack of hardcovers made a great bedside table.

As for my noticeable bookish problem, over the past week, a number of books that were destined for destroying, had found their way home. I mean, with the discount they were offering us at the emporium, how could I not bring them home like poor abandoned kittens?

Samantha, on the other hand, was heartless. She hadn't brought a single book home despite her plush savings account, rescuing absolutely nothing from the clutches of the spine grinder or page shredder. Completely. Heartless.

How many innocent books had been pulped on her watch?

Then again, she might actually leave her position at the end of our two-week stint with a pay cheque, unlike me. Again, my savings were not expanding and compounding like they should.

TAMARA

TAMARA

💰

ME

I'm not falling for this one, S.

GABBY

Wait. ur first name's Oprah!?!?! I've got to
tell Lamonte. He's going to die.

I rolled my eyes. Everything with Gabs was always about Lamonte. How had the man not yet figured out how eager she was to leap out of the friend zone? Then again, maybe he wanted her to stay there.

Just like hunky James. He probably felt I was best-suited for the friend zone, too.

Gabs and I needed to start falling for guys in our own league.

TAMARA

Her mom's a big Oprah fan.

Tam-Tam was my bestie for a good reason. She was always there for me. Just like I was with this apartment when her high school sweetheart decided—like most people in long-term relationships seemed to—that he wanted more excitement in his life. In other words, not Tamara.

We were currently in the process of showing him we were very exciting and doing just fine without him, thank you very much. (Not that I thought he was watching, but just in case.)

GABBY

How did I not know that?

SAMANTHA

Same!! FYI, we would have paid big money
for that info.

TAMARA

😶

SAMANTHA

Why u think I'm pranking u? One little time…

GABBY

Been more than once.

TAMARA

This.

ME

How come I'm the one who always falls for her jokes?

Maybe Josie, our fifth roommate, was the one pranking me. She hadn't jumped into the text string yet, and was likely busting a gut at me all the way from the Kananaskis. She'd been hired to do some inventory management for someone with a bunker in the Rockies an hour from the city in her spare time. The whole thing was so hush-hush, she'd even had to sign a nondisclosure agreement when she'd taken the job. But she'd let it slip that someone super wealthy had built a secret bunker in case of an apocalypse.

We'd all looked to Samantha upon hearing that, as her family's social circle ran a little higher than ours. As in, her family held a seat quite comfortably in the top one per cent of the city's—and province's, heck, probably Canada's—financial elite. She didn't act like it though, as she was slumming with the rest of us. But still—she probably knew whose bunker it was, and was on the list to get inside should we all face Armageddon.

TAMARA

What's YFGM?

ME

Was it Josie?

TAMARA

GABBY

SAMANTHA

What a bunch of sassy brats.

ME

You guys have to try harder. I'm on to you now.

SAMANTHA

Doubtful.

GABBY

I shoved my phone between the couch cushions and sighed in frustration. Not knowing was going to drive me nuts. Was someone stealing my identity, or was this simply a prank to wind me up? I should have waited until everyone was home and then questioned them in person. Tamara had the most obvious tells when she was hiding something, thanks to her sweet loyalty. All I'd have to do was wait until she came home from work on Tuesday night, exhausted and cranky, had yanked off her bra and made a nest of blankets on her bed to curl into while reading horse magazines and eating cookies—rice crisps if she was feeling fat. Her guard would be down and I'd see her blush, or act overly innocent, avert her eyes—anything that would tell me there was something to dig for.

But no, I'd jumped the gun and had no idea if she was in on it. Whatever *this* was.

My phone beeped with the horse neigh sound that meant a text from Tamara. I dug the phone out of the cushions and read the text she'd sent to only me.

TAMARA

Probably junk mail. Ignore it.

Junk mail was such a boring theory. I wanted it to be more. It *had* to be more. I was overdue for some excitement.

ME

I think someone is messing with me.

TAMARA

I don't think it's the girls.

ME

It's driving me 😜.

TAMARA

You're so impatient.

She was a big proponent of wait-and-see. Me? I got itchy just thinking about having to wait this one out. I wanted to know now.

TAMARA

Google the return address.

Smart.

Wait. There was also a phone number on the invoice. I could get answers even faster.

ME

I'll call them!

TAMARA

No! What if it's a scam? They want you to call them, because it's some sort of reverse charging system where it'll cost you a hundred dollars a minute.

ME

It's a 1-800.

TAMARA

It's got to be a scam—phishing for personal data. They want you to call! Don't answer anything they ask with a YES or they'll record you and edit the conversation to make it seem like you agreed to whatever their scam is.

ME

Your mom has made you paranoid. I'm calling.

Mrs. Madden, a total small-town sweetheart of a mom, watched way too many news stories about bad things, and was the number one target for dramatic clickbait headlines. Then she'd call us up and warn us about whatever she'd heard or read about. She used to video-call us, but then she got worried that someone was going to hack our call and use artificial intelligence to create an avatar that mimicked her, and then scam all of her family and friends. She'd even created a secret word, so we'd know if we were talking to the real human version of her or not.

TAMARA

I checked maps. Their address doesn't exist. No 1010B on 10 Avenue! SCAM!

Samantha was my role model in so many ways. She was an inspiring rolling stone of adventure, and nobody would ever leave her for being too boring. She was always aware of the next hot club, and by the time I'd heard of it, she was already on a first name basis with the bouncer and cutting to the front of the line. Samantha wasn't waiting for life to find her. Nope, she chased it down and make it submit.

Holding the invoice, I typed the phone number into my phone. I was not going to turn into a smoking ball of impatience! I was getting to the bottom of this, and if not, I would at least prove to my pranking roomies that I wasn't *always* the overly trusting country bumpkin.

Shaking my head, I scoffed at myself. The whole agency got the day off.... Seriously? Was I really that self-centred or gullible?

I ignored her text and hit the green button to connect me to the YFGM phone number.

"Hello," said a chirpy voice, and I almost replied before realizing it was a recording. "You have reached the offices of YFGM, Your Fairy Godmother. Have a great day." *Beep.*

I sucked in a startled breath. What on earth?

Your Fairy Godmother?

CHAPTER 2

~ *Char* ~

Tamara was still texting me as I pulled on my coat, my curiosity piqued beyond their usual safety levels. My current plan, since my maps app was clearly out of date, was to do a walk-by of the invoice's listed address. It was probably just a fun little store called Your Fairy Godmother.

Or maybe my roommates, who knew how blue I'd been lately over my dad's declining health, or how alone I felt on long weekends when they went off with family, had put together a surprise for me.

My phone neighed at me, and realizing Tamara might be freaking out about me calling YFGM and then ghosting her, I texted back.

ME

Got their voicemail.

Heading down the stairs to the locked door that opened into the main floor foyer, I typed 'Your Fairy Godmother' into my phone's web browser search bar. I rolled my eyes as fairytale references came up. What had I expected?

I tried again and added 'Calgary' to my search. Nothing

13

different. So maybe YFGM wasn't a store. However, if it was new, it wouldn't be in maps yet or have an online presence.

But then, how did I owe them so much?

A glitch?

I redialled the number out of curiosity. Maybe my friends had gotten ahold of a burner phone for this prank, and I might recognize the recorded voice if I paid attention. That would most definitely be preferable to having my identity stolen.

"Hello. You have reached the offices of YFGM *again*. Have a magical day." *Beep*.

I threw my phone, breathing hard as it bounced down the last two steps and clattered against the scarred wood door.

It knew I'd called before.

It knew.

And it was *shaming* me for not leaving a message.

I laughed at my panic and sat down on the steps, inhaling deeply. It was simple. So simple. Samantha, or whoever had the burner phone, noticed I'd called and had zipped in and changed the outgoing message. That was all.

This was simply part of an elaborate plan to stay one step ahead of the bumpkin.

Your Fairy Godmother was *not* a real place. It was probably a virtual assistant company. Because fairy godmothers? *Please*.

Pulling myself together, I collected my phone, thankful for the extra sturdy case I kept it in, and let myself out into the foyer.

I squeaked as Randy, our landlord, popped into view, two feet away. How was it he always magically appeared beside me like a poltergeist, no matter what time I came or went from the upstairs apartment?

"Hello, Char. Heading out already?"

I gave a quick smile. "Yup."

"Did you drop your phone? I heard something take a tumble. Hope it's all right."

Ugh. Randy.

I waved my phone. "Yup. Fine. Thanks."

Everyone in the building collected their mail from the entry and used the front door. Naturally, we all bumped into each other here and there. Although, do the math on this one—we ran into Randy about eight times more often than the cutie Irishman Caleb, who had the apartment below our living room, despite our best efforts to avoid Randy and to bump into McHotStuff.

Almost a year ago, when Tamara had taken Caleb a slice of homemade cake on Samantha's behalf, in an effort to find out if he was single, she'd run into Randy twice. Twice.

Sadly, those statistics were not an anomaly. They were also the reason I often contemplated the scary, wobbly fire escape that clung to the back of the building. And it wasn't because I wanted my smart watch to stop nagging me to fit more steps into my day and to increase my heart rate.

"Ah, to be young again. Friday nights!" Randy smiled like I might invite him to join me.

The man had inherited the building, collected our rent, and fixed things with a startling level of incompetence, as well as borderline stalked us. Why he thought we were all pals was beyond me.

"Have a nice night," I said, continuing to move to the front door like I had a ride waiting for me, and therefore couldn't stop.

"How's your sink draining?"

"My what?"

"Your kitchen sink?" He'd hurried his pace to catch up, stopping alongside me where I stood frozen, my immediate thoughts about our forbidden pet gopher. If faulty old plumbing called Randy into our apartment when we weren't home he'd surely get busted. Sometimes I wished I didn't have to deal with Randy any longer.

He smoothed the bits of his waving comb-over to cover his shiny, flying saucer of a scalp and waited expectantly. If he embraced his middle-aged bod rather than fighting it, he might stand a chance with the ladies. I mean, he wasn't a bad person. He was just trying way too hard. Like, Olympics level of trying too hard—and was wearing figure skates at the sailing event.

"It's fine," I said, assuming our sink truly was. No problems had been mentioned in our group chat, and it surely would have if dirty water had stopped doing what it was supposed to.

"Good, good. There was a clog in Caleb's—just below you. The young Irish fellow? Coffee grounds. You don't put coffee grounds down the sink, do you?"

Hm. I may have seen Samantha trying to wash her fancy new latte machine and running a few more grounds down the drain than usual lately.

I shrugged.

"What do you do with your grounds?"

I shrugged again. I wasn't the one who made the coffee.

"But you're a coffee drinker," he pressed. "I've seen you with Timmie's cups."

Everyone with a Canadian passport went to Tim Horton's at one point or another in their lives. That was hardly a marker of my caffeine intake habits.

"My roommates make the coffee. I'll ask them to be careful."

"Okay, good, good."

I turned the doorknob. Just a few more steps and I would be free.

"The girls are all gone for the May-long, are they?"

"Uh, yeah." Inwardly, I cringed. I knew he watched who

was coming and going from his front window, but seriously. Could he act any more creepy?

His tone became jolly and slightly parental. "Well, don't party too loud on your own tonight, or I just might show up!"

~

HANDS STUFFED in my jacket pockets against the evening's chill, I shuddered as I hustled away from Randy and the building. As I passed his red sports car, which was blaring its alarm, I resisted the urge to go back and complain to Randy about the noise. Everstone wasn't a super great neighbourhood, with all the vacant lots and lack of community pride vibes, but it wasn't what anyone would call inner city. And it wasn't so bad that someone would try to steal his cherry red beast every single day —which seemed to be how often its alarm swore a blue streak.

Everstone had potential, but it was a tiny, forgotten neighbourhood close to the downtown, boxed in by the Bow River, the Stampede grounds and Canada Pacific's main rail line. We were only a few blocks wide and long, and ranged from half-occupied, basically historic (by western Canada standards) buildings to industrial lots. We had one restaurant, one coffee shop and cheap rent. But if the revitalization bug found us, and gave us a good bite, the line of interesting old brick buildings a block from my place would become super trendy and fetch top dollar. But right now they were mostly vacant, sadly over-looking the trashy empty lot across the street. The lot's sagging chain-link fence was full of holes and had grown thick with blown-in trash. Not to mention the waist-high weeds and the abandoned warehouse sitting on the lot behind.

Nobody wanted to start a trendy business around that.

Usually I sped by, head down, trying not to notice the dumpy bits so close to home. Today, however, I slowed, worried about a group of kids playing in the empty lot. They'd created a slide out of old barrels and bent metal siding panels from the abandoned warehouse, like they were in a third world playground. One of them was going to get hurt. I paused, wondering if I should tell them not to play in there. But where else would they play? On the street? That hardly seemed better.

Before I could decide what to do, a woman came hustling up.

"Get out of there! Right now!" She had her hands on her hips and had her mom tone down pat. I startled, and out of habit, or maybe self-preservation, my spine straightened and my arms dropped to my side as though I was awaiting a command.

The kids' heads popped up like Felipe's did when he sensed danger.

"I swear," the mother muttered, as the three young boys scuttled through the break in the fence like they were being chased.

"We need a park," I said as she looked at me, head shaking.

"We need to complain to the city about this dangerous monstrosity." She was already herding her boys up the street toward the apartment building on the corner.

"Yeah," I agreed.

"Too bad it doesn't do any good." She was moving, nudging the children when they moved too slow. "What did I tell you about playing in there?"

"It's dangerous," they said in the most dejected voices. It pulled at my heartstrings.

I'd grown up in small towns all over the province, and no matter where we'd landed for Dad's jobs, or whether I fit into the close-knit communities or not, I could always assume there'd be a safe playground at my disposal. Why should it be any different for these city kids? It wasn't fair. Not at all.

I began walking again, my mind spinning, wondering how I

could help. Maybe there was nothing. Maybe this was just one more aspect of city living that I'd never get used to.

As I got closer to the downtown, the temperature drifted lower, the buildings around me growing taller. This time of year in Canada, you could be breaking out the sunblock or the parka. And tonight we were dipping toward parka weather.

My route to the other end of downtown went past my favourite place in the city, the Museum of Culture. It had been one of my first placements at Temporarily Yours, and I'd been placed with my now-roommate, Josie, who was an inventory specialist. She had since started her own business, but back then we'd worked alongside as she'd trained me on two different inventory systems. With her strategies and efficiency, we'd gotten the massive job of changing the museum's inventory system over to the new program in less time than had been budgeted. Sadly.

I'd loved poking around in the restricted areas and tagging all the display and storage pieces. Except the mummies. They gave me the shivers whenever I was in the same room with them. The ancient pottery, though? Those pieces made me slow down, inhale a little deeper and savour the warm feelings they exuded. When I looked at them, I got a comfortable feeling of belonging, of fond memories and calm assuredness. It wasn't a common sensation in my life, and it probably helped that Grecian pottery turned out to be the key to unlocking the untapped relationship between me and my dad. After nearly thirty years, we'd finally found something to talk about. However, he didn't like to daydream about the person who'd made the items. And he didn't want to imagine their family routines and home life like I did. I wanted to make up a story about the pieces, and what they'd survived in order to make it to today. Back then, was everyone just trying to survive from day or day, or were there people like me, on the lookout for adventure?

The museum's large, three-story sandstone and limestone building began to loom up from its spot on the corner. With a bounce in my step, and my original destination temporarily forgotten, I headed toward the wide stone steps that would lead me inside. James was working somewhere in the building tonight, and the only question was: go straight to the ancient pottery, do a deep dive into the new Blackfoot exhibit, or track down James and pretend he wasn't the highlight of my night.

Tamara asked me once why I didn't work at the museum, and I guess it was because I didn't know enough. Or at least, that was how I felt. Sure, I'd beaten the museum's director at history trivia at their members-only Christmas bash a few months ago. But Richard really should have known those things, such as where Kerameikos got its name—from the Greek word for pottery: keramos. As well as the recommended humidity setting for their paper archives, their mummy collection and their ancient pottery. Basics.

I reached the doors and stopped, face scrunching. I didn't have my membership card on me, and I'd pleaded one too many times with Glenda at the admission desk to bend the rules and let me in without my physical pass. Usually, if I listened to her woes about her gout, she'd eventually allow me inside. But I think Richard, the museum's director, must have busted her doing that, as she'd been cracking down on me lately.

Turning, I marched back down the steps. At least I was a bit closer to meeting my stair-climbing goal for the day.

"Char! Hey, Char!"

I turned toward James's voice and felt my lips turn upward. Spending time on the museum's inventory for those few weeks had not only allowed Josie and me to become friends, but I'd also become friends with the hunky museum security guard,

James, too. It truly had been the best job ever. Even better than the book depository, and that was a pretty sweet gig.

"Hey!"

James jogged down the steps, stopping in front of me. He was about eight inches taller than I was, and delectable in a just-friends sort of way. Because hot guys who worked out regularly—such as James—didn't go for dorky, curvy girls like me. Not that either of us was looking to cross that line. Our friendship was too important, and I was certain neither of us had lain awake at night wondering how the other person's lips rated when lined up against our own.

Right.

"You okay?" he asked, his brows pinched with worry as he reached out to tap my arm. I swear the whole limb went warm.

"Yeah, why?" I resisted the urge to wipe my face clean of any half-cocked dreamy expressions or possible drool.

"It's not often I see you walk *past* the museum."

I laughed. Oh, that. "Mark your calendar." I eyed his spiffy, navy blue security jacket. The colour suited him and his Norse, Viking-like good looks. Built, blond and with a fiercely loyal protector vibe that ran beneath his sweet kindness—that was my James. Whoever did the museum's hiring had good eyesight and even better taste. Not that anyone would hire based on appearances these days. They'd get cancelled faster than a hacked credit card.

"I set something aside for you in the gift shop."

"Really?" I caught myself leaning forward like an eager three-year-old who'd heard the word 'present.'

"Want to see?" He was already walking backward, toward the museum, certain I'd follow.

"Yes!" I hooked my arm through his, spinning him around as we hurried to the doors. Even though he was a total hunk, and I sometimes got all tongue-twisted when I was with him, I felt comfortable in ways I didn't around other guys. "I forgot my pass, though."

"Don't worry about it. You're with me." He smiled with a warmth that assured me.

As we made our way inside, I asked, "Anyone try to touch the mummies today?"

James knew I was a sucker for museum stories. I'd had a fit the first time I saw a kid climbing around the mummies. I'd abandoned my inventory chart and pulled James over to scold the boy in what turned out to be our friendship's Meet Cute.

Then, after he'd gently guided the child back to his parents, I'd chided James for his lack of severeness, even though I'd been swooning a bit for how sweet and firm he'd been. I'd given him quite the lecture about letting people climb on sacred, ancient items. His lips had quirked the whole time, like he'd been fighting a smile.

Then he'd leaned in and cemented our friendship with a tidbit I'd never once overheard while eavesdropping on the various tours throughout the museum. The mummies on display were fake. That was right. Reproductions. And not only that, he'd had a hand in making them one summer as part of the museum's student hiring program.

Total. Swoon.

Honestly, if I'd actually paused to think about it, I should have figured out that they were reproductions. The ones on display didn't send chills down my spine when I walked past them, unlike the ones in the back.

"Nobody even tried to touch a toe," James assured me.

"Really? How boring."

"And nobody tried to take a selfie from the wrong side of the rope or unravel any head wrappings."

"Ew. Has someone actually tried to do that?" I might be a

curious history nerd who was up for pretty much anything, but that idea completely grossed me out.

James smiled. It was sweet and slightly crooked in the most perfect way.

"We did have a shoplifter in the Tinkertorium." That was the poorly chosen name for the museum's gift shop—it always made me think of a bathroom. "She was trying to stuff a reproduction sword down her pants."

I cringed, hoping the blade had a sheath, or at least was dull-edged.

"Did you have to personally retrieve it?" I tried to lift my eyebrows seductively, but honestly, I was too intrigued to pull it off. Plus, I really didn't have the confidence to pull off true sexiness. You had to commit and put yourself out there, and at the last minute I always backed off, afraid I'd look like a complete idiot who had no clue she was far from what men considered sexy.

James laughed, his shoulder bumping into mine. "No." His voice dropped. "I had to call 9-1-1." He waved at Glenda. "Just showing Char the new stock."

The woman let us in; her smile way bigger than when she encountered me on my own.

"You called to have her arrested?" I asked, bringing his attention back to his unfinished story, my mind fizzing with how James kept letting his body touch mine accidentally. Or was that on purpose? A sign that indicated he was into me? Maybe that was why I'd so few dates in recent years—I was illiterate when it came to men and their I'm-interested-in-you signs.

"The repros have fairly sharp edges, apparently." He grimaced. "When she was trying to return the sword, it slid out of its sheath."

I shuddered, my imagination going wild. "You're exaggerating." He did that here and there, knowing I loved the added drama.

"You'll never know." There was a twinkle in his warm eyes and it made me think of earthy, grounded pottery pieces and a feeling of belonging I couldn't quite peg. As for the twinkle, I wasn't sure if it was his joy in teasing me, or if he was tickled to have me stumped.

"I'm going to fact check with Glenda."

James laughed, then nodded at Greg, who was covering for Kendrick in the gift shop tonight. Greg usually ran tours, asking me for random facts to sprinkle into his spiels. I loved it when I overheard him sharing the things I'd told him, and seeing it intrigue others.

Tonight, he reached under the back counter with a ring of keys before revealing a beautiful necklace with a perfect, small black and orange-red pottery fragment edged in silver. The artist, from well over a thousand years ago, had illustrated the shape of two hands on what had likely been a water jug.

James took it from Greg, proudly draping it over his palm for my inspection.

"James," I gushed, "it's perfect."

"Thought you might like it."

He knew me so well.

"Yeah, she loves everything old, doesn't she?" Greg joked.

"And yet, she doesn't like you," James muttered, his eyes flashing to mine to catch my reaction.

Was he jealous of Greg? He was outgoing and cute, and I'd crushed on him for approximately a day and a half before downgrading him to merely fun-to-flirt-with. In other words, James had nothing to worry about where Greg was concerned. But I was charmed that he might think he had competition.

"Hey!" Greg complained. "I'm the same age as you are."

I giggled as James turned his back to Greg and slipped the

piece into my hand, his fingers brushing my palm with a gentle feathering. I flipped the fragment, taking it in. Ancient Athenian clay. Differential firing. Artistic detail. Very much one of a kind. Did I mention ancient? I hefted it gently, considering whether it was a perfect reproduction. No. It was too heavy. Cracked. Carried old world vibes. It was the real deal, unlike the fakes that had replaced several of the more priceless exhibit items in the Grecian wing last week.

"This is an amazing piece," I stated.

"Why?" Greg asked.

"The illustration's detail, mainly. To have it survive for so long, and then the way it's centred in the fragment definitely increases its value." I turned the piece over again, feeling a tiny bit like I was on an episode of *Antiques Roadshow* with the guys waiting for my evaluation. "It's nicely set in the silver, and it's in amazing shape."

"So it's a good one?" Greg confirmed. He often asked me which were the best pieces so he could guide his tour patrons directly to them, and earn a commission on their purchase.

"It is very good." And I wanted it. Desperately. "How much is it?"

James flashed me the price tag, delicately stuck to the chain's clasp, and I cringed. My life had been pretty charmed lately, but not *that* level of charmed.

"I get a staff discount," he said. "I could buy it."

"I wish you would..." Realizing I sounded wistful, I quickly added what was implied, "I'd pay you back, if you did, of course." I was unable to take my eyes off the piece, even as I returned it to him.

Financially, it was out of reach. I was doing my best to stick to the plan Samantha had outlined for me, and I was still slowly saving up for the Greece trip for my dad. Assuming his health improved, we'd hopefully go sometime next year. This necklace, as gorgeous and amazing as it was, could push the trip back by at least a month in terms of my savings.

I stepped away from temptation and sighed. "I love it."

"But?"

"Come on," Greg urged. "You only live once."

"It doesn't go with any of my outfits."

"Greece," James said, and I confirmed with a quick nod, pleased he remembered that I was saving up for my dream trip. Not only was the man hot, but he listened like he cared. Total aphrodisiac.

Greg took the piece with a shake of his head, locking it up in a nearby display case. I didn't own any jewellery that belonged locked up. Obviously, today I was lusting after numerous things that were beyond my league.

"Sorry," I muttered.

"Don't apologize," James said, guiding me out of the gift shop with a warm hand on my lower back and sending a shower of sparks through me like someone had lit a sparkler.

"I appreciate you setting it aside for me."

A feeling of FOMO—otherwise known as a fear of missing out—settled into my bones, and I almost turned around to empty my savings account. That piece was one-of-a-kind. Ancient. *Special*. Nothing new would be made by that artist or his peers. Ever.

"Of course. I saw it and immediately thought of you." Outside the front doors, James asked, "Where are you heading to next?"

I hesitated before answering. There was a possibility that he could be in on the YFGM invoice prank, if it was one. On the other hand, if I confessed that I was going to peek at a place filled with fairy godmothers, or some such thing, so I could figure out my strange, hundred-thousand dollar tab, he might have me shipped off to the funny farm. He was kind and caring in that way.

"I'm checking out a business on tenth and tenth," I said casually, building a lie as I spoke. I watched James out of the corner of my eye. He was a salt of the earth sweetheart. From what I'd gathered, he came from a perfect and loving family, and he was the type of man a woman married but didn't date, or whatever the expression was. In other words, James wasn't a liar and the idea of telling him a mistruth felt like a severe violation of our tentative, museum-based friendship.

"Tenth?" He glanced in the direction I needed to go: southwest. I was still off my target by several blocks.

"Yeah. Joan wants me to do a quick walk-by of a place that's looking for a few temps for their summer rush." I cut myself off, remembering something I'd heard about liars always giving too many details.

"Oh." He nodded, his look one of obvious skepticism.

Notably, there was no flickering hint that he was hiding prank minutiae from me. I was starting to think my friends could apply to the CSIS—Canadian Security Intelligence Service—and get in. If this was a prank, it was something that would have taken some time to put together, and nobody had dropped a single hint over the past several days or weeks. Nary a moment of feigned over-interest in anything, an ill-placed eye twinkle or guilty glance away.

Right. Because it might not be a prank. It could be a scam.

Or it could be real. What would that be like? To have a fairy godmother?

The fact that I was more curious than a rational being should be meant I should keep my mouth shut. My thoughts were my secrets. Especially since they were ones that might get me shipped off to Ponoka's Centennial Centre to have my grip on reality double-checked by qualified mental health professionals.

I sighed and rubbed my face. This really was a case of identity theft, wasn't it?

"You okay?" James asked, lightly touching my forearm.

I dropped my hands to my side. "Yeah, of course. Want to tag along?" I perked up at the idea of spending some time walking and talking with James. Plus, having a big guy in a security uniform accompanying me into the unknown was not a bad plan.

He gazed off toward tenth again and winced. "Sorry. Can't."

I checked my watch. "Aren't you done your shift?" Should I admit to knowing his dayshift schedule?

"Yeah. I am." He wouldn't meet my eyes. His gaze kept darting away like he had a secret.

I gasped. "You have a date!" I gave him a shove, which I'd meant to be playful but surprisingly, given his size, nearly knocked him off balance. Good thing he caught himself, otherwise he could have broken a leg, charged me for assault and then I'd be out of a job—no longer bondable. I shook my head at my silly imagination running wild and muttered, "Sorry."

Of course he had a date. He was cute. Just because I hadn't had one in at least eight months, that didn't mean his love life had to shrivel like a raisin as well.

Sometimes I thought maybe he liked me, but clearly he wasn't secretly pining for me, waiting for me to make a move.

The man was a hunk of the highest order. I was delusional to even consider that he might be pining for me. James wanted a big, close-knit family and a woman who was steady and calm, and didn't say awkward, stupid things when she was uncomfortable. Or nearly shove him down a set of stone steps when she was actually happy for him in a sad, wishing-it-was-herself kind of way.

"That's uh, nice. Are you going to get lucky?" I asked half-heartedly, and immediately wished I hadn't. Not because I sounded a tad jealous and judgemental, but also because it was absolutely none of my business. Why he still talked to me when he made me so incredibly tongue-tied, awkward and nervous was beyond me. And to think, I was more comfortable around him than most other eligible men. It was a good thing I was already comfortable with my singleness, because it was looking like I'd be this way for the foreseeable future.

"It's a first date."

"Sorry. What?"

"I'm not really into one-night stands."

"I don't think sleeping together on the first date makes it a one-night stand."

"Well, in my experience, a relationship never really develops if you jump into things that fast."

"What do you mean? Like develop emotionally?"

He nodded. "It doesn't seem to progress beyond the physical."

"Huh." I'd always sort of gotten the vibe that James was looking for love, and not just a good time like most men his age, and his confession felt like a verification of my theory. He wanted to move slowly and deeply, and make it last forever.

That was the fantasy, wasn't it? Too bad it was just that —fantasy.

"Don't you find that?" he asked.

"I don't..." My tongue got all twisted, my imagination running wild at the suggestion of a one-night stand with James. His strong biceps like a vise around me, his weighty, muscular body.... Wow. Forget it becoming parka weather out here, break out the shorts. I resisted fanning myself and muttered, "I never. I..."

"You've never-ever?"

"No!" Out of habit, I glanced about for eavesdroppers judging me, then lowered my voice. "Not like that. I'm not a—you know. I'm just not someone who moves fast, or is into one-night stands."

"But you think I am?" James said, tone wounded.

It took me a moment to realize he was kidding, and I barely refrained from giving him another shove—this one out of frustration. What was with me tonight? Yeah, I wanted to touch the man, but shoving him? That was hardly a good way to show how I felt. The move didn't even work for fourth graders on the playground.

"You're frustrating," I grumbled.

He flashed me a triumphant grin and let his shoulder bump into mine as we meandered in the direction of the staff parking lot's entrance.

I struggled for a way to recover the conversation, so it didn't end on the note of my spectacular awkwardness.

"Where are you taking her?"

"Probably Earl's." He gave a one shoulder shrug.

"Fancy."

He gave me a dry look. "Not really, but not everyone loves Peter's."

I gave a dramatic gasp. Peter's Drive-In was a long-established burger joint in the city and had the absolute best milkshakes. Plus, when you ordered a large fries, it came in a shoebox. Mind. Blown.

Okay, so they didn't do that anymore. But still. Impression made. They meant business and I could totally climb aboard that train.

"Real women love Peter's."

"You're not real, Char." He bumped his shoulder against mine, giving me a look of affection that made me hope he'd cancel his date and see me as 'real'—whatever that meant to a single hunk like him.

~

"IT SHOULD BE RIGHT HERE," I muttered to myself, pacing outside a row of single-storey businesses. On my walk to YFGM's address, I'd promised myself I'd extricate myself from this erroneous invoice, laugh off anything fairy godmother-like, as well as act tough in the face of a potential scam.

But I hadn't expected to find nothing.

Studying the buildings coated with dust with their air of neglect, I couldn't find Your Fairy Godmother. I didn't know whether to scream in frustration or to relax in relief.

I took another scan. I wasn't a city girl, and sometimes street addresses left me muddled. If the address wasn't 'go a mile past the large pine,' I got lost, and tenth was an odd, east-west strip through the city, scattered with more parking lots than buildings. To further limit my options, the Canada Pacific's main rail line ran behind the south-facing row of buildings instead of there being an alleyway.

It was this or nothing. And it was looking like nothing—a dead end.

However, this would be a great place for an underground nightclub.

Train? What train? They'd never hear it over the thumping music.

I counted off the businesses again, determined to get to the bottom of YFGM. 810, 1210, 1410. 1010 and 1010B were completely absent.

"1010B, 1010B," I muttered to myself on the empty sidewalk. I scanned again and there it was: Photocopies and Beyond. How had I missed it the first few times?

I mean, to my credit, it was one of those skinny places that was basically the width of a door with a tiny window above it to let in a bit of light. Since there was no second level to the buildings, it was probably just a staircase that led to a basement.

Creepy.

Although...nightclubs were often in basements. But so were kidnapped women, according to awful TV shows that refused to leave my memory banks. Why couldn't every scene with Luke from *Gilmore Girls* stay rooted in my mind instead? They were *much* more pleasant.

I shivered and blinked at the door with the tiny, faded business sign. It wasn't a nightclub, and this wasn't a prank or fun puzzle for me from my roommates. I was alone in the city this weekend, and I was the victim of identity theft.

What had I expected? To find the offices of an actual fairy godmother, pressed up against the grit of a major rail line?

It would be located in a magical forest, obviously. A cute little building with magic sparkles flying out of its big, bright windows and wood nymphs flitting about, slipping inside through tiny, old-fashioned keyholes that were just their size.

I sighed, my entire spirit flagging. A teeny, grubby copy place that hadn't even made it into a maps app was a perfect front for a scam artist stealing identities.

Not quite ready to face going home and calling the police about identity fraud, I reached out to try the door. Dealing with a fairy godmother would be much preferable to dealing with scammers, and I found myself saying out loud, "I was hoping you'd be the office of Your Fairy Godmother, you stupid door!"

I squeaked and jumped back as the metal door with the crooked Photocopies and Beyond sticker transformed into a wooden one with an intricately carved handle with lifelike leaves and flowers. Above it spanned a maroon sign that stated simply, 'YFGM.'

I sucked in an unsteady breath, body trembling.

What. The.

Magical....

Okay. Get a grip. My mind was clearly playing tricks on me. Doors didn't transform like that.

Hand outstretched, and nearly touching the wood handle that was darkened from use, I hoped I wasn't about to do something incredibly dangerous. Because what if this was a trap and inside was a human trafficking ring?

I lost my nerve and dropped my hand, shaking my head at myself. Tamara's mom's constant worries about the city were starting to erode my confidence and sense of security.

Honestly, if I was going to believe in something dark and awful behind this door, I might as well believe there was a fairy godmother inside who thought I owed her money.

Right. And if she were real, and I went in there, she'd have me turned into a toad for having an overdue account. Smiling at the absurdity, I paused. Wait. Did fairy godmothers turn people into things, or was that the work of witches? I needed Josie's mental spreadsheets of the magical world as gained from her passion for reading romantasy. She'd know.

Shaking off my thoughts and ready to figure things out, I touched the door handle, my fingers moving over the bumpy grain of wood. Carefully, I tested it. Locked.

Thank goodness.

"Not going to let me in YFGM?" I laughed, relaxing as a smile stretched wide. It looked as though I didn't have to face this weird, slightly scary fiasco today. Thank you, Universe.

But as I turned to return home, I heard the telltale sound of a door's lock clicking open.

CHAPTER 3

~ *Char* ~

Open the door, or ignore it and run?

I'd never felt more like a vulnerable single woman, alone in the city at night in my entire life.

The door popped open a crack, and I jumped.

Was someone watching me? Waiting for me to make a move so they could grab me? Was it too late to scream and run? Had freezing for a few precious seconds removed the opportunity for flight, and now I was faced with fight? I pulled my fists up near my chin and widened my stance, ready to go like Tamara and I had learned in the self-defence class her mom had made us take before our high school graduation had released us out into the world.

I should walk away. No, run.

Instead, keeping my centre of balance low, I reached a toe toward the door, trying to pull it open without putting myself vulnerably close to the unknown. The door creaked open a few inches. Not enough to see what was inside or who might be waiting for me.

"Who's there?" I called, my voice weak and croaky with fear.

My call was met with silence.

Repositioning myself, I stretched my leg, hooking half my foot on the door and knocking it wide. The whole entry seemed to be thick with plants.

I straightened, feeling my face scrunch in confusion. Plants? Hardly threatening.

Was this a fairy godmother forest? Hidden inside a city building?

Wait. What was I thinking? Fairy godmothers weren't real.

But scammers wouldn't take time to load their office with living plants. They'd be ready to drop and go at a moment's notice. So what was this?

With a curiosity that would likely get me killed one day, I called out a 'hello' and stepped inside the botanical garden entry. Weird. My skills of spatial comprehension weren't tops, but even I could tell things weren't lining up. There were a lot of branches and leaves in the way, but it was obvious this room was much bigger than the narrow strip it had appeared to be from the outside.

To confirm my assessment, I stuck my head out the door and looked at the front of the building. It was still just a door wedged between two properly sized businesses. Logically, you would expect a stairwell and not much else beyond this wooden door. But there wasn't a step in sight. Just an entry thick with plants, a carpeted path that wound between them and the sound of a water feature trickling nearby.

"Close the door!" snapped a growly voice, and I jumped, releasing the door like it was red hot, most of my body still inside the office. "The heat ain't free, and you'll make it colder than a witch's tit in here. Then I'll be real mad."

I watched the door close behind me, considering whether I needed to bolt back out of it again. It clicked shut, and I tentatively followed the curved path, weaving through the plants until a half circle of three large wood desks that looked like they'd been sculpted from a giant oak tree came into view. Nobody was at them. Behind them, five veiny grained doors stood closed at various heights. Even further to the left was a wall covered in ivy that led back into the foliage entrance, and to my far right was a tall, ornately carved reception desk with a standing counter. Behind it was a gold-painted office door. There were plants everywhere and I swear, out of the corner of my eye, I saw something hummingbird-sized flit by.

"Well?" croaked the earlier voice. "What do you want?"

I peered around, not seeing anyone. "Hello? Where are you?" Was one of the plants talking to me? I half expected to sneak a peek of curtain with a wizard behind it, speaking into a microphone.

"Oh, for..." A short, witchy looking woman stood up and glared over the top of the reception desk. Well, she sort of did. She was quite short and, with the desk still between us, she probably couldn't see anything below my neck. "What? What is it that you want?"

I stared, at a loss for words. This woman seriously looked like a stereotypical witch. She had a hook nose complete with a wart at the end of it, and straw-like grey hair. All that was missing was the hat, broom and cat.

A black cat delicately landed on the top of the reception desk and I nearly fainted. The feline stared at me with its glowing amber eyes, and I mentally scratched that last bit from the witch's requirement list.

"Cat got your tongue?" The lady laughed, her voice crackling over a bubble of rusty laughter.

I would have fled if it weren't for the fact that I was pretty confident witches didn't exist. Not the fairytale kind, anyway. Wiccan witches, yes, sure. Witches that rode brooms and turned people into newts, no.

"Let me speak to your boss," I said, surprised by how no-nonsense my voice sounded.

"Oh." The witch put her hands on her narrow hips and gave me tone. "You think you can just walk in off the street and talk to *her*, do you?"

I reached into my pocket and unfolded the sheet of paper they'd mailed me, dangling it in front of the receptionist. "Yes, I do."

"Yeah? What for?"

I waved the invoice. "I need to clear this up."

"Accounting." The witch sat down, giving a little hop to get into her chair. I was pretty sure her feet didn't touch the ground, and I wondered why she didn't cast a spell to make her work station more ergonomically-sized before blinking away that crazy thought.

Because, again, witches were not real.

Just like fairy godmothers.

The receptionist leaned back in her chair, tossing back her head and hollering, "Igor!"

Was it me, or did that name evoke a mental image of a scraggle-toothed monster?

The witch leaned forward with a sigh, reading her computer screen. "He says no."

"What?"

"He's not seeing human clients tonight. Something about a headache."

Human clients?

"Then what do I do?"

"Why should I care?"

"Well, because I need to get this cleared up."

"Send an e-transfer. The email address is on the invoice."

"No." I straightened my spine. "I wish to speak with

someone who can help me understand what's going on. Because I didn't—"

"You wish?" Her eyebrows lifted.

"What?"

"You *wish* to speak to someone?"

"Erm...yes?"

"Oprah!" I turned at the sound of my legal first name. A small, hidden door had swung open beside the gold one behind the witch's desk. It had blended in like a true secret passage, and I immediately wanted one for the apartment.

A stick-straight, tall woman with beautifully shaped brows and flaming red hair that was cut into a sharp, perfect, shoulder-brushing bob, strode toward us. She wore black leather pants, a flowing white blouse and strappy red stilettos with black detailing. Her arms extended wide as if she planned to hug me even though she was still several feet away.

"Sorry." She gave her head a little shake, every strand of her hair falling right back into the perfect bob. "You go by Char, don't you?"

She pronounced it like the burned wood rather than with a sh sound, but before I could say anything, she corrected her pronunciation.

"A white girl named Oprah?" The witch snickered, eyes gleaming as her gaze scraped down my curves.

I flicked her a dirty look, and she smirked. I decided right then and there that I didn't like her, and never-ever would. Not even if she was an amazing and generous baker who tried to buy my affection with chocolate cake or brownies.

Instead of hugging me, the woman with the bob gripped my upper arms and took me in, her slashingly bright red lipstick almost disappearing as she grinned so widely. "At long last we meet."

This definitely wasn't a prank being played by my friends. They were creative, but not this creative.

Which, sadly, still left us with identity theft or some form of scam.

"Who are you?" I asked.

"Me?" The woman placed her hands on her chest and studied me for a beat. "I'm your fairy godmother." She swivelled her hips to the side and extended her arms dramatically, showcasing herself. I could have sworn pale pink sparkles rained down from her French manicured fingertips. But before I could confirm the sparkles, she whirled and entered the hidden room as though expecting me to follow.

Fairy godmother? Was that what they called people running identity theft scams these days? The label did have a certain ring to it and, deciding I had no other feasible option, I followed her.

"Next time you call, leave a message," the witch cackled after me. "You've been ticking me off."

The secret passage door closed behind me with a soft clack. The room beyond resembled an office bullpen with rows of cubicles, but all done in pink with some pale blue accents. It was like Mattel's Barbie designers had gone wild in here. Plush pink carpet, pink walls, powder blue desks and pink leather office chairs. Many of the desks were empty, but some had dainty women working at them, their perfect hair sporting some sort of pink hair accessory. Too much pink. And it clashed horribly with the lady I was following, and for some reason, that made me adore her just a little bit for being a fashion outlier.

She led me into a small meeting room. A mahogany table was pressed against the beige wall and two black leather chairs were positioned on either side of it. No pink in sight. I sat, noticing a long, narrow window several feet up the wall to my right that over-looked the bullpen. A woman with delicate features was watching us. Unlike the woman I was with, her hair was blond like the others, and its perfect waves were held back by—you guessed it—a wide pink hairband. She was dainty and looked…well, sort of fairylike.

As soon as the woman claiming to be my fairy godmother looked toward the window, the pink lady dropped out of sight.

"I expect you have questions?" she asked me, one eye still on the window.

I nodded, perching on the edge of the seat, at the ready to bolt if need be.

"Tea?" she asked, her attention returning to me.

I shook my head. I was managing to *not* freak out over the weird changing door and strangeness of this place, but I needed immediate answers. Not after water boiled and tea steeped.

"Right, no tea." She studied me. "Whiskey?"

I shook my head again.

"Good. Now's not the time to get tipsy. Canada Dry? It's my favourite. I adore the little ginger ale bubbles. They tickle my nose."

"No, thanks."

"Mind if I do?"

I shrugged, and she got up, opening a mini fridge hunkering under a thick stack of yellowing papers. This office—it wasn't actually a meeting room like I'd first thought—was unlike the cubicles in the bullpen. It resembled a private investigator's office more than anything. It was reassuringly very unfairy godmother-like.

It also seemed much too established for a scammer's headquarters. For example, on the old computer lurking on the desk behind me, there was a thick layer of undisturbed dust. And abandoned on top of the desk's scattered and faded, dog-eared papers and file folders sat a crystal tumbler containing a finger's worth of amber liquid and an ashtray holding half of a crumbly cigar. The aluminum blinds to my left were dusty as well, and a few slats were broken, weak, late evening light filtering through. Where did the window look out to? There'd been no windows on the outside of the skinny little strip of a building. Were the neighbouring businesses actually false fronts with Your Fairy Godmother extending deep and wide into what was actually one long building and not several as it had appeared?

In front of me, a tall bookshelf stretched against the entire wall, sporting a cutout to hold the mini fridge where the fairy-claimer clanked around.

I was growing frustrated by the lack of solid clues as to what this invoice was actually about.

"I hope your Friday night is keeping you...*occupied*." The redhead ceased her pop can clanking and glanced back at me, her eyes twinkling like we shared a secret.

Considering I'd never met her before, and didn't have a clue who she was, there was no secret. None that I was in on, anyway.

And why had she put special emphasis on the word 'occupied' like it should mean something to me?

She stood, suddenly red-faced. She slammed the fridge door closed and sat in her chair again, expression pinched.

"What?" I asked, clutching the edge of the table, ready to make a run for it.

She gave a sharp shake of her head.

"Is this your office?" Even with this room's down-on-his-luck, old man décor, it seemed to suit her more than the pink bullpen.

"No."

"What's your name?"

She seemed to settle, her earlier happy persona slowly returning. "I suppose you can call me Fairy Godmother, or Miss. F.G. if you're into that sort of thing."

"No, what's your *name*?"

"Estelle," she said quietly, as though unsure what she could reveal about herself.

"Estelle."

"Yes."

"Why did I get a bill from you?"

She leaned forward, one elbow on the table with a comfort born from confidence and a solid awareness of exactly where you landed in this world and what your purpose was. I was a bit in awe.

But then it all crumbled like it had been an act, and she half-stood, hands splayed on the table. Her gaze was locked on the bullpen's window and there, just before she skipped out of sight, was the fairylike woman from earlier gleefully sipping on a can of Canada Dry.

Estelle's neck flushed red, her jaw set.

"Uh, the bill?" I prompted.

Estelle's shoulders pushed up and forward and she drew in an impressive breath before letting it out in a rapid flash, her shoulders squaring again. Her focus returned to me, her smile bright and filled with purpose.

"The invoice is because you've been making wishes. And they've been granted."

I blinked.

No.

No way.

Nope.

Just. *No*.

"The bill is for your wishes," Estelle explained softly, her expression so open and fresh I felt crusty, tired and slightly jaded just sitting across from her.

I could already tell this conversation was going to be exhausting.

I leaned back, arms crossed. "Yeah, no."

"Yeah, yes," she insisted brightly.

"I'm going to need to see a detailed invoice."

"I can do that." She popped up. "It's important to do proper audits."

"Yeah," I muttered as she hurried out of the room, leaving the door open. I had a feeling that should there ever be a need, she was the type who'd volunteer to be a school hall monitor.

Moments later, the ginger ale-sipping fairylike lady from earlier appeared. "Hi. I'm Trish." Her handshake was soft, gentle, warm. "How are things going with—" She tipped her head in the direction Estelle had gone, her lips pinched together as though disgusted, "—her."

I blinked at Trish. I wasn't sure what I'd witnessed with her and the can of ginger ale, but as someone who'd moved around a lot as a kid and been the easily picked-on outsider, she sent my mean-girl radar buzzing.

"You must have so many questions." She practically floated into the room, perching on the edge of the table, hands gently clasped on her knee—which was, of course, tastefully covered by the long skirt of her pastel pink and purple floral print dress.

"Estelle's...answering them."

"She's only a trainee, you know."

"And you are...?"

"Trish." She stood with a confident laugh that tinkled. "I just wanted to introduce myself so you'll be comfortable coming to me with any questions when I take over her accounts after she fails her next levels."

"I'm not going to fail." Estelle was in the doorway, feet planted, jaw set, eyes practically shooting fire at Trish.

"Why are you meeting her here?" Trish's question seemed innocent, but her tone was like a war cry.

"I'm introducing myself to my clients."

"All of them?"

"My VIPs." When Trish didn't look convinced, Estelle added primly, "Proper notice must be instituted when clients are moved from one fairy godmother to another."

"Still having trouble with the dream spell, are you?" Trish muttered with a smirk, then gave me a tiny finger wave. "Lovely to meet you." As she passed Estelle, she whispered, "Good luck, Training Wheels."

Estelle firmly shut the door and set a pale pink file folder in front of me.

"She seems..." I paused, trying to think of the right word.

"Evil?"

"I was going to say competitive." I let out a small snort and Estelle and I shared a kindred spirit flick in the meeting of our gazes.

Opening the folder, I scanned the top sheet. Pink paper with YFGM printed along the header beside a wand shooting sparkles. There were several pages of detailed inventory, listing many granted 'wishes.'

I skimmed them quickly, trying to gather an accurate impression of what was going on. Some of the charges on the list rang a bit too true, as did their invoice date. But it didn't make any sense. How could anyone know these things? If I was a diary keeper, I'd think someone had read every page and was now using those private entries against me as a joke.

I shivered, rereading several lines and realizing that someone had taken a very, very deep dive into my life. But if they were investing that kind of time into their next mark, why not choose a better target? Say, one who actually *had* a hundred grand kicking around?

Biting my bottom lip, I slowly scanned the detailed list. A wish for a pet—so I'd have a friend no matter where we moved to. I'm sure a million kids made wishes like that. For Trevor to notice me—in a girlfriend kind of way. Then another wish to get him to quit smothering me with affection. That one sent chills down my spine with its accuracy. Vehicular repairs listed on the same snowy day I got stranded on a mountain logging road south of home when I was sixteen. My car had been kaput for over an hour and I was beginning to panic when all of a sudden it started again. On its own. You didn't forget weird stuff like that.

I closed the folder, my skin clammy, my heart pounding and vision narrowing. How did they know all of this? My brain refused to accept the possible implications of this new information, and I realized vaguely that I was nearing panic.

"Any questions?" Estelle asked.

"How do you know all of this?" I asked hoarsely. The papers were trembling in my grip and I set them down, locking my digits under my thighs, willing myself to pull it together. "This is so invasive! A complete and utter breach of privacy."

Estelle blinked at my tone. "Well, I..."

"This is an outrage!" My skin flashed with heat, my brain too big for my skull.

"But I'm your fairy godmother."

"You are not!" I blinked back the wetness in my eyes.

Estelle glanced at the window as my voice rose higher.

"But I am. I was assigned to you." Her voice remained low.

"Trish said you're a trainee."

Estelle's shoulders softened, as did her expression. "Yes. And my evaluations are at the end of the quarter along with hers, so if you have any questions about the wishes or fees before you clear up your bill we can—"

"Prove it."

"I'm sorry?"

"Prove you're a wish-granting fairy."

"Oh." Estelle sat back, then brightened. "I'd be happy to. What would you like to wish for today?"

"World peace."

Estelle blinked rapidly and her mouth moved, but no words came out.

"You can't do that?" I felt a whisper of smugness. I could feel myself one step closer to running home and forgetting all of this—except for the massive privacy breach. I'd still have to take action on that.

"Why don't we start with something a little less complicated, and with results that are a bit more expedient?" She was swaying in her chair, her breathing shaky.

"Fine." I shared the first thought that came to mind. "Make James cancel his date tonight."

"Sure!" Estelle said brightly. "Make a wish!"

"I just did."

"No, you need to wish it."

"Yeah?" I crossed my arms, my heart still thundering in my chest. "How?"

"Concentrate on what you want. Feel it. And start with 'I wish'." Her tone was oddly soothing.

I sighed. "Fine." I closed my eyes, playing along even though I knew there was no way she could jump over into James's mind and make him do something just because I wished it. That would be pure evil, and our world would be a very different place if that kind of stuff was allowed.

With my hands clasped in front of my chest, I said in a syrupy voice, "I wish I may, I wish I might, that James will cancel his date tonight."

I opened one eye. Estelle was leaning forward, nodding eagerly. "And?"

"And what?"

"Well done. But you'll want evidence, won't you?"

Good point. I'd need evidence that this weirdo made him

cancel, because I was her puppet master, and my wishes were her command.

"Fine." I closed my eyes again. "And I wish that he'll immediately call me up to take me out for a milkshake instead." I leaned back in my chair and watched her.

Estelle closed her eyes and inhaled, her lips curving up in a smile. She looked positively happy. Glowing, really. I didn't know what her makeup and skincare routine was, but I wanted it for myself.

Ha. I should wish for it.

Seconds later Estelle said, "Done."

I lifted my palms to the sky, waiting. A few long beats passed. Then my phone vibrated in my pocket. Narrowing my eyes at Estelle, I pulled out my phone to check its screen. My smugness dropped. It was James.

My body went cold, and I whispered, "What kind of sick joke is this?"

I scanned the room, on the lookout for hidden cameras or microphones. Was Trish actually Estelle's accomplice and not her rival? Because there was no way this was really James calling me. It had literally been less than a minute since I'd made my wish. They had to be spoofing his number so it would look like him on my caller ID.

"Well?" Estelle said encouragingly. "Answer it."

With sweaty, trembling fingers, I fumbled with the on-screen button to answer the call. "Hello?"

"Hey, so…my date," James said slowly, as though uncertain why he was calling me.

Like he was under a spell. Like mind control was occurring.

I swallowed and stared at Estelle.

Or maybe this phone call was just another layer of deep fake —they were simply synthesizing Trish's voice to sound like James, and they didn't realize he usually sounded confident and upbeat. Warm and friendly, and as though he had all the time in the world to focus on you. Just you.

I shook my head. This whole fairy godmother thing was getting too conspiracy theory for me. If I kept this up, within an hour I'd be wearing a tinfoil hat and burying coffee cans of cash out in the woods. This had to be nothing more than a nice stack of coincidences lining up in their favour.

"Yeah, it looks like it's not happening tonight," he continued. "Did you want to go for a milkshake?"

For the second time today, I tossed my phone as if it had become too hot to hold, and it clattered across the table, then tumbled off the edge and into Estelle's lap. She lifted the phone and placed it on the glossy wood surface between us.

"Hello? Char?" James' voice carried to me.

"How did you do that?" I whispered.

"I'm your fairy godmother," Estelle whispered back, arms out, her expression radiating happiness.

I scowled and lifted the phone to my ear, one eye on the crazy woman sitting across from me. "Where would we go?"

"Peter's."

My phone felt too heavy.

How did Estelle and her hoodlums know that was my favourite place? No, that was common knowledge. Plus, while deep diving into my life, they surely would have hacked my bank accounts, viewed my numerous Peter's Drive-In transactions, or even just hacked my phone's GPS and noted how often I landed there.

"Or," James added dryly, "we could go somewhere 'fancy' like Earl's, except tonight's water leak could be problematic." He paused a beat, his tone turning wry and playful. "Or is somewhere like Earl's not real-woman enough for you?"

CHAPTER 4

~ *James* ~

Something wasn't right with Char. She'd lied to me earlier about her walk-by. But most importantly, she was always up for milkshakes, and she'd just abruptly ended our call with a quick 'text you later' after what sounded like a scuffle with her phone, along with a whispered conversation.

Was she actually on a date? Because if she was, and had to whisper about me to some dude and fight over her own phone, I wanted to find the man and give him a good shake before punting him out of her life. A woman like Char deserved better than that. All women did.

Also, were milkshakes on the table: yes or no?

Turning my phone over in my hands, I considered the idea that she might be upset with me for waving the pricey gift shop necklace in front of her. I'd been so caught up in being the one to show it to her, anticipating the way her face would light up, that I hadn't even thought about the money part of it.

I sighed, hoping I was just being paranoid, and that Char would soon text me about meeting up.

Nothing against Alana, my date, but I'd been relieved when I'd arrived at Earl's to discover they were closed for the night due to a water leak. Obviously, like me, she'd only agreed to our date because of my mom. The two women worked together in the Salvation Army offices, and my mom had been the one to set us up. When I'd called Alana to let her know about Earl's, she hadn't suggested another place or time. And neither had I.

As for my mom, she meant well, but I could find my own dates. Preferably ones who kept me on my toes with their lust for life, and weren't too skinny. A beefy guy like me needed a woman I could hug without worrying about snapping her spine like a toothpick.

Which brought my mind back to Char and her delicious curves. What was up with her?

Why had she been so eager to get off the phone? And more to the point, why was she dishing out mistruths and keeping secrets?

And why hadn't I cancelled my date and tagged along with her when she'd asked?

CHAPTER 5

~ *Char* ~

"He was looking forward to that date," I snapped at Estelle, having ended my call with James. I still couldn't believe I'd asked this mind-controlling monster with the bright red hair to target my friend's dating life. Talk about over the line. Why had I wished for his date to fall through? And why had Estelle granted it? James rarely dated, which meant this woman had to be special, and I'd just wished her away.

No, no. None of this wishing business could be true. It wasn't real. I hadn't made that happen. I was having a dream. I'd fallen asleep on the couch after work. Or maybe I'd been hit by a car on my way to the museum and was actually in a coma.

I surreptitiously tried pinching myself. It hurt. But we felt things in our dreams, too, right? I sighed and scrubbed my face, a very real feeling of guilt for my actions against James pouring through me like lava.

"I can't believe that's allowed—to meddle in someone else's life," I grumbled.

Estelle's smile wobbled, and a flicker of uncertainty lingered in her gaze.

I opened my folder of wishes and scanned them again. There were a lot of granted wishes on my invoice surrounding my numerous crushes over the years. Had I really wished for someone to love me that many times? I read the invoice again, heart sinking, while Estelle talked through the basics of being able to hear my wishes.

There was no way that someone—anyone, even my own mother—could know about all of these so-called private wishes. But fairy godmothers? They couldn't be real. If I genuinely had one, wouldn't I already be in Greece, touring the ruins with my dad?

My eyes stung, and I clenched them shut, reminding myself that I'd figure this out like I always did when faced with a problem, because I was brave and strong.

As well as selfish—as I'd just proven with James.

But really, my selfishness was nothing new. The ultimate evidence was here, staring me in the face from the invoice's first page. My tenth birthday wish. I definitely remember how hard I'd wished for my dad to be home when he'd been out working extra shifts to repair the car after mom had slid off an icy road. I'd put my whole heart into it, and he'd surprised me by coming home and telling me exactly what I'd wanted to hear—that he hated missing my special day. That he'd been away at work and figured, what the heck? He wanted to be home, so he was going home. What would they do? Fire him?

Well, they had. Right after the three of us had gone out for brunch where the server had brought a candle-lit piece of cake to our table. I'd been so happy, and simply over the moon with the attention. My whole family together, doing something centred around me—what could have been better?

Then Dad got canned for skipping out of work, and nothing was the same for the three of us again. I'd always known it was my fault for wishing him home, and whomever wrote up this invoice knew it, too.

Money had been tight for the following six months after Dad lost his job. So tight that there'd been no renewed library membership, no sign up for baseball that summer, endless bottle picking in the ditches, and yet another move. Mom withdrew into herself and daytime TV to the point that even when Dad finally got work again, I'd basically been home alone even when she was there. Then she'd found *him*. My stepdad. Too loud, too gregarious. Plus, he had his own daughter. Perfect, slim, fun, and outgoing in an easy way that made me feel extra awkward.

I never lived with them. The only times I ever stayed with Mom and her new happy, perfect family was when Dad was working away and couldn't find someone to shuffle me off to. Eventually, I'd just started staying home alone, even though, legally, I was probably too young.

My mom and dad had never really gone on any trips when they'd been together, and I still didn't understand the super-social, excitement-loving woman my mom had become after meeting Damon. Had she always been longing to get out more and experience more thrills? All I knew was that I'd felt like an unwanted misfit, everyone just waiting for me to turn eighteen so I wouldn't be their problem any longer.

I opened my eyes, blinking away the visual stars that had appeared from keeping my eyes so tightly closed, and stared at the invoiced wish again. One greedy little wish that had started the wrecking ball swinging toward my family.

Who would ever grant such a request, knowing it would lead to familial devastation?

"When our clients reach the age of 9,125 days," Estelle was saying, "we are within the bounds of our magical laws to start billing them for their wishes."

"Nine thousand and...?" My overwhelmed mind was no longer absorbing information, stuck on that one bad wish.

"Leap years. I know." Estelle rolled her eyes. "It complicates the math. That and business days. Your world. Our world. Rules, regulations, Mrs. C.'s list."

"Mrs. C.'s list?"

"Witches. They play by their own rules and interfere with ours whenever they feel like it."

"How is it okay to grant wishes that ruin everything for others? What about their wishes and their sense of agency?"

"That's a great question. It has a very complicated and nuanced answer."

"And that is...?"

"Your life is the product of your wishes. It is made up of your past, future and present all together, all at once."

"Okay, but you just stepped into James's present and messed it up."

"We are all interconnected, and have our own destinies and sense of agency." She intertwined her fingers. "All of our pasts, presents and futures are woven together."

"I know, but I just took away his...whatever. I interfered. I did something wrong. Something bad."

She tipped her head to the side. "Did you?"

"Yes!"

"I can't grant a wish that will harm someone else."

"But you granted a wish that ruined my parents' marriage. That was harmful! Why wasn't I warned?"

"Oh, that wasn't me. Paxi was your original fairy godmother. She was very hands-off. Let the chips fall as they may. That was more her philosophy."

"I'd like to speak to her, please." I had a few things to get off my chest thanks to her granting that tenth birthday wish that had stolen my family.

Estelle's lips disappeared for a moment as she chewed on them. "She uh…"

I leaned forward, sensing a clue that, at last, might allow me to pry this whole mess open. "What?"

"Got eaten by a dragon."

I sighed in defeat. This conversation was ludicrous.

"I'm sorry," Estelle said softly.

"None of this adds up. How do you know about my birthday wish if Paxi granted it? Why would she devastate my family like that?" The idea of having someone else to blame was a reprieve from my own guilt.

"I can't know her reasoning, but often, a granted wish creates space."

"Yeah, it made space for my parents to get divorced, my dad to have his heart broken, and for my mom to find someone new. She moved on to a perfect life with a better husband and daughter. Paxi made space for me to be forgotten about." My chest was heaving, the hurt fresh like overturned soil in the spring, loamy and moist and oh-so cold. "There was plenty of harm in that stupid, childish wish, and it should never have been granted."

The sympathy in Estelle's eyes made emotion well in my eyes. "I promise to do better by you."

"I don't care! I want my family back. I want for bad things to never happen. Why would she hurt us like that?"

"We can allow a temporary harmful effect in order for long-term beneficial effects to occur. It's about energy, karma, balance and putting more good into the world than we take with each granted wish. The reach can last—"

"Explain James's ruined date." I crossed my arms. "Where's the beneficial effect for him?"

Estelle's slow smile suggested a secret.

"What?"

"You care for him."

"Of course! He's my friend, and it was *my* awful wish that ruined his night. I need to know what my carelessly tossed wish is going to do to him."

"You will see in time."

"No! I need to know now so I can stop it." My imagination was running wild with the possible consequences I'd set in motion with my wish. My lovely friend being single forever thanks to this one broken date. His faith in love demolished. It felt dramatic, but what had occurred after wishing my dad home on my birthday was evidence that things could go really bad—and fast.

"It's all good, Char. Be rest assured."

"How can you know that?"

Her smile was serene and unexpectedly reassuring. My relief took me by surprise, making me realize how worked up I'd gotten. "Why are we even talking about this?" I muttered. "You aren't real."

Her face fell, and she looked at my phone, then up at me with childlike confusion. "But I made him call you like you wished."

"You need to make this bill go away." I pushed it across the table toward her. "I didn't know I was being charged. There is no approval from me. There have to be laws. Notice. All of that stuff."

"There was notice. I saw it!" Estelle perked up. She swivelled in her chair, pushing herself across the room in her bright red heels. She grabbed a thick, battered file folder—not pink—from the files stacked on the desk, then rolled herself back to the table. Estelle dropped the stuffed folder onto the table with a flourish, sending sticky notes and small pieces of note paper fluttering out of the folder and onto the dusty carpet below.

"Why isn't anything in here pink?"

"Paxi loathed pink. She thought it was a weak colour." Estelle lifted a page from the stack. "Notice of future payment was granted to you on the eve of your thirteenth birthday. You were quite young." She smiled at me. "You'd caught the hang of the wish bug early."

"What notice?"

"It was served to you in a dream." She placed the paper on the table and spun it to face me. "Signed by Paxi."

"Yeah, no. A dream that I had when I was a—a *child*—is *not* fair warning that you plan to bill me a hundred grand well over a decade later. This isn't *real*."

A shiver ran down my spine as a remembered dream flit into my mind. An old lady had stumbled into my room in a gauzy dress, muttering about wishes and payment. It had felt ominous and had freaked me out so much I hadn't been able to sleep more than a wink for days. I'd barely made the baseball team that season thanks to my exhaustion and lack of focus.

"Dreams are discounted by humans, Estelle." Hearing the edge of panic in my voice, I inhaled a deep breath and forced myself to talk slower. "That's not serving proper notice, and this would never hold up in court."

"But the Magical Court of Rules is very strict," she whispered. "There's a process which was followed."

"Look." I closed my eyes and inhaled, aware I was arguing with a crazy person and expecting to win. "You can't just bill someone because they have the ability to focus on a wish! I *manifested* all of this!" I slapped the documents in front of me.

Logically speaking, if wishes weren't real, then I couldn't truly be to blame for the demise of my parents' marriage.

Which then begged the question of why I'd been beating myself up over that wish for so many years? It was ridiculous. All of this was.

"I'm your fairy godmother. I want to make your life better. Are you not happy with your life or wishes?"

I shook the detailed invoice. "Why are there so many more wishes over the past few months? Huh? Talk about suss. Some of these things aren't even real wishes! This is nothing but a scam!" I smacked the last page to illustrate the silliness of it all.

Wishing my colleague would shut up for five minutes. Wishing for a clean public washroom. Wishing for Randy to leave me alone. Wishing to have my apartment all to myself for the three-day weekend. A shiver zipped down my spine.

"The fact that any of these things happened is kismet, or coincidence, or whatever you want to call it. It's *not* something you can bill someone for. It isn't even creating karmic space or whatever you called it."

"There are more wishes this quarter because I took over when Paxi...um, retired."

"Got eaten."

"Well, yes. She was getting a bit senile. So? More questions, or should we get you all paid up?"

"No, aren't you listening?"

Estelle blinked at me.

"You aren't real. None of this is real. I don't understand how you know all of this stuff." I shook my head. I'd believe in a psychic right now, but not this. "Just no."

"Just yes. I am your fairy godmother."

"Then I want a new one. One who can't hear me."

She looked as if she'd been slapped. "You think you'll find someone who cares about your wishes more than I do?" Her voice was wobbly. "One with...with better rates? We're regulated, you know."

"Well, I'm not paying."

Estelle stared at me.

"I don't have this kind of money," I explained.

The colour drained from her face.

I leaned back, arms crossed. "I couldn't pay this even if you were legit. Plus, I'm going to report you for an invasion of privacy."

"No, no. We are within the bounds." She patted a thick book at her side, one I hadn't noticed earlier. Had it always been there? It was massive and worn, leather-bound and oozing old-world vibes. "And wishes aren't free, Char. There are costs involved with every wish that's granted."

"I don't have the money. I'm basically broke and have no assets. You picked the wrong mark for your little psychic scam-a-roni. I'm not paying this." I shoved the papers so hard they flew off the desk.

"But...but." She was blinking so fast her lashes were a blur. "I'm never going to pass the level to become an eighty-fourth generation fairy godmother. That is what is expected of me."

"Really not my problem."

She was spiralling, gulping air between sentences. "I can't be demoted to a tooth fairy. Teeth gross me out! And I'm too big to be a garden fairy, and my black thumb will kill everything. Garden fairies are tiny and get eaten by frogs. They'll have to shrink me. What if they do it wrong and I end up with one giant arm that didn't shrink and everyone will scream in horror?" She jammed an arm in my direction. "I'll be shunned by the family. I have to pass my levels. I have to." Her voice was low, hoarse, and desperate. "This is my only chance. You have to pay your bill. It's in arrears, Char. It's due now, and I should have told the head fairy how much you owe before I ever granted you more wishes! I'll be demoted! I'll never pass."

I blinked at her performance, unsure if she was done. "Well, I can't pay it."

"You have to! You knew what this was going to cost you!"

"Actually, no." Her spiralling was making me more calm, more assured. "I mean, I never even got a price list."

Estelle, suddenly calm, chirped, "Of course you did!" She flipped to the sheet at the bottom of the thick file folder, frowned, then skimmed a list stapled inside the front flap of the folder. It had dates typed on the left and some sort of hand-written inventory beside it. Her jaw clenched, and she rapidly flipped through the scrawled pages, blinking hard.

And that was when Estelle started intermittently crying and swearing, and black and silver glitter began raining down around us.

CHAPTER 6

~ Estelle ~

Char had bolted.

And now the head fairy was summoning me into her office for my daily report, which wasn't due for another hour. Had she heard my unfairy-like swearing? Or maybe spotted the human tearing through the bullpen? Or had it been the silver and black glitter borne of my frustration, rage, fear and futility raining down in Paxi's old office that had clued her into the need to meet with me immediately?

Holding my scattered emotions inside, I walked as slowly as possible to the head fairy's office. She was going to shrink me into a tree fairy. I only hoped she would choose someone who knew the spell this time, because I hadn't been exaggerating about the giant-arm thing.

"Hope Igor's hungry," Trish sang as I trod past her pretty desk with its prominently displayed bouquet of posies. She began smacking her perfectly shaped lips like she was eating something tasty.

What was she even talking about? I shot her a disgusted scowl and kept my focus on the head fairy's office door. Tall. Gold. Imposing. And still so far away.

"You do know what she does to bad trainees who are beyond demotion, right?" Trish whispered, falling into step beside me like she was heading over to the wish machine. That was where the wishes came in from our clients. All day long the white and gold beast sputtered out a never-ending strand of paper, striped in different colours like a random rainbow, the wishes pooling on the floor until they were doled out to their assigned fairies.

It was cute. Quaint. And glitchy. In my first week, I'd bypassed the old, hard-of-hearing machine with some tech of my own that caught many more wishes. After all, I had to prove my worth to Gram-Gram (my great-great-great-great-great-great-grandmother who was head fairy of this region), and I figured my ticket was a bit of ingenuity and innovation to boost my granted wish revenue beyond everyone else's in the region.

In other words, it was the only hope I had because in our family of eighty-three generations of fairy godmothers, they all steadfastly refused to talk about their work outside the office despite holding many of the top fairy godmother positions. They felt it was up to each new generation to prove themselves without a drop of handy nepotism or any kind of assistance.

That meant I was lagging behind pretty much every other fairy godmother trainee in my cohort as their families had sent them to fairy godmother playschool, elementary school, junior high school and then, at last, high school. They'd had thirteen or more years of tutoring, quizzes, and memorizing our giant rule book. Whereas I felt a lot like Harry Potter on his first day at Hogwarts. Every day.

And since I came from a family of high-ranking fairy godmothers, Trish, in particular, wanted to show me up. Likely because her family and mine were constant rivals for pretty much every high-ranked seat in the whole wide fairy godmother queendom. It didn't help that my family had the better fairy house with nicer shaped rocks, gems and shells on our front door as gifts from the humans, and from our back deck we could watch the water sprite games in the pond like we were royalty sitting in our private spectators' box.

Trish really wanted me to fail. And I really, really did not want that.

"She feeds them to Igor," Trish said wickedly, her face awash with a delighted smile as my legs lost their ability to propel me. She danced past. "Nice knowing you." She spun, blowing me a light kiss before disappearing around a cubicle corner.

I swallowed hard. Surely that was just a nasty little lie meant to scare me. It couldn't be true. The ogre from accounting, eating fairies? Gram-Gram wouldn't allow that.

But how many failed fairies did I know?

Not a single one.

How many had I heard about?

Also, not a single one.

I'd only ever heard about demotions. Had I messed up enough that I wasn't even worthy of a demotion from fairy godmother down to a tree or tooth fairy? Or was Trish just taking advantage of my lack of knowledge?

A nearby fairy caught my wandering, panicked gaze from where she was sitting at her desk, and she quickly went back to work, her body shivering, and my doubts multiplying.

With stiff legs, I began moving again. Would I get a chance to say goodbye to my family? Would my portrait, already half-painted in anticipation of me graduating into a fully-fledged fairy godmother, ever grace the halls of our fairy house? What would happen to it? And my beautiful shoes that had been so hard to come by in our pink world—they'd go to waste.

"Estelle. Report!" the head fairy snapped from her office.

I entered slowly through the gold door. On the opposite pink wall was another gold door that led to the reception area. I stood on the worn spot of faded pink carpet in front of Gram-Gram's rosewood desk and reluctantly met her lavender-coloured eyes. She was all in pink today again. Chiffon that rustled when she moved. Her golden hair was more silver than in the photos at home.

"What is this I hear about no price list? Did you not go through Paxi's files from top to bottom and double-check everything before you resumed the granting of wishes?"

"Paxi was a legend," I squeaked.

A crusty, perfect legend who'd rarely ever granted wishes in her final years. I'd met her at family functions and had noted the reverence. But I hadn't truly realized she was a legend and trailblazer until I'd gotten into training and everyone had greeted me with a hushed level of deference upon learning I was related to her. That had lasted until I'd failed my first quiz. Now I was at the bottom of the pack and the most eager to prove myself. But apparently I should have been going over Paxi's latter work with a fine-toothed comb.

"As not everyone is aware," the head fairy told me, "her work wasn't perfect in her final days, and she had been ailing for some time before we realized it and reduced her load. I know there were many things to check, but that is part of the job. And quite frankly, with your lineage, I expect more from you."

Everyone did. They thought the rules and regulations were running through my blood. Which they were not. Surely Gram-Gram, being a family member, knew the uphill battle I was facing for being kept in the dark for so many years and could cut me a break. Just a teeny tiny one that resulted in allowing me to continue my training.

"Paxi forgot to bill her youngest clients when they came of billable age," I reminded her. I'd been the one to catch that oopsie. Not the accounting department who'd missed the discrepancies during audits, and not Trish, who'd been dealt the other half of Paxi's small client list.

I'd thought my great-great-by-at-least-fifty-times aunt's slip-ups had been overlooked due to her status and orneriness, but it seemed Gram-Gram and others had actually been quietly keeping tabs on her. If I was part of her account's clean-up crew, was that a compliment? A severe test? Or a setup that guaranteed my failure?

Maybe Paxi had been fed to that dragon. Because how could you oust someone who went against the whole organization and practically predated it? When Your Fairy Godmother's offices had switched to more branded colours—pink, a colour my fellow trainees had been indoctrinated to wear since birth—Paxi had steadfastly refused. At the moment, her office was preserved the way she'd left it, without a stitch of pink present, but I figured one day Gram-Gram would get her hands on it and barf pink all over everything.

My new dragon theory had me rethinking my resistance to wearing pink like the others.

"I'm the one who authorized the accounting team to send the invoices," Gram-Gram reminded me right back, clearly unimpressed with my trainee position-saving argument.

"But I missed the price list," I admitted. I desperately wanted to point out that so had Trish. With Paxi's clients split between us, surely she also had clients missing price lists, too.

Come to think of it, cleaning up Paxi's accounts couldn't be hush-hush since Trish was part of it, and she'd happily smear our family name through the mud in hopes of elevating her own. Was this an act of transparency by allowing others to potentially see how bad Paxi had become at her job? Or couldn't Gram-Gram see through seemingly sweet, backstabbing suck-ups such as Trish and thought she was a trustworthy trainee?

"The checklist, Estelle." Gram-Gram gave me a stern look. "All of your assigned accounts. Run them again."

"Yes, ma'am."

"Find what else was missed and report back. No shortcuts. You're a dreamer, and floating through this job will not get you anywhere. You need to think differently. You need to see the flaws, the problems and come up with a solution. You will be treated the same as the other trainees."

I opened my mouth to tell her about the tech I'd commissioned a hobbit to create for me so I could capture more of my clients' wishes. But I held back, realizing I hadn't asked for authorization, and my initiative might actually sink me further into the hot water I was currently wading through.

"We have systems in place for a reason. You need to prove you're *worthy* of becoming a fairy godmother. There is no room for mess-ups. We are working with karma which is a very strong force. If you're not ready and can't handle it, I need to know."

"Yes, ma'am. I understand it, and I can handle it. I want to make the world a better place. I do. I really do."

"Don't suck up to me. *Prove* yourself to me."

"Yes, ma'am." I blurted out what was in my heart. "I'd also like to say that I believe Char deserves good things and that we need to do right by her." Gram-Gram nodded. "I want to create space for her in the world. I want to create a vacuum so the good flows in toward her."

"You aren't advanced enough for that." Now she was shaking her head. "You can't yet control which form of energy will flow, or which way it will go. Don't start punching above your levels and working with things you're not equipped for. You hear me?"

Her warning tone had me straightening my spine. "Yes, ma'am."

"And no more wishes."

I blinked. "Sorry?"

Was I being demoted?

"No more granting of wishes for Char until she is paid up. Her account was flagged by Igor."

But we couldn't cut her off! Char deserved a happily ever after and bright smiles, as well as someone creating space for her. All she wanted was someone in which to share the small moments of her life. She didn't need another uncaring, crusty fairy godmother assigned to her like Paxi. I mean, she'd been a legend and all, but in her final years, she'd barely allowed the good energy to bloom in people's lives.

I believed everyone had the right to be cherished and loved in a way that they could see and feel, and I wanted to be the one who granted that for Char at long last. Her world was waiting and ready to open up for her. She just needed me and a little magic. And numerous well-placed wishes.

"Do I tell her she can't wish anymore?"

"You told her about divine timing?" Gram-Gram had her fingers steepled, her eyes bright and alive as she worked out her plan.

"Yes, I think I mentioned it."

"Good. She'll just think the timing isn't right for her wishes. We don't want to scare her off. She's one of those dolphins or whatever Trish calls our best clients."

"A whale." I hated the term and, even more, I hated that Gram-Gram was now using Trish's slang.

"Yes. She's a whale of a client. She makes lots of wishes, which is good for us. So, we'll bide our time this quarter while she pays off her debt." Her voice lowered. "It should have been you who flagged her account, Estelle. As well, you should have stopped granting her more wishes. Go back to your desk and read up on the financial thresholds and protocols. Then write me a five-hundred-word summary before you leave tonight. Leave it on my desk."

I held in my groan. "Yes, ma'am."

"That's two issues in one day, Estelle," she said quietly.

"I'm sorry. I'll do better. Please don't feed me to Igor."

Gram-Gram blinked at me, then leaned forward, aiming her right ear—her better one—toward me. "I'm sorry, what?"

"I heard that Igor—"

"Nonsense. He's vegan, Estelle."

Her tone made me feel about an inch tall for believing Trish's lies. The head fairy sighed heavily as though tired of me, and embarrassment washed over me. "Is there anything else I should be aware of?"

I sucked in a breath, knowing I needed to simply blurt out my next problem. "Char doesn't believe."

"Incorrect."

"But she said—"

"Did you pass your exam on this topic?"

I nodded. She knew I'd had to pass all the introductory and midlevel tests to be given client access.

"List the reasons we know she believes."

"There's a portal into our offices which hovers between our worlds," I said slowly, thinking it through. "It's protected by a spell. If she truly didn't believe, she wouldn't have been able to see YFGM, let alone enter."

Gram-Gram nodded.

"She also wouldn't have a bill with us, because if you don't believe, we can't hear your wishes." I started to smile. "So somewhere deep down inside she believes, even if she doesn't want to."

"Very good."

"I granted her a small wish to prove my identity like it says in the training, but she still said she didn't believe me. She said it was kismet. She also said humans don't believe in what happens during dreams."

"In regards to her billable wishes notice from Paxi?"

I nodded.

Gram-Gram sighed. "That issue may be on us more than on Char. But her not wanting to believe and pay up is not an original problem. She's a valuable client—assuming she makes good on her bill. It's best we don't cut her off completely, wouldn't you say?"

She lifted her brows at me and I nodded eagerly.

"We won't cut her off then. But no more granting of expensive wishes. Only ones that will help prove to her that you are the one making her wishes come true. She needs to be inclined to pay that hefty bill of hers."

"She said she's broke."

Gram-Gram waved a hand. "They all say that."

CHAPTER 7

~ *James* ~

I checked my phone again for a text from Char, barely refraining from sending her another. She was always amped about milkshakes, so why was she ghosting me? Something was definitely wrong.

I popped onto the various apps where we were friends, checking their maps, disappointed to see she was good about her privacy, and hadn't allowed her current location to be shared. Maybe I could convince her, for safety reasons, that she should always share her location with me.

Yeah, and come off as a stalker.

I'd been playing the long game, understanding instinctively that she could be easily spooked. She was strong, smart, fun and outgoing, but when it came to love, there was a big hurt hiding behind her sunny smile. Who had hurt her? She didn't talk about her past much, and I wondered if she suffered through a broken engagement, horrible breakup, or been cheated on.

Whatever it was, I vowed to never be a repeat. And so we'd slowly become friends, and I'd let her learn to trust me. Trust was huge for her, something not freely given, and every time she let me in a bit further, I felt like I'd won a massive prize.

But, we were in the friend zone, and I feared that if I made a move that was too fast or direct, I might scare her off. Especially if she didn't want to move beyond friends. And there were several reasons why she might not want to.

First was smarmy Greg, the museum's tour guide. He was smooth and flattered Char in a way that often made her blush and run her fingers through her hair. Was she interested or merely flattered? He was always asking Char about her passion —ancient pottery. She gave him interesting tidbits which he then used in his tours, delighting her. I wasn't the kind of guy who'd knock down another to prove my worthiness to a woman, but Greg sure made me want to.

Second, Char rarely stayed in during the evenings, and always seemed to be on the go. Whereas I didn't think twice about crashing my parents' games night with the neighbours. I liked my close-knit family. I also enjoyed adventure, however Char craved it like it was oxygen. Did she see us as too different?

It also didn't help that she'd never given off the interested vibe until more recently.

But tonight, the way she'd kept touching me, and had that whisper of possible jealousy when she'd asked about my date...

She could be interested. Definitely.

It was time to make a move, but I was nervous. I'd been holding back my attraction for so long, I feared that if she gave even so much as a hint that it was okay, I'd sweep her into my arms and kiss her breathless, confess my love and ask her to move in with me.

A bit much. To say I was way ahead of her was more than an understatement.

Drumming my fingers on the steering wheel, I sat in my car, mindlessly driving, not ready to head home to my lonely basement suite.

I was worried about Char tonight, and wasn't sure why.

She'd seemed nervous and awkward, like something was off kilter in her life and had sent her thoughts elsewhere.

Who did she have looking out for her? Her roommates were busy with their own lives, and it sounded as though her family wasn't that close. How would anyone know if she was in trouble and needed help? Who would she call? Tamara, for sure. But did she know that I'd also be there, night or day?

My phone vibrated, and I leapt to check the screen at the next red light, the tension draining from my shoulders and neck as I read the message.

MUSEUM BABE (CHAR)

Hey, sorry about that. Is it 2 late for milkshakes?

ME

Never.

Where R U? Pick U up?

MUSEUM BABE (CHAR)

Walking north on 10th.

Of course. Why hadn't I thought of swinging out that way?

Well, because knowing where she'd planned to go was not an invitation to show up there. That would be overeager and send her running.

I already felt like I had no game around this woman, and it made me careful. Maybe too careful. But I'd never had to hold back while pursuing a woman like I did with Char, and it was the hardest thing I'd ever had to do.

But she was worth it.

Unable to bury the smile that came with the knowledge that I'd soon be hanging out with her, I headed south past SAIT's campus, and over the bridge into the downtown's west end.

Minutes later, I slowed along tenth before spying her walking like she was trying to put distance between her and wherever she'd been. I pulled up alongside her.

She opened the car door and leaned in when I came to a stop. "Hey, cutie! Heading my way?" She fluttered her lashes in what was probably supposed to be flirty. It was adorable and so innocent I wanted to cup her beautiful face and kiss her.

"You bat your eyes at anyone going to Peter's?"

"Pretty much." She climbed in, doing up her seatbelt with trembling fingers. She smelled like fresh spring air.

I maneuvered the car through the quiet city streets, driving north, the last of the day's sunshine long gone from the sky.

"How's it going?" I tried for casual, reading her for signs on what had happened since I'd seen her last. She seemed her usual upbeat self, but there was a stitch of preoccupation in her expression, and an atypical quiet about her. Plus, there was the whole shaking-hands thing and the speed-walking she'd been doing.

Her voice grew low, like a kid in trouble. "Sorry about your date." Her eyebrows pitched upward as if she felt personally responsible for the way things hadn't worked out with me and what's-her-face.

"It's fine. Can't even remember her name."

"Yeah, but you didn't choose for your date to get cancelled."

I shrugged. "Things happen."

"A timely coincidence?" she muttered under her breath.

"What about you? Your walk-by seemed to take a while."

Char remained silent, watching the city from the side window. Finally, she shifted, facing me. "Have you ever made a wish and had it come true?"

"Probably."

"No, for real."

"I don't know. Why?"

"Think of one."

I laughed at her intensity. What bone had she locked onto now? I knew she'd gnaw it until she was done, but I had no clue how long that would take, or what this was about. I loved that she kept me on my toes and I could never guess where her busy mind was at. "I've wished for a basketball game win."

She was quiet a second. "That's not a real wish."

"You don't know guys."

"Do you believe in paranormal...things?"

"Like ghosts?"

"More like magical beings. Like fairy godmothers." She was eyeing me in a way that suggested my answer was important, and that I should tread carefully. "Like maybe things exist that we can't see? Ogres? Unicorns? Fairies?"

"My cousin went through a fairy phase. She loved them. She believed they're real."

She'd also been six. Char was a few decades beyond that.

She hunched deeper into her seat. "I always thought fairies were winged."

"Yeah. Me, too." What on earth had she seen in the past hour and a half and why were we talking about fairies?

She shifted to watch me, face creased with concentration. "Think if they were real, they'd be our size? And have no wings?"

"Dunno. Doesn't really sound like a fairy."

"Right?" She pushed back in her seat, head shaking. "People are crazy."

I chuckled and allowed my imagination to roam. "I think, personally, if all that were real, I'd want to see fire-breathing dragons."

She watched me from the corner of her eye. "What about a witch or an ogre?"

"Nah, I'd choose to see something awe-inspiring and beautiful." As I pulled up at a red light, I met her gaze on the last word.

CHAPTER 8

~ *Char* ~

We pulled up to Peter's and parked, walking up to a window to order our shakes. Being a true drive-in, and this being the original location, there was no indoor seating, which I loved. We took our milkshakes and sat at a picnic table despite the evening's chill, the ice cream drink making me shiver.

"Sorry your date didn't work out," I said again, the guilt gnawing at me over my ill-thought-out wish. Because even though that had merely been a timely coincidence, I still felt as if I'd made it happen, just like I had when my dad was fired all those years ago.

I wasn't yet sure where I stood on the fairy godmother thing, but I did believe in manifestation, karma, kismet, and that our thoughts were powerful things. Despite that, I still couldn't wrap my head around how Estelle had formed such an intensely private list. The more I thought about it, the more it felt like fairy godmothers had to be real—simply because of the knowledge she had of my innermost thoughts, wishes and dreams. Unless she was a psychic tuning into my personal frequency and pulling out wishes and their dates. Somehow, that didn't quite sit right, either. Maybe it was the glitter that had rained down around us in the office just before I'd run out of there.

Because I was pretty sure a psychic couldn't do that.

The same with the sudden chill that had entered the office. It had been freaky and out of this world. Literally out of this world.

I mean, I *wanted* a fairy godmother to be real. But the problem was money. Wishes were supposed to be free.

"First dates are awkward," James said, pulling my mind back to the here and now. He'd taken the spot across from me at the picnic table, his large, tall frame not quite the right fit for the attached bench and table.

"First dates are so bad I haven't been on one in a year." I gave him a playfully serious look over my straw.

"You lie."

"You're right. Eight months."

"You lie."

"Your tone suggests I'm a hottie who should be getting more dating action than I am, James." I lifted a brow in his direction. Well, I tried. My brow muscles were hopelessly attached like Siamese twins, so when I tried to lift one as though I was mysterious, I probably just looked surprised or overly interested as both brows moved in unison.

He nodded thoughtfully, his kissable lips puckering in faux displeasure. "We both should be."

I sat up taller. This was where we made a marriage pact, like in the movies or romance novels. Something along the lines where if we weren't married by thirty-five, we'd marry each other.

I'd hold out for a chance at that.

Even though I was certain he wanted the warm and cozy homebody type. I mean, his parents had beaten the odds and were still together—happily, by the sounds of it—and he was putting out the marriage vibes. He wanted stability and loveable perfection. Everything I wasn't.

"I don't go out with someone I know I don't want," I explained. "Why lead them on with an awkward first date and get caught up in the hope? I have friends, and I can have fun on my own." I cast my eyes downward again, as though my milkshake needed my full concentration.

James remained silent, and I peeked up to find him looking amused, his eyebrows waggling.

"James!" I gasped. "Get your mind out of the gutter!"

"*Char.*" He placed a hand against his chest as if he was deeply wounded by my insinuation.

"But James? Answer me this: how are we going to get you married off and build your cozy little love nest if you don't go out on more dates?"

"Sorry, my what? And it sounds like I put myself out there more than you do."

"Yeah, but you're a nester. You're looking for a woman who's calm and steady and loves holding down the fort. Someone hoping to get married and start a family and settle into a routine."

"Um..." He winced as though I was severely off track. But I'd heard the wistful, confident tone when he talked about his own family growing up. I could tell he expected it for himself. Domestic harmony. Homemade cookies. Meals shared around the family table. Spouses who adored each other every single day. True love. The works. Barf. Hello, reality check? That stuff wasn't real. There was no evidence other than maybe his parents. And their relationship, by the sounds of it, was a ticking bomb. Men had midlife crises. Women ran off with other men. It was probably just a matter of time.

"No?" I asked. "Where did I assume wrong?"

"I want love and a...nest. Eventually." He looked so uncomfortable. It was cute.

"A love nest, right." I wanted to giggle, but held my face neutral.

"But I also want fun and surprises with someone special, travel and adventures," he said, his tone grumpy. "You make it sound like I want to go back to the 1950s and hunker down there."

"Fun and adventure?" I couldn't keep the skepticism from my voice. Probably because my heart was singing that maybe James and I were more alike than I'd realized.

"You're mocking me."

"No. Not really. And, to be honest, if I were a dude, I'd want the 1950s. Someone to cook and do my laundry sounds heavenly."

He sighed heavily. "Not what I said."

"But admit it. Men had it made for a while. And it would be nice to have someone take care of all that life stuff. You just work and come home and chill." I put on a deep voice and held out a hand as though cupping an invisible glass. "Honey, beer me!"

James laughed, the skin around his eyes crinkling. He was going to be such a silver fox when he got older. But, even through his mirth, his shoulders were stiff, his gaze not quite meeting mine for very long. It was like he had a secret. Like he was holding something back.

I gasped, slapping the picnic table with the palms of my hands. "You secretly want that!"

"No, I don't."

"Then what?"

"I just want a partner who's happy, self-fulfilled and content," he said with obvious discomfort. "Someone who surprises me."

"Nice list. Get it off the internet?"

"You think I can't want that?"

"I think you can, but if you truly do, it means you're perfect."

He slurped his shake and rolled his eyes at me, clearly exasperated. And something else I couldn't quite put my finger on.

"And," I continued, "it begs the vital and most important question."

"Which is," he asked dryly, undoubtedly going along with the conversation for my amusement. Did I mention he was the best?

I leaned forward, layering drama into my voice. "What is wrong with James Backstrohm?"

"Excuse me?" He actually looked a bit insulted. "I like to think I'm pretty great."

"Yeah, yeah, you present well. But it still all begs the question."

"Why I'm not married?"

"Yes. And why is that? What is your fatal flaw? Webbed feet? You secretly gaslight your girlfriends behind closed doors? Hmm?"

He choked on his shake, his brows pitched together in clear mental pain. "Do I look like the kind of man who'd do that?"

"Maybe."

He glowered at me, but there was no real heat.

"For all I know, you're insecure about your webbed feet, and afraid your girlfriend'll tell the world and then you'll never work in this town again because everyone's too freaked out to hire you."

He snorted, his lips curving upward.

But, again, the shifty eyes. I pressed against the picnic table, reaching for his hand. His was warm, unlike mine, which was freezing—even though I'd stopped holding my shake a long time ago and had been keeping my hands tucked in the cuffs of my jacket. "Tell me."

"My feet aren't webbed."

"You turn into a werewolf at every full moon? You secretly believe in fairy godmothers?"

I held my breath in case he said yes to the last one and had vital, useful information for me.

"Have you ever been engaged?"

Wait. What?

I scoffed, confused by his question.

Me? Engaged? Not even close. My hand slackened its grip on his. "Wait. Have you?" I gasped and gripped his fingers so tight he winced. He had! "When? What happened? Tell me everything."

He slipped his hand out from under mine, leaned back, the tips of his fingers hooked between the table's slats. He let out a slow breath.

"What was she like? Why did you break up? Come on, tell me. We're friends, right? I mean, you already told me you don't have webbed feet and you're not a werewolf. This is a cakewalk."

His eyes flicked up to meet my own, then flashed back to his milkshake, which he snatched up and took a long pull from. His was chocolate. Not strawberry, like mine.

So, not quite the perfect guy. But not worth tossing back into the sea of eligible men. Especially if we were both still single at age thirty-five.

He set down his milkshake. "I'm sorry about the necklace."

"The necklace?"

"Yeah. I knew it was expensive. I just thought you'd really like it."

Oh. The one from the museum. "I do! I love it. I..." I shrugged, feeling that annoying pinch of not having as much cash as I wanted. "And hey buster! I see you trying to change the subject!"

He gave me a cute grin that was half mischievous and half apologetic.

I lowered my voice, leaning forward in hopes he'd dish about his breakup. "Did you get the ring back?" How big was it? Did he plan to give it to someone else? What did men do with returned engagement rings, anyway? "Are you still on the rebound? Was tonight's date to break your rebound cherry?" How did I not know this about him?

He sighed and rolled his eyes, but I could see he didn't mind me asking. Not truly. "It's been a few years, Char."

"Oh." I nodded. "Okay."

"And we broke up because..." He let out a long slow breath, scanning the parking lot over my shoulder as though searching for an appropriate answer.

"Because why?" He was driving me crazy. Yeah, yeah, he didn't want to talk about it, obviously, but I had to know absolutely everything. Now.

"We weren't..." He shrugged and shook his head like he couldn't believe we were having this conversation, and he was afraid of scaring me. "We were good together."

"That makes no sense, James."

"Yeah, no. But we weren't *great* together. You know?"

It was clear he wasn't well-versed at explaining his failed romance. Unlike women. By now, we'd have the elevator version which was a super quick life story of the romance that could be shared in less than a minute, and then the hours-long version which dissected every tiny nuance of the relationship, building up to the tear-jerking break-up. That version was best served with lots of wine or ice cream, depending on whether you wanted to nurture a bitter or wallowing mood.

"You broke it off?" I confirmed.

He nodded.

Wow.

He really did want the fairytale. He sure was going to be disappointed when he was eighty and realized he could have settled for 'good enough' half a century sooner. And that there'd been no reason for him to spend his life alone in his little love nest, waiting for Miss Perfect because she didn't exist. Women were a hot mess of inconsistencies. We were perfect only in our ability to keep the world of men on their toes due to our whims of unpredictability.

"Why?" I asked.

"When I made future plans, I didn't assume she'd be there with me, or that she'd want to be doing what I was. Or that she'd want to try doing different things. There was a plan, and it was fine, but it held no space for other things to flow in or out of our lives."

I stared at him, fascinated. He really was the full meal deal with a side of fries. No, make that a poutine upgrade. When this guy married, it wouldn't be due to some stupid, silly pledge between friends. He was holding out for a lightning strike: true love.

Wait. Something he'd said about space tickled a memory. What had Estelle told me earlier? *Often, a granted wish creates space.*

There was a ringing in my ears as I focused on James, trying to sort out the connection between Estelle, my earlier wish, his breakup, and the eerie sense of déjà vu that was sending shivers up my spine.

"You wanted space?" I asked carefully.

"Not like that," he said with a testy edge.

"No, I know. I meant, like, for...serendipity?"

He nodded, his eyes lighting up like I'd hit on something he didn't expect most people to understand.

I reconfigured this new information into my view of James. But I still couldn't help but wonder if his words were somehow due to my earlier wish and Estelle's belief in creating space. Or serendipity, as it was. Did James truly believe what he was saying? Were these his words to explain his breakup, or was he under a spell?

I shook off my thoughts. James had broken up with his fiancée years ago. Well before my stupid date-breaking wish. Estelle had really gotten into my head back there.

Assuming what she had done to him was real and not just a timely coincidence. A cosmic joke at my expense.

"You want kids?" I asked James.

"Yeah."

"And she did, too?"

"Yeah."

"How long were you together?"

"A while." He placed his elbows on the table, dropping his arms so they were crossed along the table's edge.

"High school?"

He nodded. "We didn't get really serious until university, though."

His romance was kind of like Tamara and Kade's—started in high school, but again, the real world had proved that their so-called love wasn't enough. Was it ever?

"How about you?" he asked.

"No. Never engaged."

"Want kids?"

"Sure. If it happens. But I don't really see myself getting married."

James blinked, as if I'd suddenly switched to speaking a foreign language.

"What? I can't imagine it." I tucked my hands deeper into my jacket's sleeves.

"Can't imagine it or don't want it?"

"I never said I don't want it."

"So you do want it? Kids and a husband?"

I could feel heat tracking its way up to my cheeks, my imagination dishing up delectable images of what it might be like to have a man as steady and sure as James in my life. "Sure. Of course. Assuming I find the right person." I gave him a sly smile. "And he likes me back. I'm not into brainwashing and kidnapping."

He let out a guffaw. "Good to know."

"So what was your ex-fiancée like?"

"Nice."

"Yeah, but...like, what's your type?" When he didn't reply immediately, I suggested, "Skinny, Swedish. Smart. All the things." He and his type would make beautiful babies. That, I could see. She'd have her life together, but would also book last-minute vacations to exotic locales off the beaten path as well as know how to cook killer meals from any nationality. And maybe speak a few languages to boot.

"Actually, no."

"Then what's your type?"

He stared at me long enough my heart thundered in my ears. It felt like he was suggesting I was his type. And we all knew that couldn't possibly be true.

CHAPTER 9

~ *Char* ~

An hour later, back in my apartment, with my milkshake long gone and my mood much improved thanks to some time with James, I sat in the living room trying to sort out my thoughts.

Was I really James's type? Did he actually want more serendipity in his life and not a routine-driven, stable, cozy marriage I'd assumed?

Felipe was a horrible listener, chattering at me until I showed him I had no more lunch leftovers, then abandoning me with my unfinished thoughts about Estelle to go curl up in his shoebox nest under my bed. I sat in the dark living room, wishing my roommates were home—at least one of them—so I wouldn't be alone with the endless whirling of thoughts about James and fairy godmothers.

Fairy godmothers. Was I going to believe in the possibility or not?

Had my evening been real? Could it be that I was experiencing an intense fever and was hallucinating, or had slipped a mental cog and was now delusional? It would explain the way James had looked at me when he'd said the word 'beautiful' and also when he'd given me that meaningfully look when saying that skinny Swedish babes weren't his type.

I'd already tried walking the line of grout in the tiled bathroom and hadn't run into anything other than out of tile lines to test myself on. Now I placed a palm to my forehead. It felt about the right temperature. I covered one eye, then the other, to check my sight. That all seemed fine, too. Not very scientific testing, but nothing major was jumping out as a possible explanation. Therefore, my experience at Your Fairy Godmother's offices was likely to have been real. But if I accepted the reality of Estelle and her magical, glitter-shooting world, I also had to accept that I was massively in debt. And that made me feel a bit nauseous.

Everything on that detailed invoice was too accurate to discard as a mere coincidence. She knew things I'd wished upon that I didn't even want to admit to myself.

I sighed and dropped my head into my hands, doubting reality.

My phone beeped with a text.

My dad had replied to my earlier joke with a laughing emoji. I'd sent him an article about a 1900-year-old kiln that had been found in Corsica, which he'd ignored. He'd liked my joke about Athens, though. But who wouldn't?

Why did people living in Athens have a tough time getting up in the morning?

Because Dawn was tough on Greece.

Dawn, the dish soap. Get it? Yeah, it was bad. But I had to stay connected to my dad somehow.

A key rattled in the door at the bottom of the stairs. Randy? He wasn't allowed into our apartment without proper notice!

I quickly shut my room door, locking Felipe inside, and peered down the stairs.

"Hey," Tamara said, hustling through the main-level door as

was her habit so Randy couldn't waylay her. The trick seldom worked. The man was half ninja. And not in a cool, sexy way. "Glad to see you didn't get kidnapped."

"What? Why would I have been kidnapped?"

"That scam. Didn't you go past the address? You never texted back."

Oh, right. Texting her and the girls about the invoice from Your Fairy Godmother felt like days ago. I'd been so rattled after the silver-black glitter rain I hadn't even thought about jumping into the texting string to share an update.

"Sorry. I went for milkshakes with James right after."

"He likes you."

"As a friend." I stepped aside to let her pass me at the top of the stairs. "What happened with you?"

"What do you mean?"

"You were supposed to go camping with your family all weekend. Family reunion thingy."

She frowned at me as she hung up her coat on the rack between our bedroom doors. Our living room, kitchen and bathroom were on the street-facing side of the upper floor, and our bedrooms took up the back. "No. I told you I'm not going this year. I went out with Kade."

"Kade?" Her stupid ex?

"He was in town for an appointment so we grabbed supper." She tilted her head to one side in exasperation as she caught my expression. "Don't make that face."

"What face?" I ensured I properly schooled my expression and reopened my room door to return Felipe's freedom. My feelings about Kade were well known. He'd broken up with my best friend for the stupidest reason. Basically, he'd wanted to try something different—in other words, Jannifer Bryant.

That had worked out nicely for me though. I got to have my bestie as my roommate. Although, Tamara still hadn't embraced city living, and I worried that she was going to give up on her new city life with me if she was picking up with Kade again.

At least she hadn't brought him home with her.

Still, I was certain she'd packed a bag earlier this morning, and had planned to be gone the entire weekend. Even Randy had mentioned her being away.

Wait. Had I accidentally made a wish? I clapped a hand over my mouth to stifle a gasp. I had! When I'd returned from meeting Estelle, I'd wistfully wished one of my roomies would come home so I could talk it out with someone.

Oh, this wishing business was dangerous.

No. It was a coincidence. Just like with James and his cancelled date. I couldn't change the past with silly little wishes.

"What's up? You seem weird," Tamara said.

"Nothing," I said quickly. Too quickly. She turned, her long purse strap half-lifted to hang on a hook.

"What's wrong?"

"Nothing," I repeated, striving for a more casual air this time.

"You never say 'nothing' unless something's wrong."

"Just a weird day." I flopped onto the couch, toying with a jagged line of cuticle, pressing it back.

"Every day is weird in your world." She thought I brought home the strangest stories from my temp jobs. And sometimes I did, but she didn't understand how much I loved the constant change that came with my job. It kept me from getting stuck in repetition, the years clicking by and blending together until one day I got up from in front of the TV and ran off like my mom had.

Tamara sat in the armchair and shucked off a cowboy boot. Then the second one, dropping it onto the floor with a thud that had likely annoyed Caleb, whose suite was below our living room.

"I think I'm losing my mind," I said.

"That weird invoice?"

I nodded.

"Well, both you and the lady who came in today," Tamara said, referring to the dental office where she worked. "There are way too many people with too much dough, staring in the mirror and plotting new ways to spend it."

"Why? What happened?"

"This woman has a perfect set of chompers and she wants caps."

"So?"

"She said her real teeth weren't straight enough, big enough or white enough and that she wanted caps."

"And?"

"Dr. Gris said she could have them!"

"So?" I picked up one of Tamara's horse magazines and flipped through a few pages, relieved to be distracted from thinking about myself for a few minutes. "It's her mouth."

She slouched into the armchair. "We're going to whittle down her perfectly good teeth and put on caps. It's such a waste. It's so...so *vain*."

I laughed. "Welcome to the city. Want some Botox?"

She shot me a dark look. "Don't even start."

"A little lipo, maybe? Come on, highlights? A tattoo? Everyone's doing it."

She scowled. Her style was all-natural, and she was pretty enough with her brown eyes, matching wavy hair and a gentle spattering of freckles to pull it off. She looked like Maya Rudolph. In other words, entirely adorable.

"So what happened at the YGM place?"

"YFGM? It stands for Your Fairy Godmother."

Tamara's face lit up with delight. "Is it a store? It sounds fun! Did you get your invoice cleared up?"

I shook my head. "No. No, it's..." I sighed and sagged deeper into the couch, hands covering my eyes. "You're going to think I'm completely crazy."

~

AND THAT WAS how after explaining my super weird evening to Tamara, I ended up doing it again on Monday night for our other three roommates.

Josie, who'd been quiet for the entire story retelling, stood. "Okay."

"Okay, what?" I asked.

"We go."

"*There?*" I shivered in dread just thinking about going back to the offices of Your Fairy Godmother.

"Yes."

"Why?"

"Why not? You said you don't believe. So, let's prove it's not real."

I shared a quick look with Tamara. I'd confessed to her on Friday night that I sorta believed even though I didn't want to. It bent my mind and the logic it subscribed to, but there were too many things I couldn't explain away.

Going over all of those weird things again for my roommates had secured the idea that Estelle could somehow be telling the truth. Otherwise, how could I explain her knowing about that strange and haunting dream I'd had at age thirteen? And my car starting on the mountain road all by itself? How could she know about all of those deeply private things about me? How could I explain the magically hidden offices that transformed into a photocopy place, and then into a wooden door for YFGM? Or having James call me immediately after I'd wished he would? Or the freaky glitter rain?

There were too many unexplainable things to discount.

And, as sheepish as I was to admit it, a tiny bit of me *really* wanted to believe I had a fairy godmother.

"Do you think you can prove it's not real?" I asked Josie. She was our resident, passionate expert on imaginary worlds. She might be an inventory specialist with a super logical, analytical mind, but she was also a diehard romantasy reader. Although, to be fair, I'd often hear her scoffing while reading, complaining under her breath that the details were incorrect. Fact checking fantasy fiction. That was our Josie.

But if she felt she could prove Estelle wasn't really a fairy godmother, and put this internal mental debate to rest once and for all, I was all over it.

"Let's do it," she said, grabbing her jacket and marching toward the door.

My heart lifted at her take-charge spirit, and I followed her down the steps. She'd get to the bottom of this, and I'd never felt more grateful to anyone in my life.

Half an hour later, the five of us stood outside the spot where the door for Your Fairy Godmother had appeared for me on Friday night. There was nothing here. No number 1010B.

I paced back and forth, feeling pre-emptively stupid in case my imagination had made it all up and I'd dragged my roommates across the city's downtown for exactly nothing.

"It was like this when I first got here on Friday."

"Did you have to say something?" Josie asked me.

"To undo a spell?" Samantha scoffed. "This is too whack-a-doodle for me. I'm going home." She tossed her hair over her shoulder and pivoted to leave. She'd recently had the rebellious shade of green stripped from her Latino curls, returning it to a healthy dark, dark brown with golden heights. She looked like the millionaire trust fund babe that she was, and I bet that this gritty, rundown street was a bit too real for her. That and our whack-a-doodle behaviour. I mean, a woman could only handle so much, right?

"Wait." Josie caught her sleeve, watching me. "Think back."

I shrugged. "I was talking to myself."

"What did you say?"

"I said it was too bad YFGM didn't exist or something."

Beside me, Tamara gasped. With her mouth hanging open, she pointed to the building. "That was not here before."

It was the wooden door with the maroon YFGM sign above. Not the photocopy place like on Friday. I'd somehow skipped a step.

"What?" Samantha was frowning at the buildings. "Nothing changed."

"There's a wooden door," Josie said calmly, like this happened to her every day. "And sign for YGFM."

"How did you do that?" Tamara was shaking, and Samantha and Gabby were watching like she'd lost her mind.

"Do you see it?" Samantha asked Gabby, who shook her head. Samantha crossed her arms. "We don't see it. Are you trying to get me back for that birthday prank, Char?"

"No. The door is right here." I reached out, not quite touching it.

"It's a wall," Gabby stated flatly.

"They don't believe," Josie told me, her expression serene.

Samantha rolled her eyes. "We aren't four. Of course we don't believe in magically changing doors." She jutted out a hip, her demeanour giving off an air of exasperated impatience. "Can we go home now?"

"Yes!" I snapped, feeling freaked out and under pressure. "Go!"

"You can leave," Josie said calmly. "But I'm going to stick around."

"Why?" Samantha asked. "You have a portal to go through?"

"Something like that." Josie looked to me. "Shall we?"

I really didn't want to, but Josie was already pulling the door open, dragging a hesitant Tamara inside. At the last minute, I hopped over the threshold, turning back to see Samantha and Gabby frozen in place.

I gasped and stepped back outside again. They began moving, seemingly unharmed by the fact that moments before they'd been in an alarming state of stasis.

"Come on," Josie said impatiently, tugging me back through the doorway. "It's just a spell that bends time."

"A spell?" Wait. I thought Josie was here to help me prove this was all made up. Now she was talking about spells?

I slowly stepped into the entryway that was thick with plants, watching Samantha and Gabby freeze again. This felt like a really big thing—one of those things I couldn't rationally explain away. And especially one of those things that might prove that I really did have a fairy godmother.

"They'll be fine," Josie assured me.

"Are you sure?"

"Somewhat positive."

"How do you know?"

She shrugged, already pressing forward. "I don't."

Something in the plants to our left moved, and Tamara jumped, stumbling against me. Her eyes were wide, and she looked about ready to collapse.

"You okay?"

"What's in here?" she whispered.

"Just the stuff I told you about." I hoped. I wasn't quite so confident now that I'd seen our roommates freeze in place out on the sidewalk.

"Are you sure this is a good idea?" I asked Josie, tugging on her elbow.

"Quit worrying." She was grinning like a diehard Harry Potter fan who'd finally got to step foot in the Universal Studios' Harry Potter theme park.

"You again?" the receptionist barked once we made it as far as the desks. "And you brought along friends? How lovely for all of us."

"We'd like to see Estelle," I said, my voice embarrassingly shaky.

"Are you a witch?" Tamara asked timidly.

"Yes, of course she is," Josie replied with a brisk air of authority. She gave the receptionist a curt, businesslike nod. The receptionist said nothing, simply did something behind her desk that had Estelle appearing a second later, ready to greet us.

"Char! How lovely to see you again. Hello, I'm Estelle." She shook hands with Tamara and Josie. "So nice to meet you."

"If you're a fairy godmother, where are your wings?" Tamara asked, her expression puzzled by Estelle's black leather pants, unnaturally red hair and lack of wings.

"We don't have them," she said brightly. "It makes it too hard to sit in chairs."

"Do you have a unicorn?"

Josie gave Estelle a patient smile, like she knew the answer. And the answer was yes.

I held my breath, waiting for confirmation and cataloguing the fact that unicorns might be real. I wanted to see one. Like, last week already. Could I wish to see one? How much would it cost, because I bet it would totally be worth it.

I shook off the thought. No. No wishes. No debt. No unicorns.

And also...probably not real.

"There are consequences if you know too much about our world," Estelle said apologetically to Tamara while eyeing Josie curiously, as if she was trying to place her.

Was Josie a client? Was that how she seemed to know stuff about this magical world?

Wait. No. We were here to disprove all of this, not to reinforce my tentative longing to believe. She read tons of romantasy. And, clearly, so did Estelle. End of story.

"Do I owe you money, too?" Tamara asked as we got settled into the little office outside the pink bullpen. We were sitting on one side of the big mahogany table near the high-up bullpen window, with Estelle across from us.

This time, going through the secret door, I'd felt a shift in temperature, the bullpen warmer than reception. And I swore some of the workers in pink had been hovering above the ground while they'd walked from their cubicles to a strange machine burping rainbow paper.

"The first three wishes are always free," Estelle said. "It has a certain fairytale feel to it."

"It does," Josie agreed.

"So I haven't had any wishes granted?" Tamara sounded a bit disappointed, and I wondered if she'd forgotten our primary goal for this visit.

Estelle closed her eyes and inhaled slowly. "Let's see. There were just the three. So far. A wish for a pony. A horse. And a second chance." She opened her eyes, and Tamara turned even more pale. "Is that right?"

She slowly nodded.

"Okay, but..." I watched Tamara with a spark of worry. The horse-related wishes checked out. But a second chance? I hoped that wasn't about Kade.

"We're here about Char's bill," Josie said. "She's the only one of us three that owes you money, correct?"

I nodded, appreciating Josie's directness.

"Correct." Estelle smiled. She was looking at me with a warm fondness that made me want to like her despite our...issues. "And it's due when our quarter ends on August fifteenth."

"Q3 goes to the end of September," Josie stated. "Not August."

"Not in our world."

"Oh?" Josie considered that and I could see her mentally tucking away that little nugget, adding it to one of her mental spreadsheets of facts about the magical world.

"I'd have thought you'd use the solstices or something," I cracked.

"Eighty-seven days to pay," Josie murmured, "once we subtract the five days we've already lost this quarter. Not much time."

"But I told you I don't have money."

"Yes. I was speaking with the head fairy, as well as doing some investigating." Estelle patted the spot at the table beside her, and that thick leather-bound book from Friday was there at her side again, under her hand. I swore it hadn't been earlier. I'd been trying to keep track of details this time and clearly failing.

"And?" I asked, leaning forward.

"How many fairy godmothers are there?" Josie asked, and I shot her a look. Did she not recall that we were here to get me out of this mess?

"Not as many as there used to be," Estelle said. She leaned against the table, hands delicately clasped in front of her. "Deforestation and issues with the ozone haven't exactly been easy on us. Even the tooth fairies need human parents to help out more and more. Then there's Santa with his cholesterol."

"Santa?" Tamara whispered, the concern in her voice making me give her a second look. *Please don't tell me that this grown adult sitting beside me still believed in flying reindeer and a fat man stuffing himself down chimneys each year.*

"Thank goodness for Mastercard," I joked. Nobody laughed. "Well, it's a good thing you and the money I owe aren't real." I tried to say it with enough conviction that Estelle might disappear. Sort of like those family movies where if the kids believed in Santa, they saved Christmas. Well, I was hoping for the reverse.

"I'm real."

"No."

"Make another wish, and I'll prove I'm your fairy godmother."

"I'm not wishing again," I told Estelle, pulling my hands into the sleeves of my sweater. "Ever. I'm not giving you more opportunities to breach my privacy and charge me fake fees." I crossed my arms and sat back. "Coincidences happen. So, thanks, but no thanks. The only wish I want to make is to have you and this debt go away."

She blinked, face falling. "I can't grant those sorts of wishes."

"Of course not," I muttered.

"I want you to believe in me and my powers." She wiggled in her chair, positioning herself as upright as possible. She tugged at the cuffs of her white blouse. "Make a wish and I won't charge you for it."

Josie released an excited gasp, looking at me with hope.

"We already tried that," I reminded the group. "The James wish?"

Tamara nodded, her expression disgruntled. She'd been pretty bothered that I'd done that to James. So was I.

Josie, however, seemed way too thrilled about the possibility of seeing a wish granted, and appeared to be all in.

"Can I make one?" she asked.

"Shh! No." I elbowed her.

"Yes, of course." Estelle beamed at her.

"What's the loophole?" I asked, knowing there must be one if she was offering free wishes.

"No loophole."

"You're going to grant her a free wish?"

"Oh, no. I'm not going to grant it. If I grant it, then I have to charge her. But I'll tell you what Josie wishes for. Then you'll know I'm a real fairy godmother, and can hear wishes."

"That proves nothing," Tamara pointed out. "You could be a mind reader."

"Wait!" *No.* "You charged me to cancel James's date?"

"Don't make a wish!" Tamara said, clutching my arm. She leaned forward to glare at Josie, who looked away, cheeks pink.

"I won't," I assured Tamara. I jutted my chin in Estelle's direction. "She and her predecessor seem to enjoy destroying the lives of my friends and family." I thought of all the crappy wishes that had been granted over the years, and how they'd ruined some really great things.

Estelle gave me a hurt look. "I'm only trying to give you the life you deserve."

That wasn't saying much.

"I'll do it," Josie said. "And I don't care if you charge me for it."

"What! No!" I turned to Josie. Had she only come to help me so she could meet my fairy godmother and make wishes?

"No, I got this," she said reassuringly, and my anger faded. Maybe her analytical mind had found a way to prove this was all just make-believe.

Estelle perked up, all smiles. "Make a wish—without saying

it out loud, and really put your heart into it. I'll hear your wish and tell you what it is, but won't grant it."

"Okay," Josie said.

"You're not wishing."

"Give me a second," Josie complained.

Then she closed her eyes, and tipped her chin upward like enjoying a sunbeam, and looking even more like Anne Hathaway than usual.

"Something harmless that seems impossible," I coached Josie, one eye on Estelle. "But is consequence-free. Like a milkshake from Peter's."

"I won't be granting this wish, so wish whatever you want. Something random," Estelle suggested. She glanced at Tamara, giving her a wink. "And if you choose to wish, don't wish for another horse."

"Why not?" I asked. "She wants one."

"Divine timing isn't right," Estelle said impatiently. "And as for you, you really wish for Peter's milkshakes a lot."

Beside me, Josie giggled, her concentration broken.

"You ever had one?" I parried back to Estelle.

"No."

"Well, then. You can't judge me until you do."

"Fair enough. So? Ready, Josie?"

Josie nodded and Estelle tipped her head back slightly as though catching a scent. "Aw, that's a sweet one, Tamara." She smiled at Tamara, who immediately looked down.

"Wait," I said. "I thought Josie was the one making the wish."

"Tamara made a stronger one than Josie's."

"That's a thing?" Josie asked, giving Tamara a peeved look.

"What did you wish for?" I demanded, clutching Tamara's sleeve, instantly knowing she'd wished for Kade, a second chance, and true love. It was there in the guilty blush spreading across her cheeks like a flood.

"Oh, Tam-Tam. Him again?"

Her eyes were pleading with me. "It just kind of popped into my head."

Honestly, I wanted to be upset, but I knew she wanted love and a family of her own more than anything. Maybe even more than a horse. It didn't help that her mom was always trying to set her up with eligible bachelors and hounding her about being single.

At least Estelle said she wouldn't grant this one. But it did make me wonder if Kade being around lately was the result of Tamara's previously mentioned wish for a second chance.

"Love is good energy," Estelle said, her voice tinkling with joy.

I wasn't so sure. At least not where Kade was concerned. He'd sent her flying and crying into the city. His personality was so big, his focus so self-centred that he'd never allowed Tamara to bloom in his shadow. Surely, she could see she deserved more than what Kade could offer and a second chance would lead to nothing good. Especially since it felt like she was finally coming into her own, and figuring out what she wanted from life.

Although, as much as I loved having her here in Calgary, I knew this wasn't where my friend truly belonged.

I tangled my hands in my lap, realizing I was being just like Kade—selfish with the sweetest person I'd ever met. I wanted her to want the same things I did, so I wouldn't have to be alone. But she wanted to be a country girl with a horse and husband. She didn't crave or need big adventures and constant change in the way I did. She didn't mind sitting at home with her thoughts, and it made me wonder if I'd actually brought that romantic Kade mess on her by wishing she'd join me in the city.

If so, that seemed wholly unfair to Tamara, and I hoped that fairy godmothers had some stop gaps in place for that sort of selfish, dark magic wishing.

Then again, there was my tenth birthday wish and the one about James. So, it appeared as though they didn't.

I needed to put a halt to all wishes. Forever.

"Are you telepathic?" Tamara asked Estelle.

"I can only hear wishes."

"What about my wish?" Josie demanded.

"You wished this folder would fall off the table." Estelle swiped a hand across the table's surface, knocking the papers to the floor. "Wish granted."

Josie gasped, her expression one of tickled delight.

"You didn't charge her for that?" I confirmed, eyeing the splayed papers.

"Of course not. Where's your sense of humour?" Estelle chided and Josie nodded, taking a side that most definitely wasn't with her party-trickless friend. "Char, if you'd like another wish, you are welcome to go now."

I crossed my arms over my chest. "No, I'm good."

"Was that a spell that hid YFGM's door?" Josie asked. "And Samantha and Gabby couldn't see it when we did because they don't believe?"

"I don't believe!" The words felt heavy, like a lie.

"It's a security enchantment," Estelle said, one eye on me.

Josie smiled smugly. "Thought so!" It was as though she thought she was a step ahead of Tamara and me in regards to the whole paranormal fairy world thing and its magic. She turned to me. "Think about how long the line would be outside her door if everyone knew what she could do."

"They'd burn me at the stake," Estelle said.

"Pretty sure that ended a few centuries ago," I muttered.

"Or run me out of town."

Yeah, that could happen. Maybe less so in a city, but in a small town she'd be gone in a minute.

"Estelle could just..." I tried to think of the right word to explain what I saw as a solution, but failed to find it. "Invisible herself?"

Josie giggled.

"Well, I don't know what it's called!" I said hotly, my hands aflutter. "But you understand what I mean? Beam me up, Scotty! Or make it look like you're here, but you're actually somewhere else. Somewhere safe."

"I have to pass a few more levels before I can do high-powered magic like that," Estelle said kindly.

The idea that she might not be safe or able to protect herself made me uncomfortable. Did that mean I was starting to believe? Or was I just a softie for someone who seemed nice, even though delusional about reality?

I sighed in defeat, my brain tired of going around in circles and trying to make sense of illogical happenings. Right now, I wanted to go home and have this problem behind me. Even if that meant believing.

"Could you imagine if everyone knew about our fairy godmother services? We'd have to hire five trolls as office security and about forty more ogres and goblins to do my accounting!" Estelle laughed, Josie joining in. "It's hard to find good accountants. Especially ones that speak English and don't mind working for fairies."

"I'll bet!"

"I forgot to ask!" Estelle stood. "Would you like some Canada Dry?" She was smiling, looking more comfortable than I wanted her to be. So certain. So sure. "I have it back in stock." She opened the mini fridge to display rows and rows of green cans. She lifted her perfect eyebrows in question. She must spend a lot at the salon or time in front of the mirror trying out eyebrow-shaping tutorials she found online.

"Did you wish for it? To restock itself?" I asked. I'd die for a fridge that magically restocked itself.

"We can't grant wishes that might benefit us."

"What if we made the wish *for* you?"

Estelle shook her head.

I eyed Estelle's brows again. "So you wake up looking gorgeous? Because that really is a wasted wish area. It would be a total time saver." I needed to learn her skin care regime *and* whatever it was she did to her brows.

"Thank you," Estelle said kindly.

I rubbed my face, aware I was veering off track again. We needed to focus on details and get to the bottom of this. "You said there was a loophole or something where I don't have to pay my tab?" I noted her thick book, the layers of dust, the hum of the mini fridge, a framed photo on the desk of two women, one in pink, one in brown.

"You were warned the fees would come due, and we haven't charged you interest—"

I sat up straight, no longer hearing Estelle. The woman wearing brown in the framed photo. I knew that face. Seeing it again after so long was like being socked in the gut.

"That's her! The one from the dream," I croaked, pointing at the framed photo. That was the woman who'd stumbled into my bedroom when I was thirteen, and had thoroughly freaked me out.

Estelle twisted to look at the photo. "That's Paxi. Your former fairy godmother."

My breathing went jagged.

My vision narrowed.

There was nothing left for me, but one thing: to believe.

In a hoarse whisper, I said, "You really are my fairy godmother."

~ *Char* ~

I was still wrapping my head around the fact that I had a fairy godmother. That all of this was real. Even my debt.

But what else could I do, but believe? There were just too many things adding up that were utterly unexplainable.

A spark of delight flared in my gut. A fairy godmother. I had a fairy godmother!

"You said you're broke?" Estelle asked me, point blank.

My head snapped up, the reality of her existence, and what I'd blindly gotten myself into slapping me in the face. Was this where I could wish it all away despite her saying I couldn't? I was sure there had to be a way to get my fairy godmother to make the debt magically disappear, and then for her to send me off to the ball in the most beautiful dress where James would be waiting in a stunning tuxedo and winning smile that was just for me.

"She is broke," Josie confirmed.

I gave her a hurt look.

"What? It's true. Even with Samantha's mad money skills on your side, you're still handling that canoe without a paddle."

I frowned, trying to make sense of her analogy. I guess she

was saying I was up a creek without a paddle. Sorta true. Hurtful, but accurate.

"Your debt is very large," Estelle agreed. "But…I think I found something that will help."

Tamara, sitting on my left, was gripping my arm in support. Clearly she believed in fairy godmothers and this debt, too. I grabbed her hand, holding it.

"I think it would be worth trying non-monetary payment methods," Estelle said.

"Sorry, what?" I asked.

"Karma?" Josie inquired, head tipped to the side.

Estelle nodded, and began explaining how the world was made up of energy, and it all had to balance out in the end. But good could balance good. It wasn't necessarily good versus evil, which I liked.

In my case, I could create good energy, or good karma as it was, and have it applied to my account. If I created enough of it, it could run down the balance on my account to zero by August 15.

Happily ever after.

Fight fiction with fiction.

"But any shortfalls have to be covered with cold hard cash on the fifteenth," Estelle explained.

"No problem." Generally speaking, I was a kind and helpful person so a karma plan would be a walk in the park.

"What happens if she can't pay?" Josie asked.

"I totally can! I'm a nice person!" I elbowed Josie for her lack of loyalty.

Estelle swallowed hard. "Let's just focus on making lots of good energy happen."

"Why?" I felt a chill in the air. "What happens if I don't pay up?"

"Igor in accounting? He. Um."

"What?" She was acting like something huge and horrible would happen to me. "Bad interest rates?" I'd sat through a lecture about those with Samantha while watching her cut up all but one of my credit cards—which I now had to pay off in full each and every month like a smart adult. "Or do I get eaten by the dragon who ate Paxi?" I laughed, but Josie froze beside me.

I could have sworn Estelle went pale, muttering something about Igor eating someone or something. I wasn't totally sure, but the lightness was definitely gone from the room. "Sorry," I croaked. "What happens to me?"

"Nothing, nothing!" Estelle said brightly. "In all likelihood, your past, present and future will be placed on the scales in the Magical Court of Rules and a determination will be made at that time."

"What does that mean?"

"My advice is do your best, and stay off of Mrs. C's naughty list."

"Who's she?"

"A witch. So, are you good with the plan?"

"Um." I looked to Josie, whose brows were furrowed in thought. I didn't dare glance Tamara's way. The fingers on the hand she was holding had lost their feeling thanks to her killer grip.

"It's the only way, isn't it?" Josie said, her question more like a statement.

"Other than sending an e-transfer for the balance, yes," Estelle replied.

"Then that's that." Josie shifted, facing me. "We're done here."

As we got up to leave, I stopped at the office door. My mind was running around like an excited Felipe when we brought out a bag of Spitz—his favourite sunflower seeds—only I wasn't excited. I was confused, and I was having trouble wrapping my head around all of this new information.

"My wish about James?" Estelle nodded. "That's worn off, right? Everything he says and does—that's him, right?"

Estelle gave me a sweet, reassuring smile as she nodded.

Feeling relieved, and with my feet practically floating like the fairy crossing the pink carpet, I coasted along after Josie and Tamara. My smile grew as we made our way to the doors. James found me beautiful and, by some happy miracle, I was that sweet man's type.

OUTSIDE YFGM, Samantha and Gabby were gone. Josie tried to explain the time differences between worlds and portals. Basically, what I gathered, was that our friends hadn't actually been frozen, but time had done a slow-down and speed-up thing around the portal as part of a protection spell.

Still concerned for their wellbeing, as well as their mood for being ditched by us without apparent explanation, I called them only to discover that they were happily having drinks in a nearby Irish pub.

I still didn't get it. But they told us to go on home without them, so now Tamara was driving us back to the apartment in her convertible, Benjamin, with the top up, the May evening still too chilly for letting the wind tousle our hair. As she drove, I considered how many good deeds I needed to perform over the next three months in order to pay off all of my stupid, thoughtless wishes. If each good deed was worth a buck, I needed around one-hundred thousand of them. If my math was on target, that was over twelve-hundred good deeds a day.

I turned, looking into the back where Josie was sitting. "Josie, can you do the math on my account for me? How many good deeds do I have to do to clear my account before August 15th?"

"How much is a good deed worth?"

Tamara had been clutching the dusty, yellowed list Estelle had given us from accounting when we'd left, and I found it on the dashboard, wrinkly from being in contact with her clammy hand. I held it up to the window to catch the waning evening light.

"Gimme that," Josie demanded. She hunched over the list, mumbling numbers. "The average seems to be about seventy cents. Canadian."

I let out a squeak, causing Tamara to swerve around an invisible obstacle.

"What?" she gasped. "What?"

"Seventy *cents*!" I complained. "Why is the Canadian dollar always so weak?"

"Exchange rates suck," Josie muttered. "Although, I'm not sure what currency this would be exchanged from. Galleons? Spacebucks? Latinum?"

"Seventy cents is an outrage," Tamara complained. She was still pale and had been since the door for YGFM had appeared. I hoped this wasn't a permanent affliction, and that I hadn't accidentally broken my bestie.

"That can't be right." I reached into the back seat for the price list, but Josie pulled it further away, refusing to share. Why hadn't we noticed the prices back in Estelle's office? And why had she sold this karma plan as something feasible when it clearly was not?

"This karmic price list has to be out of date," Josie muttered. "Carrying someone's groceries for one block or less: 50 cents. Seriously? Changing a flat tire for a stranger: $1.50. Shovelling a neighbour's walkway: $0.75. Baking a treat for someone: $0.35. Where are the ideas that are worth more than a buck? And what decade is this list from?" I heard the crinkle of paper, like she was checking the back of the page for more details.

"You guys," Tamara said in an exasperated tone like we were children, "of course, being a courteous person and doing things such as helping an old lady cross the road doesn't pay well. It falls under the domain of good citizenry and being a decent human being."

"Yeah, well, it looks like I'm going to have to become Mother freaking Theresa," I muttered.

Trying to avoid the temptation to spiral into panic, I performed some quick and dirty mental math. No, that couldn't be right. I reached into the back and snatched the list, scanning it. These prices really were rock-bottom low. If this was accurate, then a good deed average was closer to seventy cents rather than a dollar. And that meant I needed to perform closer to sixteen-hundred good deeds a day, rather than a thousand. How could I ever do that?

I couldn't. Plain and simple. In August, I was still going to owe my fairy godmother a big stack of cash that I didn't have.

"Stop the car." I reached for the door handle, a tidal wave of panic hitting me, nearly pulling me under. I unclipped my seatbelt before Tamara stopped, my door swinging open.

"Whoa! Where are you going?" Josie demanded as Tamara ran one tire up over the curb in her haste to stop the car for me.

"I need to walk."

"You okay?" Josie jumped out with me.

"I need to walk." I began marching, Josie falling into step beside me as Tamara coasted slowly alongside us, windows down. "Just need a minute," I called, waving Tamara away. "Go ahead home."

"I've got her," Josie assured her, and after giving me a doubtful look, Tamara complied, pulling away.

Tugging my coat closer around me as the spring wind whistled down the street, I spied a man carrying a box into one of the brick buildings close to our apartment. I jogged ahead to hold the door for him.

Actually, maybe this was going to be a snap. I was a natural at good deeds. Only a couple more thousand left for today.

"One deed in the bank," Josie commented as we met up again.

I groaned. "I forgot to do the chant thing in my head."

Estelle had been very clear that I had to empty my mind before performing a good deed, and mentally say that I was acting to pay off my debt with Estelle. I hadn't done that, which meant the positive energy I'd just created hadn't been sent to Estelle's account.

"Next time."

"This is going to take me forever, and I have less than ninety days." I turned to her. "You believe in this stuff, right? Could good deeds actually work?" I was nodding, subconsciously encouraging her to echo me in a reassuring way.

She chewed on her bottom lip, and I could see the doubt in her big brown eyes.

I groaned. "This is impossible." I started marching again, my heels hitting the sidewalk with every step, filled with frustration and anger. Anger at myself, and at Estelle. I thought of my dad and the birthday wish that had betrayed my family's security. That wish shouldn't have happened. It shouldn't have been granted.

Josie snagged my jacket, pulling me to a stop, her look thoughtful. "You need to think bigger. A lot bigger."

"How do I do that? What's bigger?"

"Something that helps more than just one person."

"Volunteer at an animal shelter?"

"Maybe?" She didn't look convinced, and I continued walking again.

"That's got to be good karma," I argued. "It's for poor abandoned animals. It's definitely got to be better than baking cookies for a neighbour."

"Unless it's for Randy." She giggled. "That's automatically worth more."

I snorted a half-laugh.

"Maybe I could start a charity?" I suggested. Although, I wasn't sure I had the time or expertise to get one up and running before mid-August. And even if I managed that, there wouldn't be enough time for it to create the amount of good energy needed to bring down my debt.

"You need a project that benefits many, and can grow like a snowball," Josie mused.

"Pyramid scheme?" I teased.

"No, yeah, maybe. You need a snowball you can push down a hill so it can grow and lead to more beneficial effects. Karmic energy is an action cycle. It's cause and effect, cause and effect. If you can get that going, then it'll start to do most of the work for you. Sorta like compound interest."

I laughed, appreciating her optimism. "You sound like Samantha. She loves her compound interest."

"Yeah, well, even though she's a bit spoiled, she's helped me grow my inventory business's bottom line with all of her tips. I may even get to retire one day. Imagine that." She bumped her shoulder into me.

"Yeah. She sucks." We laughed, the warmth toward our friend unspoken, as was our appreciation and loyalty to her. "What will she and Gabby remember about us going into the office-portal thingy? From their perspective, did we ditch them or just vanish into thin air?"

"They won't question it. There'll be a rational story they both believe for why we parted ways outside YFGM."

"But they don't believe in..." I waved a hand in the general direction of Estelle and the office filled with fairies "...all of that?"

"No. Not yet, anyway." She winked at me, clearly loving all of this.

What a weird day.

We passed a group of teenagers milling about, aimlessly kicking their skateboards against the curb, one of them dribbling a basketball, then bouncing it off a nearby boarded up building, leaving round ball marks on its siding. The wind pushed an empty pop can across our path, clanking along before getting caught in the fence that stretched in front of the vacant lot. At least the kids weren't playing in the lot's trash again. I could still see the slide they'd made earlier though, like a tempting invitation that would surely woo them back.

Josie and I hunched further into our jackets, and for the first time, the city didn't feel full of possibilities. Our neighbourhood, Everstone, felt dirty and slightly unwelcoming. I still wished Everstone would get cleaned up and given a good dose of community pride.

That wasn't a real wish, though. I was done with those. It was more like wishful thinking, which certainly had to be different.

As the streetlights came on, three kids missing their front teeth ran by, playing tag in the street, all smiles and shouting. I thought of them growing up here with the street as their playground.

Cleaning up our neighbourhood could be one of those big snowball ideas Josie had mentioned, but the question again was, how did someone like me do that?

A car tooted at the boys as it crawled past, and I muttered to

Josie as we stuck to the sidewalk, "They're going to get run over."

A dog barked in the distance, reminding me of the shelter a block over and smaller, more achievable karmic ideas. "How much do you think volunteering at the shelter would earn me?"

She shrugged. "A dollar each time, maybe?"

"But I'm taking care of a poor, defenceless, surrendered animal!"

"You have to think bigger. There's got to be something."

I sighed and hooked my arm through hers, grateful not to be walking alone tonight.

While we walked, I took in our neighbourhood. If I were to walk dogs, where would I take them? There were no green spaces in Everstone. Just sidewalks and parking lots. Were city dogs really supposed to do their business where everyone walked? That didn't seem right somehow, and I felt as though someone ought to do something about that, too.

Sighing with an internal feeling of defeat as we reached the end of the block, I paused before crossing the street. I turned to Josie. "Do you hear that?"

"Sounds like crying?"

We both pivoted to face the direction we'd come. The kids were no longer playing tag in the street, and the teenagers were gone.

"Shh!" She grabbed my arm. "There it is again." From somewhere around the middle of the block, someone was crying.

Josie and I looked at each other and took off running, stopping in front of the abandoned lot, scanning for the kids we'd seen earlier.

"Right there." I pointed to that awful barrel and sheet metal slide they'd made last week. I bent down, cramming my curvy body through the hole in the fence, getting muddy hands as I clawed my way into the lot. I cursed under my breath. "This lot!"

"You okay?" Josie called to the three boys once we were through the fence. Josie, being tall and slim, had made it through without apparent issue, popping to her feet at almost the same moment I did.

A boy's head appeared over the barrel, his voice filled with panic. "He cut his leg."

We came around beside the children and I sucked in a breath. A boy in sweatpants, about ten-years-old, had a bad gash in his thigh.

"You." I pointed to the tallest boy. "Go get his parents." I turned to Josie. "Call an ambulance." I already had my jacket off and was pressing it to the wet wound. "You're going to be okay. Just breathe, okay?"

He nodded, his eyes filled with tears and fear.

Josie, who was dialling emergency services, whispered to me, "Say the chant."

"What?"

"The *chant*."

I shook my head. Exploiting this poor kid's awful moment for the betterment of my magical world financial situation felt wrong. So wrong. I was just doing what anyone else would do.

"It's going to be okay," I said again to the boy, hoping that I was speaking the truth. He leaned into me, tears still streaming down, and with the hand not holding pressure to his cut, I pulled him against me for a hug. He sniffled into my shoulder and I whispered reassurances and held him while we waited for help.

Despite being in a short-sleeved work blouse, I wasn't that cold, and I took in the lot. It was actually fairly spacious, and we were protected from the wind by the brick buildings standing on either side of us. There was no alley through the block, and if someone tore down the abandoned warehouse set behind this lot and cleaned everything up, the double lots would make a decent park. There would be room for basketball nets for teens, a real slide for the kids to whiz down, or grass for them to play tag on, or even just a spot for adults to take their dogs. It could be that community piece that Everstone was missing. Something to help it become more than a forgotten collection of old buildings people had decided to live in.

There were likely grants available for creating that sort of green space. But again—how did one set a project this massive into motion?

A minute later, the boy's parents came running, eyes wide with panic, the ambulance arriving shortly after. Josie and I stepped back through the fence, the paramedics having made the hole bigger with their giant wire cutters so they could bring a gurney in for the injured boy.

"They need a real park," I said to Josie as we made our way home.

"Yeah?"

"Yeah." I felt a fire in my gut, anger and injustice swirling to create a desire to help. To make a difference. To give the people of Everstone something like what I'd had back in Eagle Ridge. Safety. Community. Greenery and beauty.

Josie contemplated me for a beat. "I think you may have found your big idea."

I MIGHT HAVE FOUND AN IDEA, but the next day was a mental dumpster fire. First, I didn't know how to make a green space for our neighbourhood, and I obviously didn't have the cash to buy the lots and transform them. I'd looked up grants, but I'd need about a million of them to build the park I envisioned. It didn't help that I didn't know what I truly needed or where to start. Plus, what was to say that a park in our tiny, kinda rundown neighbourhood would even start a karmic snowball?

Second on the disaster list was my data entry shift at the Book Emporium. That had been awful for the first time in a very long time. I'd made more mistakes in one day than I had over my entire temping career. At one point, Samantha had hissed at me over her stack of books, telling me to smarten up.

How could she act so calm and like life was normal?

Yeah, I know. She didn't believe in fairy godmothers, and thought the three of us had simply headed home after not finding the source of the fake invoice while she and Gabby had gone for drinks. That was her reality. And it was a little different from mine right now.

And anyway, if she had this kind of debt, she'd pay it off herself with her fantastic money juggling and investing skills, or simply ask her mommy and daddy to take care of it.

But in my world, none of that was happening. Despite my attempts at proper financial management, I was a long way short of a hundred grand and my parents were no help. My mom had basically disowned me via rampant disinterest, and my dad was on disability and barely making ends meet.

What was really tweaking my brain, though, was the idea that if fairy godmothers were real, other things might be, too. For example, hungry dragons. Ogres. Leprechauns. Santa Claus. Witches. Maybe even garden gnomes were alive and real, like in that movie *Gnomeo and Juliet*. What about Godzilla and zombies? Where did it all end? What was truly fiction?

During my bathroom breaks, I'd half expected Moaning Myrtle to appear, because what if J.K. Rowling had been telling the truth about that particular ghost and she was actually real?

Although Myrtle was part of Hogwarts which was in

England. So chances were, I wouldn't meet Myrtle due to geographical issues. Not to mention that Hogwarts and Myrtle were both fictional.

Supposedly.

Yeah, that was where my brain was at. Doubting everything. Plus, I was tripping over myself to be exceedingly helpful to the point where I was almost knocking people out of the way to open doors for them, muttering Estelle's payback mantra under my breath, and getting sidelong looks like I was losing my grip on reality.

If only they knew.

Finally at home, eyes closed and splayed on my back, I soaked in the comfort of my bed. It was going to be a very long three months.

I'd even tried being patient with Randy when I gotten in, murmuring Estelle's chant under my breath while letting him tell me all about the dating app he was on. That had to be worth at least five bucks, right? Especially since the entire time I ignored the fact that my long-awaited order from an online pottery shop that sold ancient Grecian pieces was sitting on the mail shelf behind him.

Honestly, I needed to delete the shopping app from my phone, because whenever I got down in the dumps, I found myself mindlessly scrolling and bidding in more auctions than I should. And right now, I was in a prime mental space to do a *lot* of bidding.

I needed a distraction. Like a date with James.

I laughed in the silence of my room. Right. Talk about getting wrapped up in a fantasy world. Although, that was one I'd happily enter.

Maybe I could get lost in a good book. I rolled off the bed and went to the living room and settled onto the couch with one of my recently saved hardcover history books. Within minutes I was absorbed, my mind a few millennia away.

Samantha came home, plopped down on the chair beside me, kicking her new black boots up onto the coffee table.

"Aren't they pretty?" She angled her feet one way, then the other.

"Better take them off or Gabby'll shoot you." I turned a page, admiring the glossy photos. Gabby, when she wasn't mooning over her best friend Lamonte, scolded us for living like pigs. I swear the handheld vacuum spent more time being carted around by her than sitting in its charger.

Realizing I could do something nice for Gabs, I went to the kitchen and gave the coffee table a wipe, clearing off the dust and crumbs while mentally saying Estelle's payback chant.

"Gabby is wearing off on you," Samantha said as I sat down again.

"Just trying to be a good roommate," I said, grabbing my book again.

She reached over and flipped up the cover of my book before dropping it again. "Ew. Bor-ring."

"Hey." I hugged the book to my chest, whispering, "It can hear you."

"What's your deal? You were messing up all over the place today."

I let my head fall back against the cushions. "I'm stressed."

"About what?"

"That fairy godmother thing."

"The fake invoice? Ignore it." She began unlacing her tall boots. "I found a new restaurant. It sucks. But its bar is hopping. We should go on Friday."

I nodded to acknowledge her, but didn't ask for details like I normally would. Instead, I hugged my book, my mind back to spinning about how I was going to pay off my debt.

She pointed to the Grecian pottery book still snuggled in my arms. "Don't you already know everything there is to know about old crap made from clay?"

"Hey, we all have something quirky about us. You have an unhealthy shoe obsession, for example."

"It's a womanly right."

"Yeah, well. At least my quirk isn't..." I tried to pull up a positive quality about my thirst for knowledge and failed "putting anyone in danger."

She snorted, brows raised. "Unless you talk about the book." She threw out a few pottery terms, gave a fake yawn and sagged into the chair, making little choking sounds while flailing like she was in the throes of death.

"Ha. Ha."

She sat up again. "You need to get out more."

"Yeah, I wish. No! Not really! *Not* wishing that."

Samantha gave me a concerned look.

"So, hey." I leaned forward, realizing this would be a great time to pick her brain about the financial aspects of my karmic park plan. "Say I was going to start a charitable project. What do I need to do?"

She gave me a one-shoulder shrug. "Write some bylaws, create a board. Get signatures. Apply to become a charitable society with the provincial government. Get approved. Hold meetings and fundraisers, etcetera, etcetera."

That felt like a lot of sitting around and paper pushing.

"What if I just wanted to clean up that lot down the street where the kid got hurt last night?"

Her brows pinched. "That was awful. I'm so glad you and Josie were there."

"Yeah." I tried not to think about it, which was difficult. The boy's parents had managed to catch me coming into the apartment lobby tonight and had gifted me a homemade pie of gratitude and had returned my jacket—the blood miraculously washed out of it. Their son was going to be okay, but I couldn't ignore their teary eyes and the feeling that I needed to make a change, so stuff like that wouldn't happen again. "Could I clean up that lot, or turn it into a park without creating a charitable society?"

She shrugged again. "Complain to the city. Get the lot owner to clean it up."

"I did. And the mom said she complained weeks ago, too. Nothing's happened."

"But now that a kid has been injured, I'm sure it'll get a new fence at least."

A fence would do nothing. "It should be a park."

Samantha's brows lifted at my insistence. "So do it. Raise money. Get grants. Buy the lot. You don't have to be a charity."

"I don't?"

"No. Clarisa always does crazy stuff like this. She steps up and helps, you know?"

Samantha's stepmom was a lady who lunched. And apparently did good deeds for her community. I needed to become her, but without the lunching part. I needed to figure out how to do all of this in enough time that it could snowball some good energy right into my magical bank account over at Estelle's.

"Where would she start?"

"Call the city and find out who owns the lot. Then look up what it's worth. Take it from there, I guess."

I nodded as my phone buzzed with a message. I patted around beside me to find the device in the couch's cushions. I held it up, staring at the screen as my heart leapt with joy.

James: *Joining leisure league. Wanna help me shake the dust off my pitching arm?*

I hunched over my phone and typed out a reply.

"Ooo. Is it James?" Samantha cooed. "You're smiling and blushing."

"Shut up." I was crushing, yes. But it would never come of anything, even if he did seem to like me back. The two of us wanted different things, so why entertain the idea? We were just friends who enjoyed each other's company.

"Tell him I say hi."

"No."

Me to James: *Of course! When? Where? Think I still have a catcher's mitt around here somewhere...*

This would be a perfect way to increase my good karma, right? Say the mantra, catch a few balls....

I hesitated before hitting Send. But I *wanted* to hang out with James and I loved baseball—which he knew. So, if I wanted to do this, and took great joy from it, did that lessen its karmic payback value? Should I be spending my time on tasks I didn't enjoy but had greater payback value?

Or did doing things that made me happy increase the positive vibes and spread the good energy even further?

There was so much I still didn't understand. Shaking off my thoughts, I sent the message. If I didn't have some fun, I'd give up. Tomorrow I'd check in with Estelle and see how my account was coming along, and ask her more questions about how this whole fairy godmother thing worked.

CHAPTER 11

~ *Char* ~

Half an hour later, James and I were in front of my place, the setting sun bouncing off the windshield of his Range Rover, baseball gloves in hand.

"Got somewhere we can play?" he asked. He was wearing a soft grey, loose sweatshirt and black track pants. Instead of looking like he was giving up on life, he looked buff and athletic.

And so very handsome. Maybe part of it was the new haircut. His sandy hair was tousled and yummy, and he was grinning, a bounce in his step. He seemed so genuinely happy to see me. Was I more in need of a friendly face than I'd realized? Or was my crush worsening?

Maybe I was just blue. That point in my cycle where everything felt hopeless, coupled with the reality that it all truly was —from my finances to my dating life.

"By the time we get to the river park, it'll be dark." It was a couple of kilometres from my place—2.5km to be exact—and with no nearby parking. There was nothing close, and nothing in Everstone.

Again, we needed a park.

I sighed and James said cheerily, "The street it is."

I eyed James's Range Rover and Randy's candy-red sports car. "We should go further down."

We walked until there were fewer parked cars, stopping near the trashy empty lot and its surrounding brick buildings. It was flanked by a small, no longer functioning bread factory and a small insurance agency with grubby windows. But my eyes were drawn to the gaping section of chain-link fence from where the paramedics had cut their way into the lot last night. The landowner really needed to get down here and clean things up ASAP. But maybe they no longer wanted the land, and I could buy it and make it into a park. Or at the very least, slip in and take the sharp-edged piece of metal siding and hide it some-where so the kids would stop using it as a slide.

James and I rolled our shoulders and stretched, then started a gentle game of catch. While we moved, I practiced saying Estelle's mantra, hoping that helping out James would grant me at least a few bucks against what I owed.

"Do you have a catcher's mask?" James asked as we finished our warmup.

I shook my head. "Just don't throw it at my face." I squatted into a catcher's pose and slapped my mitt. "Come on, lay it on me. I have good reflexes."

He threw a few easy tosses as though playing with a child. Realizing I could truly catch, he started adding more heat and speed to each successive one that I caught. A few of them stung the palm, even though I was wearing a mitt.

"How fast do you pitch?" I asked, leaning to the side to catch one that was outside the strike zone.

He shrugged. "Fast enough. You're good."

"Thanks."

The zip of the ball relaxed me, and I found myself smiling, having fun. I likely wasn't putting good out into the world, just my own heart, but it felt nice and I realized there was nowhere else I'd rather be.

"You should join the team," he said. "It's co-ed."

"The team?" I shook my head, thinking of the sixteen-hundred or so good deeds a day I needed to accomplish. "I don't have the time."

"We only practice once a week, and have a game every other weekend in June and July."

"Short season."

"Leisure league." He smiled.

"I'll think about it."

"I'll send you the sign-up form."

Unable to hide my pleasure, I smiled back, warmth flowing through my veins. "Yeah? You think you've convinced me to join?"

"The team usually grabs drinks and nachos after practices and games. I'll buy you a drink after every single practice if you join us."

"Sounds fun." And expensive—drinks, nachos, baseball fees. Right now I needed to watch my pennies—even though Canada didn't have them in circulation any longer. I wasn't eager to spend any time in a weird magical court this August, and then possibly get eaten by a dragon or monster that everyone had previously, and falsely, believed was fictional.

Because, yeah, I'd overheard Estelle mutter something under her breath about Igor from accounting eating people and fairies when they misbehaved. Plus, there was already the story about a dragon eating Paxi.

I was somewhat confident I wouldn't get eaten by anything magical. But then again, there were a number of unsolved missing persons cases out there....

I wasn't very confident about discounting anything about Estelle's world at this point.

We tossed the ball back and forth, my mind half present—the other half studiously building arguments for why ogres wouldn't eat humans. Surely there was some sort of treaty in place that protected us?

James began mixing up the angles, speed and spin. He was good. He'd told me he'd played in high school, and it looked like he hadn't lost his touch. "I'll share my nachos with you, if you join."

I laughed, tickled that while I'd been fearing ogres, James had been thinking about ways to spend more time with me. "I said I'll think about it."

"Great. I'll pick you up Thursdays at seven."

"Oo. Sorry. That's too close to my bedtime."

"Liar."

"I don't have cleats anymore."

"Don't need 'em. Leisure league."

"Fine. Maybe."

"I accept."

I shook my head, flattered but also feeling shy by his attention. "You just need a girl on your team, don't you? I know how these co-ed teams work."

"Maybe I'm the token guy on the team. Ever thought of that?"

"Ha." That idea made me grumpy. A team of women all fawning over James. Because that would happen. Definitely. I much preferred the idea of being the only woman on the team —mostly ignored and working hard to prove I belonged and wasn't holding us back from a win. "Then I'd better join in order to keep you in line."

His grin was wide, his shoulder rotating as he released the ball.

The light was waning, and both of us were tiring. My legs weren't used to being in the squat position for this long anymore, and I knew I was going to be sore tomorrow. But watching him wind up and let it fly, the happiness in his expression while playing my favourite sport was worth it.

He threw another fast one, and I deflected it from hitting me, my attention flickering away to his quads at the wrong moment in order to make the catch. The ball arced high, veering off to my right. It was followed by the sound of glass cracking.

I popped upright. Oh crap.

James was already at the brick building's window, gaping at the spiderweb of fractured glass.

A window slid open above the empty store.

"What's going on down there?"

"Um, we broke your..." I said, gesturing feebly to the front of the store below him. "Sorry."

The window slammed shut, and a few seconds later, a large man filled the doorway that led onto the street. He turned to look at the crack, then whirled on us, face red.

"Sorry," I said, creeping backward.

"It was an accident," James said firmly, "and we'll—"

"You'd better."

"Do you happen to have insurance?" I asked. This was not going to be cheap. It was a big picture window.

"Excuse me? You want me to increase my premiums and pay a deductible because of your carelessness?" The man stepped closer, and James immediately slid into the space between me and the man. I clutched the fabric of James's sweatshirt where it was loose around his waist. I always forgot how tall he was, how built. He made me feel dainty. And that was one adjective nobody had ever used to describe me.

The man glowered, flames practically shooting from his nostrils. I had a passing thought that if there were fairy godmothers, maybe there were also demons.

"It wasn't her fault, and you need to back off," James said, his voice even, a hint of threat in his growly tone. His shoulders, I swear, had gotten huger. As much as I hated the situation, it had been so long since someone got bent out of shape on my behalf. It felt nice. Which was kind of sad, the more I thought about it.

Still. I got tingles at his protectiveness.

"You want me to back off?" The man reached out to push James, but he swiftly blocked the man's hands, sending him tumbling against James's chest instead. He took the force like a solid oak.

"It was an accident," James said, righting the man. "And we said we'd fix it."

The man backed off, one eye on James, complaining about how the neighbourhood was becoming even worse.

"It just needs spiffying up. A bit of pride, maybe?" I said, squeaking when his dark, unimpressed gaze hit mine. I shut up and stepped back behind James.

I mean, Everstone, while shabby, wasn't violent or beyond hope. Our neighbourhood was rarely on the news. Which was a perk, considering Tamara's mother called and fretted over us whenever it was.

Once James and the man had everything sorted, we walked toward my apartment, passing the empty lot. "That wouldn't have happened if that mess was a park." I shook my head. "Anyway. I'm sorry. I'll cover half."

"No chance," he said.

"Of it becoming a park?" I pretty much had to go big if I planned to pay off my debt. Especially seeing as anything I'd just earned with James had been eaten up by the broken window and subsequent fight with the guy. Cause and effect. That was what Josie had told me. We'd made space for good and then filled it with bad. We'd ruined that guy's day for sure. That was not the positive energy I was hoping to snowball.

That meant I really needed to do something big and wonderful.

"No chance of me letting you chip in for the window," James explained.

"What? Why? I wasn't paying attention to the ball. It was my fault."

"You're trying to go to Greece with your dad."

I stopped. Greece. I'd forgotten all about my dream trip. Was that ever going to happen now that I was in major fairy godmother debt?

"Anyway, I threw the ball too hard."

Squaring off, eyes narrowed, my tone was light but filled with challenge. "You saying I can't handle your catches because I'm a girl?"

James faced me, so close his chest brushed mine. He was still throwing off alpha boss vibes, still a bit puffed up, but honestly, I was swooning.

The skin around his eyes softened, and his body stilled. His blue eyes danced over my face and I knew mine were doing the same thing, like a butterfly seeking sweetness.

"I can handle your pitches," I said, my voice not sounding nearly as confident as I'd like it to. Sure, my palm was still stinging, but I'd never admit it.

"You're a good player."

"I know."

"Sometimes..." His words trailed off, his eyes locked on my lips. I moistened them with my tongue. His chest expanded with a slow inhale.

"Sometimes what?" I said, placing a palm against his pecs, chin tipped upward.

"Sometimes women say things."

"Like?" I wanted to roll up onto my tiptoes, make it easy for him to kiss me.

"Like they'd love to play catch with me, but don't actually know how and then want to go home."

"I'll always tell you the truth. No flirty lies to win you over."

"Yeah?"

"Yeah. I'll be honest about what I want. Even if it's different from what you want."

His focus was still on my lips, but instead of kissing me, he suddenly blinked his way out of his little spell and turned to continue walking me home.

Unkissed.

CHAPTER 12
~ *James* ~

Shoulda kissed her, man. Shoulda kissed her.

That had been an invitation.

But Char didn't want something long-term, or even marriage. On Friday she'd confessed that she couldn't picture it, whereas I could. She wasn't against it, but she clearly wasn't looking for the kind of relationship I wanted.

And yeah, maybe I was weird for feeling lonely and wanting what my parents had—their best friend, confidant, and lover all wrapped into one person, one relationship.

But who wouldn't want that? Other than Char. But I had a feeling she'd been hurt in a way that made her believe she couldn't have it.

My guy friends rode me hard for wanting to be married. But when you could see the future, there was no point screwing around. You found the right woman, someone you wanted to spend every hour with, and you took it from there. Done deal.

Char wasn't on that same page with me, which meant I needed to head home and go for a very long run to work her out of my system. Then I needed to find someone new to obsess over. And definitely not think about how Char's jeans hugged her curves in a very enticing way every time she dropped down into catcher's position.

Just imagine what kind of baseball kids we'd have. Summers spent in a fifth-wheel, travelling to games and tournaments, camping out as a family, living the baseball lifestyle.

Shake it off, man. Shake it off.

That wasn't the future she was actively looking for.

"James?"

I was almost to my car when I heard her sweet voice from her front step where I'd dropped her off like the sucker gentleman I was—not even trying to angle my way inside or finding an opportunity to see what her cherry lips tasted like.

Why couldn't I get her out of my head? She'd even told me that pursuing her would be a waste of time. On Friday she said that she saw no point in dating someone you knew wouldn't make the distance.

We were looking for different things. We weren't two people that would make the distance.

And still, I turned too fast, too eager. "Yeah? Do you want to go donate blood?"

What?

That was embarrassing. Donate blood? Total cringe, man.

"Um. Okay. Sure."

I nodded. I had no clue where you donated blood or when. "I'll, uh...text you."

"Great. So, um, that lot..." She was gazing down the street, and I craned my neck to try to see what she was referring to. "The empty one."

"Oh. Right?" She'd told me about a kid getting hurt in it last night.

"Do you think... How hard would it be to make that into a park?"

She'd left the step, moving closer. The streetlight above us clicked on, and she looked up at me with perfect eyes. Gentle. Kind. Sweet. And still totally wild and untamed. That was my Char.

She wasn't the type of woman I could run out of my system. Not even if I ran all day and all night. I had a feeling that I'd just loop right back to her each and every time I thought I was finally far enough away that she'd no longer have an effect on me.

"You want to make it into a park?" I asked.

She nodded, eyes lit up with determination and inspiration. "I'm going to find out who owns it, but I don't know what to do after that." She was holding her breath, like admitting she might be in need of help was new to her.

"I know some people."

"Yeah?" Her whole face brightened, hooking my heart like a fish on the line. I'd do anything for that smile. Anything.

CHAPTER 13

~ *Char* ~

After work on Wednesday, I waited for the walk signal to change several blocks from Estelle's office. I was feeling good. James had sent me numerous milkshake memes over the day, and I'd replied with baseball jokes. It was silly and juvenile, and I'd loved every second of it. We were flirting so hard, it was like my brain had forgotten that, romantically, he was a nonstarter because of our relationship expectations.

All it could scream at me was "HE LIKES ME!! THE HOTTIE LIKES ME!!"

So maybe it didn't matter that I'd never be the kind of woman he wanted for his long-term, love-nest plan. We were young. We had the 'right here, right now', to take advantage of. Maybe I could allow myself to forget about all the ways I wasn't the ideal woman for this hunky Viking of a man who was crushing on me, and just crush back on him and enjoy the feeling.

Flying high from my day of flirting, and the fact that I'd also managed to perform a ton of good deeds at work, from making coffee, to running out to grab lunches, and even cleaning the disgusting microwave in the staff break room. Yeah, it was probably only five dollars of good deeds, but I was eager to see what impact I'd made on my bill, as well as dreading what that cracked window from last night might have cost me.

Cause and effect. Cause and effect. That was what Josie said.

I sighed. Was I really excited about putting five dollars toward my debt? Although, maybe crushing on James and helping him out was beneficial—I mean, love was the purest form of energy, right? I could swoon over that man all day long, if need be.

Because otherwise, currently, my mission to pay off Estelle was impossible, and since I wasn't with MI6, it meant it was truly, and utterly, completely impossible. But what else could I do other than take a massive risk and try to build a neighbourhood park that may or may not put some good out into the world?

I chewed on my lip, trying to form a Plan B.

I had nothing.

My mind slipped to my happy place: Athenian pottery. I'd sent my dad a post I'd come across on my lunch break about an ancient civilizations travelling exhibit that would be coming through Alberta in a few months. Even though he rarely left the house, I was hoping he'd reply 'Let's go!'

The walk symbol changed, and I went to step out just as a blue convertible with its roof stuck halfway up, or halfway down—depending on how you looked at it—lurched onto the curb, nearly hitting me.

I jumped back, hollering, "Learn to drive!"

I turned to glare at the driver before realizing it was Tamara behind the wheel. Embarrassed for not recognizing her car, and for snapping at her, I said, "Tamara? What on earth? Are you okay?"

Peering into the car, I checked the floor of the passenger side, the common place to find Tamara's cowering passengers shivering in a heap of fear. The spot was empty.

"Don't ask, just jump in and help me navigate. I have fewer bumps when you're in Benjamin."

Benjamin being her car. Bumps meaning collisions. Usually minor. A bumper tap, jumping the curb, nudging a parking meter. And, apparently, now also almost mowing me down. The usual.

"Where are you going? Home is the other way."

She gave me a pleading look.

"Fine." I yanked open the car door, and sat down, wishing I were more religious so I could do the sign of the cross and mean it.

No, I didn't wish that. Estelle, that was not *a wish!*

"I'm having a day," Tamara said, "so I had my phone navigate me to you."

"Really? Why?"

"I got to thinking about things, and I had to make sure you're okay."

"I'm fine." I buckled up, cinching the belt nice and tight, then ensured my headrest was adjusted to a suitable height for preventing whiplash. I clutched the dashboard as the car lurched its way off the curb.

"I'm not that bad!" Tamara complained, eyeing my theatrics.

True. She wasn't. Although, with the downtown rush-hour traffic and all of its one-way streets, large delivery trucks as well as rushing, aggressive drivers, she tended to get worked up. Back home, she was a lot calmer behind the wheel and rarely hit anything.

I turned down the volume on her playlist of out-of-season Christmas carols, a sure sign she was stressed. Tamara swerved like she planned to change lanes, then changed her mind. I did my best to relax into the seat, realizing that a car accident wasn't likely to make my life that much worse at the moment. In fact, maybe I'd meet a handsome doctor. A rich one who believed in helping me pay off my fairy godmother debt.

"Where am I going?" Tamara asked.

"I don't know. What's got you stressed?"

"Because...because..." She lowered her voice as if someone might overhear her. "Because you have a fairy godmother, and I think it's finally sunk in. Like, really sunk in. All day, I couldn't stop thinking about her and wondering what else might be out there influencing our lives that we don't know about."

"Yeah. I've been thinking about that, too," I said soothingly as she swerved around a city bus, trying to remind myself to breathe and relax. And not make a wish. But Tamara was such an erratic mess of a driver today it was difficult. Making wishes seemed to be my default for pretty much every stressful situation in my life.

"You've cost me a lot of money with your driving," I mused as she jammed on the brakes for a yellow light.

"You sound like my insurance company," she muttered.

"You know how many wishes I've made, and been granted, and billed for due to your driving?" I teased.

"Have not." Tamara said, her hands committing a death grip on the leather steering wheel. "Don't even say that."

"Sorry."

Reaching up, I hit the button to close the roof. It was a gorgeous and sunny late May day, but not *that* sunny. The air still had a nip to it, flowing over the mountains only an hour away from the city.

The cloth roof closed beautifully. Not at all stuck, likely a victim of Tamara panicking and hitting every button at her disposal.

"What's else is wrong?" I asked, figuring her level of stress had to do with more than just the Estelle stuff.

She chewed her bottom lip, heading down our street. "Stuff."

"What kind of stuff?" Kade? Was he back in her life and getting her heart and brain all confused again?

Then again, it could be more Estelle stuff. She hadn't liked the James-break-a-date wish, and she hadn't liked hearing about the broken window, either. "Is it karma?"

"What if your actions are actually making things worse? What if that broken window got James tied into your karmic mess—like, in a bad way?"

My stomach dropped, my mind speeding though worst-case scenarios. "Do you think that could happen?"

"There's a lot that wasn't explained to us."

"Take a left," I said, sending her under the tracks and toward Estelle's office. "I was actually on my way to see Estelle and check on my repayments. You want to come in with me?"

Honestly, though, I wasn't sure she could handle witches, ogres, and fairies right now. She might pop a valve. But I also really appreciated that she was so worried about me. She was the best kind of friend that an in-debt gal could ask for.

She gripped the steering wheel harder, a look of ticked off determination filling her gaze as she stopped in front of the invisible Your Fairy Godmother offices. "No, but I'll wait for you in the car."

"LET'S CALL IN IGOR." Estelle seemed happy to see me, and we both had opened cans of cold Canada Dry ginger ale in front of us. Tamara, staying true to her promise, had opted to wait in the car. I was a bit curious if time would be the same for her outside the offices as it was for me inside. I'd tried to convince her to sync our watches, but she made a compelling argument that the magical world would have a workaround for any time discrepancies between us as I entered the office's portal.

Plus, she didn't wear a watch.

"Who's he? Is he the ogre?" I asked.

"Igor's from accounting." She'd pushed a button on the wall, but nothing noticeable had happened.

"Does he really..." I paused, to take a bracing breath "eat people?"

Estelle sagged, eyes rolled heavenward. "No." She waved a hand, cheeks pink. "Sorry if you heard me say that. I was—it...it was inaccurate. He doesn't eat humans or fairies, and I'm sorry if I made you think he does."

"You sure?" I felt hesitant relief, not quite ready to believe.

"I've been assured he's vegan. But I do recommend that you be very polite and don't look at his toes."

"Why?"

She gave a delicate shudder. "They're disgusting."

"Why doesn't he wear shoes?" Moments later, my jaw slackened as the door to Paxi's old office swung open and a short, green-skinned, hunch-backed...monster entered.

He dropped a pink folder on Estelle's desk, peered at me with his beady black eyes, licked his lips, and headed for the door again.

"Thank you so much, Igor. I appreciate your dedication and speed." Estelle smiled hugely, fidgeting and looking nervous.

Naturally, I couldn't help but glance down at his feet as he moved past me. Hairy, large knuckled, oddly bent toes. Honestly, not as gross as his drooling mouth with the rows of crooked teeth, and killer bad breath that smelled like an overfilled dumpster after a week-long heatwave.

"Thank you!" Estelle called again as he exited the room. She opened the pink folder he'd left behind with trembling hands. "Okay. Let's see."

"Are you sure he doesn't eat people?"

"Fairly certain. I mean, yes. He doesn't eat humans."

"He licked his lips at me."

"He likes to toy with humans."

"What?" I had an instant vision of a cat playing with a mouse before taking its life. I glanced toward the door, assuring myself that it was closed and that I was somewhat safe.

"He doesn't care much for humans. Barely even tolerates fairies." Estelle was reading the papers he'd brought her. "It looks like you've repaid $1.12. Good work! A dollar-twelve isn't bad for your first crack at the bat."

I blinked a few times, my mind letting go of the ogre business and slowly focusing on the amount I'd put toward my account.

"A buck twelve! I did way more than a couple of measly good deeds!"

"There's a note about bandwidth issues." She frowned at her paperwork. "You also added a substantial amount to your total."

I cringed. "How much?"

She ran a finger down a column. "Let's see. A few wishes and..." She winced. "That broken window while funnelling the energy into your account. That added up quite quickly."

I leaned forward, dread settling in. "How bad was it?"

"Well, the window itself wasn't too terribly expensive, but upsetting the owner—"

"But James calmed him."

"You started a bit of a cosmic energy wave." She shut the folder. "But it was a small one. All done now. I did feel it, though." She gave a shiver. "I much prefer the good energy."

"What about James? He was with me when we broke the window. Will any of this taint him?"

"What do you mean?"

"I don't know. Tamara thought it might be bad karma for him, too?"

"Yes, but no. It's complicated. You're actively channelling your positive energy toward your debt, so the impact of your actions is amplified in some ways because we are bypassing some of the universe's natural checks and balances. He isn't bypassing anything, so he will be fine."

"You're sure?"

"Yes."

Seeing I wasn't fully satisfied, she added, "He had a blip of bad karma, but it's already balanced out."

"Clearly he doesn't have fairy godmother debt like I do," I muttered, relieved that he would be okay, but a bit sad I was still handling all of this alone. I wouldn't wish a mess like this upon him, but some company would be nice.

"Of course not. Men don't have fairy godmothers."

"They don't?"

Estelle sighed and shook her head, her red hair shifting like a satin curtain. "Sexist, right? I've been advocating for equal rights, but honestly, nobody really seems to care."

I considered that. Personally, I couldn't imagine any of the men I knew getting bent out of shape for not having a fairy godmother.

"What was that bit you said about bandwidth issues?"

"Igor noted that the receiving bandwidth was weak." Estelle scratched an ear, frowning. "That's odd. I'd better look into that. Good thing you came in."

"So that means you didn't capture all of my good deeds? What I did was actually worth more than a dollar-twelve?"

"Yes, I think so. The machinery probably needs recalibration. Planets, moons, universes. Even our sun moves around over time. They're always on the go!" She gave me a cheerful grin and went to the dusty old desk in the corner. "It's been a while since we've used that machinery, as most people pay in cash. I'll ask the gnomes to make a few adjustments in their gardens, and you should be good to go." She pulled something out of a drawer that looked like a tiny transistor radio, and spoke into its speaker after fiddling with the knobs and saying 'hello, hello' a few times.

"What are you doing?"

After receiving a garbled squeak back, and taking part in a quick conversation in a tongue I didn't understand, she put it back in the drawer. "I asked the gnomes to recalibrate their sundials."

"Sundials?" Was she kidding me?

"Not the kind you use," she assured me after seeing my expression. "Ours are much more complicated, and measure things way beyond the sun and this universe."

"So it heard a bit of good, and a bit of the bad? But in the future, both of those will be heard better?"

"Oh, it heard the bad just fine." She read the notes in front of her. "It added fifty-three dollars to your amount owing."

"*What*? How could it hear the bad stuff better than the good? That's unfair!"

Estelle wrinkled her nose apologetically. "Maybe I can ask for a discount since our machinery wasn't adequately calibrated." She went to push the button that had summoned him the first time. "I'll ask Igor if that's possible."

"No! It's okay. Ask him later." I didn't think my nerves could handle seeing the ogre twice in one visit. I shifted forward in my seat. "So those cosmic energy waves. How do I get one going?"

~

Back in the car, I turned to Tamara.

"It's bad, isn't it?" She turned off the CBC comedy radio show, and with her big chocolaty eyes pinned on me, waited for a reply.

"Not horrible. But not great. The window added more to my account than I took off with my small acts of service."

She sighed and started her Sebring.

"Oh, and the whole ogre-eating-me thing was a joke or something. Not going to happen." I swallowed hard, the fearful corner of my brain reluctant to let go of the idea.

"Are you sure?" She was watching me with round eyes. She shuddered involuntarily, and I was glad she'd stayed in the car.

"Yeah. And guys don't have fairy godmothers, so James wasn't impacted."

"Whew. That's good."

"But like Josie suggested, I need to do something big to get this debt paid off," I said, buckling my seatbelt. I'd filled her in on the idea earlier and she'd agreed it might be smart. We were both overwhelmed at the scope of the project though, from buying land to transforming it into a friendly public space.

"Estelle agreed that the park would be smart. It could start a cosmic energy wave." Catching Tamara's worried expression, I added, "That's a good thing. Not without risks, but it's solid. And since I have no better ideas…"

She nodded, starting the car. "Then I'll help."

"Really?"

She smiled at me before shoulder checking and leaving her parking spot. "Of course."

"But how are we going to do something like that?"

"Are you kidding? We grew up in a small town. This community stuff is in our blood."

"Yeah, but I was only in Eagle Ridge for a few years."

She laughed at my expression. "I promise you, that town is in your blood. Plus, you're totally a smalltown girl at heart."

I crossed my arms, thinking of her meddling mom, sporting the same hairstyle for decades and being overly-focused on getting a husband for Tamara. I scrunched my nose. "No, I'm not."

"Are too! So come on. Get with the program. We have more experience than you think. You and I did grad fundraising. We organized helpers for the town's spring cleanup. We begged businesses to donate to the silent auction when the curling rink's roof collapsed. We've totally got this."

She seemed happy and calmer than usual, and as she drove us home, there was no lurching, swerving or close calls.

"You really think we could do this?"

"Yes, but we're going to need to get the girls on board. We need Samantha's richie-rich connections, Josie's organizational skills, and Gabby's physical strength."

I had wondered what Tamara had planned for our cleaning obsessed roomie. She did work out regularly—mainly to hang out with her crush, Lamonte, who was a fitness buff. But the byproduct was that she was stronger than the rest of us, which would come in handy once we got to the physical labour part of our plan.

"James says he might know some people, too."

"You really like him, don't you?"

"Yeah, but it's not like it'll go anywhere. I'm not his type." I could feel my cheeks heating, a familiar sting of rejection hurting in my chest. I wanted to change the subject, take action on the park and forget my inner ache.

"Why not?"

"He wants a functionally cozy family like his own, and I don't even know how family should work."

"Give yourself some credit."

"How? My family was a hot mess, and I don't even understand love. I'd mess up our marriage in five minutes." I felt the familiar urge to move, to distract myself from the well of feelings and inadequacies inside me. If I continued to sit here, I'd wallow and what was that going to help? Nothing. Absolutely nothing.

Tamara, as though sensing my need to move, reached over the console, clasping my left hand in her right one.

"You wouldn't mess it up," Tamara said calmly, and with a trustworthy level of authority that it settled my inner demons enough to consider her next words. Her warm hand was grounding, her assurances comforting as she squeezed before releasing her grip. "You know exactly what you want, even when you're too afraid to go for it."

I swiped at the sudden wetness in my eyes. "I don't know what I want."

Inside me, a whisper took up, calling me a liar. I wanted that same dream James had. I just didn't believe in it. Especially not on a first try. The divorce rate was around fifty percent for a reason. And I wasn't sure I could survive a romantic failure at that level. To think I'd found the huge love of my life, something I could trust like thick ice over a lake in midwinter, only to have it shatter beneath me like ice over a spring puddle and plunge me into life-threatening waters. Devastating.

"Char," Tamara said gently, reclaiming my left hand for another squeeze, "he likes you. Sometimes that's enough. You just have to be brave and say what you think and feel."

I nodded, trying to focus on the flickering cozy feeling that James's crush might be real—so real that others could see it, and verbally confirm it for my disbelieving heart.

"He said he broke up with his fiancée because there was no room for spontaneity."

"Really? That's practically your middle name!"

A surge of joy soared through me, tugging my lips into a grin. "Right?" I was Oprah Charmaine Spontaneity Adventure McDonnell.

Her voice lowered in seriousness. "Don't let your fears keep you from this guy, Char. He's special."

I nodded again, sniffing back tears. He truly was. Even if he was out of reach for someone like me, who had so much baggage that I tripped over it with every step I took forward.

"So?" Tamara asked, after we'd gone a block in silence. "You're going to try making a park?"

"Yeah, I guess." I wanted to keep talking about James, not my fairy godmother problems. But I did need to get going on a large-scale karmic project because, if Josie's math was correct, I only had eighty more days to come up with over a hundred grand. A little more pressing than my growing crush.

"What do you think a wish would cost me to get the park started?" I asked Tamara. "Would the expense outweigh what it could possibly bring in if I wished for the right kind of help?"

"*No!* No more wishes."

"Why not?"

"Because..." The car swerved slightly under her care. "All the reasons! Do I really have to list them all for you?"

"I guess not."

"Good. Now let's get home, convince the girls to help, call James over and start this work party."

"Tam-Tam, you're my favourite."

She grinned as she parked Benjamin, her convertible, outside the apartment. "I know. I'm the best, aren't I?"

"You truly are."

Less than an hour later, the five of us gals were camped out in the living room, Tamara and I having miraculously convinced everyone to help. We'd given each roommate a different pitch, playing to their interests. There'd been this amazing positive vibe like we'd all thought this might actually be possible. Like we could sit down and change our community.

Tamara had been the easiest to get on board, mostly because I was in danger, and she hated that as much as the idea of kids playing in a dangerous lot. Josie climbed on board because the project was connected to her beloved magical world, and we promised she could make all of the spreadsheets she wanted. Yeah, spreadsheets were her love language.

Gabby was a timely gold strike as she'd just learned the heart-crushing news that Lamonte was going out with a woman for the third time, and that they were rapidly approaching couple status. In other words, she needed a major distraction.

Samantha had been the hardest to convince. We needed her money skills and contacts. But what was in it for her? She strived to be as different from her stepmom Clarisa as possible, and this project had do-gooder written all over it. In the end, I'd crossed my fingers like I had with the other gals, refusing to make a wish, and instead asking the universe to please, please help me.

Samantha had said no.

But the four of us, full of energy and an upbeat connected silliness that I'd never experienced before, had all begged and pleaded with Samantha, then threatened to cash in our RRSPs if she didn't help us.

She'd laughed and relented, making us promise to never tell Clarisa.

Then she'd grabbed her MacBook and sat down at the couch, taking charge like I'd hoped she would. "First, we need to find out who owns the land. Then make an offer and buy it." She turned to me. "Did you do that yet?"

It had been twenty-four hours since she'd given me that tip, and I hadn't.

I shook my head. "Moot point. I don't have any money." I purposefully took in my roommates and their expressions in case this was when one of them decided to reveal that they'd secretly won the lottery and were sitting on millions.

Nobody spoke up. I gave Samantha a hopeful look. I had a feeling she had lots of money tucked away, and possibly even that rumoured trust fund.

"You don't want to own the park," Samantha stated. "That's a huge liability. You want to create it, and donate it to the city. So really, you just need a loan." She eyed me, and I could tell she was calculating my available credit as well as my assets. And I was coming up short. "So," she said on an intake of breath, "we'll look into some community greening grants to acquire the land. Clarisa and her various clubs do it all the time. We'll also talk to the city and see how they can help us, since I assume you'll want to donate the park to them once it's built. Then they can handle the liability and maintenance costs. Not to mention the property taxes."

I nodded slowly after looking to Tamara and Josie, who shrugged and nodded. Samantha's idea sounded smart. Get the karmic ball rolling, then hand it all over so I didn't have the ongoing risks or headaches.

"I found out who owns the lot," Josie said, hunched over her phone. "They owe back taxes, which means it's going up in a tax sale next week." She looked up, eyes wide, like she didn't quite believe the fortuitous news.

Was this an actual, honest-to-goodness timely coincidence? Or had I somehow wished for this? Because the odds were incredibly low that the land would become available right when we needed it.

"And same with the lot behind it. The one with the gross old warehouse!" she exclaimed moments later.

"I'm going to sketch the future park so we can visualize what we'll need," Tamara said, her eyes brighter than I'd seen them in some time. She disappeared into her room and returned with a sketch pad I knew was filled with horse drawings.

"Let's start researching grants," Josie suggested. I nodded, my mind still trying to track through the past several days, and whether I'd somehow wished for the two lots to come up for sale. But wishes couldn't change the past, right? The lot owners would have had to skip out on their taxes for years, meaning this was simply meant to be.

Serendipitous.

I started to feel like maybe this was going to happen. And maybe, just maybe, I hadn't even needed to make a wish.

CHAPTER 14

~ *Estelle* ~

I felt bad for not thinking about getting the gnomes to recalibrate their sundials for Char. After she left, I'd opened the giant rule book—Big Bertha—and found a way I could help without Char needing to make a wish. I just hoped Gram-Gram couldn't tell that I was circumventing the wishing system and sending positive energy to Char. But why would I get in trouble? There was no rule against it.

None at all. Not even if the recipient was human.

So now Char, who'd barely made a wish all day—thanks to all of her almost-instant take-backs—had a new wave to ride, thanks to me, and I hoped it helped her out.

Really, though, she needed to break her wishing ban and make a few. It would surely speed things up. She couldn't make direct wishes against her account's balance, but she could make a few grey-area ones around getting her karmic snowball moving. And maybe a couple around love, too, since those would be much more expedient than what I could do with my energy influencing. I really wanted to grant her a wish that would put her firmly in James's arms.

If only men had fairy godmothers. I bet James would make a really good wish.

CHAPTER 15
~ *Char* ~

"Another dud grant," Samantha muttered a half an hour later.

"Add it to the spreadsheet I shared," Josie replied, her fingers flying over her own keyboard.

"Already did." Samantha looked at the park plans over Tamara's shoulder, asking, "Did you add a checkerboard table like you see in the movies? So old men can come and play checkers or chess in the park?"

Tamara slid the drawing Samantha's way. She tapped a spot. "Right there. In the shade of the tree by the playground and not too close to the basketball nets or dog zone."

"Sweet."

Without any luck, we'd been digging around the internet, reading up on grants, trying to find the right one. My doubts were growing along with the tiny hole in the sleeve of my v-necked red blouse. A few stitches between the sleeve and cuff had come out, and without thinking, I'd been worrying the hole bigger over the past thirty minutes.

A knock on our door had us all looking up from our tablets

153

and laptops, on the lookout for our little friend Felipe. He was sitting on the arm of the couch, having climbed up a nearby stack of books. He popped up onto his haunches, studying us with his beady black eyes as our attention turned to him.

"It's probably James," I said, getting up way too fast to pass for cool or casual. "He said he'd come by and help after his shift at the museum."

"Oooo," Samantha sing-songed. "Ja-ames."

"Sadly, I'm not his type," I said to shut her up, even though I questioned the validity of my statement. I figured I was about half his type.

I hustled down the steps to let James in, chagrined to note that Randy had caught him and was grilling him about fishing, of all things.

"Not really much of a fisherman," James stated, squeezing his large frame deliciously past mine.

"Thanks, Randy!" I chirped, quickly shutting the door before he could list his preferred lures. I knew from experience it was the five-of-diamonds lure, and how he'd gone to see the monument for it in Lacombe, as that was where it had been invented or whatever. The province's smallest city was about two hours north of Calgary, and I feared that if I didn't extract James he'd find himself on a fishing trip to the stocked dugout by the monument.

"Sorry," I whispered to James. He gestured for me to lead the way, and as I climbed the steps, I became very aware that he had an excellent view of my swaying rear end.

"No problem," he said. "Glad to know someone would notice if any of you went missing."

I snorted. "Not exactly a comforting thought."

"Hey, James!" Tamara called, scooping up Felipe as he zipped between legs, eager to greet our guest.

"How's the project going?" James asked, taking in our digital battle station. It sorta looked similar to a teenager's bedroom, thanks to our collection of dirty plates and empty chip bags littering the room. We'd done a lot of damage in the past half an hour, and now Gabby was furiously trying to make the place presentable.

He shifted his weight, his shoulder brushing mine.

"Finding grants so we can buy the land has been tricky," I said.

He handed me a large plastic container. "Cookies from my mom."

"Really?"

"She likes to bake. She sent that whole thing home with me the other night."

He seriously had the best mom. I don't think my mom ever baked cookies. In fact, the first time I'd ever made some was with Tamara and her mom.

"Sweet." Gabby stole the container, opening it and diving in. "Ginger cookies! My fav." She sat down, container cradled in her arms, glaring and shifting the stash out of reach whenever anyone tried to help themselves, her cleanup tasks forgotten. She really was taking the whole Lamonte-has-a-girlfriend-thing pretty hard.

"We discovered the lot is coming up in a tax sale next week, so we need to move fast," Josie said, nose buried in her work. "Do you know of any grants that could help us out?"

"Yeah, maybe." James unzipped his coat and took my abandoned spot on the couch. I stood awkwardly outside our ring of furniture, unsure where to sit. Everywhere was taken other than a tight spot beside James.

He scanned my laptop where, earlier, I'd brought up info on local grants. Then he took out his phone and sent someone a text. Moments later, he got a ding and began typing on my laptop.

"Try this one." He looked up at me and I came around so I could read the grant's details over his shoulder. He shifted slightly, patting the small wedge of cushion beside him. I shoehorned myself into the space, embarrassed at the width of my hips. James didn't seem to notice, even though his leg was resting against mine—no *pressing*. It was incredibly distracting. So was his voice. He was speaking quietly to me, saying how cool it was that I was going to make a park for the kids. His admiration was like a microwave set to high on my melting heart. He probably thought I was an unselfish saint, and I hoped that having a primary motivation of getting out of debt —even though I really did want to clean up the lot for the neighbourhood kids—didn't reduce my much-needed big wave of cosmic energy, or whatever Estelle had called it.

"How's it look?" James asked, referring to the grant.

I startled, realizing I'd been basking in his words and daydreaming about the warmth of his thigh against mine, noting that he had a small mole on the underside of his chin that I'd never noticed before. We were so close my breath caught in my lungs. I could easily shift my weight and fall into his lap, my lips upon his. I looked down, clearing my throat.

"The deadline, um." I checked our spreadsheet. We'd already axed that one due to a few other requirements. "Is a bit late."

Josie, still not looking up from her own work, held out a hand. "Gabby, give me a cookie or die."

Gabby quickly handed the container to Josie. I scored one as it went by and took a big bite. So good. The cookie was soft, sweet, but still gingery. Just right.

"Hey, you have a hole in your shirt," James said in a low voice like it was just the two of us on this couch cushion, an island lost in a calm sea, nothing else for miles. He gently touched the inch of skin showing through the blouse's gaping hole.

"I know," I said with a sigh, trying not to think too hard about how nice his touch had felt. How electric. It was like every cell was on high alert now, ready and waiting for more James.

But I'd destroyed my shirt. I should think about that, not how yummy he was. When I wore this one, I felt gorgeous. It hung in the right way to emphasize the drop from my generous chest to my waist, giving the illusion of super sexy curves, and the jewel tone made me look healthy and vibrant even when I was tired.

There. No longer thinking about James. Instead, I was thinking about the fact that I didn't have a sewing kit to fix my beloved shirt.

His focus had gone back to his texts, and he angled his phone so I could see. "Try this one." I typed the grant name into a search engine.

"Got it," Tamara said, beating me to it. A moment later, she turned her tablet to face us so we could read about the local community greening grant.

I snatched her tablet, scanning the info. "This is amazing!"

"They meet once a month," Tamara said, and I let out a gasp of excitement.

"James, you're a godsend," Josie exclaimed, leaning out of her seat to give him a high five.

I murmured my agreement.

"I think Clarisa used to be on the board for that one," Samantha said, coming around the couch to peer over my shoulder. "Yeah, she quit because gardening was too hard on her manicures. I think she's still a member, though. I'll ask."

"I wish she was still on the board, and could give us the grant," I said wistfully. Tamara gave me a dark look. "What?"

"No wishing," she said firmly.

I clapped a hand over my mouth. I hadn't even noticed my absent wishing. It was such a part of my habits.

"Harsh," James said, coming to my defence.

"I didn't mean that wish." I looked at the ceiling as though that might help cancel out what I'd said.

"You can wish all you like, Char," James said. His leg was still against mine, an insistent pressing.

No, I really couldn't. Not any longer. I sighed, surprised at my deep, echoing sense of loss. No more semi-charmed life due to buying my way out of sticky jams, thanks to my fairy godmother. I felt so...average and blah.

"Nope. Quit wishing and take action," Tamara told James. "That's the motto."

"Only way to change the world," Josie said feebly.

"You're all weird," Gabby stated, taking another handful of cookies.

"Apply for that one," Samantha said, handing the tablet back to Tamara. She checked her smart watch for the time. "I have a date with an Irish hottie. Gotta run." She disappeared into her room to get ready.

"Caleb?" James asked. I'd given him the rundown on Samantha's unrequited crush on our downstairs neighbour a few weeks ago. I loved that he remembered me mentioning Caleb, and I wondered what other details about my life he recalled. Was there a chance he was hoovering up tidbits about me, like I was with him?

"Not Caleb," we all echoed back.

He raised his hands, palms up, as if to ask why not.

"She's scared he'll say yes if she asks him out," I said.

"What? That's not a thing." James looked at my roomies, as though seeking confirmation. Oh, he was adorable.

"It's a thing," Gabby said.

"He won't live up to the hype," I said. "The hype in her head."

"Girls are weird."

"And guys are impossible," I replied. They were like trying to piece together a broken urn that had been sitting in some farmer's field for over a thousand years and you no longer had all the pieces.

"But this new guy," Josie said, leaning forward, voice lowered, "has made it four weeks, and they've had about a dozen dates already."

"That's super huge for her," Gabby added. "She's practically married!"

"I can hear you!" Samantha called from her room.

"Quit gossiping and help me with this application," Tamara complained, and we all crowded around her, debating the wording of every sentence like we were writing the next great Canadian novel, and not applying for a grant we likely wouldn't even get.

We fired it off to the grant agency and sat back in a quiet lull. Now what? We'd pretty much exhausted all the grants we could find that fit our needs. If there were no grants, it meant no land and no park, and no karmic snowball.

I was antsy, practically able to hear the clock ticking down on me. I wanted to keep taking action to shore up my slim odds. There wasn't time to sit around and wait for the grant agency to meet and debate, and then cut me a cheque at their leisure. Assuming they even gave us the grant.

But what else was there that I could do? Find a private donor? If so, then would they get all of the good karma instead of me?

"Excuse me a sec." I went to the washroom, wondering if this was the moment to break my earlier promise to Tamara and make a wish. Because the more I thought about it, the more a small wish that could tip the odds in the park's favour would be worth it. Spend money to make money.

In the bathroom, I closed my eyes and wished for the grant agency to see our application and approve the request. Immediately. Or at least in the next two days. But preferably sooner.

I returned to the living room and Tamara eyed me like she knew what I'd just done. I looked away, and James stood.

"I've got my glove in the car. Wanna play catch before we lose the light?"

"Sure." I turned to my remaining roommates. "Are we finished for tonight?"

"Unless you know of more grants we can apply for," Gabby said, closing her laptop and sinking back in the chair with a groan. "My stomach hurts."

"That's because you ate your weight in cookies," Tamara scolded, passing the empty cookie container to James. "Thank your mom for us." She hoisted Gabby to her feet. "Come on, a walk around the block will help."

A few minutes later, James and I were on the street, ready to play catch, Gabby and Tamara starting off in the opposite direction. This time, before we warmed up, I made sure James and I were extra far from any possible breakable objects.

"I like that you're doing something big for your community with the park," James said.

"Trying to," I corrected as we slowly windmilled our arms, warming up our shoulders.

"It'll work out."

"Hopefully."

We began stretching our arms across our chests. One, then the other, facing each other. He was handsome in any light. But the fading spring sun was especially fond of him, heightening the angles of his cheeks and jaw as well as that sweet look of admiration sparkling in his gaze.

A woman could really take a gaze like that the wrong way.

"I feel like a slacker," he said, his tone light.

"Why?"

"What have I done with my life? What mark have I made?"

"Well, you don't have fairy godmother debt to pay off, so..."

He laughed at my unexpected reply. "You always keep me on my toes."

I sighed. Yeah.

We backed up, facing each other, ready to start tossing the ball, our warmup routine already an unspoken, shared habit.

"Try not to hit any windows today." His smile was lopsided, teasing and entirely the sexiest thing I'd seen all day.

"You threw that ball, I'll remind you."

And I was paying dearly for it in an alternate universe filled with ogres and fairies.

James lobbed the baseball my way.

Thunk. I caught it in my glove.

"And you, superstar, failed to catch it," James retorted, his goofy smile making me want to grin even though he was busting my chops.

I tossed the ball back with a bit more heat than I would normally use in a warmup. "Because you distracted me."

His glove snapped shut around the ball. He underhanded it back to me, loose and easy. "How so?"

"By being gorgeous."

He laughed, head back.

I waited for him to react further, but all he did was take me in with a heated gaze.

"So what did your fiancée look like?" I asked, immediately embarrassed. Obviously, I'd been obsessing about her for the past week. I'd even tried a deep dive into his social accounts to see if I could find hints of her, but he wasn't very active online. No fiancées. Lots of pretty girls, but none of them wearing rings that I thought might have been chosen by him.

"Blond."

"Naturally. Make sure you keep your Norwegian genes pure."

He chuckled. "Not Norwegian."

"Doubtful. You look like a Viking."

"Well, she was a Viking, too, then. Blue eyes."

"Slim?"

"Fit."

Dang. That was even worse.

"What did she do? Like for a living or whatever? Do you still hang out?"

Why was I torturing myself with this info? I didn't need it. He wasn't ever going to actually *choose* me. I wasn't a Suzy Homemaker like his sweet mom obviously was. But maybe he wasn't totally the man I assumed he was, either. He *had* broken up with his ex, after all. He wanted room for serendipity, just like I did. And hanging out with him was so easy. That had to mean something.

Maybe I had to make space for the possibility of James, just like Estelle said I needed to do with my karmic plan. It was all about good energy, and that was one thing James had in spades.

His lips had curved into a small smile, and I wasn't sure if it was amusement over my obsession with his ex, or in fond remembrance of her fineness.

"She's living in the Netherlands."

"Naturally, and riding her bike everywhere with that fit bod."

"Taking insta pics by windmills and tulip farms."

"Of course. And she never sweats."

"She has a healthy, rosy glow to her cheeks."

"Never an unsightly, blotchy red." I winced, knowing my pale skin often went blotchy. "She probably uses filters to give her pics that glow."

I threw the ball hard, and James had to reach as it swung out wide. I'd given up on impressing the world with my looks a long time ago. Around grade twelve, to be specific, when the boys' fastball captain kept saying I didn't look at all like my social media pics, with the flattering filters. The way he said it made me feel like a gigantic poser. And mad. He never, while I was around, ever said that to my teammate, who was popular, perky and used more filters than I ever had.

After that I'd pretty much thrown up my hands, the message clear that with my curvier build that I'd never make the cut—so why kill myself trying to reach an unattainable ideal thanks to genetics?

"I think she's doing something with geothermal," James continued. "She's into the sciences."

Sigh. A world saver. I was jealous and in awe of her already.

And yet, she still hadn't made the James-cut? He couldn't see himself with her in five years, or whatever his claim had been?

What hope did I have?

Then again, he seemed to think I was some sort of saint because of this park plan. And he didn't seem to mind my nutti-ness or pottery nerdiness.

"What about you?" I asked. "What are you into? What makes you passionate?" He was a museum security guard, but somehow that didn't quite fit him. I doubted that was the start or end of his life's passion.

"What do you mean?"

"Did you go to college?" He'd never mentioned it, even though we'd sorta hung out for over two years now.

"A few times."

"A few?"

"I have a couple of certificates. Some random classes. I haven't found what I'm passionate about yet." He looked wistful and a tiny bit sad, too. "I'm a bit envious of you."

I scoffed. "Don't be. I'm a hot mess."

"I don't see you that way." His warm gaze lingered on me, and it felt good. Whatever he saw, that was who I wished to be.

CHAPTER 16
~ *James* ~

S hortly after the streetlights came on, Char's phone rang. The grant agency.

We naturally began walking back to the apartment, Char replying to whomever was on the other end of the line with "uh huh, uh huh." We got all the way inside the apartment, and up the stairs before Char dropped her phone and turned to me, squealing and dancing.

"We got it! We got it!"

I stared at her, stunned. The grant? How was that even possible? There'd barely been enough time for the agency to gather everyone to read the proposal and vote.

She grabbed my arms, her eyes bright with joy. "They've been wanting to build something in Everstone for years, and everyone was in the office for a retirement party when our application came in! They held an emergency meeting and voted yes!"

"Unreal," I breathed, completely dumbstruck by the sheer vibrancy of the woman in front of me. Even though it sounded awful, I was grateful for the kid's injury that had spurred her into action. She was the kind of woman who could turn on a dime, rally the troops and change the world, making it a better place. She had the drive of someone who'd been mistreated, and was vowing to ensure nobody else ever had that experience. She was incredible. She was beautiful. She was an inspiration.

I lifted her in the air. Twirling her, her happiness flooding the room and making me smile. Her arms were around my neck as I squeezed her tight. I resisted kissing her neck as it came close to my mouth, instead opting for her mouth.

I kissed her fast and hard, then realizing what I was doing, and that I was kissing her for the first and possibly only time, I slowed and softened. I explored her mouth with my own, lost in the moment, letting her slide back to her feet so I could glide one hand into her soft hair.

"What's going on out—oh."

I blinked my way back to reality; the kiss broken as I took in Char's roommate. Tamara was standing awkwardly in the living room as though debating slipping back into the kitchen.

Char biting her bottom lip, glancing at Tamara then at me again, like she was considering jumping in for another kiss. Reluctantly, I allowed myself to release her from my arms, but was unable to look away from her lips and those happy eyes.

I wanted to kiss her again, and I was pretty sure she felt the same.

CHAPTER 17

~ *Char* ~

"Your parents' house?" I pushed my way deeper into the passenger seat of James's Range Rover. We'd kissed once, twenty minutes ago, out of excitement over the grant. And now I was about to meet his parents?

I gently brushed my lips, still warm and tingly from James's earlier kiss. I know, it was only my imagination telling me I could feel the effect and pressure from his lips on my own, but his kiss had been sweet, and oh-so right and I wanted to savour and stay in the after-bliss for as long as I could.

The question was: why were we at his parents'? He'd promised me a distraction after I heard back from the grant agency and hadn't been able to sit still. It hadn't helped that Tamara had been shooting visual daggers at me as I filled in the girls on the agency's decision. Somehow, she *knew* I'd made a wish.

Even though it was eight at night, I wanted to go buy the land and set to work.

And so James, ever the friend, had dragged me away—even though our kiss hadn't been a friend-zone kind of kiss. It had, in fact, been toe-curlingly delicious. The kind of kiss you shared with a soulmate. The warm, fuzzy vibes James gave me were even better than holding an old piece of Athenian pottery. Way better.

When he'd suggested a distraction, though, I'd thought we might go somewhere and make out. Not go meet his parents.

I think I'd rather be at home, pacing until the land offices opened, as well as freaking out over what our kiss meant, thanks. His parents were going to take one look at me, and know I wanted to be out of the friend zone with their son, even though it broke my own rule about dating someone I already knew I wouldn't marry. They'd instinctively know I didn't understand close-knit family vibes, or how a family should be there for you, reading your needs, and taking care of them without any apparent thought. I'd learned from watching Tamara's family how important that was, and I knew I was lacking. I didn't know how to do that. How to comfortably fit myself into that type of familial situation.

"I've got to run in and grab something." James came around the Range Rover's bumper and opened my door. "I still can't believe you got that grant. And so fast!"

I nodded, one eye on the front of the cute bungalow with its cheery potted flowers and freshly tended lawn.

"I mean, they even dipped into their emergency reserves so you can buy both lots, and tear down that warehouse. You have to be the luckiest woman in the world."

His gaze was liquid warmth spreading over me, and I nodded again. At this moment, with him looking at me like that, I *was* the luckiest woman in the world. I was also a woman out of her depth.

He held out his hand.

"I can wait here," I said, leaning further from the door.

"Aren't you coming in?"

"I thought you just had to grab something?" I knew he had

his own basement suite near SAIT, which meant this was a quick zip in and out. In other words, there was absolutely no reason for me to go inside.

"I do. But come meet my parents."

"Um..."

He was holding out his hand, insistently bouncing it, palm up, waiting for me to take it. "They don't bite. They meet all my friends."

Friends. "Right. Of course." I nodded, the friend zone reminder snapping me out of my freak-out daze. Talk about putting the cart way before the horse on that one. It wasn't like we were romantically serious about each other, and needed to meet each other's families. It wasn't like his parents would assume I was there as a potential future daughter-in-law. James was the socially sure kind of guy who brought friends home, even though he was an adult. Tamara's boyfriend, Kade, had been like that in high school. I was sure everyone in our school had been to his house at one point or another.

I mentally bolstered myself. I needed to remember that making mental room for the possibility of a relationship with a guy like James was one thing. Thinking he wanted me to meet his parents because he was in love with me was quite another.

I hopped out, my hand gently resting in James's as I slid out of the SUV. He released me sooner than I wanted, leaving a hole in my gut. He led us to the front door, letting us in with a hearty, "Just me and a friend!" He said to me, "Ditch your coat wherever."

Friend. I was starting to really dislike that word.

I glanced around the entry at the coat hooks already filled with jackets. "Aren't we just running in and out again?"

"Yup." He tossed his jacket on a filled hook, then took mine, adding it to the heap while he kicked off his shoes.

A dazzling woman in her fifties, with long sweeping

earrings, appeared. Her left earring tickled the top of her shoulder, her other was hidden in a tangle of curly black and silver hair. What her body lacked in mass, her hair more than made up for. She looked at home in a paisley wrap-around skirt and ropes of beads.

Not at all the plump, unstylish mom I'd imagined.

"I'm Sally." She offered her hand, and we shook, even though she struck me as a hugger. Maybe she was holding back, sensing that it was too early for me to be comfortable with a hug. "You must be Char."

I blinked at James. He'd mentioned me to his mother? I was charmed.

And way too hopeful.

"Nice to meet you," I said, already imagining what it might be like to be a part of her circle. Homey afternoons spent gossiping around the kitchen table with cups of tea with sunlight streaming in through the open windows....

Seriously. One kiss and, even though I wasn't cut from the same cloth as the Backstrohms, I was trying to figure out how to blend my way into this sweet family's routines?

Sally led us into the kitchen where a card game was laid out, mid-play. A woman with a spine curved by age smiled at us. James went to her side, giving her a kiss on the cheek.

"Hello, Mrs. Laven. How are you doing today?"

"Beating your mom at cards," she crowed triumphantly, her eyes sparkling.

"Good to hear it. This is my friend Char." James turned to me. "Mrs. Laven lives next door." He turned to his mom. "Where's Dad?"

"He had a later shift, but I think I just heard the garage door go."

A man stepped into the kitchen as though on cue. "James! Thought I saw your car. Nice to see you." He was tall and built, an older, more rugged Viking version of James. He gave his son a shoulder squeeze, kissed his wife sweetly, said hello to Mrs. Laven before making his way over to me. I was still in the doorway on the other side of the room, unsure where I should be and what my role was.

"Hello. I'm Otto."

"Nice to meet you. I'm Char."

"Just raiding the costume box," James said. "Back in a mo'." And with that, he ducked through the door his father had appeared through, leaving me in the kitchen. I hesitated, unsure if I was supposed to cross the airy room and follow, or stay put and be social. My index finger had found the hole in my shirt's sleeve from earlier, and I forced myself to stop worrying the spot.

"I donated most of it!" Sally called after her son. When the door didn't reopen, she shrugged and turned to me. "He'll figure it out. Cookie? They're homemade."

I stepped further into the room, accepting a chocolate chip cookie, which was still warm from the oven. Soft, gooey, sweet and utterly perfect, just like her ginger cookies had been.

"James brought us some of your ginger cookies. Thank you. They were a big hit."

Sally smiled. "I'm glad you liked them."

"She loves to bake," Mr. Backstrohm said, grabbing two cookies for himself.

"I do." Still holding the plate of warm cookies, Sally angled her cheek toward her husband, who planted another kiss on it.

The whole sweet family and doting parents were actually a real thing in James' world. And it didn't give off liar vibes like I'd half-expected. Everyone seemed happy, upbeat, and truly alive. The idea that a perfect little home life might exist left me feeling strangely alone, like an outsider looking in, wondering how the pieces all went together to create such a beautiful picture. But most of all, how to make it last?

Even during my family's better days, I didn't ever recall a settled feeling quite like this one. This was a blip in time so easily taken for granted, so mundane, and yet so heartwarmingly real.

Was it possible that my parents had always been cartwheeling, slipping and sliding toward divorce from the day they'd met? Maybe my wish had simply been the nudge that had finally tipped them over the edge to face the reality that their relationship had hit a dead end.

Watching James's parents interact, their cozy evening routine already on autopilot, I realized how easy it would be for me to say the wrong thing or make an inopportune, ill-thought-out wish—which seemed to be my specialty—and ruin it all should I ever become a part of it.

"She looks a bit rounder," Mrs. Laven said, leaning toward Sally as she sat back down at the card game, speaking as though I wasn't there, her gaze on me. "Is she expecting already?"

Instinctively, I sucked in and smoothed my blouse over my midriff.

"Greta, this isn't Sophia," Otto said awkwardly, giving me an apologetic smile as he pulled a prepared plate of leftovers from the microwave.

Sophia. The ex-fiancée who hadn't made the cut. Why? Was she too similar to this sweet life that James had had growing up? Was he looking for something different? For more excitement than this cozy routine could bring him? Because I could tell him firsthand that 'excitement' and this kind of home life didn't mix. Maybe he already knew that? So then, what did the man truly want?

"This is his friend, Char," Sally added.

"Hello," I said stiffly, edging toward the garage door on the other side of the room. "Maybe I should go help James."

"I bought them a toaster." Mrs. Laven studied me with a critical, rheumy eye. "I liked your hair better when it was shorter, although this colour suits you nicely."

"Thank you," I replied politely.

"Come sit," Sally said, patting a chair at the table. I slipped into it. "What a lovely blouse, but oh dear." She clucked and stood, one hand on the sleeve that was ripped.

When she released me, I instinctively covered the tear with my other hand and watched her leave the room, back in an instant with a small wicker basket. "Let's fix that sleeve for you."

"Oh, but..."

"It'll only take a moment. Are you wearing a cami underneath?"

"Sally," Otto warned.

"Oh, it's just us ladies here," Mrs. Laven stated.

"That's my cue," Otto said, exiting the room with his plate while giving me a look of sympathy.

I mentally checked which camisole I might be wearing under the blouse. Was it ratty? Too sexy? Ill-fitting? Basically embarrassing in any way? Probably. But with Sally already matching the thread from her kit to my shirt, I felt I had little choice but to start unbuttoning.

Sally slipped on a pair of reading glasses and set to work as soon as the red fabric was in hand. "Tell us about yourself, Char."

"Um, what would you like to know?" I ran my fingers down my bare left arm, feeling chilled despite the warmth of the cozy room.

"Did you grow up in the city?"

"No. Eagle Ridge." I'd only lived there a few years, but it

was easier telling people that was where I was from than explaining my life story.

"Lovely area. Do you know the Firestones?"

"I don't," I admitted. Sally gazed at me over her glasses, obviously in need of an explanation.

"Very pretty town," Mrs. Laven added.

"We moved there when I was in grade nine."

"Are you parents still there?" Another look over her glasses.

I shook my head.

"Oh. Where are they now? Are they retired?"

"My dad's in Lethbridge. He's retired." Again, easier than explaining that after a work accident, he was on disability, and would be for the rest of his life. Or that he rarely left the house, and despite my pushing and prodding, wasn't willing to road trip to our province's capital to take in a travelling exhibit with me. True, he'd already seen the ancient civilizations exhibit in a documentary, and taking it in would mean him travelling four-and-a-half hours each way. But I thought he loved that stuff as much as I did.

"Not too far. And your mom?"

"She..." I realized I wasn't sure where she was at the moment. She travelled a lot with Damon, often living in a different province or country for months at a time while he did consulting work. Mom and I hadn't talked in over a year, and the few times we did chat it was usually about something necessary, making the calls brief. "She lives in B.C. some of the time."

The sewing went down, and Sally's head came up. She wore a look of curiosity, as though her mom senses were sniffing out the brokenness in my past. Looks like that always cut me to the core and sent my eyes welling.

It was such a dumb reaction. I wasn't an abandoned child. If needed, I was sure Mom and Damon would bail me out of jail or let me crash there overnight. They were still family, even though I hadn't gone to their destination wedding, and didn't celebrate the holidays with them.

Sally gave my closest wrist a squeeze, her empathy so thick and real I had to blink back unexpected tears.

"Family is tricky, isn't it?"

Looking around at her cozy setting, her family and neighbour, I wasn't sure if she truly understood just how tricky it could be. How devastatingly isolating it felt to be unwanted, or to be the wrong fit in the group of people you should feel closest to.

CHAPTER 18

~ *James* ~

Char came flying into the garage, her red blouse untucked, her cheeks flushed, eyes slightly wild with fear or pain. Breathlessly, she asked, "Can I help? Please say yes."

I straightened from my crouch, heart pounding. "You okay?"

"What can I do to help? What are we looking for? Costumes? Your mom said she donated a bunch."

"Uh. Okay." I'd expected my mom and Char to hit it off, but obviously something had backfired. "I'm sorry."

"It's fine." She rubbed her palms down the thighs of her jeans, already calming. She took in my parents' garage, which was stuffed with boxes, my dad's car and tons of sporting equipment from hockey nets, downhill skis to my old skateboard.

I opened the flaps on the box I'd dug out moments ago. I quickly checked the contents. Not what I needed. "I guess my mom must have donated it." I headed back toward the house door, pausing beside Char. "You sure you're okay? Do I need to give anyone a talking to?"

She let out a choked burble of surprised laughter. "No." She held out her arm, her voice wobbling slightly as she told me, "Your mom sewed my sleeve."

"That sounds like her."

Char nodded quickly with a sniff. "She's so sweet."

I didn't get the tears. Wasn't having a sweet mom a good thing?

"She only just met me." Her voice was wobbly and my heart tore for her. A little kindness had spooked her. What had her childhood been like that a few stitches in her shirt had left her undone? It made me want to tear down walls and roar at the cruelty of the world. To hold her in my arms and never let anything bad happen to her ever again.

I cleared my throat, opting to play off my mom's kindness in hopes of reducing Char's spooked state. "She adopts all of my friends as one of her own."

Char nodded, brow furrowing, and I felt the awkwardness hang in the air over my casual use of the F word. Friends.

Char lifted a hand, twisting her wrist and opening her fist to reveal the small travel sewing kit my mom had picked up in Greece on her honeymoon. It was a small plastic box, made to look like an ancient pottery piece, and one-hundred percent Char.

"She gave me this." She sniffled again, her voice wobbly. "She told me to think of her as my own fairy godmother."

CHAR and I had made it out of the house relatively unscathed, and as we drove toward Prince's Island Park near the downtown, I explained, "Mrs. Laven is struggling with memory issues. She keeps buying me toasters thinking I'm still engaged. I've managed to return three so far, but there are still two in the garage." I aimed for some humour. "In case you ever need one."

"She did mention a toaster."

"She thought you were Sophia?"

Char nodded, her smile wavering.

"I'm sorry." I wanted to hug Char, to take that haunted glimmer from her gaze. Instead, I kept driving. I had a feeling that my mom had been herself and folded Char deep into her heart, throwing Char off balance. There didn't seem to be a lot of people looking out for Char, especially if small kindnesses threw her off. "Mrs. Laven has home care now, and my mom provides respite support here and there like tonight, so the toasters should stop."

"That's nice of your mom," Char said, her expression sad. She'd mentioned once in passing that her father wasn't well, and I wondered if it was simply age or something more.

Before I could ask how he was doing, Char's expression turned bratty in that way that warned my smile to be on red alert. "I hope you don't mind, but I told her I was letting myself go because I'm preggers with your baby. Expect baby clothes to start pouring in next."

I laughed, very much doubting she'd said any of that judging from her earlier panicked look and how quickly she'd politely extracted herself from any conversation after we'd left the garage, empty-handed.

It was surprising seeing her act so uncomfortable. I'd only ever seen her as the fun-loving, confident woman who thrived on curiosity and constant change. She lived with four interesting women, knew the museum like the back of her hand, and was always up for everything. Plus, she was practically friends with everyone at the museum. And now she was going to change her neighbourhood because she saw a need for it. She was the kind of woman who would make life an adventure. The kind of woman who'd always bring light and new perspectives to each and every day.

And my family had left her spooked.

"Your family seems really nice."

"They weren't too much?"

She laughed lightly. "Oh, they totally were. But they're good people. The way they're looking out for Mrs. Laven, and how you're all still so close, it made me think of ancient civilizations and how the extended family stuck together. One close-knit unit." She sucked in a deep breath. "I thought maybe you were wearing rose-coloured glasses when you described your family. But it's real. And it's really sweet, James." Her smile wobbled. "You think I'm lucky, but I think you are."

She tucked her hands between her knees, shoulders hunched forward, watching me shyly, and at the next red light I had to resist leaning over the console to kiss her. Instead, I simply stroked her cheek with the back of a finger, thinking how lucky I was that she'd been the one to show up at the museum all those years ago.

CHAPTER 19

~ *Char* ~

J ames. Oh, that man. He was sending my head spinning today. His sweet family, his kiss, his gentle caress and the way he kept looking at me. It was a good thing we'd had to drive to Prince's Island Park, because my legs were a bit weak with all the swooning I was doing.

"There's a run?" I asked, reading the various signs posted around the island park as we parked his SUV and began walking.

"It's to raise money for local animal shelters."

"Are we running?"

James definitely looked like a runner, but me? Not so much. I had too much painful jiggling going on to make that sport any fun. A 5K would leave me black and blue and cranky for days.

"No, no. But I thought it would make a good distraction." He grinned. His knuckles brushed against mine and I wished I'd reacted fast enough to hook my fingers in his. "There's a DJ and beer garden. Figured we could crash it."

I gasped, delighted. "You rule breaker!" I raised a hand for a high-five and he complied, but then twisted his wrist, capturing my hand, holding it while we crossed a footbridge over the Bow River. I tried not to skip along beside him, excited that he was holding my hand.

People were filing past us, many wearing cat or dog ears, as per the run's theme of raising funds for the local shelters.

"I want ears," I said, watching a man in a full black cat costume pass us.

"They have them at the registration table," he called back to me.

I gasped and turned to James. "Think we can score some?"

He laughed at my eager tone, his hand tightening around my own. "Sure? My mom used to have some—that's what I was looking for in the garage."

"How did you know about this?" I asked him as I stretched to reach the stripped-down registration table and its pile of left-over headband cat ears. I asked the person packing up, "Can we?"

She nodded and I returned to James, releasing his hand to slide a pair of ears onto my head.

"The run?" James was standing close, like he wanted to still be touching me when we weren't holding hands. "I was supposed to work security at the beer gardens."

"Why aren't you?"

"I was supposed to have the night shift at the museum this week."

"But?"

"Schedule was changed at the last minute."

"What drew you to security? It doesn't seem like your thing."

"Yeah." He untangled a lock of hair that got caught in my ears. "I didn't realize it would be so boring. I was looking for something fun, but would give me time to think."

"Time to think?" I cringed automatically. Thinking was never a good idea in my case. It was as unhealthy as sitting around. The more I did it, the more I feared becoming my mother, or the more I whirled in my own toxic thoughts, blaming myself for selfishness that had ended our cozy little family dynamic. Although, thinking about now, with James snugged up close to me, I didn't get that familiar old clenching in my gut or wash of spine prickling shame. Did that mean I was finally letting it go?

"So why don't you get another job?" I asked.

"There's this cutie," he said affectionately, adjusting my ears again, "who keeps coming into the museum and bossing everyone around. I couldn't possibly miss out on that."

Heat flowed through me as I realized he was referring to me. He'd been staying in a boring job so he could see more of me? I could faint. Swoon. Dance.

He had to be lying, right? I mean, who did that?

But I was pretty sure he was telling the truth, and it made me want to float away.

"Well," I said, reaching up to put his ears on. "If you're feeling lucky, you could call her up and arrange a meet up." I was careful not to say date, even though that was what I really wanted. It had taken us some time to get where we were tonight, slowly dipping our toes outside of the friend zone. I didn't want to mess things up by cannonballing my way into something he might not be ready for. Especially since I still wasn't sure how we'd work long-term. Did he want a cozy home life, or did he want spontaneity? He said he wanted spontaneity, but I could see that a cozy home life was important to him. And did the two go hand-in-hand? I wasn't so sure.

"I should quit, huh?" he said.

I smiled. "You should do whatever you want to do."

"Yeah." The intensity in his gaze made me feel pinned to the spot, my breath catching. His thumb was caressing my neck, just below my ear, and I realized I had an erogenous zone I hadn't known about.

"Yeah. You should." I cleared my throat, hoping he'd devour me with that mouth and those dark sexy eyes of his. "How do I look?"

"Cute."

I gave him a flirty flutter of my lashes. "I always look cute."

"And beautiful." He gently gripped my chin between his thumb and index finger, tipping it upward so he could lower his lips to mine. He kissed me slowly, like earlier. But when I kissed him back, suddenly the intensity level shot through the roof, his arms tightening around me, drawing me close like he'd been waiting to do this since the day we'd met. Like he'd lain awake for more hours than one could count, wondering just how amazing this might be.

And amazing, it was. My whole body felt light, but also very much here and now, alive in every spot that our bodies touched like I was playing with electricity.

We broke the kiss, my breathing jagged like I'd just crossed the finish line after sprinting the last half of the run.

James. Oh, James. Did he have *any* idea how sexy he was? And wearing those adorable kitty ears and owning them, not shedding them like wearing them would lessen his masculinity. He was perfect.

"Wow," I whispered.

He breathed me into another kiss, long and slow and so filled with promises I wasn't sure my legs would ever work right again.

"You're going to give me diabetes," he said, his hand finding mine.

"What?" I felt dazed, like I'd shot through a portal and into a whole new life.

"Your kisses are so sweet..." He kissed me again, like this would help him prove his point.

"I need whiskers," I whispered when he seemed done kissing me. I swung my purse off my shoulder and rummaged through it, feeling suddenly nervous and unsure what to do with my hands, my mouth, and all of these feelings I'd kept so carefully hidden for so long.

I handed him an eyeliner pencil, my hands shaking. "Give me a nose and whiskers, please."

With a slow smile, he didn't question why I didn't use one of the small mirrors hanging on the stand near us, but uncapped the pencil and shimmied his feet so he was even closer, like we might kiss again. I could feel his breath, warm on my cheek, his jacket brushing my chest.

"What do I do?"

I angled my face upward. "Triangle nose. Three whiskers each side." I mimed where I wanted the whiskers on my right cheek. His face was so near to my own, it was impossible to meet his gaze without burning up.

He was closer than he needed to be and I loved it, sucking up the pleasure of having his body so close to mine. He gently placed his left hand on the side of my face, his palm cupping my jaw. My breath hitched as his large, rough hand brushed my skin, his eyes taking in every detail of me.

He took his time, sketching a triangle on the tip of my nose, then colouring it in with gentle, patient strokes.

His eyes seemed so blue whenever I flicked my gaze to his. He finished the nose, the act of applying the makeup feeling more intimate than if he'd kissed me again.

"You have flecks of green in your eyes," he whispered, angling his hand to start on the whiskers.

Daring myself, I allowed myself to meet and hold his gaze, possibly the scariest, most intimate thing I'd done with him to date. This close I felt vulnerable, exposed. But also held and cherished and safe. I trusted this man more than any other.

"Mm. You have bits of grey." I felt dazed and dreamy, as if I could float away like one of Estelle's fairy coworkers.

Estelle. Debt.

Ooph. Unfun thoughts.

But the giant grant. The fact that the agency had wanted us to get *both* lots and had found enough money to buy the land so we could get started. Well worth any wishes added to my bill.

I felt my smile pick up again.

James was frowning, his focus narrowed as he carefully drew one gentle line from the valley of my nose and cheek outward. I giggled and moved, his line going off course.

"Stay still." He laughed.

"Sorry."

"I love that you trust me," he murmured as he carefully, stroked his thumb across my cheek where the whisker line had strayed.

"Maybe I shouldn't," I teased.

"I have no real plan."

"For what? Your life?"

"That, but also tonight."

"Who needs a plan to have fun?" I scoffed, before realizing that Sophia had left her mark on him. He'd said she had life all laid out, their routines set. He hadn't been able to see spontaneity in his future—the one thing I had in spades. Maybe I was his type, from head to toe. And maybe that whole tight knit family business could be learned. Maybe this was exactly what my heart had been waiting for.

"I don't need things laid out, James," I assured him.

"I promised you a distraction," he said, reworking the original wonky whisker.

"You're delivering." I nestled deeper into his open arms.

The whisker he was drawing went crooked again.

I laughed at his exasperated expression. "I give up."

"No, no!" I tilted my head upward for him, my smile properly schooled, eyes watching his. He was shaking his head, not truly upset if his sparkling eyes were to be the indicator. He seemed to love this every bit as much as I did.

CHAPTER 20

~ *Estelle* ~

I smiled to myself as I stood in front of Gram-Gram in her flowing pink dress. She was a pretty fairy and had a kind face. She was ageing gracefully, and I hoped that when I was in my hundreds, I looked as good as she did.

But even if I didn't age gracefully, I was still going to look really great sitting in this office when she retired. Yes, I was going to beat out Trish and her family line. I was going to be the family member who held this coveted seat, because I was rocking being a trainee fairy godmother.

"Your report?" the head fairy asked.

"Yes," I said with confidence. "I had the gnomes recalibrate their equipment. I also requested an adjustment in regards to Char's most recent charges."

"I heard."

I opened my mouth to explain, but she waved a hand. "Undecided."

"She's trying, ma'am," I argued. "I should have had the equipment recalibrated as soon as I—"

"I'm not blaming you for not thinking of that. Her increased debt for the broken window could have been much worse if the sundial had been properly calibrated." She held up a hand. "And the good deeds would have been worth more, too, I know. I think in the end, she got off easy. Let's leave things as they are with her account for the time being. I see you've been granting her small wishes?"

I crossed my fingers and nodded. The wish I'd granted so Char could get the grant hadn't been a tiny one, due to the tight time constraints she'd put on it. I'd given Agnes at the grant agency the intuitive hit to open her email and check new applications during a retirement party. Then I'd influenced her to push her colleagues to hold an impromptu emergency board meeting, interrupting their party. "Yes, small ones."

"And is she closer to believing?"

I opened my mouth, realizing that I was breaking our earlier deal, and that somewhere along the line, my confidence had overshot me. Gram-Gram had allowed me to grant Char small wishes that would help her believe in us, instead of cutting her off completely. Char now believed, and was actively working to reduce her debt. But I'd kept granting her more wishes. The question was a trap.

"She believes," I admitted.

"Estelle." The way the head fairy said my name held more disappointment than any words she could have used.

I lowered my head. "I'm sorry. I got caught up."

"You have a good heart. But until she's under the amount-owing threshold, you need to stop granting her wishes." She lifted a hand before I could speak. Cutting Char off was unfair. "And Estelle? Quit meddling in Char's love life."

My jaw dropped. How did she know what I'd been doing behind her back?

Did she also know that I'd been influencing things by sending positive energy Char's way? Just a bit here and there, nudging her life along.

"But they both want to leave the friend zone," I protested.

"She didn't wish for it, did she?"

I sighed, shaking my head. Technically, Gram-Gram was correct. There hadn't even been a wish followed by a clawback, giving me no wiggle room. For a woman who wished so much, Char really should be more strategic.

"But if men had fairy godmothers, I'm sure James would be wishing for her to kiss him."

The head fairy leaned forward, clasping her hands on top of her rosewood desk. I lowered my gaze to follow the pattern of flowers carved into the richly hued wood.

"So then, do you plan to continue to meddle throughout their lives to ensure their relationship stays on track?" she asked.

"They just needed a push."

"They need to do things in their own time."

I held in a dejected sigh. "Understood."

"Also, a reminder?"

"Yes, ma'am?"

"Stop influencing fate."

"Ma'am?"

"Your positive energy 'gifts,' shall we call them?"

No wonder she was the head of our region, and had been for centuries. I couldn't slip a thing past her.

"I appreciate your creativity in finding a workaround, seeing as wishes surrounding her debt repayment can't be granted. And, yes, I retracted the one you made in regards to the grant agency. It was flagged by the ethics committee shortly after you granted it due to a conflict of interest."

I swore the sparkle in Gram-Gram's lavender eyes suggested that a teensy bit of that wish had been granted before it had been shut down. Did she approve? She must, because, according to Big Bertha's list of rules and regulations, I should be getting a strike right now. A red mark across my forehead for all the other trainees to see and for Trish to gloat over.

"The ethics committee will be watching you very closely from here on out."

I nodded, reminding myself to act sombre. Having the ethic committee watching me was not a joke.

"Also, quit nudging all of those poor humans to help her."

"But the book said that sending positive energy—"

"I said stop. Before you leave tonight, read section 5.a. under Conflicts of Interest and be sure you understand. Then write a letter of apology to the committee."

"Yes, ma'am." I sighed, frustrated at being caught as well as always feeling one step behind my trainee counterparts. "Ma'am?"

"Yes?"

"Why didn't I get sent to fairy school like the others? I'd have thirteen years of knowledge under my belt, and wouldn't be embarrassing myself or our family by messing up all the time."

"You'd also be thinking like them," Gram-Gram retorted immediately, waving a hand dismissively toward the bullpen filled with pink clones.

"But isn't that the point?"

"No. Recall that I appreciate your creativity." One eyebrow rose in my direction in silent question.

I nodded, summoning her earlier, almost-compliment to mind. She might appreciate my creativity, but it had gotten me into trouble, hadn't it?

"Creative thinking is what differentiates a good fairy godmother from an exceptional one. Also, please remember that from here on out, until she is below the threshold, Char is on her own. No more wishes."

CHAPTER 21
~ *Char* ~

I sighed, leaning against the closed apartment door, fingers to my tingling lips. I was still in awe of how quickly James and I were moving.

He'd dropped me off, and we'd kissed out front until Randy's stupid sports car alarm had started blaring. Seriously, nobody had even come within a few feet of the vehicle.

James and I had spent hours at Prince's Island Park, cheering on runners as they crossed the finish line before heading to the beer gardens and listening to the DJ. I'd loved that James had paused to cheer on the last runners, the ones who were at the back of the pack, and who'd barely finished. Could the man make me love him more?

At one point, I'd thought of Estelle's payback chant while cheering, going over it a few times in my head. Then, realizing it was pulling me from truly being there and enjoying James and the silliness of what we were doing, I let it go and rode the wave of fun.

I shook my head at myself. I'd been giddy and happy as well as a little bit silly. James had rolled with it, encouraging it. I'd told him some bad dad jokes, and he'd claimed they were worse than his dad's. It had made me think of his mom and how sweet she'd been, teaching me a few quick stitches while fixing my shirt and then sending me home with a tiny kit of my own.

I'd then furiously buried the thought, trying not to think about what kind of man would keep a woman who didn't fit with his family when he was obviously super close with them.

I texted James a goofy gif of a woman running in a marathon with a giant margarita and told him I was already training for our next run. Then I leaned my head against the door, eyes closed, allowing myself to feel the swell of sweetness thinking about the best moment of the night. We'd been dancing with people dressed up as dogs, doing silly dances like the mashed potato, and he'd pulled me into his arms, saying with affection, "You can have fun anywhere, can't you?"

It had felt like I'd passed some sort of test. One I'd been studying for all my life.

"Did you wish for it? The grant?" Tamara demanded, and I startled, finding her standing at the top of the stairs, arms crossed like an angry mother waiting for her curfew-breaking daughter.

I started up the stairs, considering my argument. I sufficed with a simple, "Yes."

James and I had returned our kitty ears when we left, but my whiskers and nose were still drawn in place and I waited for Tamara to comment on them. That or the obvious high I was riding upon.

But she stayed quiet, chewing on her bottom lip.

"Have you been waiting for me to come home?" I asked when I reached the top.

"I've been freaking out since you and James left."

"I'm sorry." Unable to hold it in any longer, I grinned, saying, "I think we're dating."

Tamara pulled me into a fierce, quick hug. "I'm so happy for you! He's a keeper."

The idea of keeping him, and him keeping me sent a spear of unwanted reality through my bubble of happiness. It was best not to think about the future.

Tamara released me, still looking tense, despite her happiness for me. Feeling bad for how she'd been stressing out over my wish that had gotten us the land grant, I tried to explain myself. "Making a wish for the grant has to be cheaper than buying the land on my own. Especially since I don't have the money, and the grant was unlikely to come through in time. This is a win-win, right now situation, and sets me up for getting the karmic ball rolling."

"But we banned wishing! And you don't even have the money to pay Estelle for old wishes. And now you've added a new one that costs who knows how much!"

I swallowed hard, surprised by Tamara's passion. "I'm playing the long game."

"It's risky!"

"Tam-Tam. It's a little debt for a big gain."

"What if the park doesn't work?"

I felt a twinge of doubt. "It kind of has to."

"But if it doesn't?"

"Can't I just wish it into working?"

"No! You're about to buy two lots and sign agreements with the grant agency. Did you ever consider that the money might have worked out for us either way?"

"Er. No." Could we have gotten the grant without the cost of making a forbidden wish? The agency had seemed pretty excited about our project. What if that was genuine, and I hadn't needed to put Estelle on the case to get them to release the money to us?

"It feels like we're playing with fire." She wrapped her arms around her middle. "I'm scared, Char."

"I'm sorry."

"Your wishes impact other people and their lives, too. There must be ripple effects with every wish. You need to stop interfering with fate, and just be happy with the life you have. Because what if Estelle makes a mistake? What if you're breaking rules by making wishes that are related to paying off your debt?"

My body went hot, then cold at the thought that I'd missed a vital loophole, kind of like with being able to put both good and bad karma onto my account with Estelle. Had I possibly broken some rules and danced through a forbidden zone? And for what gain? Possibly more debt and trouble?

I blinked at Tamara, processing the idea that my wish habit could be interfering with fate. What if fate would've found a way to hand me the same cards, wish or no wish?

If I was influencing the future, was it possible that I was ruining my own life, sending it spinning off down a different tangent instead of the one intended for me?

And if I was, was I doing the right thing for my future self, or was I shortchanging myself—my imagination more limited than that of the Universe or whomever was in control? What if it was my own actions that were wronging my life so terribly?

My hand flew to my lips. What if I'd unconsciously wished for James to kiss me? What if none of tonight was what he wanted? What if he was under a spell?

CHAPTER 22

~ *Char* ~

Life had slowed down after Wednesday's flurry of grant-getting, and me and James kissing. Was that because I'd been a lot more careful about not making wishes?

Or was it unrelated that I'd barely seen James over the past several days, and didn't know if he was still interested in me?

Logically, not seeing James could also be explained by my sudden workload increase. Joan, my boss at the temp agency, had suddenly been sending me extra, urgent jobs on top of my usual load. I'd been working from dawn to dusk which hardly gave me time to make any wishes. Or to see James.

Maybe it was just my current life circumstances putting the brakes on our full-speed getaway into a relationship, and had nothing to do with magic. Although, if I'd accidentally wished for him to kiss me last Wednesday, that wish would have worn off at midnight, if the fairytales were correct. That would explain why he wasn't banging down my door and sweeping me into his arms.

At least keeping up with our park plans kept me from thinking about the implications of my unbreakable wishing habits, having a fairy godmother, and also a sudden boyfriend.

The city had allowed me to buy the two lots with the grant money earlier today, and the girls and I had been calling in favours where we could to create a demolition schedule for the warehouse as well as forming our landscaping plan.

It was now after six at night, and I was eager to check out my new land purchase. Samantha had agreed to come along with me, as our other three roommates had drummed up various reasons for not tromping through the abandoned warehouse, plotting its demise.

I'd begged James to tag along and be our protector since I wasn't sure what would be in the warehouse. But really, I needed an excuse to see him again and get a read on our relationship status. If there even was one.

While Samantha and I waited for him to arrive, she made us some decaf lattes in her fancy machine.

I was getting addicted. Her hot drinks were always perfect. Every time.

She handed me a mug, her metal bangles clanging against its ceramic surface. "Your latte."

I inhaled its rejuvenating aroma; the steam dampening my face. Since her adoption of the machine, our kitchen smelled like a coffee shop on most days, the scent seeping into the old wood floors. Before taking a sip, having spied a carton of skim milk in our fridge yesterday, I said, "This had better not be 'skinny'."

Samantha snorted. "Like I'd waste our time." She ran a flattened hand down her side, over the curves of her torso, and coyly batted her lashes. "I like my girlish figure."

While I have some pretty feminine curves, Samantha officially had the market cornered. The woman could double as a 1940s pinup girl. Well, except for the piercings and changing rainbow of hair colouring.

I took a sip of the milky coffee. She'd made it sweet, just the way I like it.

"Perfect, right?" she asked smugly.

"Always."

We took our cups and waited for James outside, just down the street to a spot where Randy wouldn't see us from his front window and come out to shoot the breeze.

Samantha paused, the cup halfway to her mouth. I followed her line of sight: Caleb leaving the apartment.

I cleared my throat. "How are you and Malachi?" I asked.

"Mmhm."

Clearly she was still crushing on our downstairs neighbour, and I feared that didn't bode well for Malachi.

I got it though. Caleb had wavy, longish hair that brushed his dark lashes when he looked at you. He was tall, lanky, and always in a well-loved knitted sweater. He seemed genuine and kind. Oh, and he was Irish. Had I mentioned that was Samantha's personal kryptonite?

He caught our eye from down the way, giving us a nod, his eyes sweeping over Samantha. Then he vanished into his car, Samantha's gaze following like little lost puppies who'd imprinted on the man.

"Irish," Samantha said on a sigh. "Hotness like that shouldn't be allowed."

"Samantha! You have a boyfriend." I elbowed her, spilling her latte.

She shot me a dark glance and licked the coffee from her thumb. "I still have eyes. I can look."

"You could make a wish to your fairy godmother, you know," I said slyly. Tamara, Josie and I had floated the idea of fairy godmothers past Samantha and Gabby a few times over the past two weeks, but they didn't seem inclined to start believing.

Samantha simply rolled her eyes, and I moved the conversation back to her boyfriend. "Malachi's one of those nice-guy types."

"Hm?"

"You know, he's sweet. The kind of guy you'd rather stay in with on a Saturday night instead of go out bar hopping?"

Not that I ever wanted to stay in with a guy. I was too afraid of ruining it all. Being boring, getting stuck in a rut. All of that. Life needed a bit of excitement.

Samantha got a far-off look. "We stayed in last weekend. No nightclubs. No parties."

"Really? On purpose? Were you sick or something?"

She scoffed at me. "No. We wanted to."

Wanted to. Because they were in love?

I caught myself looking down the street for James's Range Rover, wondering if he'd have a similar effect on me. I was having trouble imagining it.

Who was going to be my adventurous role model if Samantha decided to settle down?

"We stayed at home—" her tone went dry "—when I wasn't over here helping you plot the makeover." She gestured toward the warehouse and trashy lot. She turned to me with interest. "Why do you like temping?"

There was something in her tone that made me knee-jerk my standard reply: "I love it. Absolutely love it. I like the constant change."

Stay moving, don't think. Excellent plan for a life of happiness, right? I would die with no regrets, just a memory filled with fun and adventure.

Plus, now that I'd earned a solid reputation with our boss, Joan, I was being sent places where they treated their temporary employees with a little respect. It was fun.

"I keep thinking you'll accept one of those offers that comes with a steady, reliable pay cheque and decent benefits," Samantha said, watching me, something in her gaze that unnerved me. "You know, settle in, settle down."

"Me?" I snorted, suddenly uncomfortable.

"Yeah. You're the smalltown nesting type."

"Am not!" The smalltown nesting type was Tamara. Not me. "I'm not related to half the people in any town, and me and my family haven't lived in some little place since its inception. I don't fit into small towns." I knew how they worked. They were like functional families—something nice for other people to experience.

"Because you've barely stayed anywhere long enough for everyone to let their guard down and let you in. You're a small-town type." Her tone was firm. "You like people, and have friends and connections all over the city. I mean, you think I have connections in Calgary, but you probably called over a hundred people you knew to see if they'd help with the park if you got the land. And most of them told you to either keep them in the loop, or said yes."

That was true. A lot of people had offered to donate a few bucks, or to at least mention my park to a business they knew of who might help sponsor parts of its creation.

"You make everywhere *feel* like a small town. You're always doing nice things for others, like helping that hurt kid and walking shelter dogs."

Right. I'd started doing that this week, too. A mini backup plan in case the park thing didn't help the old karmic bank account.

"And now you're doing all this community building stuff."

I paused, unsure if I should mention the fairy godmother thing again. At some point, she was either going to start believing, or think I was crazy. I feared the latter was looking more likely.

"Maybe I'm like Clarisa," I said, referring to her stepmom, "and just like to do good things?"

"No. It's something more."

"Probably the fact that I owe my fairy godmother a lot of money?" I angled a look her way, and she laughed.

"No, you're the family type. And temping isn't you. It's too transient. I don't think it's what makes you happy. It's not what feels good and secure in here." She held a hand to her chest, and I wondered what had gotten into her. We talked about money and what was hot around the city, not this sort of stuff. Had Tamara put her up to this talk? Because this sounded more like Tamara to me.

"Family type?" I echoed. We'd wandered back to our front step, and I set down my empty coffee cup. It was all I could do not to scoff at Samantha's proclamation of who I was, even though a tiny part of me wanted it to be true. I loved the idea of having a place or group of people to call home. I had my roomies, yes, but I knew that wouldn't last forever.

"Yeah." She gave a small shrug. "I could see you as a really fun mom." She laughed, and I stood, not quite sure what to say to that, grateful to spy James's SUV coming down the block.

He popped out of his old Range Rover, looking handsome in a deep blue sweater, all smiles. "Congrats on getting the land!"

I gave a little squeal as he swept me into his arms, giving me a twirl there in the middle of the street. He twirled me like I weighed nothing. Absolutely nothing, and I swear I swooned a little, because who didn't love a strong man?

Maybe he hadn't been under a spell after all.

Then again, no hello kiss.

Were we back in the friend zone because my wishes had worn off? Or was it because we had an audience that he didn't give me a kiss?

I felt like I couldn't even look at him fully with Samantha's words whirling in my head about how I was the family type. Was I actually like James, but didn't realize it? Did I actually want a close-knit family, even though the idea terrified me, and I didn't know how it worked? And even if I did manage to get it, would I screw it up?

CHAPTER 23

~ James ~

The three of us walked through the tall weeds of Char's empty lot toward the metal-sided warehouse, and I was glad she'd asked me along. The former owner no longer had keys for the doors that faced the street, and Char was hoping we could get in from the back.

Near the warehouse's foundation, years of packed down garbage had clogged the life out of anything that had tried to grow close to it. There was flaked-off paint, rust, holes and loose panels that clanged in the breeze like a slow morse coder. The sun lowered in the sky, and I felt like this was somewhere we shouldn't be.

But the most troubling was Char. There were no signals that last Wednesday's passionate kisses were something she wanted to repeat. In fact, she kept eyeing me as though she wasn't sure about me and where we stood.

How could she not be sure? How could I have made myself any more clear? I'd introduced her to my parents and kissed her as if our lives depended on it. Did she need me to lay it all out for her?

And yet, if I did that, I was afraid I'd scare her off.

She was frustratingly impossible, and all I wanted was her.

Samantha checked her suede shoes for marks or mud stains for approximately the fiftieth time, and I wondered why she was here. Was she a requested buffer to be slid between me and Char?

I hoped not.

"Eleven weeks," Char muttered to herself as she wiggled the key in the rusty padlock on the warehouse' back door, unable to budge the seized inner mechanisms.

That was how much time she'd allowed herself to tear this building down and beautify the lots. Hopefully, our look around inside didn't reveal any obstacles to her tight tear-down plan.

"We can get a lock cutter tomorrow." Samantha was already retracing her earlier steps toward the street.

"Where's my fairy godmother when you need her?" Char muttered, jamming the key into the lock again.

Her love of fairies tickled me. "Do girls ever outgrow that phase?"

"What phase?" Char pulled the key back out of the lock and tried blowing into it in case loose debris was the problem. I resisted the urge to reach around her and try my hand at it.

"When I'm a dad, I hope my daughter goes through a fairy phase." I could see a little girl, so like Char. Whimsical and fun, happy and strong.

"Don't have daughters. We're a never-ending nightmare of headaches," Samantha said. "Just ask my dad."

Char gave up on the door and turned to me with a dreamy expression. Maybe she was imagining the same thing I was. Me as a dad, holding our little girl in a fairy princess dress as I flew her through the air, running around the living room, chasing Char.

She likely wasn't imagining that. In fact, I didn't even know where her head was at these days. And as for me, I was constantly putting the cart before the horse with her. When my ex had shared her future family fantasies, I'd become uncomfortable, but with Char I was the one with my head in the clouds.

"Can we go now?" Samantha had stopped to wait for us, and she brushed invisible muck from her shoes.

Unwilling to call it quits in case Char decided to come back here on her own, I reached around her, giving the lock a firm yank that shook the entire door. I stepped back, peering around the side of the building, and down the narrow space between the warehouse and the brick structure next door.

"We can get in down here." Part way down the wall, I spied a bent, loose piece of siding that might serve as an entrance.

"Nope. I'm gone." Samantha turned and left.

Maybe she wasn't here to act as a buffer between me and Char, after all. At least now maybe I'd get some answers as to why Char was acting standoffish.

Char followed me as we squeezed our way between the two buildings. She knocked on the metal siding as we shimmied. "I found a scrap company that'll take this away and recycle it."

"Smart." Free removal, and the crew got whatever the siding was worth at the reclaimers. Win-win.

At the hole in the wall, we bent at the waist, peering inside, one after the other. It was dark compared to outside, the odd shaft of light making its way in through holes in the roof.

"Let me go first. Make sure it's safe," I said, crouching beside Char and holding an arm in front of her in case she decided to get the jump on me and squeeze through first. There was no way I was letting her in before me, and I quickly angled my frame through the opening. The warehouse smelled of old motor oil and dirt.

Char followed, stopping short as her eyes adjusted to the

faint light. "Oh, no. People are living in here. That's got to be bad karma if I oust them."

I eyed the weathered sleeping bags laid out on the dirt floor. I lifted a few of the beds, sending clouds of dust into the air. "I think they've all moved on. My mom said the Salvation Army was working hard in this neighbourhood last year to home the homeless."

"Thank goodness," Char said. "I'm trying to solve problems, not create new ones, and tearing down someone's shelter would be seriously uncool."

"Yeah." I moved back to her side, as though wanting to take in the building from her point of view and allowed my knuckles to brush hers, watching her from the corner of my eye. I admired Char. Not just her heart, but the way she was willing to pour it into this self-led community project.

A slight pink flashed across her cheeks at my touch, as if she was feeling shy. We stood beside each other for a moment, eyes adjusting to the building's shadowy light as we took in details. Anything of value had been stripped from the walls a long time ago, including any plumbing, fixtures, or electrical. The warehouse's frame was wood, not steel, which should mean an easy takedown. Oddly, though, there was nothing between us and the outer metal siding. No insulation, which was weird for Canada. Then again, maybe the inner panelling and insulation had been stripped out, too.

Across the warehouse, some wooden steps led up to a small room with a door. The upper level didn't even cover an eighth of the building's footprint, and I wondered if it was an old office.

Char shivered beside me.

"You okay?" I wanted to pull her into my arms and kiss her, but the signals she'd been giving me suggested she needed me to slow it down. It felt like that was all I'd been doing since the day I'd met her, and being patient was becoming a genuine struggle.

"I'm fine. Just thinking how much work this'll be." She rubbed her hands together. "I can't wait to get started."

I took in the dimly lit open space and the giant doors on the other side of the room. "Does this place make you think of a movie set?"

"You mean where the bad guys come ripping in on motorcycles or in black SUVs to make an arms deal or to do a hostage swap?" She turned to me with a grin, knowing I was visualizing the same thing. I wanted to scoop a hand through her hair and draw her toward me and kiss those smiling lips.

"Yeah," I said, unable to look away from her mouth.

She shivered again and turned to leave. I grabbed her arm, not yet ready to leave the old building. There was still more to explore, more moments to spend together. I angled my chin toward the steps on the other side of the room. "What do you think's up there?"

Char's eyes lit up, and a thrum of adventure rumbled through us like a connection.

"Empty office?" she asked, finally meeting my eyes like she used to.

"Boring storage?" I replied dryly.

She laughed. "Okay. Fine. How about important and valuable historical documents?"

"Old journals or diaries?"

"Mysteries and gold?"

"Now you're talking!" Grabbing her hand, I dragged her across the packed dirt floor—another win, no concrete pad to bust up—and over to the steps. I kept holding her hand, not wanting to be the first to let go.

Had she simply been too shy to express her affection in front of Samantha? Or were we just taking one step back after last week's sudden jump from friends, to friends who kiss like lovers?

And did it matter? I had her with me right now, her smooth hand in mine.

"I think we've watched too many movies," I admitted as we started up the wooden steps to the second level, which really was just a sliver of space tacked up near the roof and had most likely been cleared out a long time ago.

"No such thing as too many!" she said. "Imagine if we find something! It'll be like living in *Jumanji* or *Indiana Jones*. Or even *The Mummy* or *Lost City*!"

"Do I know that last one?"

"Featuring Sandra Bullock."

"Oh, yeah. That was cute. My mom rented it."

Yes, I watched rom-coms with my mom. They made me laugh and feel good. Plus, it made my mom happy.

Char clung tighter to my hand. The poor lighting and the open wood steps with no railing were clearly making her uneasy. "What if the upper landing is rotted and we fall through?"

"Where's your sense of adventure?" I needed to see what was behind that door. My inner child had been released, and was fully in charge of checking out the abandoned building. If there had been windows and rocks, I'd surely be the first to break them just for the sheer joy of it.

Yeah, I liked rom-coms, but I also really liked smashing stuff.

"Death isn't an adventure," Char chided. "Neither is being alive, but with severely broken legs and a crippled spine."

I chuckled and slowed down, tightening my grip on her hand when she flinched as a few pigeons fluttered from a rafter.

"You okay?" I asked.

She nodded, keeping her attention on the steps, and her shoulder against the solid wall to her right.

At the top, I surveyed the warehouse from our perch.

"Aren't you dizzy?" she asked.

"Why?"

"No railings! We're up high. You could accidentally fall off, landing on the hard, stained dirt below like so many people before us. Look at all those stains! There are more of them near these railing-less steps."

She was holding my hand with both of hers now.

I chuckled. "Those are shadows, Char."

She pressed closer to the wall while I tried the door. "Locked." I stepped back, my right hand still in Char's, debating whether I could kick in the door. That would be fun. Really fun.

As I stepped back from the door, I could see through the thick dust that nobody had been up here in a very long time.

"You're not worried you'll lose your balance, and then your footing, and then your life?" Her tone was dramatic, but it failed to mask her discomfort. She was gently pulling me closer, away from the platform's edge. "One, two, three, gone."

I focused on her and the endearing concern she had for me. Then I dropped a light kiss on her lips. She didn't pull back, sending fire and happiness through my veins.

CHAPTER 24
~ *Char* ~

Before I could pull James in for another kiss, he leaned back. His jaw was tight with what seemed to be restraint, like he wanted to devour me. I felt myself involuntarily tip my weight toward him, offering myself up.

Instead, he let out a shaky breath and turned away, facing the locked door. Mischief flashed in his eyes again. "Curious what's inside?"

I nodded, one hand on the wall beside me, afraid to look over the expanse of openness to my left.

He gestured to the door. "Mind if I try?"

I wasn't sure what he meant since it was locked, but I shrugged and said, "Be my guest."

Before I could finish my sentence, he kicked the door, the loud noise ricocheting off the metal walls. I jumped, nearly falling off my step and tumbling down the rest.

He gave the door another kick, and this time the latch gave.

I gasped at his strength. "How did you do that?" Talk about sexy!

He strode into the room, leaving tracks in the thick dust.

He turned back, unimpressed by what he'd discovered, which was nothing.

I surreptitiously inspected the door and doorframe. Splintered wood bent inward. Dang. I followed him into the dark room, using my phone as a flashlight. The area was the size of my apartment bedroom—not that big—and it was empty, aside from a cardboard box and a wooden crate. There was nothing but layers of dust in the crate and box, now marred by my fingerprints. Not even a fixture was attached to the loose wire hanging where a light had once been.

Somehow it was all incredibly disappointing.

I wiped my hands on my jeans, coughing at the disturbed dust.

"No gold," James sighed, checking the empty crate.

"No gold," I echoed.

But I'd been kissed, and he'd held my hand. I felt lighter than I had in days, because now I knew that there had been no midnight-breaking kiss-me spell, and that James was still interested.

CHAPTER 25
~ *James* ~

I desperately wanted to sweep Char into my arms and show her just how much I'd thought about her over the past week. How much I desired her in this very moment.

But I feared that if I pressed too hard, I might lose her. She was skittish. Shy. One to take it slow.

There was a reason I'd booked myself a trip to Corsica next week. I needed to give the woman a bit of space, so I didn't freak her out with my readiness to march her down the aisle.

It was also entirely possible that I was reading her signs incorrectly, my own wants painting over the subtle hints she was sending me. Could her shyness be reluctance? Was her lack of recent availability a hint to back off?

I didn't think so, but I was starting to realize just how many fears she had around relationships. And that meant she had a lot more uncertainty than I did. The things I took for granted, such as a marriage that would last, were the same things she assumed she'd never have.

But it was something I wanted to give her. And in order to do that, I had to do it right. I had to move slowly.

This woman was going to be the end of me.

We left the warehouse, and I took her hand again, promising myself I could, and would, move slower than I had last week, even though I could see our future, and wanted to be there. Now.

No, last year already.

She drifted closer, letting her shoulder brush mine. As we left the lot, she kept hold of my hand, even as we made our way through the hole in the fence.

That was promising.

It just felt like the energy that had been propelling us last week had eased up, and we were back to uncertainty, neither of us braving a bold next move. She could be waiting for me, but this might also be her preferred pace.

Char said men were impossible? Try dating a woman.

"Come to the museum with me," I said, leaning against my Rover, checking my watch. I had a night shift in twenty-five minutes.

A flash of uncertainty crossed her face, and I snagged her hand, pulling her against me. I wrapped my arms around her waist, loosely, so she could wiggle free if she wanted.

Her smile was quick, and she made no moves to leave my embrace. "The museum closes soon."

I gave her a deep, long kiss that I'd been thinking about for days. When we broke apart, her eyes were half-closed, her smile dreamy.

That was better. Much better.

"Come with me," I prompted, buoyed by the signals she was sending me. I warned myself to slow down, but I wasn't sure where the brakes were. Wherever they were, I wanted to snap them off and let the momentum take us away like it had last week.

She narrowed her eyes, watching me with a mischievous expression. "Okay."

I parked in the staff lot, and as we entered the museum together, I asked her, my fingers reaching out to tap hers, "Do I need to sneak you in?"

She beamed at me like I'd said magic words. "I have my membership on me." She flashed the card at Glenda moments later, and was warned she only had fifteen minutes before closing.

Greg, one of the several guides, sidled up to us on the other side of the admission desk. Charming and good looking, but total slime. It was clear he used Char's intelligence about pottery stuff to make himself look better at his job. But he was charming. And women liked charming.

"Hey," he said to Char, leaning casually on the edge of Glenda's desk. "There's new stuff in the gift shop. Think you might like it."

That was my line.

She slowed. "Really?"

Greg did a great job of making her feel smart with his questions about her interests, so maybe that was my real problem.

Jealousy.

Around Char, I lost my game, but Greg's got better.

"What era?" she asked, ignoring the fact that I was trying to gently propel her forward and away from Smarmy McDufus.

Greg flashed her a big grin, not answering her question. Probably because he'd forgotten to look up the age of the pieces or needed to ask her. "I heard you bought some land?"

"Greg, aren't you off for the night?" I asked, renewing my attempt to move Char forward again.

"I did!" Char said brightly. "How'd you hear?"

"James told me."

Yeah, and I really regretted it, too.

At another desk off to the side, where tours gathered, Richard, the museum director, looked up, obviously eavesdropping. He always studied Char with a frown, like he failed to recognize her. Then, after a beat, his scowl would deepen as though recognition had finally dawned, and that dawn was a vile orange instead of the expected beautiful array of pastels.

It pretty much made me want to push my fist so far into his face he'd need dentures.

As far as I knew, they hadn't had a run-in other than the number of times Char had taken him to task over a few of the museum's plaques and their inaccuracies. She'd confided to me once, after giving Richard a blast, that he should read the books they kept stocked in the museum's gift shop.

I'd laughed over that one for weeks.

But if I were a betting man, I'd say it was the Christmas party for staff and members that had turned Richard. Apparently, slaughtering the museum director in an ancient history trivia game wasn't a good way to earn his friendship.

Not that I figured Char wanted to be friends with the man. She'd once said he probably drove a diesel Dodge Ram with a lift kit and oversized tires on splashy rims to compensate for 'other things.' I'd checked the staff lot and confirmed that she was correct about his choice of transportation.

"My roommates and I are going to make a park once we tear down the warehouse," Char was telling Greg.

"Why? Wait." He held out a hand to stop her from explaining, his eyes dancing in a way that made me bristle on Char's behalf. He found her amusing, something he poorly masked at times. She was smart and deserved more respect from him. She'd learned more about our exhibits than anyone else that worked here, and all so she could be closer to her dad.

"Is it an amusement park?" Greg asked, "No, no." He held up a hand, head down like he was thinking. Then he lifted his stupid smirky face and gave Char a 100-watt smile. "Make a wicked warehouse bar!"

"No. It's going to be a park." She wasn't smiling any longer, and I felt conflicted. She didn't like Greg. That was good. But the guy was being a jerk to her. That was not good.

"You know," she prompted. "Playground, benches, dog area."

I found myself edging between Greg and Char, ready to shove Greg's face into the admission desk the second he tried to belittle her and the idea. It was a huge undertaking; unrealistic, really. But if anyone could pull it off, it was Sunshine Char.

"So you're paying money to do this?"

"A bit, but a lot of great agencies and companies are helping us out."

"It's called being a nice person, Greg," I said coolly. "And I think it's awesome she's trying to improve Everstone with a green space."

"It's weird, man. Nobody we know is doing stuff like that."

"Char is."

"But why? Are you nesting or something? Move somewhere else if you hate Everstone."

"Haven't you heard of nature deprivation?" she argued, heat spreading through her cheeks. Her hands had gone to her hips and there was fire in her eyes. "My neighbourhood deserves and needs a park. Kids are getting hurt."

"But..." He was squinting at her. "Why you? This sounds really hard."

"Why not me?"

"Let's go." I pulled on Char's elbow.

"Because it's a city problem, not yours. This is why we pay taxes. You could be spending the time and money bettering yourself."

Beside me, Char gasped. I'd been successfully herding her away from Greg, but now we both whirled on him.

"Uncool, man." I was already reaching for his collar, but

stopped myself before grabbing him, aware Richard was watching.

I wanted to quit this job on my own terms, not get turfed. I eyed Greg, considering her. Getting turfed could be worth it.

"Not like that." Greg rolled his eyes like he hadn't blanched at the way I'd lunged at him.

"Then how so?" I growled.

Greg gestured toward the various exhibit rooms, his face red, words spluttering from his dumb mouth. "Go to school and nerd out over all this ancient crap. She obviously loves it." He scowled at us both and stormed off.

As much as I hated to admit it, continuing her education in an area where she was passionate wasn't a bad idea. Too bad it was Greg who'd suggested it.

I watched him until he was out of sight, then noticed Richard had stood up during the exchange, looking none too pleased. He frowned at me and my lack of uniform, pointedly checking his watch.

"Not on for another ten," I said absently, steering Char through the museum and into one of the exhibit halls. Once we were well beyond the front desk area, I pulled her close, whispering, "Go get yourself a milkshake, then meet me outside the Staff Only door by the cafeteria entrance in ten."

Her hands were in fists, cheeks red. She was glaring at the direction we'd come. "Greg is such a—"

"I know." I planted a kiss on her scowl. She looked surprised, her anger gone as though I'd washed it away. She leaned in, eyes sparkling, as if I was the best part of her day. And that was the greatest feeling in the world.

CHAPTER 26

~ *Char* ~

I was still fuming over Greg's dismissive attitude and wondering if I could sic Estelle on him, or maybe one of her demon friends, if she had any. Possibly lure Igor the ogre away from veganism and toward Gregism?

How had I ever thought that man was cute and charming?

It didn't help that the museum's cafeteria milkshakes were substandard. It wasn't even in the running for bumping Peter's Drive-In off its pedestal. I hadn't even hesitated to set the cup aside so I could do a quick cruise-by of the latest pottery fragment additions in the gift shop before waiting outside the Staff Only door for James, as instructed.

"We're closing, Char," Glenda told me as she walked past the open space that led to the cafeteria and staff area. She was already sliding into her coat as the cafeteria's folding metal doors clanked shut behind me.

"Okay. Just a sec." I eyed the door James had asked me to wait outside of and bent, placing my milkshake on the floor while I retied my shoe. I took another pull on my drink as I stood, my cheeks sucking in with the effort of getting the ice cream and strawberry up the too-thin straw and into my blood-stream. She was still waiting for me to leave.

I winced. "Sorry. James asked me to wait a second. He's grabbing something for me."

With a heavy sigh, Glenda turned, shaking her head as she left.

"Hey, we're closing," a male voice announced behind me and I jumped. Then a hand grabbed my elbow, pulling me backward into the room marked Staff Only. James.

His arms wrapped around me in the warm, dimly lit hallway. His lips landed on my neck and I swivelled in his embrace to face him. He rewarded me with a lingering kiss that sent rockets off behind my eyelids.

"Come on." He took my hand, pulling me down the corridor, passing several unmarked doors. I'd never been in here, even while working on inventory.

"As good as Peter's?" he asked, glancing at my milkshake. He knew Peter's Drive-In milkshakes were my love language.

I made a face, and he chuckled, then gave a farcical grimace, releasing my hand so he could punch a fist into his palm. "Who needs to die for this subpar milkshake recipe?"

I laughed, angling the straw in his direction. He took a pull. "Yeah, not as good. And not just because it's strawberry." He stuck out his tongue in disgust.

He pulled me along again. "Come hang out with me."

"Don't you have to kick everyone out of the museum?" The glass doors had been opening and closing moments ago, the last few stragglers leaving—like I should be.

"Oscar went home sick, and I need an extra pair of eyes on the monitors."

Despite my words, my feet were already moving further into the pleasantly dim and cozy cave of the staff area.

"Richard will make a stink," I warned.

"I can handle Richard."

"You sure? He looked cranky."

"I'm planning on quitting soon, anyway."

"You are? Why? What are you going to do?"

"I thought this job would be more exciting."

"You mean pulling kids off fake mummies isn't exciting?"

He rubbed at the side of his face. "Not really. I've been learning Spanish when I'm here at night. I was going to go to Buenos Aires for a few months."

"Really? What changed your mind? All the muggings?" Tamara's mom had given us a run down when Tamara and I had been talking about a trip to South America a couple of years back. Then again, maybe the city was all cleaned up, or Mrs. Madden had misled us about the dangers. Either were possible.

Although, you'd have to be kinda dumb to try and mug James. His shoulders were powerful, and his flat stomach had the strength to back it up. Add in his beefy quads and you knew the guy would come out on top. Plus, he had this don't-mess-with-me vibe when someone overstepped.

Sexy, sexy, sexy.

"I decided to go to Corsica instead."

"Really? Why?"

"I found a great deal." He cleared his throat as though embarrassed. "I go next week."

Next week. The suddenness of his trip hit me. We were just getting started, and he was leaving?

"How long?" My voice sounded odd.

"Less than a week."

I nodded, grateful for the shortness of his trip.

At the same time, I also appreciated the breathing room it would give us. We'd been moving fast and it was scaring me a little. Around him I could lose my grip on reality and almost believe in everlasting love.

I looked at him anew. Who knew James had this sort of spontaneity in him? It was as sexy as his uniform.

I gasped, realizing what was on the beautiful French island of Corsica. "Are you going to the excavation site of the ancient Roman tile workshop?"

"The what?"

"It's nineteen-hundred years old."

"Oh. I'll have to check it out."

"Take lots of pictures for me."

"I'll see what I can do."

"Are you still quitting, then? Since you're not going away for months?"

"I got the week off, so I'll quit some other time."

"What job do you want—if not this one?"

"Not sure yet. But something fun. Still thinking about it."

He let us into the security room, and I shivered in delight. This was like being allowed down secret rooms at MI6. And the security office lived up to my expectations. There were a few rolling chairs and tons of monitors streaming images from around the museum. Most frames were empty, but the ones by the gift shop and front doors had activity.

"I'm not allowed in here." I set down my milkshake and perched in a chair, fascinated by all I could see. It was fabulous. I sucked it all up before someone told me I was breaking some sort of privacy law due to not having the proper clearance to spy on people.

James sat in the chair beside me, pointing to one of the screens in front of me. "You watch the gift shop while I watch a few other key areas to make sure people don't try to stay in here overnight."

I gasped in glee, hands coming together. "People do that?"

Where would they hide? There were so many locked doors. Would they climb over a rope and crouch behind a large display? The mummies were too narrow to hide behind. Maybe the wooly mammoth? There were so few good places to hide! How would they pull it off?

James was the best for letting me in here with him. This was already the funnest part of my week, second to James's kisses, of course.

He gave me a look. "You're plotting how you'd get away with it, aren't you?"

I felt my face heat, and I crossed my arms. "No." I relented. "Okay, maybe just a little."

"If you're nice, I'll tell you how I'd do it."

I grinned at him, loving the fact that he had it all figured out.

If he ever proposed that as a first date, I'd marry him on the spot—my lacking wifey persona be damned.

James flicked a few switches, his eyes tracking across images with a practiced efficiency.

The camera feed from the front lobby zoomed out, showing more of the room as James worked buttons. It had been zoomed in where I'd been standing just minutes ago, waiting for him. A patter of tiny bootied feet of happiness stormed through my stomach.

My voice lifted as I asked, "Were you spying on me?"

His cheeks pinked ever so slightly and his mouth made a firm line. "No. I was waiting for you."

"Hm."

"And so you know, I'm trained to watch for unusual behaviour."

"Unusual?"

"Yup. Unusual." He smirked, then moved my abandoned milkshake where it was dribbling condensation over the black plastic console. "Watch your screens. Especially that lady touching everything. Shoplifters do that."

"What lady?" I leaned forward, studying the screens in front of me before spotting her. "Oh." I leaned back, no longer concerned. "Those are just repros."

"In the gift shop? No. Those are all real."

"I don't know who's been telling you that, but they're reproductions."

"All of them?" He looked at me as though I'd been the one who'd purposefully scammed him.

"No, not quite. Just the best ones."

"Huh."

"Yeah, I hope a collector doesn't find out you're ripping people off. They'll be miffed."

James nodded, brow furrowed. I could tell it bothered him that pieces were being sold as the real deal when they weren't.

"But that one I showed you?" He turned from his monitors for a moment. "You said that wasn't a fake?"

"It was a genuine artifact. It's gone now though. I didn't see it in the case."

He nodded, seemingly relieved.

"You know, there's a lot of Grecian pottery floating around online right now. I've bought a few pieces, and they're much cheaper than in the gift shop. They've been real, too. Some of the descriptions said they were reproductions, but they weren't. Someone out there is doing a bad job of assessing pieces. Which is weird since it's not that difficult to figure out what's real and what isn't."

"It's not?"

"I won't bore you with the details of it, but yeah. Once you know what to look for and spend some time looking at pieces..." I shrugged, being careful not to bore him.

"Know what's more fun than talking about pottery?" he

asked, flicking through the screens, one by one. They were all empty now. Even Richard was leaving.

"Letting me touch the stuff in the display cases?"

"Even better." James scooted his chair in my direction. Then, with a tug, he hauled my chair to his. He leaned over and kissed me, sending my heart rate into overdrive and had me forgetting all about pottery.

CHAPTER 27
~ *Char* ~

The warehouse was coming down. The scrap workers had started removing the metal siding yesterday, but I'd begged so many favours, applied for so many grants, and asked so many local business to sponsor the park's creation that I worried I was building more good karma for others than for my account due to their amazing generosity.

What if this didn't work? What if I made a park, and the city declined the gift—even though they'd verbally told me they'd be excited to accept it—and I ended up with more debt?

It didn't help that the scrap workers didn't seem to have made much progress today. They knew the building's frame was scheduled to be demolished next week, thanks to a favour from a backhoe company I once temped for. The owner was a great guy and, thankfully, still remembered how I'd filled in for his wife during part of her maternity leave as well as suggested he start his own backhoe school to train future employees. And he had done just that, and was now on the lookout for projects to use as training grounds for his students. Enter my warehouse, and we had a deal. I only had to pay for the gas to haul away the debris and the dumping fees.

There went my Greece trip savings. Oh, wait. No, I'd used them already to pay the property taxes for the next few months in the lawyer's office during the land transfer. I guess it was a good thing I hadn't told my dad about my hopeful travel plans, seeing as they were now on infinite delay.

At home I sprawled on the couch, wondering who might be interested in sponsoring my latest upcoming park costs involving the dumping of the warehouse frame. I propped a cushion under my head and let Felipe stand on my chest. I fed him Spitz, and he shelled the sunflower seeds with a hypnotic efficiency and speed. We were making a mess, but I was too tired to care. The last two weeks since getting the land grant had been a whirlwind of working all possible shifts for Joan to earn extra cash, signing endless paperwork around the park project's land acquisition and sponsorships, studying Josie's timelines and spreadsheets, and making pitches to sponsors. And of course, missing James this past week as he backpacked across Corsica.

The lucky duck. I admired that he was out there, exploring the world, but I was a tad jealous, too. I wanted that to be me. I wanted a job that paid better and allowed me time to travel. Because for the first time, temping had lost its glow, and I realized just how exhausting it was to be constantly learning new faces, new jobs and workplace nuances. But what else was I going to do? I hadn't gone to college and my self-learned skills around pottery weren't worth much to anyone unless it was ancient Grecian times trivia night and they wanted their team to win.

I was so wiped, I couldn't even summon the energy to add my latest Grecian pottery purchase that I'd ordered before the whole Estelle debt thing to my display case. It was still sitting on top of its packaging on the coffee table.

It wasn't a fake. Thank goodness. Seeing the number of reproductions in the museum's gift shop had made me paranoid that my next online purchase would fall under a scam since I couldn't verify the validity of the piece's age until I had it in my hands, my money already in the sender's. Swapping out originals, or selling fakes as though they were the real deal would be a brilliant scam since most people couldn't tell the difference between a good fake and a genuine artifact.

Picking up my phone, while feeding Felipe another seed, I deleted the shopping app so I wouldn't be tempted to order any new pottery. Right now, every extra dollar I could get my hands on was going toward the park, and the numerous, unanticipated extra costs that kept popping up around permits and paperwork fees. Soon, there'd also be landscaping and playground equipment costs, fencing for the two lots as well as basketball court costs. Those weren't small. Yes, we'd gathered a few minor grants and sponsorships for those things, but Josie's spreadsheets still had a thick red line at the bottom of the total column.

We were making progress, but we needed more money. Quite a bit more.

"What if asking for all this help negates what I'm creating with the park?" I asked Tamara when she joined me in the living room with a horse magazine.

Josie, overhearing us from the kitchen, came in and said, "A new car isn't worth anything to the person who ordered and paid for it until it rolls out of the factory. Same with this park. Right now we're in the cost phase."

"We need to sit back and let things flow," Tamara told me gently. "Have faith."

"It's hard. What if I've screwed up somewhere and don't realize it?"

Gabby came up the stairs, home from work. She took one look at me, left the room and returned with a handheld battery-powered vacuum. Felipe spotted it and bolted.

"Gabby!"

She took the vacuum to me and the couch. I stood up, pushing her away. She moved around me, continuing her clean up.

"I was going to take care of that, you know."

"Why do you look so stressed?" Gabby asked, sucking up one last shell fragment from my shirt. She and Samantha still believed I was making the park out of the goodness of my heart. That meant they didn't understand the pressure I felt to succeed by August 15th. To them, that date was arbitrary and somewhat self-punishing.

"Fairy godmother debt?" I mumbled, giving her a cheesy smile, like I was laughing off my ridiculous claim from weeks ago that I had a fairy godmother. One of these days, she had to start believing, right? And how would I know when that was if I didn't keep floating the idea past her?

"You are a ridiculous woman," she said with a sigh. "Take a night off. You haven't been to the museum to decompress in at least a week or two, and it shows."

"Hey!"

"Isn't it open until nine tonight?"

I sighed, acting put out even though she was right. Gazing at ancient pottery was a great way to decompress, and it always made life feel worth living again. Plus, I'd read an online article on my lunch break about glazes and I wanted to look at my favourite pieces in this new light of knowledge.

"Fine. I'll go," I grumbled without conviction. "Even though James won't be there."

I grabbed my membership card and jumped on the next bus heading toward the downtown. It was the middle of the night in France, and I was sure James would be sleeping. Having a seven-hour time difference sure didn't help us stay in touch while he was away. Ditto with him not having an international texting or calling plan. He had to wait until he was somewhere with free Wi-Fi in order to message me.

Saying hi to Glenda at the admission desk, I caught some of the highlights of her recent bout with gout. It was flaring up again, and since I already felt I knew more about her health issues than a non-family member should, I scooted away as soon as was polite.

Once freed, I zipped straight to the pottery area, my shoulders loosening as I studied the first vase depicting a hunter drawing back an arrow, done in a burnt dark brown. Movement out of the corner of my eye caught my attention. Richard. The museum director. I flashed him a quick smile and tried to study the next piece through the glass despite the annoying reflections from the lighting placed high above it. I couldn't see the cracking I'd read about. I confirmed the piece's origin date on the card beside it.

Maybe my dad would have an insightful perspective on it. I'd sent him the article earlier. I shot him a quick text.

DAD

Sorry. That was a dry one. Didn't finish it.

What? He'd had at least six hours to read it. Where was his passion?

I snapped a photo of the artifact and fired it off, but there were too many reflections in the image, thanks to the glass.

DAD

Sorry, I'm no use.

ME

np

DAD

What?

"Hey, Richard," I called. "Why can't we ever see these without glass? Do you have a key? I'd like to see the uniform cracking. Plus, I heard it varies on the inside of the piece, but I can't see that when it's locked up. And also? I'm pretty sure this is a reproduction."

"It is not."

"I think it might be." He came closer, and I stepped back, giving him room. "You've swapped a bunch out lately. Are you selling them off or something?"

"We most certainly are not!" With an indignant huff, he bent over the glass case.

"Look! The cracks aren't right, and the colouring is off. That could be this crappy lighting, though. But I bet if you weighed this vessel, it would be too light for its size." The more I studied it, the more wrong it felt.

Richard wordlessly looked at the piece, then grabbed his keys and opened the case.

I gasped, hands outstretched to accept it. Even though it was a repro.

He hugged the handled vase-like vessel to his chest. "Come along."

"Where?" I almost skipped alongside him, I was so delighted by the idea that I was about to go somewhere off limits and test one of the exhibit pieces for authenticity.

"To settle your mind and prove this is an original."

Yes! "Except, it's a fake."

Now that it was out of the case, I could definitely see the colouring was off. I wished James was here so I could share the triumph with him. But he wouldn't be back until later tonight, and anyway, I didn't make wishes any longer.

~

IT WAS A FAKE.

I'd never seen a grown man grow pale so quickly.

Richard had let me into the back rooms of the museum, and I trailed slowly, sucking in the old-world vibes that surrounded us as we passed crated artifacts on our way to his office and the stored artifact records.

Richard must have weighed that vase about eight times before bolting back to the pottery exhibit, demanding I point out all of the fakes. We'd spent a blissful hour carting pieces to his office and weighing them, and then comparing them to his meticulous records. I couldn't have been happier.

Richard, however, was losing his mind. I think he'd pulled out about half his hair before he finally dismissed me, looking like a shell of a man.

I'd asked him what he planned to do, but by that point he was beyond speech, and I'd quietly let myself out, eager for James's plane to land so I could fill him in on the drama.

~

THE NEXT MORNING, having a blessedly later start to my A.M. shift, I waited for James outside the museum. I was excited to see him before we both started work. We'd talked on the phone last night, but with his jet lag and us both working this morning, it had been short.

"Hey," I said to Greg, one of the museum's guides, as he poked his head out the front doors. I still hadn't quite forgiven him for his lack of support over making a park in Everstone.

"We're not opening today."

The change in the museum's hours tweaked my interest. Had Richard found more issues with the artifacts? "Why not?"

Greg slipped outside to join me. "Some pottery got stolen."

I stared at him, trying to figure out if this was related to Richard's discovery of the fake pieces last night. Richard had planned to do a sweep of the back rooms after I left. Greg's choice of words made it sound as though Richard hadn't found the originals.

I mentally smacked myself. In all of the excitement last night, I'd forgotten to tell Richard about the fakes I'd spotted in the gift shop. This whole thing was starting to feel pretty big and pretty real. What else was being secretly stolen from the museum?

"I can't believe it."

Greg looked left and right, then leaned in. "They were big pieces from the exhibit rooms. But Richard says they were found."

"That's a relief."

"It took the police over a day to trace the pieces back to us. It hasn't even hit the news yet."

"Wait. What?" My mind struggled with the timeline discrepancies between the reported theft and the found items.

Had I accidentally made a wish, and Estelle had gone back in time to change things so it all happened for me? But why would I have wished for this?

Quite plainly, I hadn't. I was sure of it. This was my happy place, and I wouldn't wish it any harm.

"Are you saying the theft wasn't reported by the museum?" I asked Greg. "And that the police discovered the stolen items on their own?"

Greg nodded.

That made no sense. I'd been sure Richard planned to report the fakes last night if he couldn't find the originals. Was this all some big inside job and Richard was connected to it, so he had merely gone through the motions last night to take any suspicion off himself?

No, he wasn't that great of an actor. Unless his panic had been over me spotting the artifact discrepancies, and not over the missing originals.

Either way, this was starting to sound like a real heist-type situation. I took in the museum's sand and limestone exterior anew, almost expecting to see yellow police tape or other physical signs that a robbery had taken place. I wanted to go inside and look for lasers. Ropes dangling from ceiling vents. Something. Anything.

But everything seemed perfectly normal, just like it had last night. There wasn't even a police car in sight.

A POLICE CAR came while I was talking to James.

Shortly after Greg had ducked back inside, I'd spotted James making his way to the front steps, forsaking the staff entrance to meet up with me. I'd peppered the poor man with kisses, which were quite happily returned.

"How was your trip?" I asked, barely releasing him so he could reply with a quick 'good' before kissing me again. "You look so tired."

"Jet lag is real." He gave me another squeeze, his arms feeling so good around me. "I missed you."

"I missed you too," I said shyly.

James had sent a few images and texts from the hostel's Wi-Fi, but for the most part, due to the time difference and our mutual busyness, we hadn't had much of a chance to stay caught up with each other. I was itching to see all of his photos and hear every detail of his whirlwind trip.

"Next time I leave you, I'm springing for the international phone plan, no matter how expensive." He buried his nose in my hair and I felt a surge of happiness.

When we finally broke apart, he started showing me photos of the archaeological dig tour he'd taken for me, even though we both knew we didn't have enough time before work.

It was around then that the police showed up. And within minutes, we were both being asked to come down to the local detachment for questioning. We were put in separate rooms, and I wondered if they thought we were suspects. Or maybe they got better info if people were raked over the coals on their own. In my case, there would definitely be significantly fewer distractions if James wasn't in the room.

As Officer Beddoe asked me more and more ridiculous questions about my interest in pottery, I got the sensation that a snare was slowly closing around me. His questions made me sound so guilty. What if I ended up in jail? What would happen when I failed to pay off my fairy godmother debt?

Maybe this was a smart time to make a wish.

Although, if I was in jail, that would be a great place to create good karma, seeing as it was likely a karmic black hole.

I closed my eyes and focused on what I wanted. Out of here. Innocence quickly proven for both James and me.

The officer began asking me about being in the security room with James last week. I could almost see him thinking that because I loved pottery, we'd planned the whole heist. Watching the museums cameras just before the theft was clearly a stake out by two idiots who deserved to be in jail.

Then he shifted gears.

"Richard says you identified the fakes?"

I nodded.

"Why?"

"What do you mean?"

"Why would you bring it to his attention?"

"He's the director."

"You recently purchased a warehouse in Everstone."

I nodded, unable to follow his jumping around topic-wise, and what it meant for me.

"You and James were inside."

"The warehouse? Yes. And Samantha came with us, too, but she didn't go in. We needed to see what was in there before demolition."

Officer Beddoe cleared his throat and checked his notebook. "James was recently in Corsica, at an excavation site. He has an interest in artifacts?"

"Not really. That was for me." I was still a bit taken by how, in the middle of his short trip, he'd gone out of his way to check out the site for me.

"Does he have dealer contacts in the world of artifacts or pottery?"

"No. Not that I know of."

"So, this trip? Has he expressed interest in dealing in the past?"

"No. Not to me. I don't think he stole this stuff. He didn't even know the pieces in the gift shop are fake."

"I'm sorry?"

"I forgot to tell Richard last night, but yeah. There are reproductions in the gift shop being sold as original pieces."

"How long ago did you spot the first reproduction in the museum's collection?"

"The mummies? I didn't. James told me they were fake. I should have known, though." I thought back to my Meet Cute with James when the kid had been on the wrong side of the rope and trying to climb a mummy. The memory brought up a swell of warmth that travelled all the way down to my toes. And look where the two of us were now. All happy and kissing.

And being questioned by the police.

"The mummies are reproductions?"

"Yes, James made them." Realizing how bad that sounded, I added hastily, "In high school. As part of a student work thing at the museum. Those aren't real ones on display."

"Okay, how about more recently? Have other items in the museum's collection been swapped out for reproductions? Or is it limited to the pottery items?"

"Only the pottery, as far as I know. But I'm not an expert."

"I'd like you to think hard. What day did you first notice the swapped-out items?"

"Maybe two or three weeks ago. Around May long weekend?"

He made a note in his pad. "Tell me about the scrap metal workers working on your warehouse."

"They're taking the siding off to recycle it."

"Are you paying them?"

"No. They get to keep the siding. The reclaimers pay them something for it."

"Do you know the workers?" He listed some names, and I shook my head. He studied me for a long moment. "They discovered something of value in your warehouse while stripping the siding off the one side."

"They did?" I perked up. Gold? Finally, some gold! What if it was a treasure map? Or something hidden in a rafter that had been lost for years and was culturally significant?

"The crates."

Crates? I shook my head. In the small office where James had broken down the door, there had only been one crate along with the cardboard box. Both empty. I hadn't spotted crates anywhere else and, thinking over the floorpan, there was nowhere to hide them.

"There was only one crate when we went inside. There was nothing in it."

Officer Beddoe looked grave. "The scrap workers discovered three wooden crates in your warehouse."

"Three?"

"And they were filled with the missing artifacts."

CHAPTER 28

~ *James* ~

Char and I had been released from questioning at the same time, and instead of going in to work, we'd both taken the rest of the day off to decompress. And maybe figure out who'd put the stolen pieces in the warehouse, and why.

My mom, whom I'd texted to ask for the name of our family lawyer, just in case, had insisted we stop by the house. She wasn't working today and promised us lunch.

"What if they don't clear our names?" Char asked me as we made our way to the front door. I could tell her thoughts, like mine, were slipping down Worst-Case Avenue as though it was a shortcut to somewhere good. Which it wasn't.

We were persons of interest who'd been asked to stick around the city for the next few days, as they "might have more questions."

Both Char and I had watched enough TV to know they hadn't struck our names from their suspect list. We had the means and opportunity, and Char's passion for all things ancient and made of clay gave her motive.

"We'll never get a good job again," I said in a drawl, like I was quoting an old movie.

"We'll be flipping burgers. No, just washing the floor. They wouldn't allow us to flip burgers." There was no humour in her tone despite her joking.

"Frying donuts."

"Picking trash."

"There you are." My mom opened the front door before we got to it. "Oh, you look beat. Come in, come in."

She'd already set out milk and homemade cookies for us, and Char's eyes welled at the homey warmth I took for granted. She looked like a kid who'd come home from school, but landed in the wrong house. Half ready to bolt, and half-hesitantly venturing in to test the foreign waters.

Mom fussed over us, but something was off. She seemed exasperated or annoyed. I turned to her. "What?"

"You look like you're headed to the gallows. Don't take it all so *seriously*. These things happen. If I got all wound up every time I ended up in the police station...or waiting on them to get their evidence together and realize I'm not a criminal..." She clicked her tongue and gave her head a firm shake.

"Mom." I rolled my eyes, well aware she was exaggerating. She was a sweetheart who was willing to stand up for what she believed in, fearlessly wading in where there was trouble or an abuse of minorities. As a result, she had experience with the police, and had been detained a time or two. That was all. Or at least, that was how the stories went. Maybe I was about to learn some new deep, dark secrets.

For Char's sake, I hoped not. She was still looking a bit freaked out about the whole police questioning ordeal, and my mom's suggestion that she was enjoying milk and cookies in a known criminal's home while being on the police's radar clearly wasn't helping.

"Oh, you know." Mom waved a hand, her smile wicked, the beaded bracelets on her wrist sliding downward. "The usual."

"Explain the usual, Mom."

"Protests. Sit-ins... Trust me. If it doesn't stick, it won't follow you forever. Well, probably." She gave us a cheery smile. "Another cookie?"

I sighed and shook my head. Fresh-baked cookies didn't solve everything. Although Char seemed to be coming out of her stupor with each new bite, so maybe they did.

I couldn't help loving that she dove into my mom's cookies, unlike Sophia, who'd always appeared to be mentally tallying her day's sugar and fat intake.

"I'm sorry, James," Char said finally, looking up from her cookie. "I didn't mean to get you involved in this mess."

"They interviewed everyone at the museum."

"But they found *your* prints in my warehouse where all the stuff was found."

"Because I was helping you with the park project."

That seemed to make her feel worse. "Some thanks you get for helping, huh? They interviewed us like we're viable suspects." Her hands went to her face. "Do we have a criminal record? Like a temporary one while they look into trying to convict us? Am I no longer bondable right now? I have to call Joan. I'm advertised to clients as bondable. I can't be if they seized my warehouse." She was pale, her hands starting to shake as she typed out a text message to her boss. She muttered to herself, "I can't believe I wasted all that money wishing on teddy bears and crushes."

Teddy bears and crushes?

"Wait. They seized the warehouse?"

She nodded, eyebrows pinched with worry. "I can't do anything with the lots until they're done combing it for evidence. He said it could take a while. It's going to slow everything down with making the park. I can't afford to mess up the schedule Josie made. The whole plan will collapse." She moaned into her hands. "Nobody's going to want to sponsor us after they hear about this."

She acted like a woman with numbered days whenever she talked about the park and its tight timeline, and I couldn't quite figure out why. Why didn't she just give herself more time? And as for the sponsors, she might lose a few, but the ones that were truly on board would see exactly why those two lots needed a revamp into something safer for the Everstone community.

"You'll be fine," my mom said in a firm voice. "The police aren't dumb, and they know it was someone else. They'll get to the bottom of things. It'll all be cleared up in no time."

Char nodded. "I'm a good person, right?" She looked up at me with innocent eyes. "And you are, too." Her jaw dropped, a hand flying over it. "Oh no! Your job?"

I winced. I hadn't been planning to tell her this part. At least not until later. "They asked me to stay home for a few days."

Char moaned again. "Who framed us? I keep trying to figure it out, but my brain is like an open expanse of Saskatchewan prairie—there's absolutely nothing."

"I doubt someone's trying to frame you," my mom said gently. "It's likely all just coincidental. Calgary isn't that big."

"But it's in *my* warehouse! Everyone knows I love old pottery. And the timeline of it all is so...*coincidental*." Char shivered.

"But you also alerted Richard to the fakes," I pointed out, earning a hopeful nod of agreement from Char. "If you were trying to get away with theft, you wouldn't have done that."

"You're putting so much good out into the world," my mom said, giving Char's hand a squeeze. "Focus on the positive, not the other stuff."

Char paled. "Is this karma?"

"No, no. Not karma." My mom pushed her chair back, clearly done with the panic and ready to move on. "Are you hungry? I promised the two of you some lunch." She began pulling items from the cupboards. "What would you like? Any allergies, Char?"

"I should go home." Char stood.

"You can't go home hungry," my mom insisted. "You need a meal."

Char hesitated. I could see her smalltown roots taking hold, understanding that an offer was genuine.

And as usual, my mom was right. Char needed this.

As she sat again, my mom went into full bustle mode, chatting about what she was going to make.

"You okay?" I asked Char quietly when my mom disappeared to get something from the garage freezer.

She nodded, letting out a long exhale. She put an elbow on the table and dropped a cheek against her raised hand, chewing mindlessly on another cookie.

"You don't deserve to be tied up in this," she said. "You were just helping me with the park." She muttered something about wishes under her breath again, eyes screwed tight, face pinched with what appeared to be concentration.

"I'm not tied up in it." I tapped her hand to get her attention. She slowly focused on me. "They interviewed everyone, especially if they were in a position to offer tips to the thief or colluding." I reached out, laying my hand over hers. "But really, it's you who doesn't deserve to be tied up in this. Not at all. You're just a victim in this whole mess. Your warehouse was surely just an opportune place to hide the goods for a bit."

Her smile was thankful and wobbly.

I tried for a joke, desperate to see a real smile so I'd know she was truly okay. "Maybe if they decide to put us under house arrest, we can ask to be together. Netflix all day!" I raised a hand for a high five.

She wasn't enthusiastic, but she didn't leave me hanging, her hand lifting to mine. The worry etching her face softened as our hands gently slapped each other's. Progress.

"And maybe we can have my mom bring us cookies," I added.

"What's that?" my mom called, reentering the room with a bag of frozen veggies.

"Nothing."

"You have this all planned out?" Char asked me, her eyes twinkling, and I knew she was going to be okay.

"With you, I think it could be a lot of fun."

CHAPTER 29

~ *Estelle* ~

"Report." The head fairy was in pink again today, from her ballet flats to her hairband. Just like every day. "Char is back to making wishes—"

"Are you granting them?" Gram-Gram asked, eyes narrowed.

"No. Her amount owing is still above the threshold. But something has come up that I fear will interfere with her ability to repay her debts. I was wondering if I could request an exemption on her account, and grant her a wish or two in order to increase the likelihood of reclaiming some of the amount owed to us."

"Sounds like a grey area." Gram-Gram opened Char's file. It appeared as though she was getting regular updates from Igor now, and I made a mental note to beware of how close I danced to the lines with my actions surrounding Char's case. "What are the wishes you want to grant?"

I started with the more innocent of the two. "She would like to fix James's life."

"The man you sent into her arms?" The fairy was watching

me, her delicately pointed chin still tipped down toward the file, her lavender eyes raised my way.

"Yes."

Her slow blink of I-told-you-so shamed me, and my next words were embarrassing. "She'd like to remove him from her timeline in hopes of saving him."

"Remove him?"

"Create distance." Char had really done a good job of her wish. She'd calmed her mind and pictured James as the innocent man we all knew him to be, then made her plea. "She wished him away from her and requested he be protected."

I wasn't sure why she'd done it though, as it was clear he was innocent, and was going to be fine.

"Did she ever wish for him to love her?"

"There have been several romantic-themed wishes over the past few months, but none specifically for him to love her."

"Interesting." Gram-Gram's lips formed a slow smile. "She's wishing him to her, but also away. Is she afraid to love him?"

I shrugged, unsure. Humans were complex.

"Well, all of her wishes will wear off," Gram-Gram said, "if they haven't already. Looking at these dates, he's likely back under his own agency, and choosing to be close to her. In other words, there is little to reverse." She was reading the lines of her printout, eyes flicking like she was speed reading. "Besides, reversing these would be too much work and the cost is high. Too many tendrils of effects reaching out everywhere to clean up. Let these things continue to resolve on their own." She was still skimming the long list of recent wishes.

"She is a very good wisher, isn't she?" Gram-Gram tapped a line and looked up at me. "Is this the other one you want to grant? She wants to be innocent and get the park back on track?"

I nodded. "Yes, ma'am."

"The park is her karma project to repay her debts, is it not?"

I nodded again, cringing.

"Debt repayment related." She shut the file. "Automatic no."

CHAPTER 30

~ *Char* ~

The mess with the police, the museum's stolen artifacts, and the stalled-out park were giving me a headache. And with my work hours abruptly cut back, thanks to Joan's caution surrounding my property being part of an ongoing investigation, I had few distractions.

Along with the headaches was my guilt for pulling James into it all. Everyone else had been allowed to return to work after the police questioned them, except James.

Why? Because he'd been in the warehouse with me. He'd let me into the security room. He'd shown me pricey items in the gift shop, and I'd confirmed their value. And also because I'd mentioned the swapped-out items on display, and he hadn't gone straight to Richard about it.

How was he supposed to know there were thefts happening? Yes, he was security, but he wasn't the only one watching the place. And he wasn't privy to the comings and goings of objects that were on display.

The guilty ache in my heart was more than I could handle, and so while sitting in Sally's kitchen a few days ago, with James' words about helping me with the park echoing in my head, and Tamara's earlier warning about the ripple effects of my wishes, I'd made another one. I'd wished for James to be distanced from me. For him to be declared innocent, and for whatever was going on in my own life, to not interfere with his. In other words, I wished him completely free of me. I wished to undo any wishes that I'd ever made that had him bound to me.

I knew how badly my wishes could backfire on the people I cared about, and I'd made so many wishes over the past few months. So many. From wishing him to see me as a woman he might want to date, to wishing for him and others to help me with the park.

And so now, thanks to Estelle's handiwork, he was caught in the crossfire and going down in flames. He deserved so much better than my selfishness. He deserved to be with someone who didn't make wishes that caused him harm.

I'd given Estelle several days to set my latest wish in place, and now I was ready to put it to the test.

CHAPTER 31

~ *James* ~

"Can't. I have a night class," I said regretfully into the phone. "You're feeling better?"

Char had invited me to an evening concert in Prince's Island Park. Which was nice, seeing as she'd been busy and distant since our questioning by the police. She'd even bailed out of going to our first baseball practice, claiming she had a sore throat.

"Night class?" she asked, her voice lifting, ignoring my question.

Was it my imagination, or did she sound a bit happy that I couldn't go? It felt like her asking me out was a test, and I'd just passed it. Which was wrong. So very wrong.

"Since when?" she asked. "For what?" Her interest was piqued. I was right about her. Curious. Always up for something new.

Too bad she didn't seem to want to jump into something new with yours truly. She kept dipping a toe, but it was like the water was too cold for her. It was starting to get really frustrating. I wanted to drag her off somewhere private where we could be alone, and love her until she saw that what we might have wasn't a reason to be afraid.

"I'm taking some geography and mapping courses online. Signed up and started this week."

"Oh."

"Seemed like a good time."

"I'm sorry." Her voice was soft with apology.

"I was planning to quit anyway."

"But you just spent all that money on the Corsica trip."

"It's fine." And it actually was. I had some savings. I wasn't going to miss the security work, especially now that I didn't need the museum as my wingman, making it possible to bump into Char.

I could call her.

Text her.

Probably even pop by. Especially if I had a strawberry milkshake from Peter's.

Although maybe I wasn't welcome. She was giving off weird signals. Did she blame me for the warehouse seizure? Or was she just generally down and out at the moment, the wind knocked out of her sails, and one of those types that curled inward when stuff hit the fan?

"Are you looking to become a cartographer?" she asked.

"It might be fun."

She let out a surprised burst of laughter, and it felt good to knock her perception of me.

"Yeah?" she asked.

"What?"

"You take classes for fun, don't you?"

"What's wrong with that?"

"Nothing."

"Yeah, yeah. I know."

"What?"

"I can hear you thinking." The same as everyone else. "I need a career. I should know what to do with my life by now and finish the things I start. Make up my mind already. I'm wasting time, money and talent. And for what? Don't I know who am I? Do I have ADHD or what?"

Personally, I preferred my parents' take. They'd said I had a wild streak of curiosity and had a hunger for knowledge.

My grade six teacher had explained it as having ants in my pants.

I stopped talking, realizing I'd basically confessed some of my worst fears about myself to Char.

"People think I'm a flake because I like temping," Char said quietly. "Because I like being somewhere new every few weeks."

We were silent for a long moment, as though deciding what to do with each other.

The lightness of our usual conversations wasn't with us tonight, but I didn't mind. I felt as though I was letting Char in and vice versa, like the barrier of talking without seeing each other freed us somehow.

"My parents..." Char said hesitantly, and I tightened my grip on my phone so I didn't accidentally drop it and miss whatever she was about to say. "They never really...I don't know. Lived. Especially my dad."

I stood, unable to sit. I paced the room.

"My mom was pretty checked out when I was a preteen. She'd only cook if Dad was home. The rest of the time she just sat in front of the TV until she met Damon."

"Who's that?"

"Stepdad."

"They weren't happy together? Your mom and dad?" I imagined fighting, yelling matches, tearing up a young, sensitive Char.

"I guess not. Mom left. And it was so weird. She was suddenly all alive and happy and being a mom."

"That's good then?"

"To Brynnie, my stepsister." Her voice was low and I couldn't quite pinpoint the emotion she was trying to hide. Hurt? Resentment? Anger? Rejection? So many emotions to choose from.

"How old was she—is she?"

"My age."

Ouch.

"You didn't live with them?"

"No. You know what's dumb? When my mom was in that funk before she left, sometimes I'd tell her about my school adventures. Gym class shenanigans or fights or field trip stuff and she'd half perk up."

I waited quietly for her to say more. I could almost hear the unasked question in Char's words. Was she still doing that? Looking for adventures and excitement to show others so they would take an interest in her? If so, was she stuck on a never-ending treadmill, hoping to find self-worth?

She was quiet for a moment, and when she resumed, she was upbeat. "I don't really like sitting around a ton. I need to move and do something. But at the same time, I love cozying up in the living room with my friends. Why is that? Samantha said temping isn't me, and since then it hasn't felt as much fun. I don't know if I let her words become a self-fulfilling prophecy, or if she just gave me permission to see how exhausting it actually can be." She released a self-depreciating laugh. "Maybe it's me who doesn't know who they are."

"Do any of us truly know? We're always changing. Even our cells. They get replaced at such a rate that we're physically someone new within a few months. It's hard to keep up with that."

"I like that image," she said softly.

"And I like talking to you on the phone. And in person, too." I worried my intention wasn't coming across right. "I'm glad we're talking. I don't talk on the phone much."

"Same. It's nice."

"So you're an adventure addict?" I teased, getting the feeling that she was done her mini confessional.

"Apparently," she said dryly.

"If money were no object, and you'd already been to Greece, where would you go?" I knew her more lucrative jobs had been dialled back by her boss, thanks to the museum theft business, and what money she did have would be flowing into the park once the warehouse was released.

"I don't know."

"You don't want to visit more museums?" I asked. "Fly to a remote island in the Pacific? Soak up the ambiance of a famous old hotel that costs thousands of dollars a night? You don't want to find a private waterfall in the mountains? Skydive? Learn to sail on Glenmore?"

She laughed, the sound light. "Okay, okay. There's so much to do!"

I was smiling. Grinning like a fool, actually. "You going to do it? Go on a mini adventure?"

"Every day is an adventure, James," she intoned seriously.

"Wanna go on an adventure with me?"

"Always," she said quickly, without hesitation. And for a moment, I thought maybe her heart, along with mine, was wishing, wishing—wishing that we could be each other's wingman, friend, lover, everything. We just needed to have the courage to keep trying.

CHAPTER 32

~ *Char* ~

Clearly the wish to undo my earlier wishes hadn't worked. James was still interested in me, and hadn't wandered back into his own timeline or destiny or whatever it was.

Surely, it was simply a matter of time before he did, though. Estelle probably just needed a few more days to make the magic work because she was new at all of this.

I trusted the wish. And I trusted James to drift away from me.

In the meantime, was there any good reason not to hang out with him? To enjoy the sweet, tender shoots of a relationship before James forgot his interest in me, and we veered back into our separate lives again? I might only have one more day before the wish took effect. Why not make the most of it, and allow myself the distraction from reality by sinking into the adventure of such a healthy relationship?

Anyway, it hadn't truly been much of a conscious choice. After our phone call a few nights ago, the two of us had drifted back into spending time together. We'd spent the past day and a half in his parents' kitchen, eating Sally's cookies. We'd fleshed out some contingency plans based on when the warehouse might be released by the police, and currently, we were putting the final touches on a website. James had even tested out the project's online donation system by sending a hundred bucks of his own toward the park.

Was there anything more lovable than a man who was willing to jump into your projects and support you one-hundred per cent, even though the whole thing felt precipitously close to collapsing?

The scrap workers didn't know when their next opening would be to resume the work, and it was the same with my backhoe friend—once we were allowed back onto the lots, of course. The police had no new leads or clues and were tired of me calling them every day for an update on when they'd release my property.

It had been over a week.

I was antsy and stressed about it, but sitting in the Backstrohm's kitchen, with Sally's unconditional adoption of me and my cookie addiction, even though I didn't quite know how to smoothly insert myself into the Backstrohm family dynamics, I decided this was one of my top three happy places. And, yes, I was counting the museum and Peter's in that tally.

I was enjoying it while I could and creating some sweet memories to look back on when James was gone and I was feeling down.

At eight o'clock, Sally left the kitchen, her newly adopted dog in tow for their evening walk. I was learning you could set a watch by Sally's routine. Although this time she was muttering something about having never tried skeet shooting.

I turned to James after Sally shut the front door. "Should we try skeet shooting?"

We shared a look, then shook our heads. Yeah, hitting a flying object seemed unnecessarily difficult.

"I don't get it. How are your parents still so happily married? They're so..." I tried to find the words to explain the mystery of his parents' relationship. They were routine junkies. And yet still in love. Happy. Vibrant even.

With my parents, routine had become their death. Or was their routine an indicator of a death that had occurred long before I'd been old enough to notice?

"Never mind," I muttered. "No...it's just... how are they still together? Don't they get bored with the same old routine? Where's the adventure to light up their lives? You can't wait around for life and your partner. You have to live. And they're just so..."

Ordinary.

Content.

Exceedingly happy.

Peacefully in love.

James was frowning at me like he didn't understand, and I wished I'd kept my mouth shut. He wasn't going to take this painful silence and transform it into mutual understanding. He was living in a different reality than I was. And not only because he didn't seem to have a fairy godmother.

"It's just..." I felt compelled to try and explain. "If you sit around waiting for your partner so you can go have fun, you get bored and move on. People wanted adventure and passion!"

The more I thought about it, the more worried I was for Sally and her marriage.

"They've been married for thirty-four years."

"Thirty-four years," I whispered in awe. Of course, they'd been married a long time, but I'd never stopped to figure out how many years that might be. "But...they're so happy." It didn't compute. How did they not get bored with their life and relationship if it was the same all the time?

Maybe they were bored, even though they didn't seem to be.

"How do they stay interested?" I should be embarrassed by my questions, but I was too curious. Too in need of knowing.

"They got married straight out of high school and—"

"High school!"

"—have been inseparable ever since. They don't even really fight."

"That's unbelievable, James."

Blissfully married for *that* many years. How? Didn't James see what an anomaly his parents were? Nobody could assume they'd land in a relationship like that.

And yet, he did. And I was starting to believe in its possibility.

AN HOUR LATER, our contingency plans for the park abandoned, James and I snuggled up on the couch in front of a British game show I'd never seen before. My week and the stress of the unknown had caught up with me and I was slumped against him, using him as a big, buff pillow, my mind happily glazed over as contestants jumped for joy only to groan minutes later when they lost whatever gains they'd made.

It felt like the story of my life right now, but in game show format.

I yawned, noting that out the window there was a faint rainbow, the earlier evening rain storm having eased off. I sat up when the episode was done, and James shook out a leg.

"Did your leg fall asleep?"

He winced. "Yeah."

"Why didn't you tell me to move?" I asked, feeling horrible that he'd literally allowed me to inhibit the circulation in a vital limb so I'd be comfortable.

He shrugged. "You looked cozy."

I smoothed my palms down the thighs of my jeans. Cozy. That was how I felt here, at his parents' house. I wasn't even sure where they were at the moment. We'd taken over the place and made ourselves at home like a couple of teenagers. Was this homey or just plain weird?

Then again, my place was always swarming with roommates, and James's basement suite was dark, had a permanent dampness, and lacked freshly baked cookies.

"James," I scolded, standing up, "don't let pretty girls walk all over you."

He gave me a sly smile that made my stomach flip. "Some pretty women are more than welcome to."

I choked on a laugh, not sure how to respond.

"I need to go home, eat, get ready for yet another new position tomorrow morning. Maybe Tamara will make me an omelette," I said out loud, already making a mental inventory of our fridge and what she might share with me if I timed my homecoming well.

"No."

"No?"

"Let's order pizza. I don't want to go home to my gloomy basement suite and eat supper alone. Let's keep watching trashy TV and eat. My dad will be out at poker for a few more hours, and Mom said she's checking in on Mrs. Laven after her walk."

In other words, we'd have privacy.

"Sweet talker." I dropped onto the couch beside him and opened one of my favourite apps for ordering in. "Where from?"

He was already ordering on his own phone, and I leaned over to see what he was adding to his cart.

"Whoa! Wait. You forgot the pineapple on that Hawaiian pizza."

"No, I did not because it is not Hawaiian."

"And shrimp? Ew. No. So wrong."

He looked up at me as if an alien had taken over my body.

"No shrimp," I demanded. "Add pineapple."

"No, you animal."

"Excuse me? I'm not eating that."

"Pick off the shrimp."

"No. Pick off the pineapple."

He sighed and began tapping on his phone.

"What are you doing?"

"Half and half. One half good, one half for the animal I'll be eating with."

"Thank you." I gave him a prim smile and then got up to grab a few plates from the kitchen. But before I could make it off the cushions, James snagged me, pulling me back against him, his arms around me, his lips nuzzling my neck.

I giggled and squirmed as his lips tickled me. He caught my earlobe in his teeth, his breath hot on my cheek. I wiggled until I was facing him and our kisses turned deep.

I'd planned sometime this week to institute and maintain some friendship boundaries, so I didn't start doodling his name in my notebooks. The goal was to not be completely crushed when Estelle pulled all of my wishes off of James and he went back to his own state of free will again.

But this evening had been nice. Really nice. Chill and fun, even though we hadn't done much. I didn't want to let go of these moments. They were small, but felt so right. I liked cuddling up on the couch, and found I could think about family and marriage without getting that itching feeling in my legs. Maybe I had a dormant gene that allowed me to be a homebody like James?

If this was what a steady relationship was like, then I understood why Tamara missed it so badly. Hanging out with James felt natural and I began to think that maybe I could do this after all, while loving every second of it. The idea that I could maybe make something such as marriage work with someone like James tickled me more than the idea that unicorns might be real. Or had been. I still didn't have a clear message from Estelle about their status. Real? Not real? Alive? Extinct? Maybe Josie knew.

I sighed in James's arms, spent from our kissing.

Our pizza arrived, and we snuggled, eating our respective halves before burrowing in for more TV.

"James?"

"Hm?" His arm was heavy on my shoulders, but it was pleasant, like a weight securing me against strong winds.

This was another rare moment of quiet. Of calm. Of being happy exactly where I was. Not thinking about the next thing. Not itching to get moving or questioning what it all meant. I just loved being here. Nothing to say, nothing to tell. No big story or grand adventure. Just...being.

I didn't want to dive into what I was feeling or not feeling. I didn't want to pick it apart or understand it. I only wanted to enjoy this moment with him and to no longer be afraid.

"Thanks," I said, pulling his arm tighter around me.

He kissed my cheek, saying nothing, simply holding me tight like he knew exactly what I'd warred against, and that right now, all of my internal weapons had been set aside.

I think this might be contentment.

Two hours later, feeling sleepy from the coziness of our cuddles, I sat up, stretching out my torso.

James didn't have to work in the morning, but I did. I still had Tuesday onward to grind through. A wash of guilty soot coated my mood, familiar and bitter as reality sank back in. I turned to James. "You know that if I could fix your life, I would."

I'd wished long and hard about James, asking Estelle to let him slip out of my life, and out of this mess. Untouched. Unscathed. Like we'd just been two bingo balls that had briefly bumped into each other in the space-time continuum. For a few days, I'd thought it had worked. But clearly, it hadn't.

As I sat here, the week pressing on me, the yearning to spend every moment of it with James, I mentally begged for her help. I couldn't say no to this man, and that meant I couldn't protect him from the shrapnel of my life. I needed her to put the wedge between us that was supposed to be there. The one that would be there if I hadn't made a big wish for him to like me back.

She needed to fix this. Now.

Even though it would crush me.

I put my face in my hands for a moment, elbows on knees.

Why couldn't I just have this? This evening had been bliss. Such a reprieve.

But this wasn't real. My boyfriend was under a spell.

James finally spoke, reminding me that I'd spoken earlier. "There's nothing wrong with my life."

He was frowning at me, the line between his brows a deepening canyon.

"I only meant that I bring chaos, and I ruin everything by—"

He leaned in, placing his mouth over mine to shut me up.

His lips were like a Peter's milkshake on a hot summer's day; that first hit of cold on the back of your dry throat, an instant reprieve from all the crappy things in your life.

I sighed at the sweet sensation of his lips against mine, and then we found our rhythm, the syncing of our souls or something equally poetic and I was gone. Mind blank, my hands zipping up the hard plains of pecs in front of me.

Better. Than. Fantasy.

Every time. How was that even possible?

Was this some sort of ever-intensifying, unbreakable magic spell?

His arms were strong around me, his body perfectly bigger than mine. He clutched me to him with a strength that had a delicious touch of the possibility that he could crush me in the most wonderful way.

He pulled away, whispering, "Maybe I like chaos."

What was he talking about? I grabbed a handful of blond locks and dragged his lips back to mine, demanding more.

Oh, I was the chaos.

I opened my mouth, breaking contact, sputtering words between hungry kisses. "You don't. Nobody does. Except me." I thought about it. I liked chaos, didn't I?

Change and unexpected adventures.

Was that chaos?

His lips were a firm pressure, my soul a shower of fireworks and sparks as he lit me up from the inside out.

Actually, no. I didn't like chaos. Not really.

"Okay," I said between urgent kisses, my hands under his shirt, feeling the delicious heat of his skin. "Not chaos. Adventure. Change. The unexpected. Pleasant surprises."

He shushed me, and pulled me into his lap, tipping us horizontally onto the couch, our lips a rodeo of passion.

These kisses meant business. If anything, we seemed to be falling closer rather than drifting further away from each other.

The reversal spell I'd requested was definitely not working.

～

At home that night, I wept, aware that none of what I'd felt tonight had been truly real.

It was merely what I'd wished for.

Nothing more.

Nothing real.

CHAPTER 33

~ *Estelle* ~

I marched past Trish's cubicle and the perfect little pink cardigan she kept over the back of her chair, not even phased by her whispers about Igor eating bad fairies. Whatever. She was a liar, and I was on to her.

I had a client in a spiral who needed my help.

I entered the head fairy's office, taking her by surprise.

She quickly pounded the end of a lit cigar into a nearby ashtray. Above her, smoke rings floated, losing shape. I swear two of them looked like hearts. She shot me a guilty look, dropping the ashtray and cigar into her trash can despite the fire risk of doing so.

"Was just trying to figure out what Paxi liked about these." She gave a light, fake cough and I wondered how long she'd been a smoker. Hopefully not too long. Magic couldn't protect you from everything, including the evils of lung cancer.

"Permission to enter the human world."

Gram-Gram blinked and sat forward, suddenly very alert. "Explain."

"Char's in love and frightened. I tried to summon her here,

because she doesn't understand emotional enhancement wishes, or wishes relating to the behaviours of others. But she can't hear me or is ignoring me. She doesn't know that any emotional enhancement wishes that have been granted on her behalf will have worn off by now." I paused for a breath, feeling panicked.

Gram-Gram spoke up. "We don't like humans interrupting our work day. These are private offices, and think of the example you've been setting with the others by letting her traipse in here?"

"But it's not against the rules."

"It hasn't needed to be," she said firmly.

I rubbed my forehead, desperate to express all that was weighing on me.

"I need to talk to her. The divine timing is right for old wishes that I granted before the ban. They're picking up speed and...and..." I could picture how personally Char would take some of the things that were coming down the pipe due to old wishes she'd made. The one about Randy, for one. I'd been so naïve. I had granted her wishes, not fully comprehending the impact they could make when they finally came to fruition.

Being a fairy godmother was so much more complex than I'd expected.

"He loves her, Gram-Gram," I pleaded.

"Who does?"

"James. And she's about to ruin the best thing that's ever happened to her, thinking that I'm behind it all. She doesn't know what's real anymore."

"Estelle," Gram-Gram said gently. "You're becoming too emotionally involved in the lives of your clients. You're losing your perspective."

"But she needs to know! There's so much still that she doesn't understand!"

But Gram-Gram, the head fairy and my boss, acting as stubborn as the stupid, skinflinty old Paxi, simply shook her head. "Estelle, go back to your desk."

CHAPTER 34
~ *Char* ~

Tuesday and Wednesday had been a blur of work at Temporarily Yours, and the usual new-temp-job thrill had somehow worn off completely. There had been one bright spot, and that was a quick job for CM Enterprises out of Ontario. Connor MacKenzie, some big shot out east, had asked me to do research for a startup in Calgary, then one in Edmonton, which had meant jumping on the bus to head north. I was sure to wear my Flames jersey into Oilers' territory, even though it normally wouldn't be considered work appropriate. Although, with both of the province's NHL teams in the playoffs, a Flames or Oilers jersey was currently everything appropriate.

Sure, it might be June, and late in the year for hockey fever to some people, but the teams had beaten out the San Antonio Dragons with their all-star Maverick Blades to face each other head-to-head. The Battle of Alberta never rested even outside of playoffs, but this year it was extra insane with both teams vying for the Stanley Cup.

The worst part of my week, though, hadn't been the cracks from the Oilers fans upon seeing my red and orange jersey in

Edmonton, but had been catching myself feeling dreamy and hopeful, envisioning a future with James. Predictably, it was a rude slap to the face every time I recalled that my returned amorous feelings were all due to a wish.

I'd even tried going to Estelle's office to beg for her help yesterday after getting back from Edmonton, but the witch in reception said she was off for the rest of the week.

Fairy godmothers took vacations? That seemed wholly unfair, especially while I was having a crisis.

I'd asked which day Estelle would return, but the witch had simply told me that their calendar was different than ours. And then, without even moving my feet, I'd found myself on the sidewalk outside YFGM's front door. Naturally, the door was gone, and wouldn't reappear, no matter what I did.

On Thursday night, determined to spend time with my roomies before baseball practice, I came home with a giant pizza and called out, "I'm home. I have pizza!"

I opened the box on the kitchen table, and Felipe chittered at me. I cut him a tiny piece of crust and handed it to him. He sat on his haunches and nibbled.

The pie was down a slice, as I'd given one away on my walk home as a good deed. But there was still plenty. I went to the fridge and found carrot sticks and Tamara's homemade chocolate cake. I put them on the table along with plates.

The house was quiet. "Where is everyone?" I asked Felipe.

I closed the pizza box again; the pineapple reminding me of James. I loved that he hadn't backed down about me wanting pineapple on the pizza when we'd ordered in the other night. My mom would have just shut up, and then picked it off in order to keep the peace. But James and I had stood our ground and bickered over what we each wanted, finding a perfect compromise. I liked that about us. It felt healthy.

But why weren't my wishes wearing off on him? It was starting to freak me out.

Tamara appeared in the doorway, appearing slightly grim.

"What's wrong?" I was up from my seat and across the room in a heartbeat.

She sucked in a deep breath then, blurted out, "I'm moving back home at the end of the month."

"What?"

That couldn't be right. We had to give a month's notice, and we were already into June. We'd have to find another roommate.

She bit her bottom lip, giving me a hopeful smile.

Oh, no. Kade.

Why couldn't she just go ahead and fall in love with Kade's older brother Haden instead? He was the better pick. And the way Tamara and Haden seemed to avoid each other made me wonder if they were hiding a forbidden, secret attraction.

But Kade? She was moving home for *him*?

I turned so she wouldn't see my face, sat at the table and shoved a slice of pizza in my mouth to keep me quiet, to stuff my anger and disappointment down somewhere deep, stuck under gluten and cheese so it wouldn't well up and ruin our friendship.

She crept into the room. "We're going to give us a second chance."

"Mmmph." I had way too much pizza in my mouth, thankfully. I tried for a smile, but couldn't quite get there.

Her going back to Kade felt like the end. The end of adventure. The end of Tamara's dreams. The end of having my bestie at my side making me omelettes and chocolate cake. Maybe even the end of our friendship.

But most of all, the end of Tamara standing up for what she wanted in life.

I leaned back in my chair and tried not to cry.

"Char…"

"Nothing. It's fine." I shoved more pizza in my face. It was only lukewarm now, and a bit chewy. I hope that didn't downgrade my good deed of sharing a slice with a stranger.

"Char…"

I stood and pulled back on my immaturity. I drew her into a hug and lied. "I'm happy for you." I couldn't look at her or she'd see how disappointed I was. "I'm sad, too, though. And I hope…I hope this time it works out, and that it's everything…" Wait.

I gasped. Back when we'd been trying to prove that Estelle was a fraud, Tamara had made a wish for love! Estelle had said she wouldn't grant those wishes for her and Josie, but the timeline tracked. Tamara had been happy and going out a lot more since that wish. Had Estelle snuck one by us?

I held Tamara in front of me, fearing that this second-chance business was Estelle's doing and not reality.

"If I don't try things with him again, then I'll never know," she said firmly, her speech obviously rehearsed. "We weren't happy because we were young, and we didn't know who we were. I know who I am now. I know I love the country and smalltown life."

She didn't mention love. Was that implied?

"You made a wish to Estelle." I met her eyes.

"What? No." Her cheeks flushed.

"When we first met her."

"Oh." Tamara waved the idea away. "She never granted that. She just read my mind."

"Are you sure?"

Tamara's eyes filled. "Can't you be happy for me? I don't have to live your life in order to be happy, you know."

"I know."

"And it's not like you're happy anyway! You finally found a nice guy who likes you back, and you're acting as if he's about to break up with you!"

"Because I made a wish that he'd love me. Like you did with Kade, only for me it was an accident! It was before I knew Estelle could meddle and change lives based on my stupid, immature, selfish whims! And now here I am with something that's not even real. He only likes me because I wished for it. Not because of me and who I really am."

Tamara's anger slackened, and she pulled me into her arms. "Oh, hon."

She was cozy and warm and like a giant pillow of sweet kindness. As much as I hated to admit it, I knew she didn't belong here in Calgary. She belonged back home, amongst the rolling foothills with a stable full of horses.

Just maybe not with Kade.

"I hope it's real, Tam-Tam," I whispered, tears streaking down my cheeks.

She released me, wiping her eyes. "Well, I was missing Eagle Ridge anyway, so..." She shrugged. Her voice wobbled, and I could see the way my words had destroyed her happiness.

"I know you were. I'm sorry if you stayed here for me. And I didn't mean to be unhappy about you and Kade."

Tamara shook her head hard, once. "Don't."

The door to the stairs closed and footsteps—high heels—climbed our way. Samantha.

"What's going on?" she asked, coming around the corner and taking in our somber faces.

"Tamara's moving back home."

"Oh." Samantha's tone was casual. Had she already known? "When?"

"End of the month," Tamara said.

"Huh. Well, that's um..."

"Do you know someone who'd make a good roommate?" I asked. I caught Samantha's look and cringed. Oh no. What was coming my way now?

"Is this pizza?" Samantha opened the box, helping herself to a slice. "Wait. There's cake!" She added a slice of cake to her plate.

"What?" I demanded. "What were you going to say?"

She carefully rearranged the placement of pineapple on her pizza so it was more evenly spaced. "Malachi asked me to move in with him."

"He did?"

Samantha gave a sheepish smile, but the joy on her face couldn't be masked. She was in love. And she'd said yes.

Everyone was in love.

I felt left behind. The kind of woman who could only get true love if she wished for it.

CHAPTER 35

~ *Char* ~

Finding replacements for Samantha and Tamara was going to be tricky, but it got even worse than simply trying to find someone to fill their awesome roommate shoes. Josie had come home, and said she had been thinking about moving to the mountains for her business. Which made no sense at all. Then Gabby started talking about how Lamonte had an extra room in his suite, and that maybe she'd just crash with him.

That left Felipe and me as the only ones with nowhere to go.

In other words, the GAL PAL squad, or whatever Tamara called us, was breaking up.

But to make it official, we had to tell Randy, and quickly, since we were already past giving him the required thirty-day notice. I'd joked to the girls that moving out at least would mean no more evading Randy. The joke had hit an unwelcome note of déjà vu.

Josie lost a mega round of paper, rock, scissors, and she zipped downstairs to let Randy know we were leaving.

After pizza and cake, I sat outside and waited for James to

pick me up for baseball, looking up apartments online. I figured I could sneak Felipe in wherever, but finding a place for myself was harder than I'd anticipated. And expensive. I'd gotten used to having a big space and splitting costs with four friends.

Thank goodness I had baseball to distract me. I hoped James didn't give me any of those long questioning looks I sometimes caught him sending my way. I wasn't sure I could handle it tonight. It was bad enough that I was head over heels for the man, but was constantly haunted by a mean whisper in my ear telling me it wasn't real. That none of it counted. That it would soon end.

It didn't help that his gaze would often linger on my lips, making me want to launch myself at him and kiss him senseless.

By the time James pulled up out front, I was antsy from being alone with my thoughts. I hopped in practically before he came to a complete stop. He chatted idly as he drove, and I did my best to keep up with my end of the conversation. I told him I was looking for a place, and he said he'd keep an ear out. He told me about his classes, and I asked a few questions. But by the time he parked at the diamond, I was no longer able to ignore his long looks of inquiry. If I didn't get my head sorted and my focus dialled in, I'd get slammed by a ball tonight.

"I made a wish that you'd like me," I blurted out as James cast me another one of those long looks after turning off his Range Rover. "And now it seems you do. But it's not real. So, I think you should give me some space so you don't get my hopes up and break my heart when the wish wears off."

I grabbed my equipment from the floor by my feet and went to open the car door. James hit the lock button.

I whirled on him. "Seriously?"

He was quiet. Calm.

I flicked my door handle a few times. "James?"

"When?" he asked, his demeanour calm.

"When what?"

"When did you make the wish?"

"I don't know." I fumbled the stupid lock button, releasing my door. Ha! He didn't have the child lock on. Triumph!

"Well, whenever it was, I'm pretty sure I've liked you longer."

Door open, I turned to him with a frown. "What's that supposed to mean?"

"Close the door."

"No."

"Close the door and I'll tell you."

I sighed and threw myself deep into the seat like a sulky teenager, shutting the door. "What?"

He leaned over the console between us and cupped my chin, turning my face toward his. Shivers shimmied down my spine and my breath caught. I loved the way he looked at me with such tenderness and acceptance, even when I was acting loony. His eyes were an electric blue tonight, the intensity disturbing my thoughts and shutting me down, sending me to a place of peace and calm.

He was going to kiss me and prove he loved me—even when I talked crazy. It was one of the things I loved most about him.

"Because I've had a crush on you since your inventory days," he said.

"What?" My mouth dropped open in surprise, and he landed a light kiss.

My world was spinning. He'd liked me for that long? I needed to check my invoice. There were a lot of crush-related wishes on that list, but I thought James was a more recent addition.

He had to be on there somewhere. Because I clearly wished for every little whim my heart desired, so why wouldn't I wish for an amazing man like him?

I really needed to look up that date, though.

A wish that was several years old would have worn off by now, but what about more recent ones? Estelle had said something about time, but also space and fate, and one's ability to regain the destiny of their lives. The problem was, I still didn't understand any of it.

I tipped my head down, breaking contact with James.

He'd only made a move on me recently, so why would he wait that long? Was it because I'd caused his affection to spark—not through simply being my whimsical, loony self, but by being a randomly blind wishing machine?

"You lost your crush on me?" he asked.

I couldn't look at him, but gave my head a small shake.

"Then?"

"How would we even work?" I looked up, pleading with my eyes for him to explain that what I felt was real, that it wasn't because of a wish and that we could make all of this work. Forever and ever like his parents. That he'd give me a no-broken-hearts guarantee.

He took my hand, interlacing his warm fingers between mine. "We'd kiss and spend time together and see where it all goes."

I pushed back in my seat. Not a guarantee. Not even close.

That was something a man under a spell would say, wasn't it?

Or a man who wasn't looking for long-term, which James was.

"We're very different," I stated.

"Are we though?"

"Yes!"

"Char, what if this works?"

I inhaled nosily through my nose.

"Does that scare you?"

I nodded.

"Why?"

"Because I don't want to become my mom, sitting around waiting. Waiting for love, and you, and life, and adventure, and something to snap me out of my funk. And then running off with someone else because I never once spoke up for what I truly wanted or tried to make it happen."

I jolted at the revelation. From what I'd seen, my mom had never asserted herself or spoken up for what she wanted. Had she been denied so many times she'd given up? Or again, were she and my dad not meant to stay together?

James was frowning, a deep furrow on either side of his perfect mouth. "Are you in a funk?"

"No, not now," I said distractedly, vaguely aware he was referencing my little rant. "But if I got married and was sitting at home while you work away and..."

Saying it out loud it sounded dumb. Putting the cart before the horse, and I wasn't even sure if the cart or horse were mine. I was pretty sure I was more of a Ferrari girl, to be honest. Same with James.

I turned to face him. He was not my father. I was not my mother. We were both someone completely and utterly different.

"You're the last person I could ever see sitting at home, Char."

"I sit at home." My voice was wobbling. "And I like it."

He chuckled. "Okay, let me ask you..." He thought for a moment. "How many different jobs did your mom have?"

"In her life? I don't know. Two? Three?"

"How many have you had this year?"

I snorted. Fair point. I wasn't in a rut with my work. Although, more recently, I found myself wishing for something more fulfilling, something more stable...something that I could really dig myself into and get passionate about.

Was I maturing? Growing out of this excitement phase like I'd finally managed to prove something to myself and could move on?

"What's your mom passionate about?"

"Brynnie's perfectness. Traipsing the world with Damon." I sighed at my bitterness.

A couple of our teammates walked past, knocking on the window and making weird gestures that were probably supposed to encourage us to get onto the field. Whatever they meant, I decided, should it come to it, I'd never choose them to be on my charades team.

"Has she ever cheered on runners that were dressed as cats and dogs?" James continued after giving his buddies a head nod. "Lived with a bunch of yahoos and tried to build a park for people to enjoy?"

"They're all moving on! And out! And giving up on the park." How was I going to do all of this on my own? Especially with the lots still tied up by the police investigation.

"Did she walk stray dogs who need homes?" James continued. "Adopt a gopher? Know everyone at the museum by name, and correct the director from time to time? Or point out fakes that nobody else had caught, because she'd found a passion and was learning and absorbing all she could about it?"

He made me sound amazing, and I wondered if I truly was the woman he saw. Because that woman was actually kind of cool.

"You are not your mom."

"I know," I whispered, believing it fully for the first time, and realizing that her path was not my own, and why should it be?

"And we're not your parents. We're ourselves and only ourselves," he continued. "It's all we can ever truly be."

"Promise?"

His thumb stroked the line of my jaw. "Your life will never be at risk of being like anyone else's. Because there will only ever be one Char McDonnell. You're one of a kind."

I swiped at my damp eyes. "You're making me cry."

"Good. Now kiss me."

I did. And it was heavenly, even though in the back of my mind I still worried that Estelle was behind all of these wonderful feelings, and that the rug would be pulled out from under me when I least expected it.

I HAD to be out of the apartment in a week, and I had nowhere to go. With no other ideas, I finally went over to the Backstrohms while James was at a night class, and confessed to Sally. She had to know of a place through her Salvation Army connections, right?

I'd been soaring, my life never better until Estelle had come along.

Now it had crashed and burned.

Although...had I been soaring because of my wishes and my meddling fairy godmothers? Was none of my past life truly mine? Was it only crappy now because I'd given up on wishing for better things?

I wasn't sure I liked that thought.

Sally was in the kitchen, looking at recipes, her reading glasses on the end of her nose as she inspected me after I'd blurted out my problems. I came here because Sally treated me like I was one of her own. I felt cared for, and as though I belonged. Even though I was probably just another stray she was taking in out of the goodness of her heart.

But being in her kitchen tonight made me feel a sense of loss. I should be sitting in a kitchen with my own mother, confessing my problems to her, not a woman I'd only met a month ago. Although my mom had never doted on me, with Brynnie now in the picture, I could see that she had it in her. And I felt robbed.

Sitting in Sally's kitchen, feeling helpless, it was like being a teenager all over again, my world crumbling around me and being powerless to change it. I'd swore I'd never be in this position again.

And yet, here I was.

"It sounds like you're about to turn a corner in your life," Sally said sagely, her calm delivery startling me.

"What?"

"The universe is purging what you no longer need in order to make room for something new." She scrunched her nose adorably, eyes sparkling. "Something good."

It didn't solve my issues, but I kind of liked the idea that the universe was setting me up for something new. As long as it wasn't being eaten by Igor. That wasn't the kind of new experience I was seeking at the moment.

"Just a way of thought," Sally said absently, closing her cookbook. "You don't have to believe in it."

"No, it's interesting. Comforting and a bit exciting."

Her smile was warm. She removed her reading glasses, studying me. "Do you like it here?"

"At your house? Yeah, it's lovely." Had she not noticed how difficult it was to get rid of me?

"Good. How do you feel about house-sitting?"

"Here?" I looked around for clues. "Are you going somewhere?" I needed a place that would last longer than an Alaskan cruise.

"Otto is retiring soon." She watched me over the top of her glasses. "We've been taking our motorhome on dry-run weekend trips."

I nodded. James had mentioned their RV, and how they were taking jaunts to let the dog get accustomed to its moving digs. I hadn't thought that much about it, to be honest.

"We're leaving in two weeks for a longer trip. We'll be back about mid-August. We'd love it if you'd stay here. James was going to check in on the place, water the plants, mow the lawn and all that, but the insurance company prefers someone live here during an extended vacation. Would you be interested?"

"I need a place before your trip, though."

"You can move in whenever you like."

"I have a gopher."

"Bring him and his cage."

"He kind of has free run of our apartment."

"The dog wouldn't like that."

We were silent for a moment, mentally mulling over solutions.

"Well, if you can think of a solution for your gopher, the place is yours. Rent-free."

Rent-free?

Maybe Tamara could take Felipe back to Eagle Ridge with her.

Or he could be like the pair of jeans in *The Sisterhood of Traveling Pants* by Ann Brashares and we could share him. He could come into each of our lives like a talisman of luck whenever we needed him. That was an idea I could get behind. It seemed as though, even when things were swirling down the drain, I still loved the idea of there being a bit of magic.

CHAPTER 36
~ *Char* ~

Moving was the pits. Leaving my friends was even worse. And saying goodbye to Felipe, who was going with Tamara to Eagle Ridge, also ranked pretty darn low on the happiness scale.

There was just one thing that didn't suck, and that was watching James carry my boxed things down to his Rover in an old pair of jeans and a ratty grey T-shirt that was a bit small, hugging his pecs. He was utterly delectable.

He'd caught the hungry way I'd been devouring him with my eyes. And of course I was. His shirt looked like it had been designed solely for him.

With a teasing twinkle in his baby blues, he pulled the cotton blend away from his abs and asked, "Should I see if I this comes in every colour?"

Why would he even have to ask? The answer was clearly yes. Especially since I'd been unable to resist touching his beefy arms whenever we passed on the stairs.

I gave him a lingering kiss and went back to my room with a fresh stack of black garbage bags to gather up the last bits. While I worked, I tried not to think about the fact that his parents were taking me in. Yes, I was going to be acting as their live-in house-sitter, but still. He was my boyfriend, and I was moving in with his parents. That didn't say sexy things about my state of independence.

Sure, I could argue that I was free and wild, living wherever the breeze sent me, and that I was seizing the day and opportunities for adventure. The truth was, I wanted a more permanent home base, and I knew that without Sally and Otto, I would be essentially homeless.

Gabby's parents and her two brothers had gathered up her stuff last night, moving her into Lamonte's suite on the other side of the city. Lamonte was away working at a Jeep event, and I wondered if it would be at all awkward when he returned. Surely he had to know Gabby was crushing on him in a major way. Maybe this was his big move, and the two would be married within a year. Men confused me, and I hoped Lamonte knew what he was doing, letting Gabby move in with him.

At the moment, though, she was in our bathroom with the music cranked, getting a head start on scrubbing away every bit of evidence that we'd once lived here. It didn't matter that Samantha's dad had hired cleaners to come in after the moving company departed with Samantha's things.

While I continued to throw the last of my belongings into garbage bags, Josie and a mysterious brigade appeared, looking like they'd just left a LARPing session. They must have been Live Action Role Playing dragon trainers or something. There were a lot of leather vests and tall boots, as well as a few weaponish items hanging from their thick belts. All I could think when I looked at them was, 'Were dragons living in Canada?' Either way, they whisked in and out of the house, every speck of Josie gone within fifteen minutes, as though they'd been controlled by one of her detailed spreadsheets.

I watched from the front window with a bit of awe as she

jumped into an off-road vehicle with her crew. So efficient. But what was with the goofy ride? It looked ready for an apocalypse with a big Jackall jack strapped to the hood, extra stainless-steel reinforcement around the wheel wells, big knobby tires, and a roof rack filled with water and jerry cans and other equipment like a shovel, chains and a chainsaw.

But even odder than Josie's brigade, and the guy with a futuristic-looking robotic hand, was the presence of Haden, Kade's older brother. He'd shown up to help Tamara move back to Eagle Ridge since Kade apparently had a previous commitment: one that I hoped didn't involve Jannifer Bryant again. What was so odd about Haden being here was that he and Tamara had never really hung out in the past. But, even more so, was the way Tamara studiously avoided any eye contact with the poor man. It made me doubt my theory that they'd make a good couple.

Well, until that blazing moment when the kitchen box I was carrying came apart, and I sent pots, pans and cutlery down the stairs with a resounding crash that had made a red-faced Randy curse at us. Tamara and Haden had taken one look at each other and doubled over with laughter, hanging off each other for support like they were the oldest of friends.

I still wished Tamara would choose him instead of Kade.

But that wasn't a real wish. I didn't want to mess with her world or heart. I just wanted Tamara to enjoy a long life of happiness.

After a deep hug from Tamara that made me miss her already, she stood beside Haden, closing the doors to his horse trailer, like a team that had worked alongside each other for decades. Then they both popped into their respective vehicles and drove off.

I stood on the step, watching the trailer turn a corner.

Samantha waved off her moving crew, who were also done. She looked at me, lifted her chin, and sniffed coolly. "Later."

She gave me the quickest hug known to man, and leapt into her car like none of this affected her. But I was pretty sure I saw her surreptitiously swipe some tears before she pulled away from the curb.

I sighed, feeling like a dream was coming to an end. Would the five of us even continue to hang out, now that we weren't living together? Why couldn't we just buy houses on the same street, and have drinks in each other's backyards all summer?

I opened the GAL PAL texting chat and sent a message.

ME

I miss us already.

Tamara replied instantly.

TAMARA

ME

Take good care of Felipe.

TAMARA

I will. 🤍

I WIPED my own eyes and sniffled.

GABBY

If you miss me, you could come up here and help me clean!

SAMANTHA

Gabs, stop or there'll be nothing for the cleaning people to do, and they've already been paid.

I smiled and went to pocket my phone just as it rang. Seeing the number was Officer Beddoe's, I answered it immediately. It was a Sunday, so if he was calling, it had to mean good news, right?

It was. The warehouse and lots had been released. I was free to get back to working on the park.

I lowered my phone and gazed down the empty street toward the future park, feeling like I'd lost all momentum and motivation. None of us gals lived here any longer. None of us were Everstone residents. This was no longer our community. We were now spread across the city and beyond. We couldn't just plop down onto the couch with a pizza or Tamara's chocolate cake and solve problems or brainstorm.

I still had Josie's spreadsheets and all of our plans and proposals, but it was terrifying being the one in charge. The project felt like it was solely mine without the gals up in the living room, gathered on our mismatched furniture.

I turned back to the boarding house to find James leaning against the open door's frame, watching me. Thank goodness for James and his family. Otherwise, I'd be trying to cram everything I owned into an Uber and telling the driver to stop at the first abandoned cardboard box that looked big enough to house me.

I wiped my damp eyes. There were so many emotions swirling through me I couldn't process them all. James and I moved toward each other and his arms swept me up, holding me tight like he knew how I was feeling. Knew my pain, my fear, my aching loneliness, the sensation of being untethered, of not having a nest in which to return to when I needed recalibration.

~

ON MONDAY MORNING, I ended the ninth phone call I'd made from the Backstrohm's kitchen table. I'd been begging and pleading the park's case to sponsors, demolition crews and everyone on the list that Josie had made for us back in June. I was offering to name the park after them, their business, their firstborn, or their childhood dog if they'd just tear down the warehouse frame or donate some money. Immediately.

Well, mostly I had left professional voicemails, the begging all in my head. It turned out that even in the full-on heavy season for all things constructing and deconstructing, basically nobody worked on Canada Day, July 1.

I was feeling impatient. I didn't have *time* for holidays. I needed to get the park rolling again. I was one unanswered phone call away from going down to Home Hardware and buying a crowbar and trying to take the warehouse down on my own.

"Hey! Just me." It was James, letting himself into his parents' house.

"In here if you're looking for me." I hoped that he was. I hadn't seen him yet today. And even though we'd spent most of yesterday together while moving me here, and it wasn't really my style to be clingy, I found myself longing to see or hear from him each day.

"If you're looking for your parents, they're out enjoying free Canada Day cake at some park. I can't remember which one." They'd be taking off on their trip in a few days, and the first twenty-four hours of living together had been pretty good. Otto was the quintessential quiet dad, doing his own thing. And Sally had naturally found the right balance between doting and letting me find my own way.

"Happy birthday," James said, bending to lay a kiss on the crown of my head.

"Not my birthday."

"Then happy Canada Day."

"Thanks. You, too." I half expected him to be holding a strawberry milkshake from Peter's. But instead, he had a small wrapped box.

"What's this?" I asked, immediately freaking out. We were in that undefined zone where we were dating, but not really talking about it or what it all meant to us.

I suppose we knew what the other person wanted in a relationship, although I wasn't sure he'd figured out that I was now starting to want that cozy togetherness, too.

Even though I was certain it wouldn't happen for us, seeing as, eventually, Estelle's very real magic would wear off. Then I'd be alone once again, off to find my way, off to find a new tribe to call my own.

And this pretty little box looked like a gift. The kind you'd give a serious girlfriend.

He set it beside me at the kitchen table. "It won't bite you."

No, but what it represented might.

I squeezed out a smile. "Thanks."

"Open it."

I slipped off the ribbon and opened the palm-sized box, lifting up the delicate square of cotton covering the item inside. And there, staring up at me, was a piece of the most beautiful pottery fragment, edged in silver to wear as a necklace.

The one from the museum. The one with the painted hands. The original, authentic piece. The one that was expensive. Way too expensive.

"James..." There were a lot of reasons this should not be sitting in the palm of my hand. "I know I said I'd pay you back if you bought this, but I can't. I really need to put all my money into the park right now."

Even living rent free for the next two months wasn't going to help me afford this item, as much as I longed for it.

I handed it back to him, but he only unclipped the necklace, ready to clasp it on me. "Try it."

Dangerous, dangerous game.

He came around behind me, waiting for me to sweep my hair off my neck. I scrunched my eyes shut, pushing away tears.

I distinctly remember wishing for this necklace. The strong longing I'd had for it. The words in my heart slipping from my mouth.

And now here it was. This meant my wishes were still in effect. All of them. It made me want to slam myself into the bathroom, and cry and cry until there was nothing left.

James gently fed the silver chain around my neck, doing up the clasp. His fingers brushed my skin, sending shivers down my spine. He smelled like sandalwood and reassurance. This moment felt intimate. Filled with love.

The fragment fell at just the perfect height to wear with almost everything. I angled it, peering at its authentic, ancient glaze. One of a kind.

Like James.

But it was too much. Too expensive. How could Estelle grant this wish right now? James had been without work for several weeks, even though he could probably head back now that the warehouse had been released. But there were still so many, many reasons he shouldn't have bought this necklace.

For starters, today was a holiday so the museum gift shop was closed. But most vitally, the present was too much, too pricey. Instead of spending hundreds on me, he should be buying himself groceries to feed his giant muscles. He should be planning his next spontaneous trip without the obligatory pit stops to excavation sites, just because I was enthused about them. It should be about him.

I met James's gaze, my throat dry, my brain lacking the words I needed to deliver in order to return this amazing gift that was thousands of years old, and made me feel like the kind of woman a pharaoh would build a pyramid for.

James was watching my reaction, his brow furrowed. I felt for the poor man as my eyes filled with love and gratitude. I was all over the place these days. The idea of Estelle's magic creating all of these beautiful moments between James and me was messing with my head, creeping under my skin, and making me doubt everything I felt.

I tried to say the words "I can't" but my throat locked as though under a spell.

He placed a soft kiss on my cheek, and I ducked my chin, feeling ashamed for the way I'd abused our friendship and his generous kindness with my wishes. I felt like I'd possibly made him into an amazing boyfriend against his own desires, and forced him to act toward me in the way he would for his heart's truest match. Not for a woman who could never quite make the distance.

CHAPTER 37
~ *James* ~

T he necklace had been the perfect gift.

And yet, entirely the wrong one.

Char's delight had been clear when she'd opened the box, but then there'd been a flood of about a million other emotions after that. None of them awesome.

And ever since Monday's gift, I'd felt a sliver of distance between us. We still saw each other as much as we could around our work schedules, and her smiles were always full of sunshine, but there'd been an undefinable shift, as if she were holding back a piece of herself.

Tonight, as the final inning played out on the baseball field, she unconsciously allowed her thigh to press against mine despite the July evening's lingering heat. She was the best part of my week, and the best part of baseball even though we were in the dugout and not out playing. I was here with her, and that was all I wanted.

I wove my fingers through hers and her chest heaved with a long, silent sigh. For the thousandth time this week, I wished she'd get over whatever fear it was that forced her to keep pulling away. It was like we'd take two steps forward, and then one back almost immediately. What did I need to do in order to prove to her that we were meant to be? That we had it all, right here? That we just needed to have faith and let go?

"This is good," I murmured, leaning my shoulder into hers.

She pressed back. "Yeah. It is." She smiled softly, the filtered light caressing her cheekbones like a lover. I leaned over and kissed her, not caring that our teammates sharing the bench might rib us for it. As far as I was concerned, only Char existed.

But there was that tiny wedge again, with her breaking the kiss first. I could apologize for the necklace, but there was no way I ever would. She loved it. She'd wanted it. It made her happy. That meant there was nothing to apologize for.

I'd shown her how she should be treated by her boyfriend, and I wasn't going to back down or settle for expressing less just because she'd never been shown her true worth.

"Nowhere else I'd rather be," I whispered.

She tipped her head against my shoulder for a second, and I knew she was echoing my sentiment. "We're going to lose, though," Char muttered, tightening her hand on mine as our runner narrowly made it to first base.

"Probably." I landed a light kiss above her temple. Our team was only down by one, and we were up at bat. We could take this. Well, if we had a stitch of strategy. The problem was, it was leisure league. There was no coaching, no thoroughly considered batting line-ups. We ran a fair and totally randomly rotation that was based around keeping it even.

"This is driving me nuts." She watched our worst batter approach the home plate, bat in hand. Bases were loaded. Do or die.

We were probably going to die.

"I can't watch." She buried her face in my shoulder and I smiled, thanking whatever deity was responsible for this moment.

"Competitive much?" I teased, absolutely loving that she was. I nudged her, sending us both rocking to the side, as one.

She peeked up at me, nose scrunched as she confessed, "I want that end-of-season gift certificate."

"So do I."

The league's winner got a hefty gift card for the local hangout. It meant pizza and lots of beer for the winning team. We were in the running, but only if we used a bit of strategy. Which nobody wanted to hear or implement.

She sat up again, nestling us shoulder to shoulder. We resumed watching our batter swing wildly. Strike. Another strike as they went for one outside the strike zone.

Char's eyes, despite being aimed at the batter, were unfocused, like her thoughts were elsewhere as she told me, "I ran away once."

"Where'd you go?"

We were still holding hands, and she clenched mine tightly, as if she was afraid I'd vanish. "Here. The city."

"Yeah?" I eyed her while keeping my body angled toward the field. "How old were you?"

"Fifteen. I grabbed a ride here with a friend's family. I said my dad was picking me up later. But he was away working. I stayed at a hostel for two days. Then I got bored and hitchhiked home again."

"You didn't get caught?"

"Nobody noticed."

"What?"

How was that possible? My parents would have discovered I was missing within hours, maybe even minutes.

"James, you're up," someone called from off to the right. I wanted to wave them away, stay in this moment with Char, but I could see it had already been shattered by the interruption. I took in the field, realizing I'd lost track of the game. The score was now tied, the bases still loaded, our worst batter having unexpectedly come through for us to squeak out a base hit. Now it was my chance to clear the bases and win this thing.

I stood, grabbing my favourite bat. Char was watching the pitcher, acting like she'd never revealed what I suspected was a secret. One she'd never told a soul. One where she'd learned just how invisible she was to the people in her life. It broke my heart and, when I faced the pitcher, I imagined the ball to be all the people who'd ever let her down, vowing to never join their membership.

CHAPTER 38

~ *Char* ~

I woke with a start after having a horrible temping dream. I was working at Your Fairy Godmother, and Igor, the green ogre from accounting with those freaky long arms and short legs, was at the desk beside me in reception. I still didn't know what was behind the different-sized doors, and I'd spent most of the dream watching him licking an envelope at a leisurely pace. I'd been mesmerized by the way his tongue would slowly duck out of his mouth to touch the envelope flap before sliding back in like a content lizard's. Then reappearing, re-wetted, to touch another spot.

I shivered at the image.

I'd read a book once that explained that everyone in a dream is actually just a representation of ourselves. Did that mean that Igor's slowness at licking an envelope represented the way I felt about the park?

Too slow?

Or was it one of the agency's weird messages again, like when Paxi had stumbled into my dreams to tell me I'd owe money someday? If so, what was the message? That my final notice would soon be in the mail so I'd better get cracking on my karmic project so Igor didn't have to come after me?

I crawled out of bed, the house spooky-quiet, the Backstrohms already away on their road trip. I missed Felipe's morning chittering, Samantha's lattes, and the smell of Tamara making an omelette. Living alone sucked. It was like being a teenager again. Alone, alone, alone.

Maybe this was why I liked adventure so much, because being home alone was absolutely no fun.

~

"I FORGOT SALLY'S AWAY."

A woman I'd never met was looking stressed on the front step shortly after I returned from work on Friday evening. Considering that today was the start of the Calgary Stampede—an event that went on for nine days and drew over a million people into the city's downtown Stampede grounds—the look of stress wasn't that unfamiliar to anyone who lived or worked near the area. Especially since the opening parade had been this morning, drawing over 300,000 people into the core's maze of one-way streets for several hours.

While getting to work on time had been trying due to all of the buses and CTrains being packed with parade goers, at least I hadn't had to do anything over at the Everstone park today. The neighbourhood sat at the edge of the event's swath of busyness, and crossing the downtown from where I now lived would have been nothing short of crazy-making.

James, deciding not to return to his position at the museum, had been helping the Stampede's security team with some advisement and set up, and then would be on hand for the parade as well. I hadn't seen much of him over the past few days, and it made the empty house feel all the more lonely.

"Yeah. Sorry," I said, unsure why I was apologizing to the woman. "Did you want me to pass on a message?"

"No, no. It's just that sometimes she takes my mom for an hour or two," the woman said, rubbing her brow. "And I forgot she's away."

"Right." Not Stampede related stress. I wracked my brain for the older woman's name who lived next door. I'd only wondered in passing what would happen to her with Sally gone for several weeks. "That's Mrs. Laven?"

The woman nodded.

"Um." What was the word for it? "Respite care? Sally plays card games with your mom?"

The woman nodded again, and I recognized the look. It was one of being here, but not really. In her head, she was working out alternate plans, ways to make her life work.

"Would she be comfortable hanging out with me?" I asked, realizing as I made the offer that I was completely unqualified. Was I that lonely? Already that tired of being alone with my thoughts?

"Oh, I couldn't." The neighbour looked at me with an intensity that nearly had me stepping back. "It's Friday. You're young."

"I'm just doing stuff around the house tonight. She could hang out with me for an hour or two. We could play some games. Would she be comfortable with that? Honestly, it's kind of weird being here alone." I laughed like it was a joke and not painfully true.

"Are you sure? No, I can't ask that of you," the woman added just as quickly.

"I'm offering."

The woman eyed me, from my bare feet and pink toenails, to my cut-off shorts, T-shirt, and ponytail. She opened her mouth, as though she was going to say something, but then after a beat said, "If you're sure."

"I am. "

"I'll leave you my cell phone number in case she gets out of hand."

I felt the first stirrings of panic. In what ways could someone experiencing memory loss, and possible cognitive issues that I didn't understand, get out of hand?

"Is there anything I should know?"

"Unless she's going to put herself in the way of physical harm, just go with the flow. Even if she's lying or delusional. Don't waste your breath arguing. She doesn't get angry or violent, but she gets pretty stubborn."

Five minutes later, my white-haired neighbour was sitting at the kitchen table and I was dealing cards.

"Do you know gin rummy?" Mrs. Laven asked me. She clearly wasn't quite sure who I was, and maybe still thought I was Sophia, like she had the first time we'd met.

But she hadn't made any hurtful comments about my appearance having changed, and she wasn't giving me any trouble. She actually kind of reminded me of a kid who had a new babysitter. Slightly wary, but also willing to go along with things just to see.

"Can you show me how to play?" I asked.

"Where are the cookies?" Her eyes flicked around the kitchen with a practiced gaze. The usual spots Sally left them out—table, counter corner, cookie jar near the fridge.

"I'll get some." I got up and went into the stash Sally had left for me. She'd frozen dozens of them, and I grabbed some of the oatmeal raisin ones that I'd thawed earlier in the day.

I put the kettle on for tea and returned to the table with the cookies. Mrs. Laven clucked approvingly and tapped the cards sitting facedown, waiting for me.

"How do we play?" I asked.

"You'll figure it out," she assured me. About fifteen minutes later I realized I'd been sharked. I had no clue how to play gin rummy, and Mrs. Laven, instilling a false confidence in this newbie, was using it to her advantage.

In other words, I was already out five dollars, as she'd somehow convinced me that we should bet. She'd done a good job of bolstering my confidence before destroying me.

Her attention began to flag after about forty-five minutes—around the time I'd finally sorted out the shifting rules—and I suggested we take a break.

"Good idea." She slid all the IOUs I'd written on scraps of paper toward herself. "If I go to the bank with more than this much money, they'll surely think I'm up to no good." She let out a joyful cackle.

"I'll get some cash for you and trade those in," I said, pointing to the scraps. I lived pretty much cashless, and even more so now that I was playing for money against the resident neighbourhood, memory-addled card shark.

"How long have you lived next-door?" I asked, sliding the deck of cards back into their box.

"Years and years. The Backstrohms moved in when James was just a boy. The first time I met him, he was running around in his underwear and an eye patch, claiming to be an alien pirate who lived in a submarine. It was made out of a cardboard box."

"Really?" I leaned forward, eager to hear more.

"Sweet boy," she said.

"I agree."

She patted my hand. "Of course you do, dear." Her eyes narrowed and she shook a finger at me, her brow furrowing as she worked to place me. "Make sure you treat him right, otherwise you'll be answering to me. You hear?"

I nodded solemnly, secretly adoring this little old lady and the way she was willing to take me down if I mistreated her neighbour. Her loyalty warmed my heart.

"Has he always wanted a homey woman?" I asked. I still felt a bit wobbly about the necklace he'd given me, and how invested he seemed as a boyfriend. I'd never been in a relationship like this before—one so healthy. It made me nervous, like a cat in a room full of rocking chairs.

But I'd started to wonder lately that, even if he was under Estelle's spell, if I could somehow make our love real so we could continue on after the magical effects that had brought us together wore off.

"Homey?" Mrs. Laven's faded eyes narrowed in thought. "No, James has a spark in him, like his mother." She nodded to herself as though in confirmation. Then she smiled into the distance as if she was remembering him as a small boy during his pirate phase. I'd trade a kidney for a photo of him in his alien pirate get-up. I bet he'd been heart-destroyingly adorable.

"He wants a home, yes. But don't we all?" She leaned forward, placing her cool dry hand over mine, giving it a pat. "But more than anything, I think he wants to have fun, and to have someone to love."

CHAPTER 39

~ *James* ~

I really needed to make sure Char didn't offer Mrs. Laven any more respite care. I'd been suffering through pirate jokes for two days. We were currently curled up on my parents' couch after a long, busy Sunday morning, both of us spent. Or maybe Char was just pretending, and was actually scheming more ways to tease me about the story Mrs. Laven had shared about me running around in my undies and an eye patch.

Yesterday, the scrap workers had come back to finish the warehouse siding, wedging the job between two others. Then, by some small miracle, Char had then gotten the frame levelled this morning. She had a lot of contacts for someone who'd only been in the city a few years, and I supposed working somewhere new every few weeks or months widened one's circle.

Maybe this park could truly be created in the short timespan Char had allowed herself. Although, in order to do that, the next month and a half would be packed, meaning we'd be unlikely to rummage up enough time to do things like take in the Stampede together. I'd been hoping to check out some of the concerts, the rodeo, free shows, or to simply wander the midway and feed each other cotton candy. On the flipside, I never wanted to hold her back from living her own life or following her dreams.

That didn't mean I wasn't jealous of the time she spent on the park, though.

"Okay, I have to mow the lawn." She stood, leaving the room.

"But..." The spot where she'd been leaning against me felt cold.

"Next week's a busy one," she called from the kitchen. "Joan's put me back at my old level, which means more challenging work and longer hours."

I already missed spending time with Char.

"And higher pay," I called back.

Char dipped her head around the doorjamb, smiling. "And higher pay."

There was my Char.

Before she could pull the mower from the garage, I grabbed it and started on the front, determined to help in hopes of gaining a bit more time with her today.

"I'll do the gardens," she shouted over the sound of the motor.

I kept missing strips of the lawn, my mower heading off crooked as I watched Char bend and crouch over the flower beds. It was a nice view no matter which direction she faced, and I was lucky I hadn't mowed my own feet in my distraction.

I moved to the backyard, then put the mower away. I came around to the front where Char was watering the flowers. Her eyes were slightly narrowed, bottom lip between her teeth—a sure sign she was thinking about her park. She'd shed her gardening gloves, but at some point had touched her cheek, leaving a streak of dirt.

I stepped to her side, reaching for her face. She startled, the nozzle of the sprayer turning my way along with her body. Cold water drenched my face and trickled down my chest.

I sputtered, the freezing water a shock.

"Sorry! You scared me."

She was half-laughing, and I grabbed the sprayer, wrestling it from her grip and getting drenched in the process. I turned it on her and she shrieked, pivoting a shoulder between the jet of cold water and herself.

Soaked, her shirt clinging to her curves, she lunged at me. I laughed, releasing the hose to her, then spun and ran, the jet blasting me. Grabbing the hose at my feet, I kinked it, stopping the stream. Then I stole the sprayer back and turned it on her again, chasing her into the house where I abandoned it, catching her breathlessly in my arms and kissing her in the entry.

She kicked the front door closed.

IT WAS GETTING HARDER and harder not to confess to Char that I loved her. I wanted to hold her every moment of the day, and I dreaded going home each night. But I could tell she wasn't ready yet. Not for the full power of my feelings for her.

I wished she'd hurry up.

At the same time, I was loving every second we spent together, and especially the soft quiet ones that would never make it into a memoir. Moments like this one, where we were in the kitchen, our hair still damp from our water fight.

Char was in dry shorts that hug her hips, and I was in a pair of my dad's old sweats and a tee. Bodies humming, we were making a stir fry in the kitchen, chopping veggies. I paused to offer Char a sliver of carrot, a snap pea, a sprout.

It sounded weird, but I liked feeding her. And as lame and

corny as it all was, she seemed to love it, her eyes glittering with happiness. Contentment.

With our supper made, we moved to the back patio where the heat from the day was waning, our clothes from earlier drying on the clothesline. The air was filled with the scent of freshly mowed grass, and dark clouds formed in the west. After the heat of a July day, it wasn't odd to have a rainstorm or even hail in the evening, and I was sure that in an hour or two, we'd feel the rush of cold air as the storm gained on us.

We ate slowly, and I savoured the homey feeling of spending the day with Char.

"So, Mrs. Laven says you owe her from cards?" I asked as I finished my supper. My tone was innocent, but inside I was still laughing over the way Char had been taken by my favourite childhood neighbour.

Char placed her palms flat on the tabletop and scowled. "She's a shark."

"Yeah, she cheats."

Char gasped in fake outrage and flicked a piece of broccoli at me. "Why didn't you warn me? I owe her, like, fifty bucks!"

I tried to hold in my mirth, but my shoulders were shaking, and the odd snort and chuckle was breaking loose.

"Just let it out, you little alien pirate," she said on a sigh, leaning back in her chair. Her expression was adorable, resigned but also happy, like she'd enjoyed being sharked by Mrs. Laven.

I let out a loud guffaw from the bottom of my stomach, and soon Char was laughing, too. The moment felt cleansing and light, one of my favourites from the day.

I leaned across the small bistro table and kissed her, sweet and slow.

A perfect day with the woman who'd so long ago captured my heart.

CHAPTER 40

~ *Char* ~

"Today was nice," I told James as we sat at the small patio table in the backyard. I'd allowed myself to explore the edges of my contentment without question, simply testing its edges, bouncing in the weight of it.

He found it hilarious that Mrs. Laven had conned me out of fifty dollars, and any possible sting from his mirth had been happily kissed away. Not that there was any sting. I was actually a bit tickled in the way the older woman had outmaneuvered me so smoothly.

All day, James and I had stayed fairly busy. Being with him from almost dawn until now had felt fluid and natural as well as so incredibly easy. From our work on the park, to chores around the house, to cooking supper. Normally, I'd be tired of someone by now and feeling antsy, but not with him. In fact, I wanted more.

Was this what it was like for couples like Sally and Otto?

"The afternoon was the best," I added, tentatively trusting that maybe today had been real. No wishes. No magic. Just us being us. Friendship with a relationship layered over top.

Building something that could outlast any magic Estelle sprinkled on us.

"Even better than watching the backhoe tear down the warehouse frame?"

I grinned at the memory. Seeing the strength of the machine as it cracked the strong wooden joists, tearing apart a building that had withstood so much time and weather was very cool.

But even as gratifying as it had been... "Still wasn't as nice as this afternoon."

James held my hand across the table. "It's better when we're together."

"It is. And it was fun. Being here for the afternoon." Playing house.

"You turning into a homebody, Char McDonnell?"

The word 'homebody' froze me.

"Is that what you're looking for?" I asked.

His eyes solidly met mine. "I told you what I want."

"Serendipity?"

"Yes." His thumb rubbed lines across my knuckles, grounding me, keeping me here in the moment instead of giving into my fears and freaking out.

"But you also want a homey wife," I said, voice hoarse. I blinked like I had a speck of dirt in my eye, my thoughts jumbled. Maybe my definition of homey was off. Maybe it meant something like what today had represented to me.

Homey could mean having someone at your side for both the fun and the work, similar to what Mrs. Laven had told me. It was having someone easy to love, no matter what the day brought you or where you were. Homey, but with a slice of serendipity.

"I want someone who is happy wherever she is, and no matter what she is doing."

"Nobody is happy all the time," I said absently.

"I know. But some people find fun where they are, and if they aren't enjoying themselves, they change gears. I'm just looking for a woman that I get along with. Someone I can have fun with, no matter what our days bring us."

My hands were shaking. As terrifying as it was, we wanted the same thing. Homey didn't mean a 1950s housewife to either of us.

It meant...us.

As we were.

But I didn't have the lifelong example of a healthy relationship to model after like he did. I didn't know how to resolve a fight or keep things spicy. I wasn't sure I could live up to our current dream or that, over time, I wouldn't fall short.

"I don't know how to do this," I whispered, unable to look at him.

He pulled me to my feet, drawing me to his side of the table and into his lap, where he wrapped his arms around my waist. "It looks like today. It looks like friendship. It looks like love and commitment. Kindness and trust, as well as compassion for each other."

My heart was hiccuping. I wanted all of that so desperately.

He tenderly kissed me, whispering. "That's the secret. The real magic to making it work."

I nodded, sniffing back tears. It felt doable, even though I'd consistently been pulling away and reserving a piece of my heart. Even though my wishes had nudged this relationship ball into rolling on false pretenses.

I wanted things to be messy and real, and without my wishful interference. I might not get that, but I had right now. I had this moment along with many others. And I could hope that enough of them were real, and that James truly knew who I was, and that he would still love me even when he was no longer looking at me through the lacy gauze of a magical spell.

CHAPTER 41

~ *Char* ~

I woke up with one of my many park lists stuck to my cheek. I yanked it off my face and squinted at the morning light blinding me, trying to figure out where I was.

The Backstrohm's kitchen.

Did I have work today?

Was James still in love with me? Or had Estelle finally taken him away?

There was someone in the house. My heart thundered, and I clutched the edge of the table, listening, ready to bolt in the opposite direction of the scuffling sound.

"Char?" a male voice called.

It was James. I sagged into my seat. "In here." I scrubbed my hands down my face and tried to wake up.

I swivelled in my chair, waiting for him to appear in the doorway. Moments later, there he was, fresh-faced and as handsome as ever. My heart lifted as he came over to kiss me.

He still liked me.

I smoothed my shirt, then wiped my fingers under my eyes in case my mascara had travelled in the night.

"Did you sleep here?" He took a chair close to me, swinging

it around to sit backward on it, studying my rumpled appearance. It was way too early in our relationship for him to see me like this, especially when he looked fresh, as though he'd been up for hours and was having the best day of his life.

Then again, we were doing this. We were doing real. And right now I was a very real mess and completely me. I snatched him by the hand and tugged him closer. Catching what I wanted, he leaned in, letting me kiss him again. Slowly, wonderfully. He pulled me to my feet, wrapping me in his arms, angling his jaw to deepen the kiss. Someone once told me there was always space between particles or matter. I didn't believe it. Or at least I didn't want to. I wanted no space between me and this man.

When we broke apart, I asked, "Want coffee?"

James was grinning, and he had sort of a wired, bouncy energy, like he'd already had seven cups.

"What's with you this morning?"

"Remember how I applied for grants so we could buy a play structure for your park?"

"Yeah?" When the lots had been seized by the police, we'd made contingency plans in the hopes that we could still build the park, even though our initial timeline was clearly scrapped. We'd also applied for every long shot and sent in every possible proposal to every possible sponsor we could think of.

A smile broke across James's face. "We got one."

"We did?" I was suddenly wide awake.

He nodded. "And I found a company who can install the equipment in a week."

I squealed and launched myself at him, my socks slipping on the polished tile floor. He caught me, holding me tight. But I was holding him even tighter while trying to jump in his arms.

"I love you! I love you! I love you!" I yelled, my joy

spreading through me, leaving warmth and sunshine every-where there'd ever been clouds.

I stopped jumping, James's breath on my neck sending shivers up and down my spine, suddenly very aware of the muscular man holding me in his arms. The man who was always here, always in my corner. Solid. Reliable.

My boyfriend.

The man I'd wished upon and received. The man I'd then wished away, but was still here. The man whose life had been influenced by my wishes, but didn't seem to care.

And I'd just told him three little words I'd honestly never thought I'd find anyone to say them to.

I slid from his arms, embarrassed, smoothing my shirt down over my waist. "Sorry. I'm just really excited."

He pulled me into his arms again, gently lifting my chin with a finger. His warm eyes met mine, and in them I saw all the caring, affection and tenderness that I'd ever wanted. "I love you, too."

～

I WAS in love with James.

James was in love with me.

It was perfect.

And it had been for almost two weeks.

But Estelle. My fairy godmother. Magic glitter and wishes. Unicorns, rainbows and no clue what was real.

I needed to talk to Estelle. She had to be back from her vacation by now, even though the witchy receptionist at Your Fairy Godmother kept insisting Estelle wouldn't be back for some time. Our calendars were different. Yeah, yeah, yeah. She was lying to me, and I knew it. There had to be a rule about her keeping me from my fairy godmother.

I tightened my hand around James's, listening to the kids play on the newly installed playground and letting the sun's heat seep into my pores along with the feeling of happiness. I needed this to last forever. I needed to know how to make the leap from wishes and magic into reality.

"We're literally watching cement dry," James cracked, and I smiled.

"Yeah. It's great, isn't it?"

"Because it's free?"

James's dad played poker with the owner of a local concrete company, who offered the leftovers he had from various projects. The only stipulation was that there probably wouldn't be enough for what we needed, and that he wouldn't know if he had any extra until the last minute, etcetera, etcetera. Lots of caveats.

But then today he'd shown up with enough to not only create the paths in one go, but to also put in a basketball area. I had a feeling his huge surplus from today's earlier job had actually been intentional, and I was beyond grateful.

And not just for the concrete company, but for James, too. He'd helped me make forms for the concrete last week so they'd be ready whenever the cement was, and now he was helping me guard the wet stuff against mischief. We were hot, grubby, and tired.

Happy.

The sound of the kids playing in the playground was bliss. Success. We'd done that. We'd brought them this happiness. The play equipment had been installed a few days ago, with James and I, along with Josie, Gabby, Lamonte, Tamara, Samantha and Malachi spreading several truckloads of donated pea gravel underneath the new structure. We'd had to rush, so the eager kids, who kept sneaking onto the slide before it was ready, could play safely. I was amazed at how busy the park was already. The word had spread and wow. Had there really always been this many pre-school aged kids in Everstone? It was amazing.

This was what I'd dreamed of. This was the community I'd wanted to help create. Moms talking to each other, kids playing outside and making new friends. It was perfect. Not quite done, but perfect.

And things were coming along at a quick clip even though the park's bank account was empty. Everstone was so close to having something pretty amazing. We just needed to secure landscaping, a fence, and some benches and the park would be complete.

Samantha, despite her reluctance, had decided to own up to her good deeds to Clarisa, and had asked her to take a pitch to her gardening club to help us put in flower beds.

I had faith that the rest of the project would all happen, even though so much still needed to be done. Top soil and sod. Trees. Benches. A fence. Gardens. Basketball net.

Eyes still closed, and with my head resting against the brick wall behind me, I trusted James to keep the kids and sticks out of the fresh cement. I clutched my ice-cold water bottle, lining it up against the blisters that had formed at the base of each finger from all of the gravel raking and manual labour that my little typist hands were definitely not used to.

"Uh, oh," James whispered.

I opened my eyes to see what was wrong. I glanced at the curing cement, then at him for hints. His nose was more tanned than the rest of his face in the most endearing way. Slowly, I followed his gaze. Officer Beddoe was walking toward us, and my stomach dropped. If there had been a shred of evidence on the lots regarding the still-open museum's theft case, we had destroyed it weeks ago.

"Char. James." The officer gave us a nod as we stood,

dusting the dirt from our backsides. "Do you have a moment?" he asked me.

I nodded.

"You'd mentioned you order pottery pieces online."

"Yes. Not lately, but I have."

"Have you ever had a piece arrive broken?"

I shook my head.

"Or one that was a fake when it was listed as a verified artifact?"

I shook my head again, and the officer sighed. "We seem to have a shipping insurance scam that could be based out of Calgary. Do you know anyone who could be selling and shipping pieces from the city?"

"Not that I can think of."

"I was hoping you might have insights."

"Sorry, I don't think I do."

I shot a fake scowl at a kid edging closer to the sidewalk. "I see you, Kendra! Get away from that wet cement with your stick!"

"I want to put my name in it!"

"I know. So do I."

"But you did already," she whined.

True. I also added the date. My prerogative. James had wanted to put our initials inside a heart, but I'd stopped him. I probably shouldn't have. I would have loved to be able to come back later and look at the evidence of our summer romance.

"She owns the park," James told Kendra. "She's allowed."

"Does not!"

I laughed. "I actually do. But once it's done, I'm giving it to the city so it'll be everyone's."

The girl gave me a look of distinct disbelief and returned to the play structure.

"Sorry." I turned my attention back to Officer Beddoe, who looked bemused.

"I see your park is coming along."

"Yeah. We've had some amazing support from sponsors and various grants." I loved the park, but it wasn't what I wanted to talk about with him. "Do you think this scam is related to the museum theft?"

"Could be. The fact that both of them happened here in Calgary is unusual. And no. We have no new leads," he added, cutting me off before I could ask about the museum. He unfolded a piece of paper from his breast pocket and showed it to me. "Have you ordered from this store before?"

"Grandma's China?" I nodded. "Yeah. I thought it was a weird name since they don't sell China. Some nice pieces, though. All original artifacts." Something flickered in my mind. I'd ordered a piece online that I'd seen in the museum gift shop. It had been cheaper online, but who had I ordered it from? And did the timeline fit? "I haven't bought anything since April or May."

"Do you have detailed receipts of the items you bought from Grandma's China, along with the online description?"

"Yeah. I think that should be in an email receipt. Hang on." I pulled out my phone and did a quick search through my email, showing the officer several, my mind still whirling, unable to focus. When had I seen the online pieces in the gift shop? Had it just been one? That could be explained. But more than one? Possibly not.

"Could you forward those to me?" Officer Beddoe handed me a fresh business card.

I was still focused on a receipt and its attached image of the item I'd ordered. A small, somewhat indistinct fragment of a commonly found sandy-coloured urn. Easy to reproduce and switch out for the real one in the gift shop. But had I seen this exact one in the museum before spotting it online? That would be a lot of work for a few bucks, seeing as this wasn't rare, and therefore a relatively inexpensive piece.

"It feels like I might have seen this in the museum's gift shop at one point," I said to the officer. "But I can't be sure."

His gaze sharpened. "Any others?"

I shook my head. "I can't confirm they were the same piece. Sometimes smaller fragments from the same dig site flood the market, and if they're not very distinct, it's difficult to tell them apart unless you see them side by side. It could be that both this seller and the museum bought artifacts from the same sale. Maybe check this piece against the gift shop's inventory?"

The officer nodded. "Will do. Could you come in and look at some evidence? I'd like your opinion, as well as to possibly verify the authenticity and age of a few pieces."

I gasped in pleasure. "Yes!" A thousand times, yes! "When?"

"As soon as you can."

I looked at my grubby clothes. I was dirt from head to foot.

"Tomorrow," Officer Beddoe stated.

I nodded. "Tomorrow."

He walked back to his car, stopping to talk to some kids who asked if he was a real police officer. He assured them he was, showed them his badge and even his handcuffs. The sight warmed my heart.

"Wow. That's cool." James was smiling at me, looking proud.

I nodded. Finally, my weird arcane knowledge might be worth something to someone.

"Char? Do you have more cookies?" Avery, a small boy I met yesterday, came over and leaned against my leg, his body weight pushing into me as he gave me the most adorable look of hope. His messy ringlet-like brown curls brushed his eyebrows, his mouth smeared with melted chocolate chips.

My heart flipped over at his utter cuteness. "You ate the last one an hour ago, Avery." I showed him the empty container that had held close to the end of Sally's cookie stash from the freezer. I'd made a lot of friends thanks to the treats, but I wasn't sure what I'd do when I ran out. Sally and Otto weren't due home again for a few more weeks.

"Bake more," Avery said.

"Sally made these, and she's away, but I'll ask her when she gets home."

"I like chocolate chip cookies."

"I'll let her know. But it's going to be a week or two."

"My mom said she'd buy some. She stole a bite."

"They're pretty good, right?"

"Sally should open a cookie store! I have five cents and I could buy one for my mom so she can have her own." Avery was doing his very convincing puppy dog expression with his big brown eyes. Little did he know I'd already grown immune to it.

Nah, I wasn't immune. I was a total sucker where Avery was concerned.

"I'll pass that idea on to her, okay?"

"I'll bring my money tomorrow!" Avery shouted, racing off to tell his friends.

"Looks like your mom has a new career if she wants it," I told James.

"She looked into opening a bakery once."

"Really? Why didn't she?"

He shrugged. "I was born."

"You ruined her dreams." I sighed dramatically.

"I'm better than a bakery," James pointed out playfully.

"Well..."

He bumped me with an elbow. "Meanie."

I giggled and bumped him back.

Avery returned, feet dragging, head down.

"What's wrong, Avery?"

"I have to go home now. My mom says it's too hot out."

"You know what?" James leaned over as though he had a secret to share with Avery. "Char's trying to buy trees for the park, so there'll be shade for the moms and babies to sit in. Then kids like you will be able to play longer."

Avery's eyes lit up, and I nodded when he looked at me for confirmation.

He took off across the bare dirt to where his mom was sitting in a lawn chair. He was back in seconds.

"Here." He laid a nickel on my palm.

"What's this?"

"For a tree." He watched me expectantly. "Or a cookie."

"That's very sweet. But I think you should keep it." I tried returning it to him.

He shook his head, hands locked behind his back. "I want to play longer."

"Right." I studied the nickel, aware that the truth about the cost of trees might break his heart. That and the fact that I couldn't get one here in the next minute. "I'll, uh. I'll get a tree here as soon as I can, okay?"

"Today?" He rubbed his cheek, leaving a smudge behind. His shorts were dirty and so was he. We all were. Every kid playing here was going to need a bath. I needed to get them some grass.

"I can't today, but soon. Okay? And in the meantime, you hold on to this." I took his hand and placed the warm nickel against his grubby palm. "When I have a tree, then you can pay your share. Or buy a cookie."

"Okay." Avery turned, hollering at everyone at the playground. "I just bought a tree! We're going to have shade here tomorrow! And Sally's bringing cookies. Bring your money tomorrow!"

"Oh, no," I mumbled to James.

He chuckled. "The kid's adorable."

"You bought a tree?" a kid asked Avery.

"And you can't climb it!" Avery yelled back.

"Hey!" I hollered. This was turning dark quickly.

"The park is for everyone," James said, standing up as though worried he'd have to break up a fight. "Nobody owns anything. Not even the trees. We're all working together to make this park so everyone can share it. Understand?"

The kids muttered under their breath and sulked off. Within seconds, their grudge was forgotten as they raced for the slide, while Avery's mother tried to coax him out of the park.

"Not sure that helps the argument for parenthood," James grumbled as he sat beside me again.

I laughed and hugged his arm. "You'll make a great dad."

And for the first time, I could envision being a mom. As long as James was at my side.

CHAPTER 42

~ *Estelle* ~

"**I**s it real?" Char had busted past reception, and somehow figured out how to get into the bullpen. Then she'd found me in my barf-a-rific pink cubicle where I'd been stressing over something I'd done weeks ago at a summer solstice party. How was I supposed to know that the sweet, white-haired daddy flirting with me was married? Now his powerful wife was upset with me. When it came to the rules of my own magical world, why couldn't I get it right? It felt like I kept messing up everywhere.

Without even a hello, Char startled me with her abrupt question, causing me to promptly spill my can of Canada Dry all over my desk.

"Is what real?" I whispered, ducking low so nobody would see me over the edge of my cubicle. Grabbing Char's wrist, I yanked her into a hunched position.

Reaching across the aisle between cubicles, I snagged the pink cardigan Trish left over the back of her chair, even though our offices are always the perfect temperature. Glancing around, and aware of how much trouble Char and I could get in with her being in here, I mopped up the spilled ginger ale.

Technically, Char was a suspended client because of her overdue account. Technically, reception was supposed to tell her I was away if she ever stopped in—which clearly she had. And, technically, I was super glad she'd forced her way in. It was so nice to see her.

"James," Char demanded. "Our love? Is it real?"

I beamed at her and nodded, dropping Trish's ruined sweater in my wastebasket, then toed the whole thing around the edge of my cubicle and into the one beside us.

"But I made a wish. Lots of them."

I shook my head. "Not for him to love you. Not specifically. Just other romantic stuff."

"Like the necklace?"

I thought for a second, mentally going through her long list of wishes. Yes, she'd wished for that necklace made of pottery. Ancient in her world. She hadn't wished for him to buy it for her, though. That was my handiwork.

I smiled and nodded.

"Estelle," she said with a sigh. "That was really expensive."

The pretty little blond heads of other fairies were popping over cubicle walls, and I pulled Char under my desk and yanked my chair closer in hopes of using it to hide us. My legs were long, and Char was bigger than I realized. We'd both bonked our heads on the underside of the desk, and my elbow was in her ribs, her foot jammed into my thigh. Her running shoes needed new laces, as well as a good washing.

"No matter what you wish," I said urgently, "James still has control over his life. This isn't black magic. It's white. It's good. He retains determination."

"What are you two doing under there?" Trish growled, grabbing the chair and shoving it away. It rolled across the pink carpet, banging into a fairy who'd crept out of her cubicle to peek at the unravelling drama.

"Nothing!" I snapped.

"Is that Char?" Trish's eyes narrowed. She gasped indignantly and super dramatically loud. "I'm telling the head fairy." Hands on her hips, she turned and flounced off.

"You'd better go." I pushed Char out from under my desk. "Just remember—no matter what you wish, he always has choice."

CHAPTER 43
~ *Char* ~

When I'd scooted out of Estelle's office over a week ago, still confused about why I suddenly wasn't allowed in there, Estelle had pressed a piece of paper in my hand. It was an update on my account. I'd sort of forgotten about my debt in my desperation to know whether James was in love with me of his own volition.

The latest update stated that the park, even though incomplete, was starting to bring down my tally. Hallelujah.

There were still two weeks to go, and still tens and tens of thousands of dollars to pay back. Who knew if I could do it in time? I was exhausted, and there was a lot that needed to be done. I felt hungover, deflated and drained from the stress of trying to make it all happen with very little money and in such a short period.

Exhaustion overtaking me, I dropped onto a bench near the Calgary Tower, struggling to summon the energy to carry on to work. My extended lunch break, which I'd spent down at the police station helping them identify three final pottery pieces of various sizes and conditions, was over. It was my third time looking at artifacts for them, and it sounded as though they had apprehended someone a few hours ago. Today's pieces, it seemed, had the power to either make or break their case against the suspect in custody. No pressure.

Officer Beddoe was supposed to fill me in on the case and the results of it all before I left, but he'd been called away to an emergency, leaving me wondering who they'd arrested.

My own personal hunch was that the thefts were an inside job. But who was behind it all? Kendrick in the gift shop? Greg, the tour guide who also worked in the Tinkertorium sometimes? Oscar the security guard who always called in sick? Glenda in admissions? Richard? Who was it?

Traffic and pedestrians streamed around me, the melting heat from the day trapped between the buildings.

My thoughts drifted away from the thefts, and a smile tilted my lips upward. James made his own choices. He was truly in love with me somewhere under the magic spell. He was choosing to be with me.

I tipped my head back, staring up at the dizzying tower above. Things were changing in my life and who knew where I'd be in a year.

Baseball had wrapped up—our team hadn't won leisure league. Sally and Otto would be home from their trip soon, and I needed to find a new place to live. My job was officially boring me, but I didn't know what else to do. Mrs. Laven had been admitted into a memory care facility and was no longer around to shark me on Friday nights. Tamara was happily back home with Felipe, surrounded by her parents, Kade and his family. Happy and in love.

I was alone.

But I wasn't. Not completely. James loved me.

Had my life changed so much over the recent weeks because of my wishes, or because the universe was clearing everything out in order to make room for goodness? Isn't that what Sally had suggested?

My phone rang, and I looked at caller ID as well as the time. I needed to get to the office. I was already late getting back, and surely Joan would hear about it. But it was my mom's number, and she never called me.

Wait. There was also a missed call from Officer Beddoe.

I stood, my heart beating hard. I answered, alert to incoming disaster, because that was what my mind did when seeing a call from both the police and my mom within a minute or two of each other. Even though I knew it was likely just Officer Beddoe getting back to me, and my mom needing to brag about something.

"Hello?"

"You were on the news!" she chirped.

"I was?" I frowned, wondering if I'd been caught in the background of some local footage.

"Yes! It was a short piece. But they said you helped solve the museum thefts."

"Sorry. What?" I stopped walking, plugging one ear. The case had been solved? It was already on the news? I looked back toward the police station, now blocks away, where I'd been looking at the case's linchpin pieces only twenty minutes ago.

"You identified fakes! I didn't know you were an ancient history buff." My mom was using the proud tone she usually used when talking about Brynnie, and I felt the urge to shrink, to deflect the attention.

"Oh, I'm not really," I mumbled. "I just kind of lucked out by being in the right place."

"I have to go," my mom chirped merrily. "We're about to get on a cruise ship with Brynnie here in the Mediterranean, along with her new fiancé. Oh, did I tell you she's engaged? He's amazing. He coordinates million-dollar contracts all over the world! Can you imagine? She's getting married in two months. There's so much to do!"

She hung up before I could reply. Brynnie was engaged? Getting married in two months? Taking Mediterranean vacations? Why wasn't that my life?

I thought of Greece. The trip I'd once been saving up for. Truthfully, I wasn't even sure the trip was something my dad wanted. He'd never left Canada and didn't even have a passport. Would he want to go? Or was the trip idea my own personal Band-Aid, meant to make me feel like my dad and I were exciting, that we'd have something to throw in my mom's face? Because if I was honest with myself, my dad didn't really know that much about ancient civilizations, and I don't think he had a desire to learn more than he'd enjoyed on TV from the comfort of his easy chair.

The Greece trip had always been about me. Not him. Not us.

My phone rang again, and I nearly silenced it, fearing it was my mom calling me back. But it was Officer Beddoe.

"Char. We got him. I wanted to be the first to tell you—before the news piece went live."

I didn't have the heart to inform him I'd already heard about it. I put a little lift in my voice as I answered, "That's great! Who was it?"

"Greg coordinated the thefts."

I swore under my breath. How had I ever crushed on that worthless man?

"He tried to frame me?" He'd known I'd bought the warehouse and had immediately moved his stolen goods into it? Some friend he was. My heart raged and adrenaline flowed through my quads.

Officer Beddoe explained how Greg had been swapping out pieces in the museum for months. He was also behind the online scam, putting shipping insurance on the artifacts he'd accidentally broken, before sending them all off on the same day to make it look like something had happened in the post office. He then blamed Canada Post for breaking the shipped pieces and claimed the insurance.

As for my warehouse, he'd only planned to leave the stolen goods in there overnight before meeting up with a dealer. Unfortunately, due to the timing of the siding removal, the items had been immediately found.

"The timing is crazy!" I said, thinking about the string of events that had happened in order for him to get caught. How had it all stacked up so neatly? So many things had needed to happen. From me spotting the fakes, to Greg hearing about my warehouse and putting the items in there after James and I had gone through, to me being at the museum to talk to Richard on the right night about the fakes, and to the most coincidental— the siding people finding the cases of pottery... it was all so incredibly unbelievable.

"Kismet," the officer said. "Someone up above must have been looking out for the museum."

God?

Or had it been Estelle?

I smiled, my gut telling me she'd had something to do with it all. I had my own fairy godmother, and I had a feeling she'd just helped me catch a man who'd been ruining one of my happiest places. I grinned up at the Calgary Tower, feeling incredibly lucky and incredibly blessed to have Estelle as my fairy godmother.

CHAPTER 44

~ *James* ~

Char looked happy, lighter than she had in weeks, but also exhausted. I wanted to sweep her away for a weekend camping trip to the Lower Kananaskis Lake with me. I wanted to enjoy the last heated days of summer in the mountains before the evenings got frosty, but she couldn't. She was ramping up for the final push to finish her park.

But she needed a break before a break took her.

"Can you push everything back a week? Come out and play with me," I begged. I'd been supportive since the park's inception. Surely she could weasel out of one or two days of park work. Weren't her friends still helping her? They could take over for a short stint.

This week Char had seemed to finally let go of her fears around us, and I wanted to celebrate. I wanted to revel in every moment. I wanted to stand on top of a mountain and tell the world that she was mine, mine, mine. That I'd found the woman I was going to spend the rest of my life with.

Char rubbed her forehead, and it was clear I was adding to her stress. Why was I pushing her? She'd come and found me in my basement suite, where I'd been studying for tonight's cartography exam. She'd been happy and buoyed about the news from the museum, and I was ruining it.

And yet I couldn't seem to stop myself. I was like the fat kid in that Willy Wonka book. I was greedy for more, unable to stop. But instead of wanting chocolate and sweets, I wanted Char.

"I'm sorry. It won't be forever." She leaned against me on my black leather couch, her eyes pleading. "It's just right now I have a lot of deadlines and reports and receipts to send into sponsors and the various grants that have supported the park. There's already a playground, and it's been amazing, but the kids are getting filthy because there's no top soil or sod. I promised the kids trees and grass and basketball nets. I'm so close, James. I'm sorry. It's just two more weeks."

"I know." I gave her a hopeful look, wiggling her leg. "Maybe you could quit your job tonight and get a new one? One with better hours?"

She gave me a light snort. "Yeah, those fall out of the sky. I wish!" She sighed, her body softening as though visualizing the perfect job.

"One where you can nerd out on old things."

"It would be incredible to work around artifacts all day, but I don't have a degree." She looked so wistful, I wanted to fulfill that dream for her. Right now. Forget cartography. I had a new mission: find her an amazing job.

She smiled and added, "What if I found a job that included some travel? I could go places for free!"

"Or we could save up and go to Mexico for Christmas. Just you and me."

"What?" Her unfocused gaze snapped to me. "A trip? For us?"

Okay, so a couple's Christmas destination vacation might be

moving a bit too fast. But I'd seen the hopeful spark in her eyes. She wanted it.

"Well, I mean..." I acted casual, my heart thrumming like I was about to ask her to marry me. "If you can't get away for some camping, then maybe Mexico at Christmas? You should be free by then, right?"

I gave her my best smile, and she laughed, her body pressed against my side. "Sure. You buying?"

"Nah. You'll be rolling in the dough by then."

She was smiling for real now, her spirit lifted, the stress of her day seemingly shed.

"You really do love me, don't you?" She rocked her shoulder into mine, giving me a secret smile like she couldn't quite believe it was true. She reached over and mussed up my hair. I grabbed her hands and tipped her backward onto the cushions, my body pressed over hers. She giggled. "If I'm around all the time, you're going to get so tired of me."

"Hm." I kissed her once on the lips. "I think we need to experiment with that." I trailed my lips down her neck. "Explore the limits." Another kiss, this one along her collarbone. "See where the boundaries are." My lips met hers again, and I sunk into the haven of enjoying the last woman I'd ever kiss. She was the one my heart had been waiting for. I was done searching. I'd found her.

She sighed against me, and I shifted so I was wedged between her and the couch's back, taking my weight off her.

"You have everything," she said, her voice sad with longing.

I stopped my kissing and looked at her. "I do?"

"You have all these fun new jobs that work around your classes."

It was true that I'd been trying different ones lately, picking up short-term contracts like I was testing pages from Char's book. It was fun, but it wasn't a long-term thing. I wanted adventure in my personal life, not just in my work. I wanted to explore the city as well as the world with Char. That was what I craved the most.

"Savings and money," she continued. "Spontaneous trips to Corsica and beyond."

"You're going to get this park finished, Char. And then all the amazing goodness you've been putting into the world is going to flood back to you. I bet you and your dad will be travelling through Greece before you know it."

She shook her head, her forehead crinkling. I brushed a few strands of her hair from her cheek.

"Why not?"

"I realized the trip was about me. If I want to be closer to my dad, we don't need an expensive excursion that he probably wouldn't enjoy. I should get in a car and go down there and visit him. It's not even that far. We could sit around and play cards or something." She smiled playfully. "I think I finally have gin rummy figured out."

"You sure? Mrs. Laven might have misled you with the rules."

"I'm sure she did—to her own benefit, of course."

"Of course." I gently trailed the back of my index finger down the round of her cheek. "Tell me how else I have it made?" I was curious if she'd mention us.

"You have an apartment and a car." Her voice grew quiet. "And a family who loves you."

"In case you didn't notice, my mom has adopted you. You're a Backstrohm for life, whether you like it or not." She'd belonged since the day she'd walked through the front door with the hole in her sleeve. Her status wasn't quite as permanent or official as I'd like, but I'd get her there. I'd slide a ring onto her finger and take the easiest vows of my life. Love. Cherish. Hold.

Done, done, and done.

Char blushed, looking shy, but also unafraid of the fact that she was one of us now, a part of our clan.

"You forget something," I murmured, my attention drawn back to her lips. She was wearing a coconut lip balm today, and it made kissing her even more delicious.

"Hm?"

"The most important thing."

"What's that, my little pirate?" She gave me a tentative, teasing smile, like she knew what I was going to say.

"I have a girlfriend who finally," I tipped my head back and added an extra 'finally' for drama, "loves me back."

She rolled the corner of her bottom lip between her lips on a laugh, and said, "Yeah. You've got that, too."

CHAPTER 45

~ *Estelle* ~

Char was back to wishing! I ran to the head fairy's office at report time, just about knocking over Trish who was on her way out—no regrets—and stopped breathlessly on the worn spot of carpet in front of Gram-Gram's rosewood desk.

"She's below thresholds!" I almost bellowed in my excitement. "Her new wishes? Can I grant them?" So many good ones had come in. Big, juicy ones like a new job, travel and vacations... Oh, they were so wonderful! They had the power to change her life, and I couldn't wait to grant them all.

I wouldn't mess up these ones. Not like I had with her landlord, when she'd wished she'd no longer have to deal with him. I'd dealt with Randy, but had accidentally made Char homeless.

I was better at this now. I could create a positive impact without nasty side effects.

Gram-Gram lifted her new reading glasses, delicate pink half-moons, onto her nose. "What's this?"

She was toying with me. She knew who I meant.

"Char McDonnell, ma'am." I was fidgeting, unable to stay still.

With Char back in the running for making wishes this quarter, I could finally blast past Trish, and all the extra wishes she'd been able to grant while I'd had to wait this out. I could take the prize for the most wishing income for the quarter. I could taste it. Smell it. Feel that victory.

"We need to discuss what you did to Trish's sweater."

Dang it.

What were my options here? Deny it? No. Gram-Gram had a good ear for lies. Deflect?

No. I was in the wrong. Again.

"I'll apologize."

"Just wash the sweater."

"She already took care of it." Trish had created a huge show out of her sweater having been used as a mop. It was like nobody hugged her enough, and she needed to compensate by being a drama queen about stupid stuff.

She'd made such a loud production out of finding it in the trash, rinsing it out in the bathroom sink, complaining about it losing its shape, then taking it home and bringing it back all pristine and perfectly pressed the next day. Who ironed a sweater? Seriously.

The cardigan was totally fine, of course, because it had only been ginger ale. She'd announced to anyone who would listen that she was putting it over her chair, and that the haters better not touch it ever again.

So, there was that.

"Figure it out," Gram-Gram said, her tone suggesting she was already tired of this conversation and the immature battle between Trish and myself. "As for Char, you are free to initiate the granting of some of her *smaller* wishes. But keep her under the amount-owing threshold."

Internally, I fist pumped in triumph and skipped to the

door in my cherry red high heels. I knew these were lucky shoes the minute I'd spotted them.

"Estelle?"

I turned from the door. "Yes?"

"You have developed a very good ear for hearing wishes." Her eyes narrowed slightly, and I gulped. She knew about the tech I'd commissioned to hear more wishes than the old, hard-of-hearing wishing machine did. I braced myself for the backlash.

But she merely shooed me away with a hand, saying, "For heaven's sake, don't grant her every little wish. Dial it back this time."

CHAPTER 46
~ *Char* ~

Two days. I had just two days before my deadline to pay back everything I owed to Estelle. I was possibly on track, but it was impossible to know since karma math wasn't like regular addition. It compounded. It dipped and flowed.

But I had a feeling I might get my account with Your Fairy Godmother to zero by Thursday's deadline. Or at least close enough that I wouldn't be hauled into a magical court or whatever Estelle had called it.

Or so I hoped. I'd studiously not thought about it for two whole months, focusing instead on doing what I could.

And now it was all coming together like the final scenes of a book.

"The biggest trees go over there, near the playground. The area's marked out." I directed the idling tree planter, then turned to the man with the flatbed loaded with benches.

Samantha's stepmom's gardening club had donated trees from one of their tea fundraisers, which was incredible because who knew trees over a foot tall were so expensive? At the moment, the club was standing in their gardening couture next to their luxury cars, which were stuffed with potted flowers, and giving the dirt lot looks of apprehension.

Josie and her spreadsheets were supposed to be here, directing everyone. Where was she?

I gave the bench man directions, then stood back. So much was going on. Too much for one day. Top soil had been delivered and raked out, my hands aching with blisters. Anywhere someone went, they trailed black dirt with them. The paths and basketball court were already coated with the stuff. But, I reminded myself, trees were going in along with benches. Flower beds next. The fence was partway finished. Sod was tomorrow.

Then it would be done. Complete.

The biggest issue was keeping the kids out of the park while the big machines worked.

Although it was a Tuesday, so at least many of them were at daycare or school. Still, the number of parents and small kids that had come by the park today was astounding. It still surprised me how many children were tucked away in my old, tiny neighbourhood. I supposed it made sense, though. The families were young, just starting out. Where else could you afford in the city, other than Everstone?

"How's it going?" Tamara asked, sliding on a pair of brand-new work gloves. I gave her a giant hug, happy to see her. She'd taken most of the day off from her new job as an educational assistant in order to be here.

"It's coming together. Did Kade come?"

"He couldn't get off work. He says hi."

"Hi back."

Tamara surveyed the lots. "I guess in two days we find out if this all worked."

"Cross your fingers for me."

"Where's James?" she asked, gazing around the park.

"Also at work." I felt a flicker of fear due to his absence, my mind leaping to the erroneous, persistent assumption that Estelle's magic had finally worn off on him and he was in the process of leaving me. My old wishes no longer mattered where he and his love were concerned. It was real, and he was really mine and here to stay. But it was so hard to retrain my mind to remember that, to fully trust this blissful reality. I was still learning to love with all of my heart, and with nothing held back, and some days were easier than others.

"He's at the new one already?"

"No, this is an event at the Saddledome. He's doing security. He starts the new one tomorrow." He'd landed a very cool job with a mapping company. "I think he'll enjoy it. He said he wasn't sure about sitting at a desk, but it sounds like once he's been there a few months, and knows the map software a bit better, he can go out in the field for some projects. Honestly, it sounds perfect for him." The right blend of homey routine and adventure.

Personally, this week, I was avoiding work to spend more time here at the lot or working on last-minute details or paperwork. It was annoying Joan, who'd lined me up for a few different temp jobs this week in hopes of dazzling me with variety. I think she could tell my heart wasn't in it any longer.

The man installing the benches had made us a chess table, even though we hadn't ordered it due to a lack of funds. He sent us to check it out, letting us climb onto the back of his flatbed truck.

"How did he know we wanted one of these?" Tamara asked, running a hand over the table's surface. It was beautiful. The top was alternately covered with black-and-white, one-inch by one-inch tiles. It was similar to the table in her plans, only more intricate.

"The park can't afford this," I said, well aware that my latest pay cheque would be covering the last few costs that donations and grants hadn't covered.

"He's donating it."

I met Tamara's brown eyes, and she pulled me into a warm hug as we sniffed back tears of gratitude. She rubbed my back, knowing I was completely overcome by the man's generosity.

She released me so we could admire the table again. "This is exactly what I had in mind." Tamara dragged a finger over the etched design that ran along the table's wide metal edging. "Even better with this detail." She stopped and bent over, peering at the artwork. "Are those..."

Tamara straightened, and we looked at each other. We bent over it again. The table maker had added fairies. They were among cute, squat mushrooms and tiny doors set into tree trunks all along the edge of the table.

"Estelle?" I whispered.

We both looked up as though expecting to see her waiting off to the side in her leather pants and bright red hair. She was nowhere to be found. But from our new vantage point on the truck, the difference in the old lots was astounding.

"Wow," I breathed.

No more weeds. No warehouse. No garbage. No sagging chain-link.

I looked at the street and beyond. Was it my imagination, or was there less garbage in the streets than before? Had the windows been washed on the empty brick buildings? Even the one James and I cracked had been fixed.

I glanced back at the park. Community pride?

Was it already starting to happen in Everstone?

The park looked great. And this was such a perfect, central spot for it. And sure, there was a heck of a lot of topsoil being tracked around, but there were several leafed out trees already in place, a playground, a half-basketball court, a doggy area, and even concrete paths that wound through it all. Soon there would be fencing, flowers, and grass. There'd be places to sit as well as a chessboard.

It was going to be perfect. A small community neighbourhood park.

We might even finish a full day ahead of schedule.

My eyes dampened as I realized that the lots were starting to look exactly like Tamara's drawing.

We'd done it.

I hugged Tamara tightly, overcome again by everyone's generosity.

"I want to move back," I said.

She swayed me from side to side, her arms clamped around me. "I knew you could do it!"

"Did not."

"Didn't I tell you you're a small-town girl at heart?"

"I still don't see that."

She released me, pointing to my chest. "The smalltown spirit is right here. Caring, kindness, community and," she paused dramatically, her tone turning triumphantly teasing, "a big ol' squishy heart!"

ON WEDNESDAY MORNING, the sod had arrived an hour early. I was alone. And I had about a million rolls of heavy grass to lay out over a half-acre, and tomorrow was my repayment deadline over at Your Fairy Godmother. I needed to get a move on, and trust that volunteers had heard my online call-out and would appear. If not, at least the GAL PALs would be coming by later on.

Next week, my life was going to look totally different. And not just because I'd have the park off my hands. Sally and Otto had returned home. I had a lead on an apartment. Joan was miffed at me for taking another day off to work on the park, and we both knew it was time for me to find something else. James was starting his new job today, and the training was taking him to Edmonton, meaning he was gone from summer's early dawn to summer's late dusk.

By next week, would I be penniless, jobless and homeless?

Or would I somehow have it all?

Sighing, I pushed my work gloves deeper onto my hands and inhaled the city and the scent of rolled up grass on the pallets beside me. I heaved a piece of turf off the top of a nearby pallet. It was heavier than I'd expected, and I hugged it to my body, not caring if the front of my t-shirt was a wall of dirt by the end of the day. I dropped the sod at the corner and walked back for more. Then, when I had a small pile, I got down on my hands and knees and began rolling out the pieces, staggering the rows, my mind blissfully blank as I got into the physical routine.

No thinking about James and how we were indeed better when we were together. No thinking about how hard these past two months had been with my whole being poured into the park.

I was almost there. Almost done.

Next week, it was all me. All James.

I could barely wait.

~

I WORKED STEADILY ALL DAY, volunteers coming and going to help me lay out the sod, the sounds of happy kids on the playground filling the air with happiness. Bliss. I loved it. There was something so wonderful about hearing children play, laugh, and shriek.

Behind me, the expanse of bright green grass grew, eating up the massive empty stretch of dirt.

By six, I was utterly exhausted, the grass almost finished. Someone had shown up with two pizzas and a case of cold water. As we ate, more people appeared. Then a few more. As people got off work, they put on their grubbies and came to help. Several of them helped while their kids played in the playground and I felt pride for creating a green space in the middle of the city for people to gather. But most of all, this was Everstone's park, and always would be. And creating something like this, I felt like I could do anything.

I sat in the shade, sucking back water, my limbs heavy with exhaustion, watching the community of Everstone interact with each other. Gabby and Josie had come to sit beside me, having come straight from work to lay sod with me, Samantha, and Tamara.

Two men introduced themselves, then gestured toward the playground where young women were sitting on a bench, watching their kids play. I smiled and caught Tamara's look. For a moment, a current of understanding passed between us. This was it, right here. Community. People getting to know their neighbours. If you knew them, you cared. And if you cared, the entire world opened up to kindness.

Tamara leaned against me, resting her head on my shoulder. "You've done a good thing."

"We all have."

I felt a stab of sorrow just under my ribcage that James wasn't here to see it all come together. He'd worked so hard on the park, and he deserved the satisfaction of seeing it completed. All day I'd expected to see him and his strong shoulders in that tight tee of his coming to help out.

All day I'd been disappointed.

Even though I knew today was the first day at his new job,

and he had a ten-hour safety training session up in Edmonton, which was a three-hour drive, each way.

Clearly, he wasn't going to magically show up, but it hadn't kept me from watching for him.

"I've been doing that payback chant thing while I've been working," Tamara said, looking out over our progress. "You know, to send all of today's good deeds toward your debt with Estelle."

"Aw. Thank you."

"I don't think that would work," Josie said sagely.

"Yeah, but there's no harm in it," Tamara protested.

"What happened to your arm?" I pointed at the dirt-stained bandage peeking out from Josie's long-sleeve shirt cuff. I'd been meaning to ask since she'd shown up earlier.

"Oh?" She tugged the sleeve up, revealing a white bandage, then shoved it back down. "Burned myself."

"It looks nasty!" The edge of the bandage had been stained green. "You should get that looked at. It might be infected."

Josie's cheeks turned pink. "No, no. That's an herbal remedy from the medicine man."

"Medicine man?"

"I work with him."

"Doing inventory?" This was seriously not adding up. What was she and her LARPing friends up to in the mountainous woods, anyway? Things were getting weird.

She looked me dead in the eye. "Yes, inventory."

I relented, something still feeling off about her wound. "Well, I hope it heals okay."

"I'm sure it will."

Samantha was nearby, arguing with someone on the phone, waving a hand around, looking like her usual million bucks in her poshly patched overalls. Gabby was near the street, joking with Lamonte and giving his dark arm a touch, push or tug whenever she had half an excuse. She was crushing hard. Obviously, living with the man hadn't burst her bubble of infatuation.

"I think we're going to get this done tonight," Tamara said.

Done.

The word felt like a mirage after days spent in the gruelling heat of a desert.

A man was walking toward us, who reminded me of our old landlord, Randy. Except this guy didn't have a bad comb-over and seemed slimmer. He was also carrying a shoebox.

"Ladies," he said, stopping in front of us.

"Randy?" It was actually him.

"This is nice. A park so close by." He gave me a sly look. "Now I can raise my rents." My jaw dropped, and he laughed. "Just kidding."

I didn't think so.

"Randy, get out of here," Gabby said, rejoining us. In the distance, I could see Lamonte getting into his Jeep.

"This came for Samantha. I thought I saw her when I drove by earlier."

"You can leave it with us," Tamara said, snatching the box.

We watched Randy move across the park, sliding an arm around the waist of a woman about his age, giving her a peck on the cheek.

We all screeched, falling over each other as we giggled and stole extra peeks at our old landlord, and what apparently was the new love of his life.

"Well, good for him," Samantha said, coming back to our circle. She didn't have a speck of dirt on her.

"How have you been here for two hours and you're still clean?" Gabby complained, scrubbing her hands down the front of her dirty jeans, like it would make her as clean and tidy as Samantha. "Haven't you been helping?"

Samantha glowered. "Um, *yeah*. I've been doing tons."

"Well?" demanded Josie.

"All of this grass is going to die if it doesn't get watered."

I felt my jaw loosen. Oh, no.

"But it'll be the city's by then," Tamara said. She patted the shoebox. "Also, Randy left this for you."

Samantha's eyes lit up. "I thought these were lost in the mail! I must have used our old address." She ripped open the box, pulling out a pair of old-fashioned, stitched leather shoes.

"Are those used?" Gabby asked, mouth creased into a look of disgust. "That's disgusting. Think of all the foot germies."

"They're gorgeous," Samantha said, trying one on. "Vintage." She pointed a toe, showing off the shoe. They were nice, even if odd and old. She took the shoe off again and put it back in the box. "You have to water in the sod or it'll be dead in two days. Less if it's hot."

"It'll die that fast?" I asked. That couldn't be right. I scanned the two lots. How could we even water this much grass? And why hadn't I thought about that? I'd been so focused on getting this done and handed over that I hadn't considered anything beyond the time I'd be freeing up to spend with James.

I did some mental calculations. Tomorrow was Thursday, which was my deadline with Estelle, and I also had an appointment to turn the park over to the city.

A park with already dying grass.

The kids would be back to playing in dirt within a year. "Ugh. What do we do? How do we water all of this?"

Samantha waved her phone. "Taken care of. Forget Estelle or whoever. I'm your real fairy godmother." She gave a flirty little twist of her torso and winked at me over her shoulder while blowing a kiss. "The city's coming by with a watering truck in forty minutes as an act of good faith, since the property isn't actually theirs yet. So, I suggest you get the rest of this sod in place before he turns it into a mud pit. Also, he's off shift at eight-thirty, and won't water a second past then."

~

As the city's truck sprayed water over the park in the waning sun, I resisted the strong temptation to run through the spray to clean myself off.

The volunteers and families with children were starting to trickle home as the sun lowered in the sky, filled with tired smiles and goodbyes.

It had been nice spending the evening with my friends again. I sagged onto one of the new benches, admiring the park. My body ached, and I wondered if I'd even be able to drag myself out of bed tomorrow morning.

From my back pocket, my phone rang, and I stretched a protesting arm to retrieve it.

It was Joan. Surely to nag me into working tomorrow even though I'd booked it off?

"Hello?"

"Char? Something unusual has come in, and I think you'd be perfect for it. Can I put your name forward?"

My heart sank. When it came to temping, I felt so done. *C'est fini*, as the Québécois would say.

"I know, you're looking for change," Joan said hurriedly when I remained quiet. "And this isn't temping."

That made no sense. She ran a temp agency.

"Great benefits and pay. It also follows your interests. It's an international company who's opening a hub here. They saw you on the news and tracked you down to my agency somehow. They've requested an interview."

"They saw me on the news?" I pushed myself more upright,

every muscle in my body protesting. The only time I'd ever been on the news was when the police said I'd helped identify genuine artifacts in the museum's pottery heist.

"Yes, and they were impressed. They need someone who knows about pottery artifacts or collectables or some-such, and is willing to travel."

"But..." I began, feeling the pull of interest. There was a job like that opening up here? In Calgary? What were the chances? "Okay, you have to tell me every detail." Working with Joan for as long as I had, I knew she had some super serious skills when it came to upselling a job and making it sound exotic and niche. I worried this was truly a retail position in disguise.

"I don't have them yet. Can I set up an interview for you for tomorrow?"

"Uh. Sure?" What was the harm?

"I'll arrange it all. Be in touch."

She ended the call, and my mind whirled with questions.

"Hey," Samantha said, coming over to join me, dusting dirt off her butt. "This looks really good. Like a real park."

"It does, doesn't it?"

"It's missing something, though."

I frowned, my mood darkening. "I don't want to add anything more to this project. I'm done. I'm exhausted. I'm ready to sign it over to the city. Oh, crap." I pulled out my phone and texted Joan, asking for her to request a Friday interview instead. Tomorrow was booked up with lawyers, the land office, the city, and lots of paperwork. Okay, so I'd probably just be signing one or two documents to turn the park over to the city. But it felt like it should be a full day affair. Especially if I was too stiff and sore to move.

Samantha laughed and gave me a playful shove. "No. This." She held up a shiny new loonie.

"What are you talking about?" For a second I thought she

was going to stick the one-dollar coin in the sidewalk like some Canadian hockey arenas did at centre ice for good luck. But the park's sidewalks were already set, meaning she couldn't press it into the surface. Anyway, somebody would likely chip the concrete to dig out the loonie, leaving a hole in our pretty new sidewalks.

"Bury a coin to bring good luck," Samantha said, traipsing over to the shade of a new tree. Earlier, she'd given the playground kids the box from her new shoes for some game they were playing. Since then, she'd been carting them around by their laces. Now she tied them together and slung them from a branch above her before bending to scoop a hole in the dirt by the tree trunk and planting the coin.

Beside me, the man working the water truck's sprayer stopped to watch. "Did she just plant a coin?"

"Yes."

"Yee like leprechauns?" he called out to Samantha as she straightened from her work. His accent was a thick Irish one, and Samantha bounded to his side, her new shoes completely forgotten.

"Why?" she asked, eyes sparkling with mischief and intrigue.

"Don't forget your shoes," I muttered, but her focus was on the man beside me.

"You just buried a coin, dinnya?"

"It'll bring the park luck." Samantha squared her shoulders and flicked her recently dyed blue streak behind her ear.

"It'll also summon some wee leprechauns on St. Patrick's Day."

"They're not real." She narrowed her eyes, glancing at me for confirmation. What did I know about leprechauns? And was she finally starting to believe in the magical world? I'd have to remember to ask her later.

"I don't make up the legends," the man claimed, hands out in surrender.

"Well, whatever. St. Patrick's Day isn't for another eight months. I'm hardly worried about it."

"Like I said, I don't make up the legends," the man repeated like a warning.

I eyed the tree where Samantha had buried the coin. She might not yet believe in the magical world, but I knew I believed in the possibility of leprechauns.

BODY ACHING, I cuddled under one of Sally's fluffy blankets in front of the TV after my long day of finishing the sod. The park was done. The fencing was in. The flowers looked pretty. The grass was watered.

I was done. I still couldn't believe it. It felt surreal.

Tomorrow, I'd take care of transferring the land to the city. On Friday, I had a job interview. And next week, thanks to my bank account's overdraft, I could move into a newly created, sunny, above-the-garage suite over at the edge of Kensington, not that far from James, the downtown, or Sally and Otto's.

Otto was clicking through the channels, waiting for the late-night news to come on. Us watching together had become a nightly habit with him in his favourite armchair and me on the couch. I was going to miss this. Hanging out with James's dad seemed to fill a void I hadn't even realized existed.

There was something grounding about living here with Sally and Otto and becoming part of their routines. Maybe because there were enough unexpected moments where they took off on road trips, or suddenly knocked out a wall to join two rooms together like they'd done as soon as they'd got back.

Otto increased the volume on the TV as the news started. "There was a teaser about your park."

"Really?" I leaned forward, kicking the fuzzy cocoon off me, as if I'd be able to hear better without it. I pressed my palm against my hot cheeks, barely breathing.

I'd given the local television crew a soundbite when they'd popped by, but they'd made it sound like it wouldn't air as there was some bigger international news blowing up at the moment.

The front door opened, and James called out a hello.

I popped up; the TV forgotten.

"In here," Otto said.

"Got you this." James passed me a strawberry milkshake from Peter's after kissing me hello, one arm squeezed tight around my waist like he'd missed me.

I gasped in delight, taking the chilly cup in hand. "My love language!"

"Your love language," he confirmed, leaning in to give me a more heated, lingering kiss that made me want to drag him away for more privacy.

"Also my love language," I murmured, like a contented cat who'd found the perfect sunbeam.

"Keep it down!" Otto grumbled, cranking the volume.

"Come watch," I said, pulling James over to the couch. "There's a bit about the park!"

The clip finally played, and Otto hollered to Sally, "The kids' park is on!"

The kids. I was part of 'the kids,' and it felt great.

I leaned into James, who was working his way through his chocolate shake. The soundbite was good. I looked exhausted and grubby from laying the sod. But even I could tell how happy and proud I was.

Sally beamed at me from the doorway. "I'm going to bake you some celebratory cookies. Confetti chip with macadamia nuts." She reached into the room, giving my shoulder an affectionate squeeze, her eyes damp with pride.

"Well done," Otto said, looking at me like I'd impressed him. "Really impressive."

"Thanks. I didn't do it alone. James helped a lot."

"I know. But we also know how hard you worked."

"Yeah." I felt my eyes well from the recognition. From the feeling of being part of their circle, of feeling like family. Someone who they wanted to share the triumphs with, the people who'd backed me and housed me when I'd needed it the most.

I tipped my head back, sniffing discretely as Otto's attention went back to the television. James wrapped an arm around my shoulders, drawing me in, placing a tender kiss on the crown of my head.

It didn't really matter what next week brought. I could be broke, homeless, and jobless, and I wasn't scared. Because now I had it all. All that mattered.

Family.

Coziness.

Home.

CHAPTER 47
~ *Char* ~

Thursday morning, I transferred the park to the city, feeling relieved, but also like I was handing my newborn baby over to a babysitter for the first time.

Unexpectedly, I'd left the lawyer's office with a cheque. The city had changed the zoning of my two lots from Industrial to Special Purpose, and had adjusted my already-paid property taxes accordingly. In other words, I'd overpaid and now had enough for the deposit on the little garage apartment without going into overdraft. Samantha, my sweet, moneyed friend, would be so proud.

I kissed the cheque while I walked, feeling unbelievably lucky.

Today I was free at last. I didn't have to work. I was no longer on dog-walking duty as I'd quit a few weeks back due to a lack of time, and I had nothing to do for the park other than send off a few reports and thank-you notes to sponsors.

Well, except for one more tiny thing, and, no, it wasn't cash the cheque—I'd already done that with my banking app before leaving the lawyer's office.

It was time to go see Estelle over at Your Fairy Godmother to find out if the park had brought my account down to zero.

I walked over to 10th and 10th, enjoying the mid-August sunshine and the feeling of having my life back.

Or so I hoped.

I stood in front of what I knew to be 1010B, muttering the secret password for what might be the last time. The wooden door appeared and popped open a crack.

I filed inside, navigating the plants until I was with the witch at reception.

"Oh, you again," she grumbled.

"Do I need to sprint past you again today, or are you going to let me in to see Estelle?"

She cracked a surprising smile, and tapped around on her keyboard. Moments later, the hidden door opened behind her and Estelle came out, looking bubbly in her black leather pants and bright red hair.

She led me through the pink bullpen and into Paxi's old office, where we'd have more privacy than in her cubicle. As we moved, a fairy with white hair and pink reading glasses watched us from an office with a gold door that matched the one behind the witch's desk. She gave Estelle a serious nod.

"Who's she?" I asked, as Estelle closed Paxi's door.

"The head fairy."

"Cool. I came to tell you the park's done." I flopped into a chair, noting that the office seemed cleaner than it had been during other visits. And was that a new pink computer monitor on the desk? The first time I'd come in here, scared and doubting, seemed like a lifetime ago. I'd been afraid back then and had felt so alone in the world.

So much had changed. But there was still one more thing in my life that I was really, really hoping had changed.

"Did I pay off my debt?" I asked Estelle.

"Things have really shifted for you over the past few days," she replied, sliding a can of ginger ale my way. I opened it, taking a sip. It had been a hot walk over here, and the pop's crisp coldness was heavenly.

"Yeah, I was penniless and almost homeless and now—"

"No," Estelle interrupted, her tone serious. "Energy has piled up."

I was instantly wary. "What kind of energy?"

"When you start a project like your park, initially, you don't create a lot of karmic energy."

I nodded. "Tell me about it. I asked for a lot of favours. For a bit I was worried I was creating more good karma for others than for my account."

"You were. Your project was like getting a very large, and very heavy, ball rolling."

Josie's analogy of a car not being worth anything until it left the factory came to mind.

Estelle shifted in her seat, looking uncomfortable. "But then, eventually, good begets more good."

"Right," I said. "It's like smiling at people in the grocery store. Some smile back, and then they smile at someone else and it gets passed on."

"As you began making changes in your neighbourhood with your park—people meeting each other, giving the kids a place to play—it brought positive energy and created abundance."

I crept to the edge of my seat, breath held.

"You reached a tipping point of sorts and created an avalanche."

I nodded, not quite following, but hoping an avalanche was a positive thing.

"Basically, in the past few days, the widening effect of your good deeds has had an enormous impact."

I leaned forward. "That's great! I'm out of debt?"

She nodded slowly, and I whooped. I'd done it! I'd put good energy into the world without a day to spare. It was like someone had lit a rocket under me. I leapt up, grabbing Estelle, pulling her into a hug. I released her and danced around the cramped room.

"I love the new monitor," I said, giving it an affectionate pat before sitting again.

"I need you to call it off," Estelle said loudly. Too loudly. Something was wrong. Like, record screeching on my good mood kind of wrong.

"What? Call what off? I'm done. I made the park and gave it away."

Estelle was leaning hard on her desk, eyes piercing, her look desperate. "I need you to concentrate like you never have before, and stop the karmic intake."

"I don't understand. What do you mean?"

"You're flooding the system."

I placed a hand on my chest. "I am?" Wasn't that a good thing?

"I need you to do a new mantra. Repeat in your mind that you've paid your debt to Estelle." Her heavy, ominous expression was making me feel a bit sweaty. She stood, hands clenched. She began pacing, looking like a caged lion in a pen that was too small. "Please repeat that mantra: I've repaid my debt to Estelle."

"Okay. I repeat it before I do a good deed?"

"*No*. Do it *now*."

"Oh. To, like, sever our connection or something?"

"Yes. I think so." Her hand went to her perfect brows, massaging them.

"You don't know?"

"Nobody does! This has *never* happened before!" She threw her hands in the air and a few pieces of silver and black glitter rained down. I cringed, shrinking in my chair, still very much aware that she had the power to turn me into a newt.

Probably.

Estelle placed her fingertips firmly against her temples and sat down, elbows on the big mahogany table. "You paid everything back about thirty-two hours ago."

"Really?"

"And then you donated the park."

"Yeah."

"All that happiness you created over the past two days..." She was almost moaning.

"Yeah," I said wistfully. I'd never forget the bubbly warmth in my chest as I laid the last of the sod with my friends, putting the final touches on the park. I'd received so many hugs from the little kids playing in the playground, and they'd been so delighted to have somewhere safe to play close to home.

There'd been a lot of handshaking and thank-yous as we all left the park that night. At one point, two older gentlemen had made Tamara tear up when they'd shown up with their lawn chairs to play on the chessboard table. Then a large, extended family had rolled a barbecue into the park just before sunset, cooking hotdogs for whomever was still there. It had been like a giant, impromptu party among strangers where everyone left as friends. Honestly, it made my eyes a little damp remembering it all. I wanted every day to be like that in the new park. A place to gather, to share and connect and create a sense of community.

I'd done that. I'd transformed a dangerous eyesore into something a bit magical. I'd put good out into the world and created happiness out of thin air.

It made up for my past selfishness, and I felt powerful and finally in control of my life.

I lifted my attention to Estelle. "Why did Paxi grant my tenth birthday wish? The one that got my dad fired?"

Estelle blinked at me a few times. "What? We really need to stop this flow. Now."

"I need to know."

There must have been something in my tone because she sighed and said, "It wasn't just your wish at play back then. Fate and destiny needed space in order to act upon your family's timeline. Your wish was simply the vehicle to let destiny unroll."

I blinked a few times. "Destiny?"

"You weren't to blame."

I sat in the new knowledge. My parents' breakup had actually been fated or in the stars or whatever, meaning it was all going to happen somehow, with or without my wish?

"It wasn't my fault?"

Estelle shook her head and softly whispered, "No. Not at all."

I sat back, remembering the joy of sitting in that restaurant booth, the two people I loved most in the world singing to me around a candle-lit piece of cake. I wouldn't take that moment back for anything, and it was so much sweeter now, knowing that I wasn't truly to blame for the ensuing unravelling that had occurred. If I hadn't made that wish, I might not have created that warm, fond memory.

"Now please do it!" Estelle said desperately, and I jumped.

"Oh! What? Right. The new chant thing." I closed my eyes, concentrating on the new mantra to sever the connection between my good deeds and Estelle's little karmic vacuuming system. I started to giggle, imagining flowers, rainbows and glitter hearts pouring into a dusty old 1950s Hoover that was all tubes and metal, making it bulge and groan, finally breaking open and sending love across the universe.

"You done?" Estelle asked dryly, like she'd been able to see what had been playing out in my imagination and found it less than amusing.

"Yes."

"So here's the problem." She leaned forward, hands clasped on the table. "You've already paid back your debt by about three times."

I blinked. Wait. No. That couldn't be right. What were the implications of something like that?

"Everything compounded over the past day and a half. And we fairy godmothers make it a habit to never owe anyone anything."

CHAPTER 48
~ *Estelle* ~

I closed my eyes, wavering on the spot in front of Gram-Gram's rosewood desk. Today, I didn't want to even focus on its intricately carved flowers. I wanted to disappear. I wanted this hellish feeling of being between life and death to be over.

Minutes ago, Trish had found me in my cubicle, sipping Canada Dry and trying to settle my nerves after a little run-in with Igor.

He always drooled. And always licked his lips. It didn't mean anything that he'd been doing that *a lot* during our recent conversation.

Except then Trish had leaned over the back of my chair, whispering, "The head fairy wants to see you."

And it wasn't report time. And she never whispered unless it was something mean she didn't want others to overhear. Then, when I'd turned around to face her, she'd lacked her usual too-sweet, slightly gloating look. But I hadn't been able to put a pin in her emotion. Was it envy? No, why would she feel that? Was it defeat? It looked a lot like defeat. Defeat because her main rival was about to get fed to the ogre in accounting and who would she compete against if I was dead?

It was likely that. Especially since you couldn't name a rule or regulation I hadn't bent, broken or bastardized lately.

"Well," the head fairy said calmly as I wavered in her office, eyes still closed, "Char is an adventure, isn't she?"

I nodded mutely.

"Are you wishing right now?" Gram-Gram asked curiously.

I shook my head. We weren't allowed to make wishes.

"Then why are your eyes closed?"

"So I don't cry when you feed me to Igor."

She let out a giant, very unladylike snort. "Estelle," she reprimanded, "we have been through this. He's *vegan*."

"Yes, but he licked his lips when he told me I fried the system."

Gram-Gram laughed. "Yes. You did do that."

I cracked one eye open, my freaking out temporarily waylaid by her mirth.

"Our payment systems just needed a reset. Nothing permanent. Nobody is going anywhere." She gathered up a stack of papers beside her and thumped them into a neat stack.

"But we owe Char, and you said we never owe our clients anything."

"Yes." She adjusted her half-moons lower on her nose. "Owing her would be problematic, for sure. But not beyond solution."

"How do we fix it?"

She smiled and gestured like she was pulling a plug out of a bathtub. She made a whooshing sound. "I'll take care of it."

"What? How?"

"Char will help make the world a better place with her overflow, because..." she explained patiently, her voice dropping low like she was afraid of being overheard, "we never carry debt.

Clients are allowed a very small overpayment which can only be applied toward future wishes. The rest..." She swooped an arm through the air and a shower of sparkles lit up the room. They were dazzling. So much prettier than my frustrated rage glitter. "Is shared. The world is now a slightly better place."

"But that's not in the book."

"Not everything is." She scanned the top sheet in her stack, then flipped through a few more before speaking again. "I do see that you stopped the flow into her account. So, I think we're done here. Nice work."

Nice work. Was that a compliment?

I felt the kindness of her words seep under my skin like much-needed rain after a drought.

"As you may have heard, I also put your name forward for the creativity award."

I held in a gasp. Trainees never got nominated in their first year. This was huge. "No, I didn't hear."

Gram-Gram lifted an eyebrow. "Interesting. I told Trish to tell you." She held my gaze for a beat, and I could see the edges of her lips wavering like she was trying to hold back a smile.

"Does that mean I'm no longer a fairy godmother trainee?"

Gram-Gram gave me a dry look. "Don't push it, kid."

CHAPTER 49

~ *Char* ~

On Friday, with a stomach full of Peter's, I headed downtown for my afternoon job interview. I crossed the pedestrian bridge over the Bow River, and watched the people below floating on the current in their inflatable rafts and tubes, beating the August day's increasing heat.

The interview was for a company that bought and sold artifacts around the world, and they needed a pottery specialist. That person was possibly me.

But how could it be? There were so many trained experts out there. Were they all super busy?

As I walked, I allowed myself to daydream that I had the job. I could see myself strolling down the Stephen Avenue Walk, the trees along the street's edges providing shade as I searched for a new restaurant to try on my lunch break. I was wearing a crisp suit from Banker's Hall, feeling like a million bucks, and talking on my cell phone about pottery with a European buyer who had a fabulous accent.

I inhaled, savouring the feel of this new life. I could taste the cooling latte I'd picked up from an artisan coffee shop near my office. See the brightly coloured koi, or whatever they were, in the Devonian Garden's fish pond where I stopped to sit. I could even feel the gust of air from the CTrain as it passed me en route, filled with other businessmen and women. I had a modern, gorgeous office decorated with lovely, lush ferns and lots of product—otherwise known as priceless pottery pieces worth more than many of the homes lining Springbank Hill.

Okay, maybe not quite that much. Maybe in total they'd be worth the amount those homes went for in the growing insanity called Calgary housing prices.

I stopped in front of Ruckles' temporary office and pumped myself up. So what if I didn't have a degree? I could show the interviewer that I had enough field experience and reasonable knowledge. I'd helped the police, after all. Who else in Calgary could do that? Plus, I was a fast learner who was very curious, and could learn on the job.

Thirty minutes later, I left the interview, smiling. I had a new BFF, Mira, who didn't mind nerding out over mutually favourite eras. It had been so nice to hold a conversation about ancient pottery that lasted longer than approximately fifteen seconds.

At first, I'd thought I'd blown it. It had been as though the job was on the platform waving at me; the train tooting its whistle, ready to leave the station. I'd been pleased over spotting a fake Ming right off the hop. I'd asked Mira if they sold many knock-offs, then had gotten nervous and said I knew it was a fake because it was placed within sight of the windows, and they didn't have high-end security.

Fearing that I was coming across like a thief casing the place, and very aware that I'd come onto their radar thanks to the museum heist, I'd quickly muttered that the glaze also wasn't consistent enough, and that a real Ming's glaze didn't crack. About

Thankfully, she'd been pleased that I knew a bit about

porcelain as well as pottery. And even though I'd never been a buyer, or assessed the value of various pieces, I'd been offered a three-month contract where we'd try each other out with the stipulation that I would take some classes to round out my knowledge.

I was terrified. What if this was my dream, and I smashed it like I'd smashed so many other things in my life over the past few months?

Or, maybe, just maybe, it was like Sally had told me. I'd only smashed that old life so I could move forward into something so much better, such as this career.

And such as being able to let go of my fear and finally risk my heart on the man I knew was worthy of it.

I BURST INTO THE HOUSE, eager to tell Sally my job news. I'd texted James already, but he hadn't replied, probably because he was knee-deep in maps or all the training he had to do.

"I got the job!"

Sally whooped from the kitchen.

"Congratulations!" She met me in the kitchen doorway, with a tray of sugar cookies. "Look what I made." The cookies were giant, and decorated with different messages. *Congratulations! Way to go! New job!*

"What?" I looked at her in wonder. Talk about confidence.

"I knew you'd get it." She held the tray out to the side and gave me a big, one-armed hug.

We moved to the counter to try the cookies. They were tender and amazing. There was a hint of cinnamon and I was in love. I could sit down and eat the whole batch.

I brushed the crumbs from my lips and stole a second

cookie. "I don't know what I'm going to do without your cookies."

"You'll just have to stop by my bakery," Sally said, wiping her hands on her apron.

"What?"

She grabbed a folder off the counter, and with a flourish, handed it to me.

"What is this?" I flipped through the typed pages, searching for clues.

"A lease."

"For what? Where?"

"For my bakery, silly! You convinced me to follow my dream."

"I did?"

"Of course you did!" Sally was wearing a cute, frowning smile, her eyelids lowered as though skeptical of my so-called act. "With you working so hard to make that park a reality, I realized I was just sitting here, dreaming when I could be out there doing."

"You did?"

"And you got all of those kids and moms excited about my cookies." Her cheeks pinked. "So, I started thinking, why not? What am I afraid of?"

"That's really great, Sally." I set the folder back on the counter and gave her a giant hug.

She poured so much love into me with that one embrace it made me homesick for her, for this, for the family I'd found during my toughest months. Was this the emotional struggle most of my friends had gone through when leaving home for the first time? Because it really sucked.

I was glad I wasn't moving very far away.

"But I thought you and Otto wanted to travel? You just got the motorhome."

She waved a hand. "We decided we're more the weekend warrior types. And Otto says he's always wanted to run a business, so he'll do the paperwork side of things while I bake."

"That sounds perfect. I promise to buy dozens and dozens of your cookies."

Sally laughed, delighted. "I'll be in that brick building right beside your park. It used to be a bread factory."

"That's perfect!"

"Fair warning—I'm going to rope you into helping me clean the place up."

"I'm so totally down for that."

"I think Everstone is an up-and-coming community, and the rent is cheap. Plus, I got permission from the building's owner to make a walk-up window." Sally gave a little body wiggle, smiles overtaking her face, the next one bigger than the last. "People can grab goodies and coffee to enjoy in your park. I'll make sandwiches, too, so people can picnic."

"Sally, that's fabulous!"

"It's such a perfect location. Tell me you'll come for the grand opening?"

"Wouldn't miss it for the world."

MOMENTS LATER, the front door opened and a fistful of balloons was pushed inside, masking the man behind them. A blue dress shirt appeared as a few balloons were knocked out of the way, then James with his blond hair in a rumply Viking-of-a-mess.

"Congratulations!" He swept me up in a bear hug, releasing the balloons to the ceiling where they bobbed and dancing above us.

From of the corner of my eyes, I spied Sally backtracking into the kitchen to give us privacy.

I relaxed into James's arms. They felt so right, so safe. How could I have ever been afraid of how I felt about this man? How could I have believed this wasn't real?

He set me on my feet and kissed me long and slow. He reluctantly pulled away, and I placed a hand on either side of his mouth and drew his lips back to mine. He slid his fingers into my hair, and without letting go of me, kissed me deeper. I held him tight to me, and his palm was warm, flush across my lower back, signalling that he had absolutely no plans of going anywhere else.

When we broke apart, I bit my bottom lip. "There's just one thing about my new job."

His arms tightened around me. "What's that?"

"There's travel involved. Not always. But sometimes."

"And?"

"And I don't want to be away from you. I want to be with you all cozy and homey, and in our routine, with fun little adventures. I'm not scared of my feelings anymore. But I'm afraid this is too much for us. I just finished the park and want to spend time with you. It's not a lot of travel, but between this and you going out on projects, too..."

"We are better when we're together," he whispered, angling his mouth down to mine for another kiss. "But you're the kind of woman worth waiting for, and we will figure it all out."

"Promise?"

"I promise."

I breathed him in, losing myself in the moment.

"Will you tell me when you're scared?" he asked.

I nodded. "But just so you know, I'm always scared."

He gripped my chin, gently tipping it upward, but I found I couldn't look at him. I felt shy and nervous.

"Right now?"

I laughed, voice shaking. "Terrified." I smoothed a hand over the jut of his cheekbone and down to his jaw, avoiding his gaze as best I could. "I love you such an incredible amount. I'm afraid I'll work too much and we'll lose our connection, or I'll wake up and find that this was all just a dream."

I felt vulnerable confessing how open and raw I was around him. Fear was like a giant iceberg floating through my chest, on the prowl for the Titanic, A.K.A. my heart.

"This isn't a dream." He was holding me steady, one hand on my hip. He gave me a deep kiss that removed all doubt. "Char," he said seriously, "would you be my forever girlfriend?"

I smiled against his lips, my hands tangled in his hair. "You're never going to get rid of me."

"I look forward to handling that."

My heart soared above the icebergs, the heat of happiness melting away the ice.

"So, um. Speaking of girlfriends..." I dragged out the last word.

"Like you?" He dropped another kiss on my lips.

"Like me. But what's the real reason you broke it off with Sophia?"

James looked at me with such seriousness, the icebergs of fear started reforming in the frigid waters.

"I broke up with her because I met you."

No. There was no way.

He stroked my cheek, his smile soft and wistful. "When you hauled me over to chew out that kid for climbing on the mummies, for the first time, I could see my future."

"Really?" He was taking my breath away, clearing the waters for all time.

"I could see it all with you. The adventure, the fun, but also the quiet moments. All of it. I could see you there, no matter my mood, no matter which course I decided to take next. I knew you wouldn't think me crazy. You'd jump in and join the absurdity of it all." He stroked my cheek with a tenderness I could get used to. "I love you and your curiosity, Char. And I started falling for you the first time I ever saw you."

Oh, wow. I think my legs were going to give out like they did in romance novels. The wobbly leg thing was real. As real as my affection for this man.

James chuckled, his eyes sparkling. "Also, I was smitten by how, while doing inventory, you were trying to slyly peek inside a tomb."

"I wasn't!" My face went hot. "I was looking for barcodes to replace."

His smile told me he'd caught me the one time I'd pried my fingers under the edge and tried lifting. The one and only time. I sighed. "Okay. But I only did that once."

He chuckled, drawing me deeper into his arms again, into the place I truly belonged and could forever call home. "I saw all sorts of things in that job. But mostly I saw you."

Epilogue
CHRISTMAS

~ *Char* ~

I'd been texting the GAL PAL group, halfheartedly trying to talk Samantha down out of breaking up with Malachi, when my phone rang. Tamara! Maybe she had some good advice about our freaking-out friend.

"Merry Christmas, Tam-Tam! I think Samantha's totally going to break up with him. Don't you?" The last of the Mexican sun's rays had faded, but the heat was still radiating from the poolside concrete, warming me. Mexico was marvellous, whereas back home they were having a blizzard.

Yeah, I was in the right place, and not just because I was curled up on a lounge chair by the pool, wrapped up in James' bronzed arms. The water was a sparkling fake blue, but beyond it was the ocean, a deep, dark shade, changing with the wind and sun. With dusk it had become a whispering backdrop to what would surely be an amazing evening with James and his parents, who'd adopted me into the family and had even overlapped one of their own vacations so we could all spend Christmas together. Even my dad was going to fly down here for a few days, thanks to my new income bracket as a pottery expert, and his stabilized health. This holiday was perfect. Heaven. Everything I would have wished for—if not afraid of the possible ripple effects.

James placed a warm kiss on my shoulder, brushing my cover-up out of the way in order to do so. My favourite song began playing on the speakers around the pool and an adorable toddler giggled and squealed while splashing his sister. My drink cool and refreshing. I was happy. I had everything.

I couldn't have wished for this. I couldn't have imagined anything this good, this sweetly small and normal thing that would fill me with so much.

"I hit something," Tamara said, a tremor in her voice. "With Benjamin."

Benjamin was her Sebring. He'd hit a lot of things, but it had never left a tremor in Tamara's voice. I sat up, my euphoria caving in upon itself, my drink spilling.

"I'm serious, Char."

My mind struggled to compute. Tamara was back in Eagle Ridge, which meant her driving was less stressed than when she was in Calgary. That meant hitting fewer things, and not just because there was less to run into out there. No, usually Tamara laughed off her vehicular oopsies. But she wasn't laughing. She was calling me.

I plugged an ear to drown out the pool music and got up, padding further from the sounds of splashing kids.

"What's wrong?" James asked, sitting up.

I shook my head, moving toward the quiet beach so I could hear Tamara better.

"Christmas is doomed."

"Doomed?" I giggled at her dramatic tone. "Why? Was there a sleigh involved?"

"I hit Rudolph. He's on the road."

What?

My humour came up short, my heart crab-crawling its way into my throat. My mind immediately skipped to thoughts of Estelle and the magical world.

Could Santa and his herd of flying reindeer be real? It was the evening of December twenty-third. There was less than twenty-four hours before Rudolph had to do his around-the-world thing. This was hardly a good time for a Christmas crisis. Surely I was misunderstanding what my bestie was saying.

I mustered as much calm as I could, but with a growing sense of foreboding, I said, "Tell me everything. From the beginning."

THANK you for reading FAIRY GODMOTHERS AREN'T CHEAP. I hope you loved the touch of magic in Char's story! But what happens next? How does Tamara solve her Rudolph and Christmas problem?

Find out in RUN, RUN RUDOLPH!

Christmas is the best time of the year...except when you accidentally hit Rudolph with your car.

Glossary of Canadianocity

Sorry, but here are some things you should probably know, eh?

Some of these terms may be familiar to you already, as well as to my commonwealth readers, but just in case, here is a list of a few things in this story that I believe some readers might wonder about.

ALSO NOTE: This book uses Canadian spelling which is basically British spelling. *(Except when we spell the odd word like 'artifact.' Then we use American spelling.)*

Let's start with this fun one:
Yeah: Ya/Yeah/Yes
Yeah, no: No.
Yeah, maybe: Maybe.
Yeah, no. Maybe: Maybe.
No, yeah: Depends on context and emphasis. Could be no. But probably yeah.

Geography and such:
Kananaskis: An area in the Rockies, about an hour west from the city of Calgary, Alberta, where this story is set.

Rockies: The Rocky Mountain range. Big, craggy, gorgeous mountains with glaciers and snowcaps even in the summer.

Saskatchewan: (Pronounce it sorta like: Sass-catch-ew-on.) A Canadian prairie province noted for its flatness. It's actually a great place to view your dog running away for days. (Yeah, that's a joke.) Truly, it is a beautiful expanse of unbroken summer sky and beautiful fields.

B.C.: Short for British Columbia, a western Canadian province with shores along the Pacific Ocean. Pretty much everyone calls it B.C. and not British Columbia.

Battle of Alberta: Calgary Flames vs. Edmonton Oilers. Get your provincially issued license plate and represent your team! Two cities, two NHL (National Hockey League) teams, and one province of approximately 5 million people. Pick a side, stay loyal and loud! Get your jersey, car flags, flags for the house, hats, stickers, baby clothes, blankets, etc..

Calgary Stampede: Huge event held in Calgary each July. It lasts over a week. It includes, but is not limited to: high-level rodeo, performances by famous bands, Indigenous drumming and dancing, a huge midway, numerous events, live shows, a big parade and so much more.

Québécois: People who live in Quebec, another of Canada's beautiful provinces where French is spoken alongside English. Sometimes. Sometimes it's just French. Good luck ordering your Timmies, ya anglophone!

Food:

Timmies: Tim Horton's. A popular coffee/donut shop that was started by a hockey player by the name of Tim Horton. It is not confirmed if this Horton ever heard a Who.

Canada Dry: A brand of ginger ale that originated in Toronto, Canada, in 1890. Hands down, the best drink when you have the flu. Clearly, it is also favoured by fairy godmothers.

Pop: A sugary, carbonated drink. Some countries call it soda.

Poutine: Yes, please! Traditionally, French fries with gravy and cheese curds, but feel free to experiment and mix it up by adding meat or try different cheeses. These loaded fries are considered a Quebec thing, but try and find a Canadian who hasn't had it. Quebec, FYI, tends to elevate this side dish and even has entire restaurants dedicated to this form of yumminess.

Spitz: A brand of flavoured, shelled sunflower seeds founded in Alberta, Canada, in 1982. Their fields of sunflowers are something to behold.

Money stuff:

RRSP: Registered Retirement Savings Plan.

Cheque: One of those paper things you write on to give people money from your bank account. Americans call it a check. We (and Aussies) pronounce it the same, but spell it differently because we're sassy like that.

Loonie: One dollar coin. Named for the loon (water bird) on it. Naturally, we call our two-dollar coin a toonie even though it has polar bears on it.

Bottle picking: In Canada, provinces pay for returned, empty drink containers so they can be recycled. Picking bottles/cans that have been tossed out of vehicles (bad!) can be collected and returned for a refund between ten and twenty-five cents each (good!). Prices depend on the container.

Education:

Playschool: A play-based year of casual schooling for four-year-olds for the purpose of socializing and get the kiddos used to routines before entering the formal school system. Not mandatory, and it's paid for by parents. Like daycare, but with a learning focus.

Elementary school: In most areas, this is kindergarten to grade six.

Junior High/Middle school: Typically, junior high years are grades seven to nine. However, some towns have a middle school that can include a range of grades anywhere from grades five to nine...or, really, whatever fits best into the buildings they have.

High school: Grades 10 to 12. Sometimes grade nine can be included in a high school.

University/College: Two different things in Canada. Traditionally and typically, university is a four-year program where you graduate with a degree. You can use this to head on to post-graduate school. College is a two-year program (or less) and you graduate with a ticket or diploma.

SAIT: Southern Alberta Institute of Technology. Located in Calgary.

Grad: Short for graduation. In small towns, they tend to be held in May, and are more of a commencement ceremony as the provincial exams have not yet been written. Typically, with small town grads—pre-pandemic—the class dresses in formal wear, has a class photo taken in the school gym or in front of some shiny pickup trucks (Hello, Acme-Linden bicampus. I see you). This is followed by a ceremony where students cross the stage and get a certificate, eat dinner, have a dance and then, of course, the big party.

Travel:

Couple of K: Couple of kilometres.
KM: Short for kilometre. 1 km = 0.6 miles.
5K: 5 kilometres.

CTrains: Calgary's public transit system that uses light trains. Their answer to cable cars or subways.

Fifth-wheel: A holiday trailer that has a heavy-duty hitch that sits in the box of a pickup truck. (Instead of being a "bumper-pull.")

Jerry can: A container for transporting gasoline. Usually red. Other countries might call it a petrol can or gas can.

Miscellaneous:

CBC: Canadian Broadcasting Corporation. Publicly funded television and radio programming that you could argue is the heart of Canada. Well, if you're old. Not sure the young 'uns have discovered just how hilarious some of the comedy is. Or maybe they're just too young to get the jokes. (I recommend The Debaters—you can listen to it in podcast format.)

Curling rink: Where you curl.

Curling: A sport where two teams of four compete. Where? On a sheet of ice, that's skinny and long with a bullseye on each end of the ice. You "throw" a rock (kind of shove it) and let it glide down to the other end, hoping it will stop in the centre of the rings and the other team won't knock it out during their turn. Your team can "hurry hard" (sweep hard and fast) with brooms to melt a thin layer of ice in front of the rock to help it glide faster and further. A popular sport in small towns, probably because a bar is often attached to the ice. What doesn't make you too tipsy to stand on the ice, just makes you a better curler.

Dugout/stocked dugout: Not to be confused with a baseball dugout where the off-field players sit. Typically, a dugout is a manmade watering hole for cattle and other livestock that fills with runoff (melting snow/rainwater). They can also be used as a reservoir for irrigation, or possibly even stocked with fish each spring so it can be used as a casual fishing pond.

Hail: Not specifically Canadian, but I include it here in case you don't get this weather phenomenon. Balls of ice that fall from the sky in the summer. (Not to be confused with snow which can also fall in the summer.) Sometimes hail is small and fairly harmless, but other times hail can be as big as a softball and tear holes in siding, dent vehicles, break glass, devastate crops, etc.. Good luck with your umbrella.

Chinook: Warm air that flows over the Rocky mountains from the Pacific coast. In Calgary you can have a temperature change in the winter that goes from -20C to +20C in a 24-hour period, melting the snow and causing optimistic Calgarians to don their shorts.

Jackall: (Not the animal.) A jack that is responsible for a lot of injuries according to an agricultural session I went to as a teenager. Essentially, it is a tall jack that sits on one leg and has a lip that can be ratcheted upward. Clearly, unstable. Great for getting high-centred vehicles unstuck and breaking jaws.

High-centred: When a vehicle's underside gets stuck on something and the wheels can no longer propel the vehicle forward or backward.

Home Hardware: A Canadian chain of hardware stores.

Per cent: (%). Exact same thing as percent, but with a space between the syllables. It's a weird Canadian thing where we put a gap in the word. Don't worry, it looks wrong to me, too.

The Cowboy's Second Chance (Ryan)

The Cowboy's Sweet Elopement (Brant)

The Cowboy's Surprise Return (Cole)

The Summer Sisters

Falling for the Movie Star

Falling for the Boss

Falling for the Single Dad

Falling for the Bodyguard

Falling for the Firefighter

Veils and Vows

The Promise (Bonus prequel: Devon & Olivia)

The Surprise Wedding (Devon & Olivia)

A Pinch of Commitment (Ethan & Lily)

The Wedding Plan (Luke & Emma)

Accidentally Married (Burke & Jill)

The Marriage Pledge (Moe & Amy)

Mail Order Soulmate (Zach & Catherine)

Blueberry Springs

Whiskey and Gumdrops (Mandy & Frankie)

Rum and Raindrops (Jen & Rob)

Eggnog and Candy Canes (Katie & Nash)

Sweet Treats (3 short stories—Mandy, Amber, & Nicola)

Vodka and Chocolate Drops (Amber & Scott)

Tequila and Candy Drops (Nicola & Todd)

Champagne and Lemon Drops (Beth & Oz)

Indigo Bay

Sweet Matchmaker (Ginger and Logan)

Sweet Holiday Surprise (Cash & Alexa)

Sweet Forgiveness (Ashton & Zoe)

Sweet Troublemaker (Nick & Polly)

Sweet Joymaker (Maria & Clint)

For the Kids

1,001 Boredom Busting Play Ideas

Acknowledgements

Thank you to this giant book for not breaking me when you could have. (And almost did.)

I began working on this book as a reprieve to refill the well that years of dealing with long-covid had wrung dry. In January 2024, I started an island series. It was all planned out, but the jam never showed up. Neither did the peanut butter (if you're asking). So, I sat back and thought...what do I really want to write?

This book came to mind. Back in 2008—yes, over ten years ago—I'd played around with this story. Back then I was still learning to write, and was figuring out things such as character development and how to write a flowing plot. Ultimately, I'd set this story aside. But in the dawn of 2024, I couldn't stop thinking about a woman being in debt to her fairy godmother.

And so I pulled out this book, thinking I could spend maybe two months polishing and rewriting, and then send it out into the world.

Ha!

Almost a year and a half later... (Dear Universe, really? That long? Thanks for that.)

Now, this story is finally ready, and this is the longest a book has taken me. It is the longest I've gone between releases. This story, which was supposed to be oh-so easy and fun, became the single most difficult book of my life.

I still don't know why.

It's also the longest book in terms of word count.

And yes, it was fun. But then it got hard. And then harder again.

I think I wrote this book at least four times. Maybe five times, or even more if we count the times I rewrote it in 2008. And when I say rewrite, I mean a *complete* rewrite. I've written well over half a million words, just trying to find these 96,000. Man, I hope these words still make sense and are funny. It used to be funny. The first version, my ever-so-patient editor Brenda Chin read was, as she put it, a "smart ass." She meant that affectionately, and she didn't use the same tone my parents used when calling me a "smart ass" as a kid. So there was that to cling to as I struggled through several more rewrites.

As for the thank-yous, I'd firstly like to thank Brenda for her read-throughs, suggestions, and edits. As well as for her reminder that if it's a romance, they should maybe do some falling in love. Right. I'd also like to thank her for the much needed compliments and encouragement, especially when I was so deep into the forest I couldn't see the trees or even the hand in front of my face. Also, thank you for naming this book. The title is a chef's kiss! Thank you for letting me borrow your brain. (Or at least rent it.)

To my readers, who have waited for so long. And also my Jeansters reader group for voting on the pet the girls should have. Felipe is sort of a squirrel...right? Speaking of Jeansters, thank you to Sue Hamann for inspiring the embarrassing things that Mrs. Laven says when Char meets her for the first time.

A thank you to my beta readers, Margaret, Lucy, Erika and Donna. Thank you, thank you! I am still so amazed you finished the book so quickly. Also, thank you for your helpful comments and suggestions and helping me see the story from a reader's perspective.

Thank you to my error finding team who dazzle me each and every time. A special thanks to Audrey Burger for making me laugh with her notes as well as this beautiful nugget she left on the author's note in regards to fitting in: "It's difficult to be yourself trying to fit in, because parts of you get left behind."

Any remaining errors in this manuscript are likely just strange Canadian word spellings. Ha! That'll be my excuse.

For my massage therapist, Maureen Dick, for being excited when I announced the book was DONE, and for massaging the kinks out of my hands and arms and shoulders that formed while pouring over this beast month after month.

A magical thank you to authors Lee Savino and Renee Rose. In some ways, pieces of this story were just waiting for me to meet you.

And hey, thanks for reading this. I appreciate you spending time with my words. Sometimes an author feels alone. We spend so much time at our desk with our fictional worlds, it feels as though we are writing into the void since we may never 'meet' our readers. So thank you for reading, and thank you so much for your messages and kind reviews. I appreciate knowing you're out there, and that you have enjoyed my work. It means the world to me and, honestly, when I feel like there's no point to writing, it reminds me that someone out there enjoys what I'm doing. Thank you.

Side note I didn't know where to put: In a random online search I discovered that actress Melanie Paxson played a fairy godmother in the movie *Descendants*. Paxi is named for her.

About the Author

Jean Oram is a *New York Times* and *USA Today* bestselling romance author. Inspiration for her small town series came from her own upbringing on the Canadian prairies. Although, so far, none of her characters have grown up in an old schoolhouse or worked on a bee farm. Jean still lives on the prairie with her husband, two kids, and big shaggy dog where she can be found out playing in the snow or hiking.

Shop Jean's store: *Shop.JeanOram.com*

Jean's Newsletter: www.jeanoram.com/signup

Become an Official Fan: www.facebook.com/groups/jeanoramfans

Website & blog: www.jeanoram.com
YouTube: www.youtube.com/@authorjeanoram
Instagram: www.instagram.com/author_jeanoram
Facebook: www.facebook.com/JeanOramAuthor

www.ingramcontent.com/pod-product-compliance
Lightning Source LLC
Chambersburg PA
CBHW010605310726
48969CB00010B/2566